D1221833

the cracker factory

Joyce Rebeta-Burditt

BANTAM BOOKS
TORONTO · NEW YORK · LONDON

For:
Paul, Jack and Ellen, my children
Collette Supp, my mother
and
George, who laughs at my jokes and never gave up

This low-priced Bantam Book
has been completely reset in a type face
designed for easy reading, and was printed
from new plates. It contains the complete
text of the original hard-cover edition.
NOT ONE WORD HAS BEEN OMITTED.

THE CRACKER FACTORY
A Bantam Book / published by arrangement with
Macmillan Publishing Co.

PRINTING HISTORY
Macmillan edition / January 1977
2nd printing .... April 1977   3rd printing .... July 1977
4th printing .... August 1977
Condensation appeared in REDBOOK MAGAZINE / *April 1977*

Bantam edition / March 1978
2nd printing .... March 1978   8th printing .... January 1979
3rd printing .... March 1978   9th printing .... April 1979
4th printing .... March 1978   10th printing ...... March 1979
5th printing .... April 1978   11th printing ...... March 1979
6th printing .... May 1978   12th printing ...... March 1979
7th printing .... July 1978   13th printing .. December 1979

Bantam Books are published by Bantam Books, Inc. Its trade-
mark, consisting of the words "Bantam Books" and the por-
trayal of a bantam, is Registered in U.S. Patent and Trademark
Office and in other countries. Marca Registrada. Bantam
Books, Inc., 666 Fifth Avenue, New York, New York 10019.

PRINTED IN THE UNITED STATES OF AMERICA

ACKNOWLEDGMENTS

Though no man is an island, some of us are inner tubes. With love and thanks to those whose oceans of warmth and encouragement kept me afloat:

Marcey Carsey	*Burt Prelutsky*
Michael Denneny	*Marion Rees*
Pat Gritzner	*Carol Ann Rebeta*
Ann Hopkins	*James Rebeta*
Mary Ann McKinnon	*Roy Warren*
Matthew McKinnon	*Peri Winkler*

J. T. Ungerleider, MD.

and

The ladies and gentlemen of Alcoholics Anonymous, without whose willingness to share their experience, strength and hope there would have been no Cassie Barrett.

1

I woke up, rolled over carefully to prevent the pincushion in my head from doing major damage, opened the eye with the astigmatism, and focused on the window with its mesh screen and bars.

"Oh, no," I groaned, "I've fallen down the rabbit hole again." I curled up in a ball, or more appropriately, since I was in a psychiatric ward, the fetal position. I huddled under the covers while fragments of memory staged midair collisions. The pieces settled and locked and it all came back to me.

This was my second trip to Wonderland. At my first admission I'd clung to my husband's arm, frozen with fear. My arrival was the result of clever coercion by my shrink, who'd been saying for weeks, "Cassie, you're falling apart. You'd better go to the hospital."

Ever the cooperative patient, I fell apart as quickly as I could and went to the hospital, sure that I'd be surrounded by loonies doing weird things. All I could remember was poor old Olivia de Havilland wandering around the Snake Pit being vague, an out-of-focus Dante in hell. I pictured myself dramatically tied to a bed while sadistic attendants forced gruel down my throat with a tube.

Then I signed myself in and found a private psychiatric ward artfully disguised as a Holiday Inn, done in soothing shades of green, with family-motel furniture, carpeting, and famous artists' prints on the wall.

The patients who could verbalize at all pretended that they were really fine, thank you, just terribly in

1

need of a "rest." They successfully ignored less fortunate patients like old Mrs. Walker, who remained tied in a wheelchair and thought everyone was her granddaughter.

I could understand how they felt. As a child I'd tried to ignore some of Aunt Lily's more embarrassing outbursts, such as the time she threw the Thanksgiving turkey at Dad because no one passed her the gravy, or the day she set the broom closet on fire because no one wanted to discuss Catherine the Great. ("She's high-strung," Dad said. "She's crazy, Fred, a real lunatic," Mother replied, scrubbing the smoke off the walls after the fire department left. "Goddammit, no one in my family is crazy," Dad bellowed, throwing his coffee cup at Mother.)

The rooms are semiprivate, the beds are comfortable, the gruel, in disposable trays, is attractively surrounded by parsley, and the staff, composed of essentially pragmatic people, never expends the energy required for sadism.

So my terror had abated and I did what was expected. I learned the game and how to play it. When the staff said, "You should feel better by now," I learned to say, "I do, I surely do," as I shuffled off to occupational therapy to gather approval by making crooked mosaic ashtrays, bumpy with ridges of grout. I hoped that by acting better I would eventually feel better, or at least deceive the staff into thinking I did, because, after all, they were doing their best and if I still felt rotten it was my own damn fault.

I was given hospital privileges and went, unescorted, to the gift shop for candy, cigarettes, and an astrology book that foretold a career change and a move close to water, which made perfect sense to a novice whacko in a nuthouse near the lake. Forging ever onward, I was given grounds privileges entitling me to slog through the slush on Shaker Heights Boulevard where I flapped my arms to ward off frostbite while berating myself for not having delayed falling apart until spring. I smiled and chuckled, made references to maturity and even got to believing some of it.

The staff observed, and duly noted, that I ambulated, communicated, and ate my dinner. One day Dr. Alexander, motivated either by the cheerful chirpings of the staff or a need for my bed, said, "You are decidedly better. I am sending you home."

So I departed with the staff waving bye-bye, clutching a prescription for a lifetime supply of Antabuse, and wondering who it was who decided I was better. And why I felt so lousy.

Charlie welcomed me home with dinner at a Chinese restaurant, a movie, and the wariness accorded the recently weird.

"You look fine," he said, eyeing me over his menu. "In fact, you look great. You must feel better."

I dipped a noodle in hot mustard and crunched. "I guess so, Charlie."

"You guess? You must know. After all, if you weren't cured, they wouldn't have let you out."

I nodded agreeably. "Well, now that I'm cured, there's just one thing I'd like to know."

Charlie smiled. "What's that?"

"What was I cured of, Charlie?"

Charlie frowned, his eagerness to have me "better" deflated. We ordered egg rolls and spareribs.

I devoted the next six weeks to acting cured. Before dawn I was in the kitchen whisking lumps out of oatmeal which the kids dutifully ate, though they made wistful references to the days when breakfast had consisted of a bowl of Rice Krispies topped with chocolate ice cream. Or eight-year-old Steve's favorite, hot dogs and soup.

Everyone had clean underwear and socks, enough towels for a dozen consecutive baths, and homemade brownies after school. In the bottom of the ironing basket I discovered Jenny's misplaced pink booties and cap, somewhat late since she was in kindergarten, but found nonetheless.

On Tuesday mornings between eleven and twelve, Alexander nodded approvingly as I regaled him with reports of my "progress." Even Mother was pleased with my newfound domesticity.

"This house is finally beginning to look like something," she beamed, high praise indeed from one who does for a household what Mussolini did for trains. "Now, why don't you wash down the walls?"

With a collective sigh of relief, everyone returned to functioning in an orderly way, comfortably content with me. Thank God, that's over, they seemed to say. I put one foot in front of the other and marched through my days, wondering why I felt as though red-hot barbed wire was shredding up my stomach. And I stopped taking the Antabuse, telling myself that it made my food taste tinny and I didn't need the threat of its deadly effect in combination with alcohol to keep me sober.

One morning I put two poached eggs in front of Charlie, who looked up briefly from his newspaper.

"You've really shaped up, Cassie," he smiled. "A dreadful lady went to the hospital and a very nice Cassie came back. I think you've learned a lesson and honey, I'm proud of you."

He went to work and I started the dishes, trying to feel thrilled at having shaped up for Charlie. *He sounds as though the hospital performed some sort of exorcism,* I mused, scraping egg off the dish with my fingernail. *Evil is banished, goodness restored. Then why don't I feel transformed?*

The dish slipped out of my hand and smashed into the sink, spraying chips over the counter. I looked down at the mess, then at the cluttered kitchen table, and beyond that to the dust on the television set in the den. I pictured the four unmade beds and the three clothes-strewn bedrooms and the toys in the living room and last night's newspaper on the floor next to Charlie's reclining chair and I yelled at the cat who was licking milk out of a cereal bowl, "What lesson? What goddamn lesson was I supposed to learn?"

I grabbed my coat and the grocery money and was waiting at the liquor store when it opened.

"You find a place where they give it away free?" the man behind the counter leered. "We haven't seen you for weeks. Where you been?"

"Nowhere," I answered. "I've been nowhere." He gave me my bottle and I walked out thinking that I'd have to start trading at another store where the creeps weren't so free with their remarks.

Once home I pulled the curtains, put on a stack of records and curled up in front of the stereo with a tumbler full of scotch. I sipped and listened and sipped some more, until the barbed wire dissolved and a soft, mellow fog replaced the ache behind my eyes. I must have fallen asleep because the next thing I knew the kids were home and Charlie was due. I knew I'd have to scramble frantically to get to the market and home again, get dinner started and some of the clutter cleared away before he walked in the door. But first, I needed a drink.

And after the drink, I decided, *What the hell. I can open a couple of cans for dinner and if Charlie doesn't like the way the house looks he can clean it up himself.*

I was stirring soup and burning toast when Charlie came in the back door. He looked at the mess, then at me.

"You're drunk," he accused. "You're drinking again."

"Am not," I said, waving the butter knife at him. "I learned my lesson." I gave him my best "nice Cassie" grin.

"Where are the kids?" he demanded.

"In the den watching television. Why?"

"You wouldn't know if the kids were playing in the middle of the street," Charlie snapped, pushing past me.

Charlie called the kids. Greg was the first to arrive.

"I got an A in arithmetic, Daddy," he announced, "the only one in first grade."

"Fine, son," Charlie said absently, stuffing him into his coat.

"Where are you going?" I asked, while Jenny looked from Charlie to me and back again and Steve leaned against the doorway with his arms folded and eyes on the ceiling.

"I'm taking the kids somewhere to dinner, seeing as their mother is too drunk to cook."

"Isn't Mommy coming?" Jenny asked, as Charlie hustled them out the door.

"No," Charlie snapped.

"You can go to hell, too!" I shouted at the closing door. In the kitchen I reached for the bottle I'd hidden behind the oatmeal box and leaned against the sink, drinking and crying, while the soup burned black in the pan.

Later, after the children were asleep, Charlie approached me as I sat staring blankly at television.

"I don't understand, Cass." He shook his head. "Everything was going so well for us."

I took another sip. "For you, Charlie. Everything was going well for you."

"What he wants is a housekeeper," I told Alexander. "Someone to clean up the messes and see to the details while he does the important things. So long as meals are on the table, the house is neat and the kids in their places with bright shiny faces, Charlie sails serene." I stubbed my cigarette out in the ashtray.

"I tell him I'm lonely and he walks away," I continued. "He shuts me out of his life and then tells me that my loneliness is all in my head. He's good at his work and he loves it. He plays poker and golf with his friends. Neither work nor recreation includes me. I thought marriage was sharing and growing together. How can I share with someone I never see? I ask him what he's thinking and he says 'Nothing.' Nothing! Nobody thinks about nothing! Whatever he's thinking, it's nothing he cares to confide in me." I lit another cigarette.

"He tells me what I should do. He tells me what I should want. He tells me how I should *feel*, for God's sake, how I should feel! And when I say I want to do something else, want to want something else, and further, I feel what I feel, he says that I'm wrong. Wrong! Do you know what it's like to feel *wrong* twenty-four hours a day? Do you know what it's like to be disapproved of, not only for what you do and say and think, but for what you *are*? Well, do you?"

"Hmmm," Alexander said.

"I didn't think so," I said, looking out the window. "Charlie encourages me to come here, concerned that my behavior improve, while I bring a tentative hope that somehow I'll sort out my feelings or at least find out what they are. So far, Charlie's disappointed and I'm still confused. But even if we were successful, Doctor, if eventually I could march to Charlie's drummer with all of my feelings intact, there's something he won't understand."

"Hmmm? What's that?"

Tears washed out the view from the window. "The dreadful lady he can't accept and wants gone, and the nice Cassie he loves and I'm unable to sustain—that's what I am, not one or the other. Together, both of those people are me."

"You may have a point," he said, glancing at the clock. "I'll see you next Tuesday."

I set some arbitrary rules for myself. I wouldn't drink until 5 P.M. I wouldn't drink before leaving the house to go shopping. I would drink only on alternate days. For months I made myself crazy, adhering to these self-imposed restrictions.

I had varying degrees of success. The house was usually dusted, but the wax on the floors grew dimmer by the day—along with Mother's approval. Clothes were generally clean, but the ironing basket filled up again and I stashed the overflow in shopping bags behind the furnace.

I tried to convince Charlie that no one would notice if he wore one brown and one black sock; it wasn't the end of the world.

"Know what you are, Cassie?" he thundered. "You're incompetent, that's what you are." He planted his golf cap square on his head and slammed out the door.

Meals were a mixture of four-course productions and quickies picked up from the store. Either way, the children didn't seem to mind, but Charlie, who holds the opinion that the breakdown of American home life is caused by take-out food, was less than happy.

One night Steve grabbed my arm as I leaned over the sink with a steaming pot in my hand.

"Mom, what are you doing? You're throwing our dinner down the sink."

"No, I'm not, Stevie," I said, puzzled. "This is just leftover noodles I'm throwing away."

"But we haven't had dinner!" he insisted. "Daddy isn't home from work yet."

I looked at the noodles slithering down the garbage disposal. "Are you sure we haven't eaten, Steve? I could have sworn we had."

"Mommy threw our dinner away," Steve greeted Charlie.

"I made a mistake," I said. "Nobody's perfect."

"I've never asked for perfect," Charlie frowned. "I'd be happy to settle for sane. Tell Alexander I want my money back."

These occasional lapses bothered me and I stayed up late night after night, pondering probable causes and possible solutions. There had to be reasons for this constant depression, reasons and a way out.

"Wake up, Charlie," I said, shaking his shoulder one night.

Charlie glanced at the clock and tried to pull the blanket over his ears. "Please let me sleep," he moaned. "I have to get up in three hours."

"This is important, Charlie. You must listen."

"Will it take long?" He peeped at me over the blanket.

"No, just a minute."

"All right. What is it?"

"It all started when I was eleven—"

"When you were eleven! I have to be at work in four hours."

"Shut up, Charlie. Listen. A friend of the family, an acquaintance really, told me that my father had been married before—"

"I know, I know," Charlie groaned. "You've told me."

"—and he said that he never knew what happened to the first wife because one day Dad just showed up with Mother. The friend—he owned a shoe store, his name was Al—said that Dad must have simply liked Mother better. Then he asked if I minded him talking about my parents that way, probably because I looked so startled. And I said I didn't mind, I just didn't know Dad had been married before—"

"I know, I know," moaned Charlie

"—and I planned to ask Dad about it. I wanted him to say Al was crazy or had him mixed up with somebody else, but when I saw Dad that evening I froze. I couldn't ask and knew I never would. I thought about that woman all the time. I named her Lydia and thought she was ten feet tall. I thought someday she would come and take Daddy away—"

"And your mother told you all about her when you were eighteen, right before we got married," Charlie interrupted, trying to end the story.

"She said that there had been a first wife named Helga who died long before Mother married Dad."

"A happy ending," Charlie mumbled. "Good night."

I tugged at Charlie's sleeve. "But you don't understand. That was a long time, seven years of thinking that some monstrous lady will fall out of the past and claim my father. I would lie awake and watch for her at night. I would get paralyzed with fear when he was late coming home from work. Maybe that's why I get so frightened over nothing, so terrified that something horrible is about to happen."

"Ask Alexander," Charlie said. "That's what he gets paid for, to listen to you." And the blanket went over his ears.

I told Alexander.

"Hmmm," he said. "Interesting."

I grow up haunted by phantoms and all he can say is "hmmm." So much for childhood traumas and the mysteries contained therein.

One Sunday Charlie arrived home from the golf course as Mother and I were fixing dinner.

"Make us a drink, Cass," he said, heading for the shower. "It must be ninety degrees out there today."

I handed a glass to Mother, who remarked, "Not having any?"

"I'd better not," I said, not wanting to explain about alternate days.

"One won't hurt you, for heaven's sake," she fussed. "It's only when you go overboard that you get into trouble."

So I said, "Why not?" and had another drink, wondering who told Mother when she went overboard. And wondering why everyone seemed to think I should live my life by their definitions.

My Sunday bastion crumbled. Proving the domino theory, the other days caved in behind. I dragged through days that telescoped and days that seemed to have no end, struggling up an invisible hill with a weight around my neck.

In autumn Charlie packed an overnight bag for a weekend retreat.

"I'll pray for you, Cassie," he said at the door.

"I'm sure you will, Charlie. You're always talking about me behind my back."

He returned, shielded by an impenetrable serenity and ready to "understand my problem."

"What problem are you ready to understand, Charlie?" I asked, throwing his dirty clothes in the hamper.

He frowned. "Well, you know, um . . . whatever it is that's wrong with you." He was pacing up and down, avoiding my eyes. "I know that you drink too much sometimes. And I never knew anyone who gets drunk so fast. One whiff and you're gone. But it's more than that."

I breathed sharply, surprised. "What is it, Charlie? What more?"

He shrugged. "You're unhappy, Cassie. That's obvious to everyone who knows you."

I sat on the edge of the bed watching his fine-featured face with its sensitive mouth.

"Why would that be? Why would I be unhappy?" I asked.

He rubbed the back of his neck and stared at the

floor. "Beats the hell out of me. Maybe you were born that way."

I picked lint off the bedspread. "It has nothing to do with you, Charlie? Or with us?"

His hazel eyes widened. "You'd like to believe that. Blaming our marriage and me would make it simpler for you. But it isn't that simple. You were unhappy when I met you and your mother says you were always unhappy. You grew up that way, with a warped view of life."

"Mother says I was always unhappy?" I repeated, wondering when Mother and Charlie had begun this in-depth analysis of me.

"She says you were an unhappy child and an unhappy adolescent. Now you're an unhappy woman."

"At least I'm consistent. But you make 'unhappy' sound like something I'm permanently stuck with, like having blue eyes."

"Maybe it is," Charlie agreed. "But whatever it is, it has nothing to do with me. I'm going to take a shower."

"Then what is it you plan to understand, Charlie?"

"That's it," he said, throwing a towel over his shoulder. "I understand that it's your problem, not mine."

I sat on the bed, pondering the bleak and barren landscape of Charlie's diagnosis. And Mother's. I remembered my childhood and my sister, Mary Kay, hanging upside-down from the jungle gym, eyes peacefully closed and hands folded across her chest, a meditating wombat. And Bobby and me nestled in the branches of the tree behind our house, hurling crab apples at invisible Huns. And the hot summer days when Dad came home at noon and took us all swimming; cinnamon-dusted pies cooling on the counter after school; fairyland snowfalls, and Bobby shrieking while I jammed ice down his neck; long rides through the park with a bologna sandwich and an apple in my pocket; afternoons in my room, lost in a book.

"It's a good thing I didn't know then that I was always unhappy," I muttered to myself. "I wouldn't have had so much fun."

There was one rule I considered worth keeping. When I was drinking I stayed out of the car. Then, one night Charlie called.

"I can't make it home for dinner, Cass. I've got a deadline on one book tomorrow and I have to begin editing another right away."

"Why didn't you call earlier?" I demanded. "I would have made hamburgers for the kids and myself. I have a roast and everything, and you know damn well the kids aren't going to eat it."

"I've been up to my elbows in work all day, didn't even have time for lunch. Some problems came up that I wasn't expecting. It's very complicated."

"It's always complicated where you're concerned, Charlie. How long would it have taken you to pick up the phone and let me know before I got this dinner all ready?"

"I'm sorry," he said, placatingly. "I didn't know this was going to happen. My deadline date got moved up. Why don't you and the kids have dinner and go to a movie? Just keep something warm for me." He hesitated for a moment. "How are you feeling?" he asked cautiously.

I knew what he meant. "If you really gave a damn how I feel, you'd come home and find out!" I slammed down the receiver.

"Son of a bitch!" I yelled at no one in particular and finished the drink I'd been sipping. I called to the kids who were watching a cartoon show on television.

"Come on, kids; Daddy isn't coming home for dinner and we're going out."

"Why isn't Daddy coming home?" Stevie asked.

"He has something more important to do," I answered. "Get your coats on."

"What are you going to do with the stuff you cooked?" Greg asked.

"It can sit there and grow green mold for all I care. Hurry up. Sitting through a Disney movie is bad enough without being late for it too."

I rushed the kids out the door, pausing only to retrieve an unopened pint bottle I'd hidden in the linen closet. We stopped at McDonald's. The kids gobbled hamburgers and french fries while I sipped a liberally spiked Coke.

Damn Charlie anyway, always off somewhere, expecting me to hold down the fort without a grownup to talk to from one end of the week to the next.

The movie was relentlessly cute, bearable only because I made several quick trips to the ladies' room.

As the theater lights went up, Steve shook me awake. "You've done it again, Walt," I said, getting to my feet. "Put me right to sleep."

In the parking lot I cautioned the children to fasten their safety belts. Ten minutes later I was speeding down a dark, narrow road, seldom used since the opening of the new freeway. The kids were tired, cranky, and bickering, and I was anxious to be home.

"Shut up back there," I screamed at Jenny and Greg, who were poking each other in the back seat.

In the front seat, Steve, who had been very quiet, said, "Mommy, slow down, we're going too fast!"

Just to be aggravating, the other two joined in. "We're going too fast. We're going too fast."

"You kids shut up! You're driving me crazy!" I half twisted in the driver's seat, furiously flailing my arm behind me, trying to catch one or both of the little monsters with a smack. They never pulled this when their father was driving.

Steve was saying, "Mom, Mom, watch out!" as Jenny and Greg squealed, trying to avoid my hand. A huge semirig loomed out of nowhere. I was over the yellow line and headed directly toward the oncoming truck, half turned in my seat and frozen to the wheel.

With an incoherent shriek, Steve yanked the wheel hard to the right and we careened off the road, bouncing and jostling on the soft shoulder dirt while the children's screams pierced the air and my foot scrambled madly for the brake. Steve fell forward, striking his head on the dashboard as we plowed through some low, scrubby bushes and came to a bone-jarring halt. I turned off the ignition and grabbed Steve, who had fallen under the seat.

"Are you all right?" I screamed at him. There was a gash on his forehead, and when he realized that his head was bleeding he began to cry in fright, adding to the terrified bellowing of the children in the back seat, both of whom had tumbled to the floor.

"Sit still and let me look at it," I told Steve. He pulled away and I shook him sharply. Trembling, I examined the cut. It seemed superficial, just a deep scratch. I wiped the blood away with a handkerchief. Quickly, I checked the kids in the back seat.

"Get up here," I ordered, pulling them both off the floor. "Are you hurt? For God's sake, shut up and tell me if you're hurt!"

"My arm's all hurt, Mommy," Jenny cried, thrusting it into my face. There was a slight bruise above the small elbow but that was all. Greg was either unhurt or keeping his bruises to himself.

I was suddenly furious. "Look what you brats made me do!" I screamed at them. "With all your fighting and fooling around, we could have been killed!" Shaking and abruptly weak, I began to cry.

"You didn't see that truck, Mommy," Steve said, holding the handkerchief to his head. "You didn't see the truck and you couldn't turn the wheel and we almost got killed."

"That's your fault," I sobbed.

"You weren't paying attention," Steve insisted. "You never pay attention and you never know what's going on."

"You sound like your father, Steve."

He nodded wisely. "Dad says you shouldn't drink."

"Enough!" I shouted, beside myself with anger. I reached out to slap his pale face, then jerked my arm back. My fingertips barely brushed his cheek but the gesture set the children into another storm of wailing. I sat with my head in my hands, groaning. *I give up,* I thought. *I just give up.*

I tried to calm the children. "Mommy's sorry," I said. "We almost had a terrible accident and Mommy's very upset. We'll go home and I'll make some cocoa. Okay? Okay, kids?"

No one said it was okay, but they quieted down as I turned on the ignition and carefully eased the car onto the road.

We drove slowly home. The children were silent. *It isn't really their fault,* I thought, *that they've picked up their father's attitudes. They're young and Charlie's references to me are liberally sprinkled with words like childish, selfish, incompetent, and crazy, overlaid with allusions to drinking. What else are they going to think?*

Once home, I put ice on Steve's head, gave him aspirin and made cocoa. Jenny and Greg were too tired to drink it, so, inspecting them once again for bruises and cuts, I tucked them into bed. Jenny hugged me good night, but Greg pulled up his blanket and turned his back without a word.

"I'm awfully sorry I yelled at you, Stevie," I said as he quietly finished his cocoa. "I was terribly upset."

"Yeah," he said, walking past me to bed, "you're terribly upset a lot."

I let him go. Thoroughly exhausted, I fixed a drink and carried it into the darkened living room, where I sat staring into space until Charlie came home.

"A truck almost ran us off the road," I said, "on the way home from the movie."

"Oh, no. Is everyone all right? The kids?"

"Just shook up. A few bruises. The car is making a strange noise though, underneath."

"To hell with the car," Charlie said. "As long as you and the kids are all right."

"We're dandy, Charlie. Just fine."

He looked at me closely. "You weren't drinking tonight, before you went out, were you?"

I sipped. "No, no, I wasn't. I wouldn't do that."

"I didn't think so." Charlie relaxed.

The kids never said a word.

Weeks later, Mother sat in my kitchen nursing a drink while I scraped carrots.

"For the life of me, I don't know why you're seeing

a psychiatrist," she said. "You have everything a woman could want."

"Oh?"

She held up her hand and began counting off fingers. "Three wonderful children . . ."

"True."

". . . a husband who loves you . . ."

"He may love me in his own way, Mother, but I suspect he doesn't like me."

"Nonsense." Her brown curls bounced. "A lovely house . . ."

"Charlie's house, Mother," I snapped, annoyed.

"He bought it for you, Cassie," she said, smiling sweetly.

"Sure he bought it for me. He also bought it without me."

"You should be grateful, Cassie."

"How would you feel, Mother, if *you* were in the hospital having a baby and your husband came in and said he'd bought a terrific house, you'll just love it? And you don't love it, hate it in fact, but have to live in it anyway."

"I wouldn't resent it," Mother said, sipping her drink.

"Like hell you wouldn't, Mother. He picks out a house I haven't even seen, tells the owners we'll take it and then *informs* me and I'm supposed to fall out of bed with gratitude. Come on, Mother. You'd have set fire to his hat."

"He had to decide in a hurry, Cassie. He got a good deal on the house. And besides, we agreed that it would be perfect for you and the kids. And it is."

I stopped scraping. "We agreed. Who's we, Mother?"

"Charlie and I," she smiled. "We looked at the house together before we went to the hospital."

"My husband and my mother picked out my house! And I'm supposed to say thank you. No wonder I don't feel like a person! What the hell am I doing here, anyway?"

"Be quiet, Cassie," Mother said. "Behave yourself. Cut out the shrink and get yourself together."

I told Alexander that things were getting worse with Charlie and me.

"Mother whispers at Charlie and Charlie lectures at me. Everyone makes pronouncements and no one talks *to* anyone. Especially me. Every time I try to tell Charlie I'm depressed, he tells me why I shouldn't be. I'm rolling a stone uphill."

"Hmmm," said Alexander.

"Oh, well," I sighed. "What can I say about a relationship where he calls me goosepot and I call him Daddy."

"You've lost weight," Alexander remarked.

Late one afternoon in early November I found myself in my usual supermarket, staring helplessly at row after row of cereal boxes, confused and unable to make up my mind. A stock boy was replenishing boxes on the lower shelf.

"What's the matter, Mrs. Barrett?" he asked cheerfully. "Can't you find what you want?"

"I . . . I . . . I can't decide," I sniffed, tears pouring down my face.

He got to his feet. "What's wrong? I'll go get the manager. You just stay here." He patted me awkwardly on the shoulder and started for the front of the store.

I couldn't wait for the manager, couldn't stand and explain to some staring stranger that I was incapable of purchasing cereal, incapable of making a decision. Blinded by tears, I ran to the parking lot and drove home.

I called Mother, who answered with a distracted you've-caught-me-in-the-middle-of-something voice. "I can't stand it anymore," I screamed into the phone. "I can't. I can't."

"Can't stand what?" she wanted to know.

"Anything. Anything." I screamed and hung up.

By the time Mother arrived I was in some sort of

daze, still semihysterical, but foggy. I couldn't remember what I'd done before she arrived, though I did remember calling Alexander. And Charlie, maybe, though I couldn't recall having spoken to either of them. I just knew that I'd reached the end of my rope. Whatever it was, I couldn't stand it anymore.

So, here I was again, scrunched up under the covers and praying for death. With the hangover I had, death could only be an improvement, but my prayers are never answered. All those novenas, for what? I hauled my battered and demented body out of bed, pulled on my bilious green terry robe, and wobbled into the hall. I didn't want to talk to anyone, and I blanched at the idea of encountering someone I knew or who knew me, but at that point I would have endured any humiliation for two aspirins and a glass of something cold.

2

There's always a great hustle of activity around the nurses' station early in the morning. Nurses' aides and orderlies bump into each other, racing to get everything in order before the shrinks arrive. The real business of the place is to keep the shrinks from getting upset, and God help the patient who has a trauma before 9 A.M. Or even, as in my case, a headache.

I leaned woozily on the counter and watched Miss Pomeroy pour pills into little paper cups on a tray. She glanced up, gave me a You again? look, and kept pouring. Pomeroy is a pretty face set atop a mountainous body. It looks as though there are at least three people trapped inside her uniform, all trying to escape in different directions. During my last stay here, I dubbed her O.F. (for oral fixation) Pomeroy, and it caught on with the rest of the patients. I am not one of her favorite people.

I gave her an obsequious smile, and feeling like Oliver Twist asking for porridge, humbly requested aspirin.

"Hung over, Cassie?" she asked, smiling archly and looking wise.

"Certainly not," I replied, grimacing against the light. "I just have a headache." *Why don't you hire out as a blimp, Pomeroy? They could paint "DRINK BUD" on your side and float you over the stadium during ball games.* You'll *never hear me say I have a hangover, not while you stand there looking vastly superior and grossly obese.*

She gave me the aspirin and said, "Well?"

I ignored her need to hear "thank you" and was saying "When will Dr. Alexander be in?" when my right knee buckled and I found myself sprawled on the floor with that blasted pincushion ricocheting from one side of my head to the other.

I was immediately surrounded by people, including Dalton, the floor supervisor.

"Good morning, Miss Dalton." I squinted up at her. "I see your skin cleared up."

"What happened?" she asked, looking concerned. She was good at it, having taken courses in Concerned I and II, followed by Totally Concerned and the biggie, Complete Empathy. "Let me help you up." She tugged on my arm.

She hoisted me up. The cast of thousands went back to bumping into each other and I was once again asking when the doctor would be in when my leg turned to rubber and I fell to the floor.

"Oh, dear. Oh, my. Oh, goodness," Dalton exclaimed, having skipped Totally Concerned and gone straight to Complete Empathy. She reached for my arm, which I promptly pulled away. I didn't know what was wrong but was in no hurry to be standing again on unpredictable legs. In fact, I was quite prepared to spend my second round in the psychiatric ward on the floor in front of the nurses' station.

"Don't just stand there gawking, Dalton. Bring me my breakfast."

But no such luck. This time she piled me in a wheelchair, zipped me down the hall, threw me into bed and warned me not to move until Dr. Alexander arrived.

"Move? I won't breathe, ma'am." *Change your perfume, Dalton. You smell like a Shell Pest Strip*.

I lay rigid under the blanket, panic-stricken and trying to remember if I'd ever experienced anything like this before. The hangover part was ghastly, but totally familiar. I was on intimate terms with the thumping and throbbing that made my head feel as though it had been jammed inside a bell, the churning, sour and oily queasiness in my stomach, the profuse sweating and icy chill, the flulike ache in bone and muscle. And the shaking, the embarrassing-as-hell, impossible-to-control, dead-give-away tremors that made me sit on my hands or clasp them tightly behind my back. And the peculiar sensation I always get, as though I'd been hollowed out from neck to toes, my spirit and substance either removed or flown away and nobody left at home.

I lay watching my feet twitch and wondering vaguely where I had gone. And why I was falling down. And why I couldn't concentrate well enough to worry about it for five consecutive seconds without being distracted by a fly on the ceiling or the particles of dust floating in a shaft of watery winter sunlight coming through the window or the outline of what I assumed to be a female body in the next bed. All I could see were tufts of matted white hair scattered over a bright pink scalp. Whoever she was, she had buried herself beneath blanket and pillow, and was sleeping on her nose. I wondered why I always get roommates who have lost the war with creeping senility, who have either reverted to the cucumber stage or think they're four years old and call me Mother. Either the staff, and Alexander, think I have a very low tolerance for stimulation, or the sadism here is just more subtle than anything Olivia encountered.

Alexander eventually arrived, followed by Dalton, who hopped around behind his back, anxiously clasping and unclasping her hands. My persistent falling down had definitely thrown a monkey wrench into her day's schedule of events, and therefore into Alexander's, and she looked as though she thought she was going to be blamed for the whole thing.

Alexander nodded at me curtly.

"It certainly is nice to see you again, too," I said, flashing what I hoped was a radiant smile. The effort caused my stomach to slip sideways and bubbles of nausea rose in my throat.

"I want to check you out," he said, reaching for my arm. Alexander took my pulse as though he knew what he was doing. He grasped my wrist tightly, pressing the bone and peering intently at his watch while he counted. His lips moved.

I pretended to close my eyes and watched him through my lashes. *You look like a negative Sidney Poitier, Doctor. You are identical, except that you are blond and blue-eyed where Poitier is black and brown-eyed. It's more than a resemblance. You're the same person with a different paint job. Someday I'll run into a green one and then a purple one and maybe one with stripes or spots. But I'll keep my observation to myself. You have my particular form of derangement planted firmly in your mind and I wouldn't want to confuse you. Or upset you. Maybe you're unaware of the way you look. Maybe you're bigoted and would be appalled. Or maybe you would head straight for Hollywood to do an updated version of the Corsican Brothers—"They were as different as day and night, but they shared one soul!"—Then where would I be? Up a creek without a shrink, which is only slightly worse than where I am—in a nuthouse with one.*

"Hmmmm," he said and released my wrist. The

pulse-taking over, Alexander pulled a flashlight from his breast pocket. Either it's standard equipment or he has an obsessive fear of power failures. He shined the light in my eyes, making my pupils contract and setting the pincushion aquiver. I gritted my teeth and continued to smile.

"What happened?" he inquired. "When did this start?"

"About an hour ago. Every time I start to ask when you're coming in, I fall down. That question is obviously against the rules. Therefore I shall never ask again and I shall never fall down again. Simple?" I smiled serenely, feigning indifference.

"Be serious," he frowned. "Have you fallen at any time in the past few weeks, or have you received a blow to the head? Something is causing this."

He stared solemnly at me, and entering into the spirit of the occasion, I stared solemnly back at him. *You say something is causing this, Doctor? Well, if you must know, I am under the direct control of super-intelligent extraterrestrial beings who have permeated my brain in an attempt to discover the nature of the human mind. The beam they have teletransported from their solar system is intended only to suck out my memory banks, but due to the time warp and the rapid depletion of the ozone layer caused by the indiscriminate use of armpit sprays by people who want to be nice to be near, the gamma doohickey has slopped over into the psychomotor area, shaded red on your phrenology chart.* "I don't know whether or not I had a blow to the head. I mean, I don't remember. I suppose it's possible, but I don't know. I wish you would go away. You're making me nervous."

Alexander rubbed his chin and looked thoughtful. "I think you know more about what's going on than you're willing to admit."

Lord, save me from his staring. He can see through my eyes. He reads the thoughts on the back of my skull. He knows everything. I am constantly changing direction, fracturing and scattering my thoughts in an attempt to confuse him.

"You don't remember coming in here last night, do you?" he asked.

I glanced at Dalton and wished she would disappear. She reminded me of the principal of St. Theresa's Academy, all stern-eyed and hook-beaked and forever clucking in her throat.

"I remember sitting in the front seat of the car," I answered Alexander, "between Charlie and Mother. They were talking back and forth over my head. Charlie was asking Mother why she let me get out of the house and Mother was saying it wasn't her fault. She just turned around for a minute and I was out the door and who needs a twenty-eight-year-old daughter you have to watch like a hawk anyway and she didn't know where I got the vodka and she didn't think I'd taken *that* many pills, if any, and she wished I'd cut out all this crap, I was making her old before her time. Charlie was poking me every two seconds telling me to wake up and tell him what kind of pills I'd taken before we got to the hospital and they started asking *him*. I got tired of listening to it all and just drifted off and that's the last thing I remember until I woke up this morning and started falling down." I smiled blithely and clenched my teeth. Storm troopers of pain were assaulting my head with bayonets fixed.

"All right." Alexander sighed, looking like the statue of St. Sebastian with eight million arrows through his body. "Yesterday afternoon you called my office to tell me that you had taken an unspecified number of un-identified medication but before you died you wanted to tell me what a son of a bitch I am. I told you to stay where you were and called your husband. He arrived home to find you out cold and your mother hysterical. They got you to the hospital where you stopped dying long enough to sign yourself in and punch the orderly in the nose. We pumped out your stomach and found that you'd tried to overdose on St. Joseph's Aspirin for Children. We didn't need a blood test to determine that you were inebriated. You reeked of alcohol and passed out in the elevator."

"We had to hold the elevator while the orderly and

your husband dragged you out," Dalton interjected. "Your mother tried to convince the other passengers that you were in a diabetic coma."

That's Mother. Death before dishonor. Mortified beyond any but four-letter words, I flopped over in bed, pulling the blanket over my head. *Stop telling me what I did and how I looked and who said what to whom.*

Alexander continued, ignoring my retreat. "Don't get me wrong. I'm taking your 'suicide' attempt seriously and I expect you to, also. You are doing what people do when they are coming to the end of their rope. I'm just trying to point out to you what's going on."

How can I thank you, Edwin? Thank all of you, in fact. I am blessed with battalions of people who are ever willing, nay, enthusiastic, to point out to me their version of what is going on. "The trouble with you is . . ." I curled myself deeper under the blanket.

"Sit up and listen to me, Cassie. You are being childish."

I bolted upright, promptly obeying, as I always do, a direct command from anyone who speaks with authority (eat your meat . . . kiss your mother . . . go to confession . . . change the baby . . . shut your mouth . . . spread your legs . . .).

Alexander patted the incipient bald spot on the top of his head, something he does when he's making a decision.

"I'm going to order some tests for you, including an EEG, a brain wave. Until we get the results I want you to remain quiet. And tell Miss Dalton if anything unusual happens."

"Like what?" I wanted to know what other terrible betrayals I could expect from my body.

"If I tell you," he said with a trace of a smile, "you'll be sure to make it happen."

And with that he walked out of the room. Dalton tagged after him but not before she'd leaned over me and whispered, "He means convulsions."

I watched through the open door as they stood in the hall mumbling at each other. I'd never felt sicker. I was terrified that it would get worse, much worse, and more than Alexander, or EEGs, or a semiprivate room with bars on the windows and a door down the hall that locks in the ward and locks out Charlie and Mother and the kids and the chaos I have no defenses against, more than all that, I needed a drink.

Needing a drink, sorry to be here, and angry that I'd been railroaded by Mother and Charlie, who evidently had dumped me, washed their hands and run like thieves.

I could hear them on their way home: Mother sighing, "God knows we did all we could."

And Charlie agreeing. "Let *them* handle her and see how far *they* get."

And Mother, brightening at the thought of having my children all to herself, asking Charlie, "What would you like for dinner?" And Charlie saying, "Chicken would be nice unless there's time to make stuffed peppers." And Mother saying, "Of cousre, there's time. I'll even bake a cake." And Charlie smiling and turning on the car radio. Having locked the evil dragon securely in a cage deep in the forest, Mama Bear and Papa Bear skip happily home to eat porridge out of blue china bowls.

I glanced over at my roommate, who hadn't moved, and wondered how long she'd been that way and if anyone ever came in to check her out. I shivered. What I'd told Alexander was true. I couldn't remember having taken aspirin or calling him or most of the drive to the hospital. If I had taken anything else, if I hadn't called, if, if, if. . . . I could have been dead, dead without wanting it or willing it.

"Oh, Christ," I moaned, "is there no end to the shit?" I pulled the blanket over my head and gave myself over to shaking. Rivers of cold sweat ran down my back as I lay curled up and drowning in my bed.

I was trying to will myself to sleep when a nasal whine broke my already shredded concentration.

"Miz Barrett. Yoo hoo, Miz Barrett." I shuddered, recognizing the voice. "I'm suppoze to take you for your EEG, Miz Barrett. Rise and shine."

Rise I did, painfully, but I saw no reason to shine, especially for old Gloria, the peanut-brained aide who stood jiggling a wheelchair and grinning lopsidedly.

"Sure is nice to see y'all back again. I wish we'd get nothing but young ones. Some days I think if I have to give one more old lady a bath I'm gonna scream. Course there ain't so many old people here right now. It's much more lively than the last time you was here. You feeling poorly? You don't look too good."

I slumped to one side of the wheelchair. "I feel terrific, Gloria. I've had a very hectic year and I'm here for a rest. Just a little rest."

"Sure wish I could go somewheres for a rest," she sighed. "Ever since last June when I had the hysterectomy, my back's been acting up and I feel like I been kicked in the stomach by a horse. Five months and I swear I ain't feeling no better than I was before they cut me."

She jerked and jolted me into the elevator where I sat facing the back wall and holding my head in my hands.

"My feet are just plain killing me," Gloria went on. "I went downstairs to the foot department and the doctor, he says, get orthopedic shoes for thirty-two dollars and goldang, my feet are still killing me."

"Tell you what, Gloria," I said. "You sit down in the chair and I'll push."

She stared. "They'd fire me in a minute but it sure is nice of you to offer. Why you having this test? You got epilepsy?"

I sat up straight. "Christ, I hope not!"

"Well, it's the epilepsy test you're gonna have. The last guy I brought down here, they got him all wired up and turned on the machine, and about the time the lights started flashing he went stiff as a board. His eyes rolled around in his head and the nurse, she had to jump in there and jam a stick in his mouth to keep his tongue from goin' down his throat. Well, here we are."

She pushed me through the open door and bowed out with a wave. "I'll be right out here taking a little rest."

"Wonderful," I called after her, looking around to see if there was an escape hatch. *I am going to kill you, Alexander. I'm going to hang you upside down and skin you alive. I'm going to—*

"Hello there, I'm Miss De Angelo, and you are—?"

"Mrs. Barrett," I replied to the efficient-looking lady who presumably was going to provide me with my first fit.

"What's your problem?" she wanted to know.

Well, you see, lady, it all started when I was born, the only child of poor, but honest, perverts who traveled over the countryside giving flagellation lessons to fledgling sadomasochists. Lady, wake up, lady! "I fall down," I said, smiling as though it was something I wanted to do.

"Well, we'll see about that." She bustled me out of the wheelchair and into what looked like a dentist's chair placed beneath what seemed to be a floor lamp with dangling snaky wires.

"We're just going to attach these electrodes to your scalp," she said, in a meant-to-be-soothing voice. "You'll just feel a tiny prick as each one goes in."

I clenched my teeth and held on to the chair as she plunged spikes through my brain, setting my nervous system on fire and dissolving my spinal cord.

"There, now," she purred. "We're all ready. Just lie back and relax."

"I'd like sort of a medium curl," I said. "Nothing too frizzy."

"This machine doesn't curl your hair," she explained patiently. "It records the pattern of your brain waves."

You've been dealing with loonies too long, Frankenstein. You don't know a joke when you hear one. I sat back and tried to relax. When the lights began to flash I tensed, waiting for spasms and a stick down my throat. Instead I fell asleep.

"Wake up. You're all done." Her cheerful voice shattered the first peaceful moment I'd had all day.

"How did I do?" I asked, relieved that nothing terrible had happened.

She shook her head. "I can't tell you that. Your doctor will give you the results. I just take them. I don't interpret them."

She yanked the spikes out of my scalp and called Gloria, who yawned her way back to the seventh floor.

"You probably ain't got epilepsy, seeing as you didn't even twitch or nothing," she said, depositing me in my room. "Maybe it's a brain tumor."

I turned green at the word "tumor" and began rooting for epilepsy.

"One can only hope, Gloria," I said. "I'd hate to put you to all this trouble for nothing."

She smiled. "No trouble, honey. Just part of my job." And she left to spread cheer among the weak and weary.

Later, Dalton arrived with two aspirin. "I thought you might want these," she said.

I gulped them down gratefully. "Is there anything else for discomfort on my chart?" Discomfort is the official medical euphemism for unbearable pain.

"No, aspirin is all he prescribed. Plus Thorazine if you go into convulsions."

Shit! I'd forgotten about those. Convulsions and epilepsy and brain tumors! There's just too much to worry about!

"Would you please check out that lady in the next bed?" I asked. "She hasn't moved and it's making me nervous."

Dalton glanced briefly at the bed next to mine. "That's Mrs. Caliguire. She's fine. You just worry about yourself. And stay in bed until the doctor arrives."

"When will that be?" I asked.

"As soon as your tests are in. Probably tomorrow."

"Do you suppose," I said, "that I could have some paper and a pen? As long as I'm stuck in this bed I may as well write to my brother."

Dalton beamed. Communication of any kind, except yelling and screaming, which gives the staff headaches, is considered positive activity and encouraged.

"Of course you may," she said, scurrying off to get writing materials and put a gold star on my chart under "Relationships—Interpersonal."

"Here," she said minutes later, and for reasons known only to her, winked at me as she went out the door. Maybe working in the looney bin has given her a twitch.

I propped up my pillow and pushed the damp hair out of my eyes. *Here goes,* I thought, beginning to write.

Dear Bobby,

Why aren't you here? You are the only human being I really want to talk to and there you are diddling around in the California sunshine while I am locked up in the Shaker Heights version of Bedlam. If I were you and my one and only twin sister had landed, once again, in the Cracker Factory, I would fly to her side with words of comfort and a dozen Mounds bars. But that's the difference. You are an unfeeling clod while I am much too sensitive for this miserable world. You plod. I founder.

I suppose that Mother has called you, presenting the scenario of my latest disaster with her in the heroine's role. But I know that you are aware of how she is and you also know me, so I feel no need to defend myself against her, not to you.

It's been one hell of a year. I've been running around half crazy, trying to remember whatever it is Alexander said I learned in the hospital last time, trying to find the answer to it all. Bob, I don't even know the goddamn question. I just know that I'm coming unraveled and can't seem to stop it.

It's been a whole year of Charlie running off and

slamming doors when I need him. I tell him I'm sick
and he says, "You're telling me? I'm sick of your sick-
ness." And bam, out the door.

He looked at me one night and said, "Cassie, you're
a loser." Bob, when I stand on Judgment Day to hear
myself condemned to hell, it will be no more devastating and irrevocable than Charlie's "You're a loser."
Forever defective. Forever doomed. No hope at all.

I've lied to Alexander about how much I drink because I was afraid he would shake his head and frown
at me. There are other things I haven't told him. Officially, you can tell your shrink anything—he's not
supposed to judge and you're not supposed to care—
but there are times when I've told him things and he's
looked down his nose and said, "Really?" Who the hell
needs that? It's been some time since I've left his office
feeling that I've dumped a load and I resent it. I'd like
to start over with someone else, some stranger I don't
care about. But I can't. It may not be working, but he's
all I've got.

I can't talk to Charlie because he'd kill me if he knew
some of the things I've done and because he isn't talking to me anyway, good riddance. Mother is out for the
same reasons and because I can't look her straight in
the eye without wanting to leap and kill or jump in a
six-foot hole and cover myself with guilt and dirt.

I tried Mary Kay. I got drunk one night while Charlie
was playing poker and called our sweet little sibling in
Detroit. I started to cry, telling her how miserable I
felt about getting loaded at her most recent commence-
ment ceremony, when she interrupted me with "I accept
your apology, but I don't think you should visit me
again until you're feeling better. Anyway, I'm busy
working on my master's degree. Why don't you call
Father Dunhill? He can help you."

"If I wanted to talk to Father Dunhill, I would have
called him. I wanted to talk to you. Forget it. I won't
call you again."

I slammed down the receiver, furious at myself for
having apologized to Miss Holier-Than-Thou and wondering how she's managed to grow up doing everything
right while I've gone steadily downhill since I won the

penmanship prize in third grade. It doesn't pay to peak early.

I don't have any girl friends. I don't feel comfortable with women or understand their priorities. What is it that makes them look so smug and satisfied all the time? It's a private club. I don't have the key.

And I'll be damned if I'll discuss my life and my problems with what passes as angels of mercy around this place. Most of them are none too bright, and the ones who are gossip like crones at a wake, so eventually you hear your life's story from the gnome who pushes the electric floor polisher.

So you're it, buddy. I need someone to talk to, someone to confide in and be straight with before I find myself permanently welded into a straightjacket. You never preach or seem to judge. What I assume to be love may only be apathy, but I'm going to hang on to the belief that we're still "the twins," as close as we were curled up in Mother's tummy cooing secrets in each other's ears. Or growing up like two halves of a whole, knowing one another's thoughts and no need for words.

You owe me. Going back to when we were four and had our tonsils out and I screamed for the nurse to give you a drink of water, because as sick as I was and hurting, what bothered me most was hearing you cry. You owe me for that and for all the years Mother said, "Take care of Bobby, he's weaker than you."

And I did, Bobby, bossing you and loving you and feeling important and competent because of you. Now I need some of that back.

Just read what I write, then throw it away. When you write back, I don't want to hear any lectures or advice. I want to hear that you care and you're with me and you understand how I feel. Remember, someday your crazy chromosomes may surface and talking to me may be the only thing that stands between you and the rubber room.

I'm frightened. I'm afraid that I'll die any second. I'm anxious about the EEG, though I don't think real diseases are allowed here. If I ran down the hall with blood spurting from my jugular vein some official shrink type would tell me that it's an outer manifestation of my inner anxiety and recommend a hot bath.

Write to me, Bob. I've really gone and done it this time. This is for real.

Love,
Cassie

P.S. I was furious with you two years ago when you went to California instead of taking one of the jobs you were offered here. I felt deserted. But I understand—and I'm jealous. It must be wonderful to go where you want and do what you want without having to consider anyone else or come up with an explanation. And who, except maybe me, would even suspect that a grown man accepting a fabulous offer from a national insurance company was doing nothing more or less than running away from home.

3

Two days later I was still waiting for Alexander and convulsions. The hangover was even worse and I had wrenching pains in my legs, as though someone was beating on my kneecaps with a baseball bat.

I asked Dalton about it.

"It's part of your withdrawal," she said.

"Withdrawal hell," I insisted. "There's something *wrong*."

"I'll get you some aspirin," she offered.

Aspirin! The minute Alexander arrives I'm going to leap out of bed and attach my teeth to his neck.

I picked at my breakfast, grumpy and unable to get comfortable in my bed. Dalton reappeared bearing my aspirin and wearing a condescending smile. I lost control.

"Please, please, please, let me out of this goddamn bed and this goddamn room," I said, all teary and clutching at her sharp, starched sleeve. "I can't take it anymore, lying here with this dead person waiting for that fink Alexander."

She regarded me sternly. "Mrs. Caliguire is not dead and that's no way to talk about Dr. Alexander. He will be talking to you this morning."

"Would it be possible for me to get up and wait in the parlor with the rest of the patients? I haven't fallen down since day before yesterday. Please?" I whined, aware that demands would get me nowhere. Since I was properly humble and subservient, she considered my request.

"I'll go check," she decided and departed, leaving me to wonder if she'd flip a coin or attempt to discern the answer in the entrails of a slain wildebeest. She was back in a few minutes smelling of the licorice that bulged out her cheek.

"You tin det up," she munched.

My spirit leaped out of bed while my body doddered slowly behind. A hot shower removed some of the ache. By the time I pulled on my old jeans and black sweater, I was beginning to feel like Cassie, bloody, but only semibowed.

I tried to get past the nurses' station without being noticed, but Pomeroy stopped me in mid-slink.

"Oh," she called. "You're up."

No, actually I'm still in my bed. This is my aura.

"How do you feel?"

"Terrific," I replied, surreptitiously hanging on to the counter.

"Good. After you see your doctor, Kenny will take you down for a chest X ray. If you promise not to punch him in the nose." She laughed merrily.

"Of course, I won't," I said, just like someone who would never think of doing such a thing.

Patients sat in the parlor staring into space waiting

to see their shrinks. Nothing had changed since the last time. It could easily be the same group of people playing out the same ritual, like a mental illness repertory company. Another opening, another show.

I was looking for a place to settle myself when I heard "Cassie, Cassie, you're back!"

The Wicked Witch of the West lurched at me from across the room.

"Oh, shit," I mumbled to myself. If there was anyone I *didn't* want to see, it was Margaret, my former roommate, with her straggly black hair, warty nose, and boasts of perpetual mental illness.

("I opened this floor twelve years ago with old Dr. Snyder. I was the very first patient they had. I've seen them all come and go and, believe me, I know where all the bodies are buried."

I'd refrained from asking, "What bodies?" though I'm sure there's a room someplace where they stack the carcasses of those who remain obstinately demented in the face of modern medicine.)

"I knew you'd be back," Margaret crowed, falling into my lap. "I wish we were roommates again. You were so funny, always yelling, 'Hello there voice in the wall,' when they called you on the PA system. Always joking. Are you still with Charlie?"

"I'm still with Charlie, Margaret," I said, lighting a cigarette with shaking hands. *Don't tell me how "funny" I was, Margaret. Don't tell me about the "cute" things I said and the "cute" things I did or I will tell Dalton that your husband sneaks barbiturates into the ward, that he slips you a handful of junk every other night. Anything you want so long as you stay quiet and happy and peaceful and HERE. Don't tell me about me, Margaret, or goddammit, I'll wreck your game.*

"Why are you still with Charlie?" she persisted. "I thought you couldn't stand him."

"Charlie isn't *that* bad, Margaret, and besides we're working it out." *I'm with Charlie because after eleven years of being a housewife I have nowhere else to go.*

I'm too sick to get a job and I wouldn't know where to start anyway. And if I left Charlie one week, I'd have breast cancer the next and then who would want me? I'm with Charlie for all the right reasons, Margaret.

Margaret shook her head. "That's sure different than you were talking the last time. You were going to go home and get a divorce and—"

"What's happening around here, Margaret?" I interrupted.

"Oh. Do you remember Amy Dalmeyer?" she said. "She was the one with the enormous stuffed cat who wouldn't go to occupational therapy. Her, not the cat. You missed her by only a week. She just sat in her room for six weeks and cried. The staff couldn't get her to participate in anything. I even tried to talk to her, what with my experience and all, but the little snip just threw her cat at me and slammed the door. Well, her shrink—you know, Dr. Fisher—his wife died last summer and it took all the stuffing out of him. He just runs in twice a week and prescribes shock treatments for his patients so he won't have to talk to them; no way to practice psychiatry, if you ask me. Anyway, he was threatening to have her transferred to Turney Road State when one morning a Mark Eden Bust Developer arrived in the mail. Well, Amy took to developing her bust in the parlor during group therapy. That upset most of the women and all of the men. Pretty soon everyone was talking about breasts and breast fixations, even though Amy was the only one who had one in the first place. So they asked her to cut it out and she got all huffy and took her bust developer and signed herself out. How about that?"

I laughed. "I'm sorry I missed her. She had a nice sense of humor. She wasn't a looney anyway, Margaret. If I had a thirty-AA bust, I'd sit in my room and cry for six weeks too. If that infernal machine works she could give one hell of a testimonial. 'How I gained nine inches and lost a psychotic depression with the Mark Eden Bust Developer.' Whoopee."

"A bigger bust won't cure depression, Cassie. It's what's inside that counts."

May I quote you, Margaret? May I write that down and call the newspaper and quote you? The world is waiting to hear that, Margaret. "What's with my roommate?" I asked. "She doesn't speak or eat or go to the bathroom, for God's sake. She just lies there like the living dead and it's making me nervous."

"Let's see. You're in seven twenty-three. That's Mrs. Caliguire. She's in one of those 'back to the womb' things, you know. Her brother brought her in, a real old geezer with a hearing aid sticking out of each ear, looked like a Martian. He said she'd been acting like she couldn't hear a thing for months, when she can hear as well as anyone can, except for her brother, of course. Then she wouldn't get out of bed or open her eyes or anything. He said he'd even taken her to church. They belong to one of those really strict churches where they believe that God strikes you sick when you've sinned and strikes you well when you repent, although what kind of sin an old lady like that could have committed I don't know. It didn't do any good. She didn't even know she was in church. So he brought her here because he's getting along in years and can't take care of her. I heard Miss Dalton say that sometimes when people are afraid of something, like going deaf, they pretend that it's already happened and act accordingly."

"Then she's afraid of dying, too," I said. "I've seen people laid out for three days who looked more alive than that one."

"Her minister used to come in every few days and pray over her, but he hasn't been around lately. I don't know what they're going to do with her."

"Don't worry, Margaret. They'll get her somehow. Have any of the shrinks come in yet?"

Before Margaret could answer, Gloria appeared in the doorway announcing, "Mrs. Ambrose, the doctor will see you now."

"Me? Really?" said Margaret, as though it was a

big surprise and a singular honor. She patted my knee, then dipped after Gloria.

I settled back and lit another cigarette, ignoring my fellow patients the way you do strangers on a bus. The waiting wouldn't be so bad if the results were worth the effort, but I'd never been able to make any particular sense out of what happens. I've seen patients enter the interview room belligerently, having psyched themselves up and been encouraged by their peers demanding to be released. They emerge, reduced to mush and agreeing with "the doctor" that they're not "quite ready."

I've seen them creep in timidly, pathetically squeezing a tear from each eye, only to appear in seconds, discharge slip in hand and stark terror on their faces, officially designated "able to cope." RELEASED TO THE WORLD!

Sweet little old ladies and men, never known to utter a word above a whisper, find their tranquilizer dosage increased by Dr. Farraday, a nerd who looks like Cesar Romero and has the bad taste to be proud of it. By afternoon they're sitting in the parlor drooling on the potted plants.

I've seen Farraday take a patient who is clearly coming unglued and, inspired by the latest *Psychology Today* article, "Running Amuck Is the Patient's Way of Saying He's Lonely," reduce the poor bastard's tranquilizers, which sends him running through the halls and the rest of us into anxiety attacks.

If you have the temerity to ask a shrink the reasons behind these arbitrary decisions, he says, "Why do you want to know?"

Rule 1 at Shrink School states: All questions are to be answered with questions—except those to be answered with "Hmmmmm." The patient psyche is too fragile to deal with answers.

So I was surprised, elated, and fearful when my fixed and unfocused gaze fell upon the black shoes and gray tweed kneecaps of Dr. Edwin Alexander.

"Come with me," he intoned. I followed him out

with every patient's eye glued to my back. Psychiatrists *do not* come after patients. Patients sometimes prostrate themselves in the halls like demented Gandhis in a vain attempt to gain their shrink's attention, but all they ever get is stepped on—or Thorazine.

I continued to follow the gray tweedy Presence in the direction of my room. It all became perfectly clear. Alexander planned to throw me on my bed and ravish me thoroughly, not out of lust for my body, but solely as therapy for Mrs. Caliguire. Well, this ought to do it. She may be in the throes of catatonia, but she is, after all, a Baptist!

I felt both proud and humble, participating in the cure of Mrs. Caliguire. And, looking at Alexander's ostentatiously masculine back, a little horny. The stuff they put in the food only works for Margaret, who was last horny in 1921 and thought it was a gas attack.

Once again, I was wrong. Alexander sat on a chair. I sat, self-consciously, on my bed. Omens and portents filled the air, competing with the Lysol.

Alexander cleared his throat.

"I have some bad news for you," he said, looking honest-to-God distressed.

Don't look at me like that. You're scaring the living hell out of me. "What is it?" I asked, trying to be casual.

"Your EEG came back. You have some damage to the left temporal lobe. Not extensive, maybe not even permanent. But, it's there."

"Damage?" I whispered.

Oh, God, the fear! My mind had always been the best part of me, even foggy and filled with distorted perceptions. Now it was shriveling up and rotting away. *I'll spend the rest of my days strapped in a wheelchair like Mrs. Walker and calling everyone Geraldine!* Tears filled my eyes and I fought to hold on to my nonchalance.

Alexander watched my reaction, then leaned over and patted my hand. HE TOUCHED ME! MY PSYCHIATRIST TOUCHED ME! Falling instantaneously in love distracted me—for three seconds.

He went on. "It's like trauma-induced epilepsy. Probably reversible. That's why you're falling down and having muscle spasms."

I continued to cry. Maybe he'd pat me again.

"Why?" I asked.

"Who knows. Maybe it's from drinking. Anyway, it's not important. We'll give you Dilantin, the epilepsy medication. Your symptoms will improve and we'll take another EEG before you leave here. It's likely to be better. I'm sorry."

He looked uncomfortable but he also looked like a person who truly gave a damn and for that I was grateful.

Stop clearing your throat and pat me, you fool.
"Look," I sniffed, feeling impelled to comfort him, "it's okay. I did it to myself. I'll learn to live with it."

He straightened, becoming abrupt and official. "Of course you will," he said cheerfully. "It could be worse."

Sure, I could have been run over by a double-decker bus and be lying in the gutter with my head squashed. Get out of here, Edwin, with your goddamn "could be worse."

He stopped at the door. "By the way, Tom Donnerly called me this morning. He said that you called him yesterday. I thought you'd stopped seeing him."

I blushed. *Here come all my chickens, flying home to roost!*

"He told me that you sounded very upset. He wanted to know if there was anything he could do." Alexander's eyes narrowed. "I asked him if he wanted to take responsibility for you and he hesitated, so I told him he's safe. You're not out of control. He said thanks and hung up. Get rid of him, Cassie."

"What?"

"He's only concerned that Charlie will find out you've been seeing him. He doesn't really care."

"He doesn't want to marry me, but he's not cold and he does care," I protested. "As much as anyone ever does."

The muscles in Alexander's face twitched. "I know

what I'm talking about. Relationships like this aren't good for you. Get rid of him."

I had no answer. He stared at me for a moment, then disappeared. I stretched out on my bed.

I'd called Tom, looking for what? Reassurance? Commitment? Words of affection?

"If Charlie makes you that unhappy, then leave him," he'd said.

I'd thought to myself, *Don't you realize, Tom, that without somewhere to go and someone to go to I have no alternative!* but instead I said, "I'll have to think about that. I'll call when I can."

And I hung up, obscurely disappointed and exasperated with myself for being so unrealistic.

I folded my pillow under me. "I won't give you up, Tom Donnerly," I whispered into the softness. "I won't give up your hands and your mouth, the way you laugh and slap my fanny, the way you make your arms a warm, soft cave for me to vanish into, the stories you tell and the way you have of watching me when I'm talking, all tenderness and patience, even when all I can talk about is my therapy and Alexander. No, I won't give you up. Not even for him."

I was sighing deeply and nearly asleep when a voice next to my bed said, "C'mon, it's time for your chest X ray."

I opened my eyes to see Kenny, the day orderly, eyeing me warily.

I rolled slowly out of bed wondering why people think that a hospital is a place where you rest. I hadn't been so busy since Charlie and I took a two-week cruise with a dozen physical fitness nuts, led by a hyperthyroid social director.

Kenny refrained from mentioning my violent attack on his person, but he walked well behind me. Once there, I changed into a gown and stood against the wall while the technician jammed the machine tight to my chest.

"Take a breath in," she said distractedly, evidently uneasy with a seventh-floor patient. Breathing in must not be that simple. I collapsed on the floor. Thinking that I was having a fit, the technician ran into the hall, calling for help.

Kenny came running, assessed the situation, and helped me up.

"She's okay," he assured the girl. "She just falls down sometimes."

"If you say so," she replied, approaching me with a look generally reserved for mass murderers and the congenitally uncool.

All right, lady. If it's crazy you want, it's crazy you'll get. I screamed full in her face. "Arrrgh!"

With a panic-stricken shriek that satisfied my soul, she galloped into the hall. Kenny couldn't persuade her to return, so, thoroughly disgusted, he escorted me upstairs, where Dalton gave me a scolding to the effect that nonloonies have feelings too. She also gave me Dilantin. I walked to my room, where Mrs. Caliguire's nose was pointed at the ceiling.

I leaned over her form and softly chanted, "There was an old man from Nantucket . . ." She never turned a hair.

4

Several days later I sat in the parlor talking to some of the other patients.

"What time is it?" Joanne asked, sighing with each inhalation. A pretty woman, she'd been hauled in, bleeding from every orifice and half dead from self-induced malnutrition. They'd given her six pints of blood from the Red Cross, Euclid Avenue, wino division, and she'd perked up enough to go into a terrible depression.

"What does it matter?" Frank answered. "We're not going anywhere." He flipped through the newspapers on the coffee table. "Where is the newspaper? I want to see how the Browns are doing."

"I just wanted to know what time it is so I can fix my hair before Ronnie gets here," Joanne continued, twisting on the couch so she could see through the glass partition separating the parlor from the nurses' station.

Jesus Christ, not again, I thought. Every other night Husband Ronnie staggers in drunk with some babe's lipstick on his collar, tells Joanne how awful she looks and how much this is costing and then splits, leaving her sighing like an asthmatic calliope.

"Why do you put up with that schmuck, Joanne?" I asked with my usual tact and diplomacy.

"What am I going to do?" she said. "If I was a better wife, Ronnie wouldn't need booze and other women."

Go ahead, Joanne, forgive him. Play victim for the rest of your life. Just don't be surprised when someone picks up your unworthiness vibrations and kicks your teeth down your throat. Stop smiling at me. I don't feel guilty because you're helpless. Stop looking like my mother. I can't stand it. "Ronnie needs a social call from a competent hit man," I said.

Joanne stared, aghast. "He's really very sweet when he isn't drinking."

Frank continued his search. "One thing you've got to say about Barbara. She may not be much of a wife in some respects, but she never loses the newspaper."

Joanne joined in the hunt, making Frank feel guilty.

"Sit down. Sit down." He waved her back to the couch. "It's not all that important."

He turned to me. "Alexander is your doctor too, isn't he?"

I nodded.

"What do you think of him?" he asked. "I mean, he seems awfully young to me. It's hard for me to talk to someone that age. He can't be more than, oh, thirty-five. I keep thinking, What can he know? D'ya know what I mean? But he seems okay. He makes sense and all. And God knows I waited long enough to get here."

"Why did you have to wait so long?" I asked. "I was admitted in a matter of hours without even wanting to be."

Frank looked down at his large square hands and shrugged. "I never had any trouble before, so when this came up my wife called the family doctor. He found Alexander for me. I waited a week for a bed to be available. I didn't think I was going to make it." He squeezed his hands together, cracking his knuckles.

"What happened? What came up?" I asked, ignoring Frank's embarrassment.

He flushed. "Well, you see, I'm a bus driver for the CTS. Their policy is that when you're fifty you have to retire to a desk job. I never could stand being closed in, confined, you might say. D'ya know what I mean? I started to worry about it. I couldn't sleep. As my birthday got closer, I couldn't even eat. I kept seeing myself chained to a desk in a little room for-ever, well, until I was sixty-five. Two days before my birthday, I picked up a load at the West Side Market. People were packed in the aisles talking all their different languages, like friends, like neighbors. All of a sudden I realized that this is what I would miss most— the people, their jabbering and the good-smelling food, the cheeses and sausage and bread in their shopping bags. Something inside of me snapped.

"I started the bus, locked all the doors and wouldn't let anyone off at their stops. It was terrible. There I was, driving hell-bent-for-leather over the bridge with people yelling and screaming and banging on the doors. A police car started chasing me on Euclid Avenue. By the time I got to the yard there were five cops be-hind me and a 'copter circling overhead.

"My supervisor was waiting with a bunch of cops. I

just fell off the bus into his arms, crying ilke a baby."
Frank shook his head in wonderment. "And here I
am."

"What does Alexander say?" I asked. Somehow, I'd
never pictured Alexander closeted in an interview
room staring raptly at anyone other than me.

Frank gestured resignation. "He says that it's 'involutional melancholia,'" he said, tripping over his
diagnosis as we are all wont to do. "If I'm not better
soon, he's going to order shock treatments."

"What's involutional melancholia?" Joanne asked.

"That's middle-aged depression," I answered.

"Since when did a time of life become a disease?"
Frank inquired. "Come to think of it, though, it is
goddamn depressing." He gazed mournfully at Joanne
and joined her in sighing.

*Shit! Stereo sighing. I might as well be home with
Mother.*

Pomeroy waddled into the parlor and waved a pink
slip under my nose.

"Another call from your mother," she announced,
peering at me intently.

*Get out of here with your pink slip. In the outside
world, a phone call is a phone call. Here it's a Testing
Situation. If you return it, you're allowing yourself to
be manipulated. If you don't, you're evading reality.
I know that game, Pomeroy.* "I'll return the call," I
said. *The door is locked. She can't get me here.*

Mother must have been sitting on the phone.

"Hello, who's this?" she bellowed. I could hear a cartoon program blasting away.

"It's Cassie," I shrilled. "Please turn down the TV."
She didn't. Legitimate chances to bellow don't come
along too often.

"Come home. Your children need you."

"I can't come home yet. The doctor won't let me."

"What does he know! You'd rather be there with a
bunch of crazy people than at home with your children who need you!"

"Mother," I struggled to explain, "I am sick and I
need to be better before I can come home. The chil-

dren don't need a sick mother. Besides, I thought you agreed with Charlie that I should come. You were in a big enough hurry to get me here."

"That's because you scared the bejesus out of me with your damn foolishness. You are not sick. The trouble with you is, you're stubborn. You've always been stubborn. You used to stamp your feet and yell at me when you were two. When you were five I told you not to climb on the garage roof. Did you listen? Oh no, not you. You fell off and broke your arm and I had to sit up with you for weeks. You wouldn't wear your raincoat and got pneumonia and I had to go back and forth on the bus to the hospital. You got a kidney infection when we were moving to the West Side, as if moving wasn't enough for me to contend with. Then you got that liver disease from drinking bad water and who had to take care of you? You were told not to drink from a pump. Now you're in the nuthouse for the second time and who's here taking care of your children and your house? Me. I'm exhausted from your stubbornness. You're making me crazy with your stubbornness."

"You've had a hard life, Mother. Someday God will reward you."

"I don't want God to reward me. I want you to come home."

Mother was beginning to cry. I changed the subject.

"Would you like to hear about my EEG, Mother?" I asked.

"My God!" she gasped. "What's the matter with your heart!"

"An EEG isn't a heart thing. It's a brain thing." I reassured her.

"I don't want to hear about any brain thing. If you had a brain in your head, you'd come home. If you had any consideration—"

I hung up, chopping off the sentence. It gave me a zingy little thrill, as if I'd managed to strangle her.

In my room I wavered between longing for aspirin and aversion to a confrontation with Pomeroy. She'd stand, with the aspirin suspended just out of my reach, like a trainer with a doggie biscuit, watching me salivate and waiting for my trick. I'd perform with a revised edition of my phone call to Mother, bending it in the direction of either reconciliation (mature acceptance of Mother as an autonomous being) or rejection (working through adolescent dependence on Mother to an ultimately independent lifestyle).

Tell me what you want, Pomeroy. Grunt, and I'll slog through the swamp. Nod, and I'll skip through the nettles. Frown, and I'll retreat from paradise. The aspirin isn't worth it.

I sat on my bed, contemplating Caliguire the Comatose. *How peaceful you look, with your body pseudo-dead and your spirit off wandering. Don't come back, Caliguire. All you have to look forward to is a brother who doesn't want you and eventually an autopsy.*

"Please come to the nurses' station, Cassie. I mean, Mrs. Barrett. Cassie?"

The nurse on the PA system couldn't decide which one of me she wanted. They use "Mrs. Barrett" to remind me I'm married (just because I occasionally rhapsodize over other men doesn't mean I've forgotten. See my ring?) and "Cassie" to project an attitude of quasi-parental concern (now see here, young lady) or phony familiarity (you're not a patient and I am not a staff person. We are two equals having a nice chat).

"We're both on our way." I heaved to my feet, suppressing a sigh. With the patients all sighing and the staff following suit, the hallway sounded like a canyon with the wind whistling through.

At the desk, Miss Merriweather, a gorgeous redhead, pursed her Barbie-doll lips. "Doctor Proctor is waiting for you," she said, blinking exquisite green eyes. "He's going to give you a neurological workup."

"Now?"

"Oh, yes, he's waiting for you," she replied and took her cameo profile off to the lounge.

I hope you get pimples and all the veins in your nose break and spread all over your alabaster puss, Merriweather.

I lingered in the hall, deliberately keeping him waiting. As I crept timidly into the room, the Proctor Doctor glanced up from the chart he was scanning and frowned.

I'm sorry I made you wait. Honest. Here, I'll slash my wrists.

"Mrs. Barrett? Cassie?" he asked.

NOW I understand. It's their method of informing me I'm schizophrenic. Call me by two names and hope that after a few weeks I'll catch on. That way nothing specific has been said and there's no worry that I'll busily engage in acting out my diagnosis—and the doctor can later change his mind. "The latest tests show that you have tuberculosis, cancer, and Reynards disease."

"I'm Mrs. Barrett. Cassie." Why not?

"Haven't I seen you before?" he quizzed. "Weren't you here about a year ago?"

You have my chart in your hands, you imbecile. "Yes."

"And?" he encouraged.

"And I'm back."

He sighed resignedly.

An epidemic of sighing swept Shaker Heights Hospital, wiping out the entire staff, who died of carbon monoxide poisoning. They lay on the floor turning blue, closely observed by the patients who had swiftly fashioned gas masks out of bedpans. The patients, who took notes, agreed that the final agony of the staff was indeed an awesome spectacle and ran off to write up the experience for the APA Journal. The article, entitled "The Psychological Dynamic Underlying Involuntary Asphyxiation," written by Ralph Waldo Ross, registered weirdo and world-renowned lecturer, is currently in its seventeenth reprint.

"All right. You're familiar with the tests. Name all the presidents since Roosevelt."

I named them, adding political affiliation. He scribbled.

"Repeat these numbers after me: four, eight, six, seven, two, nine, five, three, one."

I got as far as nine and gave up.

"Okay, now repeat these numbers backwards . . ." and he droned on while I sat on what looked like a small milking stool, unable to remember a thing.

He got through the number game and the history game and the sentence completion and the physical.

"Your lips are dry. Are you thirsty?" he asked.

I nodded affirmatively.

"Why don't you drink water?"

"Why should I bother? I'll only get thirsty again."

He scribbled madly.

"Just one last thing. Interpret this for me. 'A rolling stone gathers no moss.' "

"I did that one last time," I said, annoyed.

"Okay, how about, 'A golden key unlocks all doors.' "

Well, you see, Doctor, the appearance of the magic, manifestly phallic key causes the locks securing the doors or vaginas, to vaporize instantaneously, which means that if you meet up with the right penis you'll open up, which usually happens whether it's the golden key or not because how can you tell if you don't let it in your lock. "I think it means that if you determine your basic problem and try to resolve it, you might find your other problems becoming resolved also," I said, flushed with embarrassment. I hadn't meant to take it seriously.

He peered at me. "That's interesting." He tapped his pen against his clipboard.

"You know, I really like to talk to you," he said. "You're bright and inquisitive. But I dislike seeing you here. I feel that you've made an unconscious decision to vegetate for the rest of your life, coming here once or twice a year to get away from it all and drinking in the meantime. You probably intend to go on this way until you die, which may not be as long as you think, but may turn out to be longer than you want. Don't you look forward to anything?"

"Only menopause and senility," I snapped. "And with my luck, they'll overlap."

His shrug underscored his exasperation and he was gone, leaving me on the milking stool.

I'm so goddamned tired of this mess, tired of waiting for calamities, of having no control over anything, over myself. I'm tired of feeling guilty every moment that I breathe.

I buried my head in my arms and sobbed, sobbed over the untidy debacle of my life: the husband I didn't want and couldn't function in the world without (guilty), the children I loved but with whom I felt unable to cope (guilty), the mother with whom I hovered suspended between a desperate need to please and an urge to commit matricide (guilty), and the lover whom I didn't love and who didn't love me, but whose participation in our mutual game of "let's pretend" was vital to my sanity (guilty).

Oh, shit, I thought, wiping my face on my sweater. *I really need help.* One hell of a conclusion to come to after four years of therapy. I dragged myself to my feet and doddered into the hall.

Proctor sat at the nurses' station, chewing on the end of his pen. Either he was working on my chart or writing his memoirs.

He focused on my face and jumped.

"You've been crying," he observed with rigorously trained scientific accuracy.

"No," I said. "I never cry. I was sitting there minding my own business and thinking how gorgeous you are when Kenny ran in, yelled 'Fire,' and doused me with a bucket of water. You should do something about that boy."

"Okay, if that's the way you want it," he replied.

"When can I expect my schizophrenia to clear up?" I asked.

"Who said you're schizophrenic? You're not schizophrenic."

"What am I then?"

"You're . . . never mind. You're NOT schizophrenic."

Damn! Almost got him that time.

5

"They think I don't know what's in the medication, but I do. They can't fool me," Ludwig said, tapping the side of his head with his finger.

"What's in the medication, Ludwig?" I asked, putting on a serious face.

"It's stuff that makes you weak," he replied ominously. "It saps all your strength and your will to resist. Then when they've got you down to jelly, wham! They move in and finish you off."

"Who's them?" I asked, already knowing the answer.

"THEM! THEM! The conspiracy!" Ludwig shouted angrily. "They're after us all and you don't even care!"

I was playing five-card stud with Ludwig, who was a dead ringer for Jack Palance, a resemblance which somehow caused several of the patients to lend some credence to his claim of having chosen our haven as a temporary sanctuary in his flight from a sinister international cartel. It seemed like something Jack Palance would do. He also said his mother-in-law was the leader of this conspiracy, which spoiled the story for me, but caused many patients, who had learned through seeing *The Godfather* that familial affiliation can be fatal, to become further enmeshed in his tale. We were divided into two camps: those of us who knew words like "paranoia," and those of us who went to Charles Bronson movies and believed every frame.

"It's tranquilizers, Ludwig," Frank interrupted. "You're a real fruitcake." Being depressed made Frank unafraid, even of a man who'd been wrestled into the ward by three giant cops and claimed to own a collection of weapons that ranged from a club to anti-missile missiles.

"Up yours," Ludwig replied, glowering. "Any man who goes bananas over losing a lousy little job driving a lousy little bus is no man at all."

John Wayne lives, I thought.

"What do you do?" Frank asked Ludwig.

"Why do you want to know?" Emile asked suspiciously.

"Shazam, Shazam, Shazam." Abdul waved his cards under Frank's nose, impatient to get on with the game. A new arrival, Abdul was an eight-foot-tall black, masculine person who seemed to be in a semistupor and claimed to be a prophet.

"He's nothing but a junkie," Ludwig had declared, but I had my fingers crossed for a prophet, as junkies we already had. Despite the stupor, Abdul was winning the game, which made the veins in Ludwig's neck stick out. Pomeroy was hanging around, clutching a bottle of Thorazine and looking twitchy. Joanne sat in a corner chair busily crocheting a red bouclé something, hopefully a shroud for Rotten Ronnie. Another new arrival, Norma, who gave off a sulphurous odor and snarled when anyone approached, sat on the sofa with her purse in her lap, like a dog protecting its bone. Other patients wandered lethargically up and down the halls.

Playing cards was better than sitting with nothing to do. Charlie was scheduled to come in around noon for what's called a "spouse-interview," and I'd spent the morning worrying and wondering why. It seemed that always, somewhere, there were two people (Mother and Charlie, Charlie and Alexander, Alexander and Proctor, Proctor and Pomeroy) actively engaged in a solemn discussion, the topic of which was "What should we do about Cassie?" I was being dissected and reassembled behind closed doors, at meetings where I was denied entrance, my life and future decided by an invisible committee composed of "interested parties" who were sincerely concerned from their point of view, but who consistently neglected to ask me what I thought about the whole thing.

So I sat, engaged in time-passing and communication with my fellow patients, most of whom I wanted to give a swift kick in the ass. *Divorce that creep, Joanne, and start acting like a person with some self-respect. Shape up, Abdul, lay off the smack. Either get used to the desk job, Frank, or retire on a medical disability and take long drives in the country. Change your name to Luigi and join the Mafia, Ludwig, where your talents and predilections will be put to good use. Bring in the next patient, Pomeroy. I'll have this place cleared in fifteen minutes flat.*

Gloria materialized out of nowhere, yawning. "Ya'll has a phone call, Miz Barrett. Git it on up there to the phone." She leaned against the table, knocking Abdul's chips to the floor. "Shazam," he said with a look that could kill.

Mother again, I thought. *What is it this time?*

"Better hurry," Gloria mumbled from under the table where she was picking up chips. "It's long distance."

"Why didn't you say so?" I shrieked, making a miraculous recovery from catatonia. I tore down the hall, waving my arms and yelling "Bobby, Bobby, Bobby" like a true maniac, an action which delighted the wandering patients and scared the shit out of Dalton, who assumed I'd totally flipped.

"Hi, Bob," I screamed into the phone. "How the hell are you?"

"How the hell are *you* is more to the point?" he said, his deep, easy laugh rolling through the phone accompanied by static.

"Oh, I'm okay. I'm getting there," I replied, then lowered my voice. "To tell you the truth, I feel awful."

"I didn't think you were there because you feel terrific, Cass. Is there anything I can do—other than write you letters?"

I started to cry softly, turning my back on the

nurses' station and Pomeroy, who was eyeing me curiously.

"If I knew what you could do, I'd ask you to do it," I said. "The trouble is that I don't think there's anything anyone can do. Everything is one hell of a mess and everyone is furious at me. Charlie keeps saying that he doesn't believe in divorce but he doesn't want to live this way anymore. He says he's going to keep the kids and I can't do anything about it because of my psychiatric history—and he's right. I can't. And I don't know what I'd do with the kids all alone anyway. And I get the god-awful feeling that Alexander is going to kick me out of here as soon as I'm better physically."

"What's wrong with you physically?" Bobby interrupted.

"Oh, I have a problem with my legs, some sort of neuritis, and a few things like that," I answered vaguely. "Anyway, Alexander just gives me the old fisheye and asks me what I'm going to do about my problems and when I start to come out with some ideas he just shakes his head and tells me that I'm confused. And Mother is madder than hell, but calls me all the time anyway."

Bobby laughed. "She called me yesterday and demanded that I come home. She said that everything was a mess and what kind of a son moves across country and leaves his mother to cope all alone and if Dad was alive he would be sorry that he spent five thousand dollars on my braces, I could have teeth coming out of my ears for all she cared. And then she hung up. How are the kids?"

"Fine," I answered, not wanting to talk about the kids. "Mother is still mad at you for breaking your deathbed promise to Dad," I said. *See, I can play the guilt game as well as Mother. Please come home, Bobby. I need you. I need somebody.*

"I know she is," he said evenly, rejecting the game. "Still, I didn't know it was his deathbed and neither did Dad. He asked me if I would take care of Mother while he had his hernia operation and I said I would, and by God, I did. No one knew he would have a heart attack, least of all him. Mother turned a two-week commitment into a pledge of lifelong servitude. Besides," he continued, "do you really think that Mother needs taking care of?"

"Hell, no," I replied, wondering why this had become a "Mother" discussion. "She reminds me of a piece of cork on the sea. She looks tiny and frail, but she sails through lightning and thunder and when the storm's all gone, there she is bobbing along on the waves."

"Yup," he agreed. "And if she ever truly needs me, I'll be there."

What about ME, Bob, what about ME? "Where did we go wrong, Bob?" I sighed.

"What?"

"I mean, everything is out of kilter. It always was. You got that blond curly hair and mine is just brown and straight as a snake. I loved school and got straight A's and you hated studying and had to go to college because you were the boy——"

"And Dad made you stop playing football when your boobs started flopping up and down under your sweatshirt," Bob picked it up, laughing. "And he broke all my crayons because he said that no son of his was going to sit around and draw flowers——"

"And you were always so damn *pretty*, Bobby, with your long eyelashes and fair complexion, so slender and graceful. I felt like a big, fat moose next to you."

"You're pretty now, Cassie," he said softly.

"I don't *feel* pretty," I mourned. "Where do we go to register a complaint, Bob? Just where do we go to complain?"

"Damned if I know," he answered, "but from what I hear you've been taking your complaints to the liquor store. Is that true, Cassie?" I didn't answer. "Cassie, what are you going to do about your drinking?"

"You've been listening to Mother," I accused.

"She isn't *always* wrong, Cass. And the last time I was home I thought you were hitting it heavy. You told me that one day you were having a drink in your kitchen and the next thing you knew you were out in a boat on Lake Erie with a guy who sold pig iron to fourteen smelting plants in the Ohio-Pennsylvania area. You said that you didn't think anything had happened but I wasn't to tell Charlie. Remember?"

Jesus, I thought, not remembering that I'd told him about that.

"What are you going to do, Cass?" he persisted.

"I'm going to immolate myself in Public Square in front of the Soldiers and Sailors Monument," I said. "I'll drench myself in vodka and set myself on fire in atonement for my sins. The headline will read 'Bad Lady Burns'! Look, I'm awfully glad you called but this is costing you a fortune. Write to me, will you?"

"Of course I will," he answered. "Just remember, Cass. I'm on your side."

"Thanks, Bobby. I'll let you know how it all turns out. *If* it all turns out."

" 'Bye, honey. Take care." The phone clicked and I stood with the receiver in my hand feeling simultaneously loved and cared for, lectured at and abandoned.

Charlie was just emerging from the interview room looking unhappy, followed by Alexander, looking superior.

"Hi, Cass," Charlie said. "You're looking better than the last time I saw you."

"You mean when you ran off and left me for dead? I should hope so."

Charlie sighed.

Charlie's got it too. It's catching!

Dalton handed me a signed pass permitting me to have lunch in the cafeteria accompanied by my husband (certified keeper). Lunching in the cafeteria is considered a privilege, something akin to an extra bowl of gruel at the orphanage. So off we went, Charlie glancing surreptitiously and warily at me, and me, dressed primly in a black skirt and white blouse, trying to stop shaking and look normal.

The cafeteria was full of volunteers with pink aprons

and blue hair, all eating tuna fish sandwiches and warding off involutional melancholia. I looked around at the chrome, sunny-yellow and brilliant-orange decor, meant to be an oasis of cheerfulness in a building devoted to disease, death, and dementia. It was like being trapped inside a plastic orange.

Charlie cleared his throat. I was beginning to think that throat clearing was a solidly entrenched male characteristic, perhaps transmitted through the genes. Or maybe it's something they do instead of crying.

"Order tuna fish. You like tuna fish."

"I'm too young for tuna fish. I want grilled cheese."

"Okay, grilled cheese—and chicken noodle soup. You're skinny." He ordered for us while I watched him.

Look, Charlie, why don't we admit that it was all a mistake. I don't understand you and you don't understand me and our priorities are different. We're two horses pulling the same cart in opposite directions. I'm tired of lying to you, Charlie. I lie to you all the time and I'm afraid you'll find out and I wish you'd find out so you'd DO something about it, Charlie. Just tell me it's over and mean it, so I don't have to live like this anymore. DO something, Charlie.

Charlie looked directly at me, his intelligent face weary.

"Alexander says that you're arrested emotionally."

"Better than for drunk driving."

Charlie scowled. "He says you're about twelve emotionally."

"No wonder I have pimples. I thought it was the Mounds bars I've been eating."

The soup and sandwiches arrived, and we found a corner table.

"He says you'll never get better, or emotionally older anyway." Charlie slumped, looking totally miserable and three inches shorter. He began munching his sandwich.

Despair filled my chest like a cold, wet mist, and somewhere behind it, little flashes of anger, like heartburn. *How dare Alexander! How dare he say NEVER —and, oh God, what if he's right. But NEVER! Never is a word reserved for lung cancer and mongolian idiots. And that pompous proponent of positive thinking has the temerity to say NEVER about ME to Charlie!* I looked at Charlie woefully munching ham on rye and trying to accept being shackled, maybe forever, to a boozy Lolita, and my heart broke for both of us.

I burst into tears, sending a shower of chicken noodle soup blasting through my nose, and sat, noodles cascading down my chin, weeping copiously onto my grilled cheese.

"If you don't like that, you can have a hamburger," Charlie soothed.

"I want to go upstairs," I wailed, as everyone turned around to stare.

"All right," Charlie said, relieved.

Outside in the hall I stood sobbing while doctors, nurses, and visitors passed by with nary a glance. In the elevator, Charlie patted me as if I were an agitated sheep dog while I wailed. Our fellow passengers stared at the ceiling. Dalton buzzed us into the ward and I fell into her stiff, starched arms. She looked over my head at Charlie.

Charlie nodded and went, looking defeated.

"What's wrong?" Dalton asked.

"Charlie's shrinking," I wailed. "Last week he was only a little shorter than me and now he only comes up to my shoulder. Every time I see him, he's shrunk more and more. Pretty soon he'll disappear altogether. Or someone will step on him. Squash. No more Charlie."

Dalton smiled, helping me down the hall to my room.

"Sounds like guilt to me," she decided. She rolled me on my bed, pulled off my shoes and threw the blanket over me as I continued to sob. She stepped to the door.

"You aren't laughing, Cassie," she remarked and vanished.

"Go to hell," I bellowed. As I fell asleep, it occurred to me that Charlie hadn't once mentioned divorce.

I woke with a rotten headache, feeling as embarrassed as though I'd walked down the hall stark naked.
And thirsty. I lumbered down to the nurses' station,
where I grabbed Merriweather's peaches-and-cream
arm and whispered, "Quick—apple juice. I feel a psychotic break coming on."

She smiled kindly and got the juice. They all—Dalton, Pomeroy, Kenny, Gloria, Merriweather, the gnome
with his polisher—smiled kindly. It was awful. I felt
like the new kid on the block who'd survived the ini-
tiation ceremony where everyone gathers round and
kicks the shit out of you—only around here the name
of the game is letting your defenses down. So there I
was sipping my juice and feeling thoroughly shit-kicked,
while Dalton jotted wonderful comments in my folder: "Made an ass of herself in elevator, showing defi-
nite improvement."

But goddamn Alexander, anyway. Even he should
realize that Charlie is not ready for insights, especially
insights so negatively constructed. But there he is.
Wind him up and out comes Freudian garbage, all
day, every day, falling like a less than gentle rain,
wreaking havoc on people's psychic countryside. And
there goes Charlie, schlepping along on a cloud of
free-flowing guilt—for nothing. Having insights
dropped in my lap is the price I must pay for being
bad, but Charlie, who's a model of goodness, could be
absolutely destroyed by insights.

6

"Why can't I have shock treatments, too?" I asked Alexander, who sat behind the desk, patting his head, pursing his lips and tapping his pencil, in an amazing exhibition of manual dexterity.

"No," he said. "They are not for you."

"But why?" I insisted. "I never get any of the good stuff. I don't even get tranquilizers. All I get are aspirins and vitamins. I can take aspirins and vitamins at home and not have to put up with this aggravation. I want to get zapped like everyone else."

"Shock treatments are for specific trauma. You have a life problem. They wouldn't do you any good."

I'd always suspected that my problem was life, but I didn't really need to hear it from One Who Knows.

He continued, "You're all right when you don't drink."

That, Edwin, is debatable. If "all right" means crying nine hours a day and trying to think of ways to commit suicide without God, Charlie, and the insurance company finding out, then I'm Miss Mental Health.

"But when you drink you become out of control and engage in undesirable activities."

If it wasn't for my undesirable activities I would have long since jumped off the High Level Bridge, you ass.

"Why the sudden interest in shock treatments, Cassie?"

"Everyone else here gets them," I said, knowing it

was an exaggeration. "I feel left out. Three times a week I have to haul myself out of my room early so Dalton can buzz in and pop a Seconal down Caliguire's throat. Dalton says she won't go to sleep while I'm in the room, which is ridiculous. Then I have to wait in the parlor with the one or two other rejects for hours while Farraday shocks the shit out of the whackos with his magic machine. The patients call him Reddy Kilowatt.

"Then I go back to my room where Caliguire is staring up at the ceiling in a state of suspended animation with smoke coming out of her ears. Believe me, one more treatment and that woman won't have to pretend she's deaf. Her circuits will be burned out."

Alexander interrupted, frowning, "Shock treatments don't burn anything in the brain."

"What do they do?"

"Well, we don't know *exactly* what they do, but we do know that they're often helpful in relieving depression. They make the patient more amenable to therapy."

"That's a wonderful reason to shoot electricity through somebody's head, so you can explain to him in Freudian terms why he's depressed. Who the hell cares? Knowing why I feel rotten isn't too terribly terrific as long as I'm sitting here still too depressed to move."

"With awareness comes insight, with insight comes the ability to choose more constructive alternatives," Alexander pronounced, reading from the notes on his cuff.

With three you get egg roll. That's one hell of a theory, Edwin. You try to practice it when your life is falling apart.

"And I resent the ritual I have to go through with the shock treatment people," I continued. "They're like mutants in a Japanese monster movie. They wake up with their brain cells or whatever all rearranged and peer around, pop-eyed with confusion and squinting from the headache they all have. They say 'Where am I?' and 'Who are you?' or else they don't say anything at all. They just stare and wait for me to supply the information. And I feel sorry for them—they all look misplaced, as if they'd been run backwards in a time machine—so I end up introducing myself for the third time in a week. I say, 'Hi there. This is Shaker Heights Hospital. This is the psychiatric ward. I am Cassie Barrett. You are . . . whoever. You have a headache and can't remember anything because you had a shock treatment this morning. You will feel better tomorrow.' Believe me, I'm getting tired of it. I should wear a uniform and a button that says 'Information.' You should build me a booth in front of the nurses' station. I should charge for my services."

"Who asked you to do it?" Alexander said.

"Don't give me that 'You must get something out of it or you wouldn't do it' crap. How can I avoid it? Your treatments don't work anyway. They are supposed to forget what's made them depressed, but not knowing makes them crazy, so after they take a shower and start to feel better they start harassing everyone they think might give them a clue, and that definitely includes me. Sometimes it's a temptation not to tell them. Norma spent half the afternoon yesterday probing and poking, trying to get her life story out of me. I wanted to tell her that she's just a mean, bitter bitch and there's no cure for that, but I didn't. Next time I'm going to tell her that the reason she's in here is because she ax-murdered her entire family in a fit of pique and got morbidly depressed because she hates cooking for one."

Alexander's eyes were focused somewhere over my left shoulder. He was wearing the expression he uses when he knows I'm blowing smoke, creating a diversion, and has decided to be tolerant of my tactics.

Jesus, Edwin, I hate the way my emotions flow through you without causing a ripple. Do you ever consider that scores of my responses may be generated by and end solely with you? That in this room and your office we have a life set apart from the one we purport to discuss so interminably, a life that exists only in shadows and echoes and the palpable vibra-

tions that hang in the air between us? I know and I know that you know, and I know that you know that I know. Say something. Stop staring at me.

"How did your lunch with Charlie go? I heard you got upset."

"Of course I got upset. He makes me feel like crawling under a rock. He sits there exuding sufferance and I feel like I should be spanked and sent to my room. He would be wholly ecstatic if Roman centurions would vault out of a bush and nail him to a cross. I like it better when he's angry. Then he gets genuinely vicious and I don't have to react with massive outpourings of guilt. I can defend myself more easily."

"Defend yourself against what?"

I inspected the question, scanning my motives. What was I defending myself against? Charlie's low opinion of me? His disappointment in me? Mine in myself? But defend myself I did, interminably.

Late one Saturday night we were in the bedroom. I'd been pacing up and down, drunkenly loquacious and fervently dumping my guts. I glanced up to see Charlie hugging his pillow and gently snoring. In an absolute fury of frustration I removed my shoe and, yelling, "Wake up you goddamn son of a bitch!" bashed Charlie as hard as I could, square on his temple.

With a roar of rage, he'd bounded out of bed and chased me down the hallway threatening murder. I locked myself in the bathroom and stood shivering with fright while Charlie pounded on the door screaming, "Come out, come out." I didn't, and he finally went back to bed after rummaging in the refrigerator for ice. I slept in the bathtub on top of sheets I pulled out of the linen closet.

In the morning I waited until the kids got up before I unlocked the door. They were unusually quiet that morning, no yelling and shoving while they ate Froot Loops out of Mickey Mouse bowls. Charlie walked into the kitchen with a jagged cut surrounded by a purply-red bruise sticking six inches out on his forehead.

"We're going to ten o'clock mass this morning,"

he'd said to the kids, and to me, "Cass, get them ready." And we'd gone off to church, where we stood together in the first pew and sang hymns just like the Waltons.

I had never told Alexander about that, and, as he waited for my reply, I realized that I never would. There were things that would remain between Charlie and me. Besides, I didn't want him to know I was capable of assault.

"I don't know what I'm defending myself against," I finally acknowledged. "I just know that I have this constant picture of myself with my arms over my head warding off slings and arrows."

"Perhaps if you modified your behavior somewhat you wouldn't feel the need to be continually on the defensive." He gave me one of those "significant" looks.

Shove your significant look, sweetheart. I'm aware that according to the script this is the part where I leap out of my seat shouting, "Eureka, Doctor, you've solved my dilemma!" and kiss your hand out of gratitude. Modify your own behavior, Edwin. I'd love to sit on your lap. It would do wonders for you. "Perhaps," I replied, then added, "Charlie didn't mention divorce." It was more a question than a comment. Charlie's ways are often mysterious to behold, at least to me.

"Charlie isn't the type of man who asks his wife for a divorce while she's in the hospital. He may think it's foolish and self-indulgent, and perhaps even unnecessary, but a hospital is still a hospital to him, and he'll wait. That's just the way he is. Decent."

"Or maybe just worried about what people will think. He couldn't stand 'he took the best years of her life and abandoned her when she went bananas' type gossip. It would wreck his long-suffering act."

"Perhaps." Alexander shrugged. "What are you going to do about Donnerly?"

Throw me another curve, why don't you, Edwin? I'm not ready to field this one. "What do you mean, what am I going to do? I can't do *anything* while I'm here."

"You could write him a letter and tell him you don't want to see him anymore. Now, or when you go home, or ever."

"No," I replied. "I don't want to do that."

"Why not?" he insisted. "This relationship causes you conflict. What are you getting out of it?"

What can I tell you, Edwin? That he makes me feel good and whole and stable? That when I'm with him I don't drink, he doesn't know that I drink? That for one day a week I'm a woman I enjoy being, desirable and intelligent, mature and independent, uninhibited and normal, goddammit NORMAL. And if much of it is an illusion, a role that I'm playing, then so be it, what does it matter? For one day a week I can soar above myself and be only the best of me.

"He's a fantastic lay," I retorted, grinning.

He rose from his chair, clearly exasperated.

"All right, Cassie. That's enough for today. Just think about what we've discussed. One of these days you'll have to decide what you want."

I sat for a long time after he'd gone, thinking about Donnerly, kind, generous, and possessing an enormously attractive vitality; Donnerly who didn't know me at all. And Charlie, who under his hurt and frustration loved me with a single-minded, almost archaic devotion and yearned for the marriage that could have been. And Alexander with his authoritative manner, his orthodox cant, and his eloquent eyes. And then there was me, married to one, involved with another, and irrevocably, mystically tied to the third. What to do? What to do?

I decided to worry about it tomorrow and departed for the parlor to watch television like real people do.

Pomeroy passed the early evening medication looking frazzled and happy that her shift was nearly over. I began picking the aspirin and Dilantin out of my pill cup, making my meager portion last as long as possible. Even the addicts get a rainbow assortment, an astounding array. I can only conclude that some addictions are better for you than others, or maybe more socially acceptable, like burping being better than farting.

I was about to swallow the Dilantin, when a bright little voice behind me chirped, "That's a schizophrenic pill. You're a schizo."

I turned and looked into a young, pretty, swollen-from-crying face with the biggest, most mischievous brown eyes I'd ever seen.

"That's Dilantin," I retorted, annoyed. "It's for epilepsy. Trauma-induced." I popped it down.

"Is not," she persisted, flopping down beside me, her legs crossed before her fanny hit the floor. "Don't worry. I adore schizos. They're more interesting than almost anyone. Except manic depressives. And then only in their manic phase."

"I am not schizophrenic," I yelled. "I am alcoholic." *Jesus Christ! I've never said* that, *not even to myself, and here I am yelling at this funky kid, in front of God, the staff, and the patients. Do I really believe that? If I don't, why would I say it? Why do I feel relieved? Ponder. Ponder.*

"Okay, okay, simmer down." She was prepared to be agreeable. "I'm Cara. I was admitted this morning. I'm depressed," she offered, eyes atwinkle. She pulled her pink mohair down tight over remarkable breasts, catching the simultaneous attention of Ludwig and Abdul.

"Was that you crying all day?" I asked. "And crying is not the word. My six-year-old Jenny has more subdued temper tantrums." The noises that emanated from this kid's room all day included shrieking, head-banging, and outright screams—an Academy Award winner, this one.

"Yup, that's me. Who are you?"

"I'm Cassie. Why are you so depressed?"

She looked cheerfully puzzled. "I don't know. Alexander says it has something to do with my father." Her lower lip trembled. "He's dead, you know."

"Alexander?" I jumped up, alarmed.

"No, dummy—my father," Cara pouted.

I was irritated at having been frightened. "Well, my father is dead too, and if you want to know the truth, almost *everyone's* father is dead, so that's no goddamn reason to fall in here and create an all-day racket. Nobody has had a minute's peace since you arrived. Shape up, girl."

"You sound like my mother," she began to whimper.

Hot damn, I sound like MY mother, too. "So Alexander is your shrink, too. How do you like him?" I said, trying to make amends.

The brown eyes flashed. "I *hate* him. HATE. HATE. HATE! He thinks he knows everything. He thinks he knows ME."

"Then go to someone else," I suggested.

"I can't," she whispered, looking lost.

Aha, what we have here is a clear-cut case of transference. She is madly in love with Super-Shrink, knotted with frustration and adrip with lust.

I resisted an urge to pat this little Cara-person. *I've got problems of my own, kid. Go somewhere else and look forlorn.* I tried another approach.

"Alexander is okay. In fact, he's good. But he's nothing special. They're all pretty much alike." With a straight face yet.

Cara bristled like a disturbed hen.

"He is *too* special," she insisted. "I ought to know. I've been going to shrinks since I was fifteen. All kinds."

I smiled condescendingly. "How old are you now?"

"Twenty-five," she said.

"Twenty-five! I would have guessed eighteen." I was truly surprised.

Cara sighed. "There's a theory that schizophrenics always look younger than they are. But I'm not schizophrenic." She sighed again.

"Maybe you are," I said, seeing as she liked them so well.

"No, I've tried, but I haven't got any auditory hallucinations, or olfactory hallucinations—not even a distortion. I see colors. And planes. And, unfortunately, I'm reality-based. I just cry a lot and try to kill myself."

"You've done that often?"

"Well, four or five times, anyway." She brightened. "It's actually a *cry for help*. Once I took six of the Seconal that my current shrink had prescribed and I had a dozen more in my hand."

Shrink School Rule #2: Give barbiturates to depressives. They will either calm down, enabling you to claim a "cure," or commit suicide, thereby bringing to an end those annoying night calls.

"Looking back," Cara continued, "I'm not positive I wanted to kill myself. I just didn't know what else to do. Anyway, I called the Suicide Prevention Center and a croaky-voiced lady said 'Suicide Prevention Center—one moment please.' Can you believe it, the bitch put me on hold! So there I stood, getting all sleepy and petrified, with the Seconal turning gluey in my hand. Scared the hell out of me, I'll tell you."

"I guess it would," I replied inadequately. "What did you do then?"

She lit a cigarette. "Oh, I hung up and called the operator, who called the Rescue Squad, who came with siren blaring and hauled me off to have my stomach pumped. I told them that I was in therapy and had a regular psychiatrist, but they couldn't reach him, so they just let me go in the morning. I called Dr. Einstein and yelled at him. He said, 'Vy doodn't you cull me?' I said, 'I did, you bastard—and you were at a Barons hockey game. I'm dying and you're getting your jollies watching a bunch of cretins getting their teeth pucked out.' So I fired him and called the APA exchange. The secretary gave me a choice between Edwin Alexander and Nardowitz Horsetter. Who would you have chosen? I figured a guy named Nardowitz has problems enough and sure as hell doesn't need me. So I chose Alexander and here I am. Do you think Alexander has any probelms? Outstanding ones I mean?"

Besides you and me, my dear, I doubt it. Alexander

lives in a vacuum on a red dwarf star that rotates
sluggishly beyond the seventh sun, where troubles melt
like lemon drops. "Your last shrink sounds terrible,"
I remarked.

She shook her head. "Oh, he was a wizard compared to some others. We, my mother and I, lived in
California for a while and I got into the group encounter scene. Then Mother got homesick for interminable
winters and industrial pollution and we came back
to Cleveland two years ago. I didn't want to return
with the holy terror, but the rotten old bat still con-
trols the money, so what could I do?" She looked
fearfully around as though she expected a monster to
jump out of the woodwork and pounce on her. I wondered if her problem was father, the obstinately deceased, or mother, the termagantly alive.

"What's it like, the group thing?" I asked.

Cara puffed. "Well, you're supposed to get in touch
with your Real Self. That means you get to act as pu-
tridly as you want, really get into hostility and spew
off language your mother would slap your face for,
and everyone stands around saying, 'We accept you
as you are and cherish your humanness.' You're supposed to find your identity by dredging up your Real
Self and confronting all the facets of your personality.
After months of torturous dredging I looked around
at all the kooks expressing their Real Selves and decided I liked their façades better. The vibes were so
bad that I had insomnia and felt nauseated all the
time, and some nut was always trying to lay his trip
on me. We had a guy named Ronald who kept saying,
'Cara rejects me because she is basically afraid of men
and can't relate on an interpersonal basis.' Finally one
day I'd had enough of the bullshit and said, 'Ronald,
I reject you because you are a stupid, hideous, ob-
noxious, loud creep. I am sick of your shit and your
Real Self sucks!' I left that group and joined another
one where they beat on ratty old mattresses with tennis rackets."

"Whatever for?" I interrupted.

"Oh, that's to release your inner hostilities. You

pretend that the mattress is your mother, or husband, or whatever, and you beat the shit out of it. That way you express your anger without anyone getting hurt. Except once, there was a toady old salesman, Jim, whose wife just couldn't resist telling him how ugly he was at least twice a week, and twice a week Jim came to group to beat up the mattress. Smart move. His wife looked like Muhammed Ali and could've creamed him into a pulp. One night he was whaling away, mad as a hornet, yelling 'Take this, you bitch!' and enjoying it so much that he wouldn't stop when the group leader told him that that was enough. Before anyone could do anything, he clutched his chest and keeled over. We called the police but before they arrived, he'd croaked of a heart attack right there on top of his mattress wife."

I was stunned. "Jesus, that's awful!"

"Yeah, well, our group leader said that it could have been worse. At least he died with his head together and in tune with his karma. Some people never get their heads together, you know." She was serious.

"That's one way to look at it. What else happens in group?" I encouraged, rabid with curiosity.

"Well, you learn to bathe naked with repulsively gross strangers who aren't supposed to notice your boobs bobbing up and down, because they tell you that it's natural to be naked and all bodies are beautiful, which they sure as hell aren't. Most of the guys and some of the women play grab-ass under the water when the group leader has his eyes shut and everyone is supposed to be meditating. I caught a cold and got scratches on my bottom from the 'naturally aged redwood togetherness tub' and some old guy's fingernails. And you're supposed to express your Innermost Desires without shame, which means letting yourself get laid by self-styled gurus, the not-so-latent homosexuals, and the plain horny dudes who come to these things just to get banged. And a couple of dykes," she added as an afterthought.

"Sounds creepy."

Cara shrugged. "Yeah, at my last encounter thing,

I came away with an awareness of my sexuality, an acceptance of my masochism, and syphilis from someone named Fast Eddie from San Diego. The syphilis was the only thing that took." Cara looked teary again, ready to overflow.

I changed the subject. "Are you married?"

"No," she said. "I'm devoting my life to being a psychiatric patient. It's a vocation, like being a nun, only a lot more expensive." She laughed and shook her crisp, brown curls. There was a sparkly humor in her eyes and electric currents of life zinging through her lithe young body.

This is a depressive?

"Why aren't there any locks on the bathroom doors?" Cara wanted to know. That was something that incoming patients *always* wanted to know.

"Well," I said, putting on my Information Lady hat, "the official version is that this is a 'mild' psychiatric ward and everyone is so well behaved. Actually, the staff breaks out in a cold sweat at the idea of anyone having any privacy. And they vigorously promote communication with our fellow man, which in this case means all the loonies you see wandering up and down the halls. So the result is that everyone either gets completely constipated or learns to sing at the top of their lungs in the bathroom."

"I'll sing," Cara decided.

"They get you there, too," I elaborated. "If you get constipated, they mark you down as an anal retentive. If you sing, it's listed as bizarre behavior. If you ignore the whole silly thing and someone walks in on you in the bathroom, you're designated an exhibitionist and spoken to sternly. Exhibitionism is a funny-farm no-no."

Cara laughed. "This is definitely different. In group, exhibitionism gets you an A and tons of approval." She gazed around the room and lowered her voice. "Nobody here seems too awfully bent out of shape. Is there much weird stuff?"

"Nothing that's going to bother you a lot," I said. "Most of the patients are in contact with reality, warped though it may be, at least part of the time, and things seldom get out of hand. Watch out for Eleanor, though."

"Which one is she?"

"She must be back in her room resting up for to-night. Until last week she was one of your run-of-the-mill depressives. Well, something must have gone wrong with her last set of shock treatments because now she wafts around all night, like a resident ghost, trying to get into bed with everyone. Just to sleep, you understand. Still, it's disconcerting to wake up around three A.M. with old Eleanor nudging you over. Several of the men are getting very anxious. The staff says they're keeping a close watch on her and we'll just have to put up with it until she gets better. If they're keeping such a close watch on her, how does she manage to crawl into three or four different beds every night? That to me is weird stuff."

"Nitpicker," Cara laughed.

Lulled by Seconal and Pomeroy's promise that "to-morrow will be a better day," the other patients had shambled off to bed. What Pomeroy meant was that she, unlike the patients, has Wednesdays off.

Cara and I were alone in the parlor. We sat in the dark and smoked silently, and I thanked whatever fates there were for sending this bright and bubbly girl-woman to distract me from my seemingly endless agonizing over my labyrinthine dilemma. Or my lilliputian problems, which is Charlie's version.

Suddenly, Cara grabbed my knee. "Let's hide all the potted plants before we go to bed," she giggled. "They'll go nuts."

"Let's," I agreed. I can sometimes resist temptation, but never mischief.

After checking the nurses' station we carefully timed our forays to coincide with the periodic bed checks made by Miss Andover, a tiny nurse whom I'd dubbed Tinkerbell, and her officious, idiot orderly, Abel. We spirited the plants out of the parlor, depositing them in the main bathroom (tub and shower), the patients' rooms ("Be quiet, Cassie, you'll wake

her up." "Don't worry. That's Caliguire. She's dead."),
and behind the parlor piano, which was covered by
an ancient gypsy shawl. Together we lugged the rubber tree to the foyer of the shock treatment room and
left a sign, "I think I'm a German Shepherd. Help
me before I bite someone or pee on my roots," nestled
in its leaves.

We accomplished our mission without being caught,
hugged each other gleefully and walked soberly past
the nurses' station, where we handed our matches politely to Abel, who immediately became suspicious.
We said a pleasant good night to Tinkerbell, who
waved her itsy-bitsy hand at us.

"Sleep well," she called.

"We will," we answered, and without another
glance at each other, we went off to our respective
rooms.

Next morning the process of elimination pointed the
finger at us. We were spoken to sternly by Dalton,
who made us hunt all the plants up and put them
back, apologize, and swear to be good, which we did
with our fingers crossed behind our backs. It was worth
it. The other patients laughed about it all day—except for Mrs. Walker, who thought that the rubber
tree was her granddaughter.

7

For several days I had been telling Dalton that I had
a bladder infection.

"What makes you think so?" she asked, writing

down notes about urinary fixations in my official folder, called Nut Notes by patients.

I persevered in describing my symptoms, insisting that they were real. "How would you know? You're not a doctor," she said.

Finally I got angry. "Goddammit," I shrieked, "I know I'm not a doctor. I'm a person who has had at least three thousand bladder infections, which is more than the goddamn doctor can say!"

"I suppose it could be possible," she capitulated. "You'd better tell Alexander."

So I had to wait for God's gift to the latently sane, spasmodically doubling up with pain and hoping that the infection wouldn't spread in the meantime. In a hospital crammed with more doctors than Medical Center, I had to wait to report a malfunctioning bladder to a goddamn psychiatrist!

"How long have you had these symptoms?" he asked, his eyes gleaming.

You just love to play Real Doctor! "Since I was fourteen," I answered. "You keep your paws off me."

"Now just a darn minute." He was indignant. "You are forgetting I'm also an M.D."

"So, who's forgetting?" I replied, also indignant. "But you can't be good at everything. I wouldn't want my gynecologist messing around with my psyche. How many pelvics do you give in the course of a psychiatric career? How do you know *where* everything is or *what* everything is, or where everything should be, or what's missing, or what's been added. I bet your wife wouldn't like it either."

"I had no intention of treating your possible infection myself," he said, disgruntled, "though I am perfectly competent to do so. I'm ordering a urine test. If it's positive, I'll send you downstairs to Bainbridge."

I was relieved. If someone didn't nip his medical proclivities in the bud, he'd soon be running around here capping teeth and performing appendectomies. *You didn't nibble on my wifey hint, Edwin. Have you got a wife somewhere, a sweet little thing who's*

*worked through her Electra complex and is in tune
with her karma?*

The specimen was positive. I was sent downstairs
where they keep the real people and introduced to a
kidney person named Bainbridge, who assiduously
avoided eye contact and examined me swiftly. I had
the uncomfortable sensation that while he was checking me, there was a still, small voice inside him saying,
"Ickypoo." And then came the questions.

"How often have you had this infection?"

"Oh, huh—uh—dozens of times."

"Do you usually urinate after you have inter-
course?"

"Sometimes. Sometimes not. Sometimes I go to
sleep. Sometimes I laugh. Sometimes I get up and go
home. Is this a psychological test?"

"No, of course not. You see, you should urinate.
You have a short urethra. Bacteria gets trapped and
later you have an infection. Do you ever get irritated?"

"Only when he—never mind."

"Seriously, you should urinate. You also have a
short vagina."

"How can that be. I'm nearly five-eight."

He sighed with dismay. "That has nothing whatsoever to do with it."

I was suddenly inspired. "Do you suppose," I
asked, "that everything on the outside being tall and
everything on the inside being short has anything to
do with my emotional problems? How could I possibly
be well balanced with everything out of line? Maybe
I have a tall brain and short emotions, or a short
psyche and tall inhibitions, or short conflicts and—"

He cut me off. "I'm going to order an antibiotic
for you and I want you to drink a lot of water, as
much as you can get down. I'll call the orderly."

Which he did, posthaste. I bored Kenny with the
details all the way upstairs. Once there I couldn't wait
to find Pomeroy and tell her that my imaginary disease was being treated with ampicillin.

"Big deal," she snapped, dropping her professional

stance of loving concern. "For once it isn't narcissism and you want a medal. Drink your water and shut up."

"Maybe you ought to go back to nurses' school, Pomeroy," I prodded, gleefully aware that I'd pushed the right button. "They can teach you all about infections and the rest of the stuff you slept through last time."

"I'd only sleep through it again," she smiled, her façade restored. "Besides, it's hard to tell when you people are ill and when you aren't. You're like everyone else. You do your best to develop illnesses."

"Why would I do that?" I asked.

"To justify being sick," she smiled sweetly.

"That's crap," I declared, and departed to find Cara, who might be more suitably impressed by my ailment.

It was lunchtime and I found her in Joanne's room, watching Joanne eat.

"Look at this, will you?" Cara said, all agog.

"Get outta my room." Joanne was trying to wave us away with one hand as she shoveled down food, like a pig at a trough, with the other.

"I've never seen anyone eat like that before," Cara commented, as though Joanne was invisible and deaf. "What's wrong with her?"

"Mmfghmf ghrg," Joanne gurgled and sloshed, spitting squash through her teeth. She couldn't stop wolfing long enough to answer.

"If they leave her alone, she doesn't have any appetite," I explained. "She was half dead from starvation when she got here, and the thought of eating still revolts her."

"Sure doesn't look like it," Cara said, continuing to gape at Joanne, who was jamming unidentifiable substances down her throat at incredible speed.

"That's because Dalton comes in fifteen minutes before every meal and gives the poor thing an insulin shot. It sets up one hell of a reaction, a super-diabetic-type response. She breaks out in a sweat and her eyes bulge. By the time Gloria brings in her tray, she'd be willing to eat a live chicken. She'll be all right when she gets enough food in her to counter the reaction." Joanne nodded vehemently at us, both confirming my explanation and gesturing for us to go away.

"C'mon, Cara. Let's leave her alone. I wouldn't want to be stared at if I was chowing up like that. She can't help it, anyway."

We walked down the hall toward our rooms and our lunches, which were getting cold on the tray tables next to our beds.

"What's going to happen when she goes home?" Cara asked. "Will she have to come running back here for a shot three times a day so she can eat?"

"Alexander told her that they'll have her physical condition stabilized to the point where she has a healthy appetite before she goes home. Then she'll return to Rotten Ronnie and his bag of tricks and lose it again."

"Who's Rotten Ronnie?"

I was explaining Rotten Ronnie in obscene detail when Kenny came trotting down the hall, breathless and carrying an envelope and package.

"Mail for you, Cassie," he said, and thrust the letter and mushy package into my arms. The brown wrapped box smelled like the air that envelops Hershey, Pennsylvania.

"Candy!" Cara trilled. "From your husband?"

"No," I said, inspecting the postmark, "from my brother. I'll split it with you later. See you after lunch."

I sat on the edge of my bed, reading the letter. My smile faded and resentment stiffened my fingers as I tore the pages apart.

"Christ!"

I pulled paper and pen from my dresser, and shoving my untouched tray aside, began to write.

Dear Bob,

Your letter has just arrived. Do you think I'm such a fool or so damned crazy that you can write me this kind of garbage and I'll thank you for it? Mother pours crap down your throat with a funnel and you solemnly chew it up and spit it back at me trying to convince me that it's chuck-full of vitamins and I should swallow it, too.

Shit is shit, buddy, no matter how it sparkles in the sun, and Mother's truth is not my truth. I am so goddamn tired of trying to accept, of being told that I MUST accept other people's views of the way it is, and what went wrong—where *I* went wrong, and what it is that must be done about it. And what it invariably comes down to is that *I* have to shape up, *I* have to "get well," *I* have to stop drinking and start living up to my responsibilities—so that everyone else can breathe a sigh of relief and get back to the really important things in their lives.

I am everyone's pain in the ass, everyone's worry, everyone's albatross. If it wasn't for me, Charlie and Mother would be oh, so happy; oh, so productive; oh, so pain-free. I am the officially designated sickie, the disrupter, the source of everyone's torment, the reason why Mother sighs a thousand times a day and pulls her crown of thorns tight around her ears. I'm the reason why Charlie ducks out of the office early to rush home and play mother and father to the kids, pretending at grieving loneliness and solicitude for me, when, in truth, isolation is his secret heart's desire and his relief at not having to cope with my presence has unscrunched his face and made him look five years younger. Everything is my fault. Everything will be perfect if only I will "come to my senses and start doing what's right." Or, as Mother says, "Be good."

You echo Mother's words when you say that Charlie is a good man. What gives YOU the right, or Mother whom you heard it from, to assume that I am blind to the goodness in Charlie? Charlie is a good, kind, decent man who is totally unaware that he is beating me to death with his decency and goodness. If awareness burst over him like a rainstorm, he'd ignore it, saying that what he does is right and he does it for my own good and if I am lying here bleeding to death from his kindness, mashed and crumpled under the weight of his goodness, then it is my problem and not his. Because there is nothing wrong with HIM.

Therefore my misery is of my making and my choosing, in no way the result of eleven years spent with a man who denies my feelings, belittles my ideas and tromps all over *my* truth.

I tell him I'm lonely and he says, "I'm here almost every night. You have no reason to be lonely." And I tell him that the lamp is there, too, and it takes more than a body in a chair with a newspaper in front of its face. It takes someone who knows you're alive and is happy you're there, who needs YOU to be there, to talk and to listen, to share with and laugh with, to make plans with and be crazy with. Someone who understands how you feel and thinks that how you feel is important, more important than what the world thinks of you and might think of him for marrying you. Someone who's not too proud or too arrogant or too goddamn masculine to say, "I'm not doing very well right now. I need your help." And once having gotten the emotional support he needs, says, "Thank you. It made all the difference." Someone who respects the person you are and the person you want to be, and encourages you to be the best you can be even if it means you might have to change. Someone who isn't afraid to be close.

But Charlie stands staunchly behind the barricades of his goodness with giant, red, flashing "Keep Out" signs erected around his perimeters, clothed in rectitude, and awash with righteousness. I say, "I'm frustrated, Charlie. I want more than this. I want to do more, be more." And Charlie says, "You have a wonderful life. Other women would give a lot to have what you have. You have no reason to feel frustrated."

And I say, "Things are awful, Charlie," and Charlie says, "Things have never been better." And I say, "I'm angry," and he says, "No, you're not" or, "You have no reason to be angry."

And I crumble with confusion. Charlie is "good," so Charlie must know. Charlie is mature, so his perceptions must be more accurate than mine, his judgments more objective and precise, his actions more worthy. If Charlie says that it's all my fault, then it must be true.

Except that somewhere deep down inside where the me who could have been still lives, the Cassie who saved you from bullies and told Sister Delores, who sneered in sixth grade and said you were dumb, to fly straight to hell, the self that got lost along the way, shouts, "No, that's not MY truth! That's not the way it is!"

And I feel the bitter, green, hot and sour rage boil up and threaten to gush over and I know if it does something terrible will happen. So I grab a bottle and drink till the barbed wire relaxes, and then I drink some more to drown the despair that follows the anger, fog on the fire. And, after a time, the alcohol makes me sleepy and I go to bed crying, wondering why it has to be this way, will always be this way. I wake up next to Charlie, hung over and dressed in my clothes from the night before, irrefutable proof that Charlie is right, it's all my fault and I've screwed up again. And always will.

And so it's gone, for the last few years. But not here. Here in the hospital, I am not the family sickie, not the source of everyone's dismay. Here, relatively speaking, I'm in fair shape, and relatively speaking is the way I've always lived—in relation to everyone else. Always asking someone else, "How am I doing? How do I feel? What should I do now?"

Here, because what I do will ultimately affect no one but me, and no one has any vested interests to protect, everyone says, "Do what YOU want. Decide what it is YOU want to do and do it." Which all sounds grand and tolerant and mature and psychologically sound until you realize that when you come down to the bottom line, no one here truly gives a shit if you get well enough to give testimonials to the effectiveness of psychotherapy or jump out the goddamn window. It isn't going to alter the course of anyone's life—not the therapists, or nurses, or the lady with the library cart—no one. So they say, "Go to it. Find your own truth," knowing you can't come back later and dump your shitty truth all over their nice, clean floor. It's goodbye and good luck and see you around, maybe.

But right now, it's just what I need. I need to hear from someone, always from someone, that somewhere there is a me with integrity, a whole person with validity and value, that I am entitled to try to find my own way, no matter how I founder and screw up, that I don't have to live my life with someone else's values, that I can live inside my own skin. That someday I'll look in the mirror and say, "You're okay," and feel it in my guts where I live. I need to be given permission to find a me I can live with sober. I need to be given the idea that somewhere there is such a thing as ME.

I need, right now, to be away from the people who make me feel like a bad little girl who refuses to do better. So when you write me that Mother makes a good point when she says that perhaps I should leave the hospital and go home to be "looked after" by herself and Charlie, who "care about me," I can only assume that you, of all people, have bought the whole bag of bullshit and gone over to the other side.

Sure they CARE about me. As long as I do what they want, their way. I'll tell you how much they care about me.

About three months ago I called Mother one night and begged her to come over. I had been drinking and arguing with Charlie all evening, one of those round and round things without any end and damn little point, mostly name-calling. I was upset and desperate and needed someone who understood, someone who would stand up for me. I told her that I couldn't live this way anymore. I was ready to kill myself.

Well, she came, and by the time she blew in the door like an avenging angel, I'd already calmed down, and though drunk, was a little ashamed of myself—and ready to tell Mother that I was sorry I'd upset her. I never had the chance.

She flew across the room and screamed in my face, "How dare you do this to me. How dare you do this to Charlie. And the kids. You're a brat. A selfish, self-centered, good-for-nothing brat! All the while you were growing up I told your father that you were defiant and rebellious and no damn good to anyone but he wouldn't listen to any criticism of his pet. Oh, no. Nothing was too good for his princess. I'm just glad he didn't live to see you like this. No! No! I wish he HAD lived to see you like this. He would beat some sense into your thick head."

"You don't understand!" I screamed, pulling away from her. "You never understand!" I turned and ran down the hall to the bedroom. She came after me.

"You're goddamn right I don't understand," she screeched. "I worked myself sick for you kids, for your father. I gave up everything so you brats would have a nice home. I put up with your father's temper and his tantrums and his illnesses, and I never complained. I had his family to dinner every Sunday and never had any help from anyone. When I asked you to help me you thought you were too damn good for housework, and I had to do it myself. And your father never, never once backed me up. I did what's right and did it all my life and got nothing but a kick in the ass from you kids and everyone else. And now you tell me that I don't understand. I understand that you're rotten and selfish and ungrateful and never think of anyone but yourself. I understand that you're wrecking your husband's life and ruining your kids and you don't give a damn about any of it and by God someday you'll pay for it. Someday you'll get punished the way you deserve and then, by God, you'll understand how *I* feel . . ."

I was lying on my bed through her harangue and suddenly I wasn't drunk enough, not nearly drunk enough, and the rage and bile exploded through my teeth. I rolled over and caught Mother full in the face with a backhanded slap. She gasped and held her face as though it was shattered glass and screamed, "Charlie, Charlie, come quick! Cassie hit her mother!"

Charlie ran through the door, yelling, "You bitch! You goddamn bitch!" and pulled me off the bed. He held me by the hair with one hand, shaking my head violently back and forth, and slapped my face with the other while Mother shrieked, "Hit her, Charlie, hit her!"

I don't remember much more. I know that I woke up the next morning, in bed, fully dressed, with the taste of blood in my mouth and unable to move my head. Charlie had gotten the kids off to school and gone to work. I dragged myself out of bed and managed to make it to the bathroom before I threw up. Blood came up and pain shot through my neck and down my right arm. I leaned over the toilet and tears flowed into the bloody vomit. I wanted to die, right then, right there, without thinking another thought or living through another pain. But people never die when they're ready or when they want, and I knew I wouldn't either, so I pried the lid off the toilet tank and lifted out the bottle I had hidden inside. I sat on the floor and drank until the pain diminished and I could decide what to do.

When I could move I took my bottle and my car keys and drove to the community hospital, where I told the emergency-room doctor that I'd fallen down the stairs. He smelled my breath and looked disgusted. He didn't offer to call my husband.

He took X rays and he told me that there was some sort of damage, I don't remember what kind. He gave me a cervical collar and some pain pills and told me to go home. Directly home.

I went home and got into bed with my bottle and my pills. Shortly before the kids were due home from school, Mother walked in.

"Get up," she said, "the kids will be home any minute and the house looks like a pigsty. And you look like a pig."

She looked at the cervical collar and the bruises on my face and began to pick up Charlie's discarded clothes.

"Charlie shouldn't have hit you so hard," she commented.

So you see, Bobby, you'll have to forgive me when I say I don't care about their caring. I don't give a fuck about being "looked after" by people who mean to rip me to bloody little shreds "for my own good." And I am madder than hell at you for buying the bullshit.

You just stay there in California, above it all, and decide for yourself what's reasonable and what's right and what isn't. But, if you're going to buy someone else's truth, don't try to sell it to me. I've had enough of it for a lifetime and I'm no longer in the market for secondhand shit.

I need you right now too much to slam any doors in your face or tell you to buzz off. But, goddammit, listen to me. To ME.

Cassie

Afternoon shadows were lengthening across the beige tiles of the floor by the time I'd finished the letter. I held it in my hand, crying softly and knowing that if I waited until morning to mail it the bitterness and vituperation in the letter would frighten and embarrass me and I'd tear it up. *I've never been able to tell anyone the way it is for me,* I thought, *the anguish I've felt and the horrible way I've behaved. I'm so damn tired, so sick and tired of pretending.*

Resolutely I walked down the hall to the nurses' station, blowing my nose on the pulpy cardboard that passed for Kleenex. Cara was hanging over the counter harassing Tinkerbell, who had just come on duty.

"Why can't I look at my folder? The patients should be able to look at their folders. How do we know what symptoms to shoot for?" she was saying. She looked up as I approached.

"Why, you've been crying, Cassie," she said, startled. "Why have you been crying? What's wrong?"

I knew I looked like a cave-in, with puffy eyes and a swollen face. I tried to think of something clever to say, but my head was short-circuited, and nothing came.

Finally, "Do you think you have the crying concession around here, Cara?" Feeble, feeble.

She bristled. "No, of course not. I was just worried about you."

I smiled, feeling strangely peaceful. "Thanks, honey. Look, I'm going to take a walk down to the mailbox and mail this letter. Would you like to come along for the walk?"

She shook her head. "No, it's too cold, and besides, I don't have any boots. It's been snowing."

"All right, I'll see you later," I said, and as she turned to go, "On the table in my room is a box full of Mounds bars, Cara. Just go in and help yourself. And while you're at it, dust Mrs. Caliguire. She's gathering cobwebs."

Cara grinned and waved and vanished in the direction of my room.

"Do you have a stamp I can borrow or buy from you?" I asked Tinkerbell. "I have to mail this letter right away or I won't do it at all."

She regarded me steadily. "I don't know what's in

that letter or to whom you've written it, Cassie, but you're obviously paying a high price for writing it. Are you sure this is something you want to do?"

I smiled, understanding the question. "Don't worry, Tinkerbell. This isn't a suicide note or a letter to Charlie asking for a divorce, not yet anyway, or a message to Donnerly telling him I want to run off and be his forever." I laughed. "He would turn green and expire. No, this is basically an epistle to my faithful disciple, an expression of my deepest feelings. Even Alexander would approve."

She started at the name. "That reminds me," she said. "He called a while ago and said that he was going to stop in and see you this evening, and to make sure you would be here."

"I was planning to attend the mixed quilting-bee and annual orgy, but I'll stick around if he's coming in. What does he want?"

"Beats me. Didn't you see him this morning at the regular time?"

"Yes, I did, but I didn't feel like talking. I really couldn't think of a thing to say. So we just had one of those Mexican stand-off things where he stared at me and I stared at him and the first one to flinch gets to spend the night in the padded room. As usual he won. That man never blinks, Tinkerbell. How do his other patients stand it?"

"Maybe he doesn't stare like that at everyone."

"Sure he does. It's Rule Number Three at Shrink School: If the patient's refusal to respond is making diagnosis difficult, stare at him fixedly until he goes into a conniption fit, whereupon you can diagnose him manic and order him hosed down. It's basic technique."

"Perhaps," she smiled, falling back on the great psychiatric all-purpose noncommittal.

I walked the three blocks to the mailbox, first slowly, with my hospital walk, shuffling along with eyes downcast. Then, as the cold air stung my face and filled my lungs, I straightened my shoulders and began to stride rapidly, enjoying the bracing air and the crunch of the snow underfoot. Shaker Boulevard glowed softly gray in the lowering dusk, and scattered snowflakes fell, outlined against the dim early-evening street lights. I leaned on the mailbox watching the rush hour traffic creep bumper to bumper, then speed up again, only to be caught at the next intersection and brought to a crawl. I wondered where the drivers were going, riding alone in their arks.

I thought of the times I'd driven past this hospital, rushing off to somewhere, to Alexander's office most likely, or dashing back toward home, in a hurry to get to the liquor store and then safely into my kitchen before the kids got home from school. I'd never given the hospital a glance, not a thought, and now here I was firmly entrenched in its routine, in the life of its encapsulated society. The world of rush hour traffic seemed long ago and far away.

"I'll never forget," I told myself, as I started back toward the hospital. "I'll never drive past here again without remembering." I smiled to myself. "And being curious about what's going on on the seventh floor."

I rode up in the elevator with visitors who had strong ethnic faces and damp, musty-smelling overcoats, wondering to myself if I wanted to get out, and how I would feel if tonight Alexander offered me my release. I briefly panicked. *Not yet, please God, not yet,* I prayed. *I'm not ready. I'm a long way from ready. Not yet.* Having no faith in prayers, I crossed my fingers and decided that I'd be safe if the first person I encountered was smiling. A frowner, however, would be a clear indication of imminent danger.

The first person I saw was sullen Norma, who didn't even say hello. My heart sank and I crept off to my room. *Curse you, superstitious Irish ancestors! I hope Norma's next shock treatment will french-fry her brain!*

Throughout my dinner I chattered at the ubiquitous Caliguire, who lay like a toppled Easter Island statue, unimpressed by my wit and effectively deaf to the world.

"You say you're planning a trip to Tahiti, Mrs. Caliguire? Well, do stop in and see the Finsterwalds, dear people. They own a banana plantation and three hundred slaves, whom they have converted to High Episcopalianism and quaintly call 'darkies.' "

It took my mind off Alexander and impending doom. I was scraping the last of my chocolate pudding out of its plastic container and regaling Caliguire with my theory of what the pudding actually contained, when Tinkerbell called me on the PA.

"Be right there," I called, and dumped my tray on the cart.

Alexander was sitting in the interview room with his head in his hands. He looked somewhat weary, which surprised me, as it had never occurred to me that he got tired like us mere mortals. He glanced up and quickly straightened, evidently ill at ease at having been caught unawares.

"Sit down, sit down," he said brusquely, gesturing me to the chair.

I sat in the chair, feeling, as usual, as if I were eight years old.

"You wouldn't talk to me this morning. Why?" He went right to the point.

"I couldn't think of anything to say. Nothing personal."

"I see." He paused, regarding me intently. *What is it, Edwin? Talk to me, love.* He shifted his gaze.

"I heard you were quite upset this afternoon. You cried for a long time."

"Who told you that? Where did you hear that?"

"That's not important. Is it true? What happened?" He waited expectantly.

I wiggled restlessly in my seat wishing I were somewhere else. Anywhere else.

I hate it when you ask these questions. I want to tell you and I'm afraid to tell you, Edwin. I'm afraid I'll get too emotional. Why am I afraid to get emotional now? Isn't that what you're for? "I received a letter from my brother," I said. "He'd heard from my mother and was repeating some of her sentiments back to me.

He seemed to agree with them. It upset me." My lower lip began to quiver. *Damn! I knew it!*

"What sentiments?"

"He said that Mother thought I should come home where she and Charlie can look after me—"

"Out of the question," he interrupted. "You're not ready. What else?"

I breathed a deep, relieved sigh. *Take that, sullen Norma. Who needs your goddamn smile?*

"What else?" he prodded again.

"He talked about drinking," I reported in a whisper, sinking as deep as I could in the chair. "He asked me if I could still control my drinking, you know, when and how much."

"Can you?" he asked solemnly, as though I was a stranger he'd just met on a corner, as though he hadn't heard my stories of dwindling control, week after week, for months.

Still, have I really told you, Edwin, or have I shied away from the subject when you've asked, skirting the issue or changing direction entirely, propelling the conversation into safer channels, such as my affair with Donnerly or latest fight with Charlie?

I contemplated his serious, passive face, unable to fathom the thoughts in his head. My lower lip quivered and I filled up with tears.

"No, I can't control it anymore," I answered, and covered my face with my hands while the dam inside me dissolved and tears flooded through my fingers. "And I don't know what to do about it," I wailed.

He allowed me to cry for several minutes without saying a word. The storm in me gradually subsided and I sat, sniffing and soggy and wishing for a Klee-nex. He riffled through the bottom drawer of the desk and came up with some tissues. "Here," he said.

"Thanks."

"Several months ago you told me that you were drinking more and enjoying it less." He smiled. "Is that still true?"

"Yes," I replied, "only more so. Now it takes very

little to get me drunk. I drink when I don't want to. I mean really, truly, don't want to, not just when I tell Charlie I don't want to. I can't even go to the damn supermarket anymore without having a drink. And once I do have one, I can't stop. There are so many days when I have a drink in the morning, just one— and I can't remember anything I say or do all day. I go shopping or pick the kids up from school or cook meals and talk to people on the phone and I can't remember any of it later on—"

"That's a blackout," Alexander interrupted. "It's like a spell of amnesia where you function, but can't remember later on. I didn't know you were having them."

"I never told you," I replied. "Sometimes, the next day, or a few days later, things come back to me, bits and pieces. And sometimes I wish that they hadn't," I added ruefully. "I don't know what I'm going to do." I started to cry again. "If Charlie gets a divorce I can't even take care of myself. And even with Charlie, I'm so goddamn sick of living this way. I can't even commit suicide right. Who ever heard of trying to overdose on children's aspirin? It's disgusting. I'm so damned tired. What can I do?"

He leaned forward, over the desk, looking sincere and flashing all four hundred perfect teeth.

"Why don't you try Alcoholics Anonymous?" he suggested

"Good Lord!" I shrieked. "I have spent four years of my life and thousands of dollars with you. When I first came to see you I was mildly depressed and had a few drinks every Saturday night. Now I drink like a fish, have been here twice, tried suicide, alienated friends, family, and spouse, act like a nut, have a dent in my head, and sometimes I'm a little irritable. And you say, 'Try Alcoholics Anonymous'! Four years with you and now you want me to join a bunch of winos in some cellar sitting around doing God knows what." I waved my arms over my head like a demented bird.

"Only two or three per cent of them are winos,"

he said. "If you go you'll find people pretty much like yourself. Alcoholics."

Alcoholics! No matter what I blurted out to Cara, "alcoholic" is so . . . so final. Yet, would I be here right now with pains in my knees and dents in my head, sleeping in a room with an immovable object, listening to Cara's prattle and introducing myself to weirdos, so overwrought with guilt that I can't even ask for an afternoon pass to go home and see my children, not wanting to live and not able to kill myself, if it wasn't for drinking? I've got to do something about it. I may be all I have left, and I sure as hell can't do it alone.

In Alexander's face I recognized the look of a man who's thrown out his net and is waiting for the fish to swim by. *Here I come.*

"Does this Alcoholics Anonymous thing really work?" I asked, and waited.

He stood up. "I've seen it work in cases where we doctors haven't been able to accomplish much of anything," he said. He walked to the door. "The number is in the phone book. You can call them if you'd like. It's up to you." And he walked out, leaving me dangling on the end of his words.

8

I awoke after having slept only briefly, a sleep plagued by nightmares and an imbecilic Freudian dream wherein Alexander had taken me to a narrow high-walled room and shown me a triple bunk bed. He told me that my place was on the top, and said, in sepul-

chral tones, "I've taken you this far, Cassie. You'll
have to go the rest of the way yourself."

"Nuts," I said, groggily heaving myself out of bed.
"I'm so brainwashed with therapy that I'm having
textbook dreams." Brainwashed or not, I knew that
I'd soon be reporting this drivel to Alexander and
sighing over its implications. He'd say, "What do you
think that means?" and I would deftly reply with a
gerrymandered insight hastily constructed to gain his
approval.

An hour later I was sitting in a corner chair in the
parlor, dressed in sweatshirt and jeans, arms clasped
around my knees, hunched over and blocking out the
world. I became aware that someone was standing next
to me but refused to look up.

*Go away, whoever you are. I am practicing the
fetal position found on page seventy-three of the
Kama-sutra.*

It was Gloria. "C'mon, Miz Barrett. You got to go
downstairs again. See Dr. Bainbridge."

I made no effort to disguise my aggravation. "What
the hell for? The infection is gone and I'm fine. What
kind of a hospital is this? You have to wait forever to
see a doctor when you need one, and then when you
don't, it's hi ho, off to see the wizard time. Go away."

"I ain't the one sayin' you gotta go. Don't complain to me. Miz Dalton, she says you on the schedule
for a checkup and I should go with you. So c'mon."

"Okay, okay," I grumbled, "but it sure as hell is a
waste of time."

"You got any aspirin?" Gloria inquired as we left
the parlor. "I got a headache that's makin' my teeth
rattle."

"You belong in a hospital, Gloria. Ask Dalton for
aspirin. It's against the rules for patients to carry their
own medication." I swung my purse, containing its
hidden cache of Excedrin, over my shoulder.

Downstairs, Gloria chattered on about her aches and
pains while I sat slumped on the waiting room bench
scrutinizing the floor. Finally, her motor ran down and
there was silence.

"What's buggin' you, honey?" Gloria asked softly. "You lookin' like a faceful of bad news."

I gestured helplessly. "Alexander suggested that I call Alcoholics Anonymous. I can't decide."

"You got a drinkin' problem?" she asked. Somehow she didn't sound surprised.

"I suppose you could call it that. Anyway, after all this therapy and the hospital twice, and everything else, Alexander says, 'Try AA.' I guess I'm angry, too. It seems to me that the bastard has just given up."

"Maybe he thinks that AA can help ya out with the drinkin' thing and he can help with the rest of your problems. I know maybe two or three people in AA right now, and let me tell ya, they doin' fine. One of them is my cousin on my mother's side, name of Bill, used to spend all the money on liquor. His poor wife an' the chillen, they didn't have nothin'. And he used to beat up on them all the time. Well, he finally comes up in front of the judge once too often, and the judge, he sends him to AA. Once Bill got there and settled down a bit he liked it and stuck around. He ain't had a drink for over a year. His wife left him, though."

"Why did she leave him if he sobered up?"

"Oh, he still used to come home and beat on her and the kids. She said that before she thought it was because of the drinkin'. Then he quit and she found out he's a mean son of a bitch sober, too."

"My goodness!" I went back to my floor-pacing, wondering if that was a success story I'd just heard. Bainbridge's secretary called my name and I entered the office.

"How are you feeling?" he asked, looking at the lamp on his desk.

"Fine, everything's cleared up. Nothing hurts." *I have a pain here and a pain here and my psyche is battered and bent. My emotions are raw and torn like a gutted deer and my mind reels with chaotic confusion, but you don't carry a map to this territory, Bainbridge, so to you, I'm just fine.*

He rubbed his hands together, looking relieved. "Excellent," he said to his stethoscope. "Continue to drink as much water as you can. That will prevent a recurrence. And if you have any more problems while you're here be sure to have a nurse notify me."

Sure I will, Bainbridge. By the time they get me back down here, all you'll have to do is perform the autopsy and sign the death certificate. "Okay," I agreed, and turned to go. "By the way, can drinking too much alcohol cause bladder infections?" I asked.

"It doesn't cause them but it sure does contribute to perpetuating them. Why?" He asked his shoe. "Do you have a drinking problem?"

"Certainly not," I replied. "I'm inquiring for a friend."

In the waiting room I found Gloria curled up on the couch with a magazine over her face.

"Rise and shine, Gloria." *There, how do you like it?*

Gloria mumbled sleepily and got to her feet. "You decided about callin' AA?" she asked. "You kin call from the lobby before we go up."

Gloria's laconic expression said, "Are you or aren't you, make up your mind." So, willy-nilly, and with some trepidation, I made up my mind.

I'm only calling for information. Just because I call doesn't mean I have to go.

I was assailed by an attack of the shakes. Gloria made no comment on my condition as we walked toward the phone. I leaned against the wall breathing in shallow pants, while Gloria, with unexpected sensitivity, mutely looked up the number and dialed the phone. She thrust the ringing receiver into my hand, and walked away, leaving me and my trembles in privacy.

A man's voice answered. "Alcahoolics Ananamus. Don Valdez spikin'. Kin I hep youl?" His Mexican accent was so thick and he spoke so slowly that I could hardly understand him.

"I'm Cassie Barrett. I'm in Shaker Heights Hospital, psychiatric ward. My shri—er, doctor said that maybe

I should call you." My voice shook so badly that I was sure he was having similar difficulty in understanding me.

"Youl gut a drinkin' prublum?"

I hedged. "Well, I might." I cleared my throat, what the hell, and spoke up. "Yes, I have a drinking problem."

"Wul, ya culled the ri plac. I'm spikin' as when who knos. How lung ya gung be in da looney bin?"

Jesus, that's really calling a spade a spade. "I don't know," I answered truthfully. "Probably not long," I amended. If I was going to get into this thing, it had to be SOON—before I changed my mind.

"Ho kay. Where do ya lif?"

"I live in Parma Heights. Why?"

"Eet's bist to start out klos to hum—in yur hum grup. I'll send a lady to see ya and thin ya kin go to a meetin'."

"Okay," I mumbled, realizing that I would have agreed to anything he suggested. "That sounds fine."

"Gud luck," he said, and hung up. I stood with the phone in my hand, desperately hoping that I hadn't just made a commitment and unexpectedly anticipating what would happen next.

"There now, honey, don't you feel better?" Gloria questioned, smiling and flashing her gold caps.

"Hell no," I spit. "It was probably a dumb idea that'll never work out." And I tromped off ahead of Gloria, who made no effort to catch up with me.

I was going down the hall toward my room wondering what the hell I was getting myself into, when Alexander fell into step beside me, matching his stride to mine.

See how well we fit, Edwin, both tall and slender? Don't we make a lovely couple? "I called AA," I said, making it sound like a challenge. *Okay, I did what you wanted me to, you bastard. When do I begin to feel better?*

"And . . . ?"

"And they're going to send a lady to talk to me. I

can hardly wait to see what apparition shows up. Probably a little old lady with a bottle sticking out of her pocket."

"Maybe. Maybe not." He laughed.

"So what if this AA thing *does* work, Dr. Alexander? What do I do about the rest of my mess?"

"You'll manage," he said decisively, coming to a halt in front of Joanne's door. He regarded my troubled and frowning face speculatively. "You're not as fragile as you think, Cassie." He blessed me with a paternal, maternal, fraternal, omniscient smile, and vanished into Joanne's room, leaving me staring after him.

In my room I surveyed my image in the mirror. "Hello there, tiger," I whispered. "Hello there, brave, courageous lady who is going to go forth and manage. Hello there, functional person. Hello there, future teetotaler of America." I glimpsed the bars on the windows reflected in the mirror and I sagged against the sink. *Who am I trying to kid?* I thought.

I stayed on tenterhooks, awaiting the arrival of "the AA lady," who promptly showed up—four days later. Her name was Marjorie and she peered around apprehensively as she crept down the hall to my room. Obviously she'd seen *Psycho* and was expecting momentary attack.

I reassured her as best I could, advising her to ignore Mrs. Caliguire, who looked like a candidate for the pathology department. Marjorie seemed dubious, but resolutely sat in the chair I offered while I perched on my bed with my legs crossed, yoga-style.

"Does it work?" I asked. That's all I really wanted to know. I didn't really care what they did or how they went about it. I knew that they held meetings but that's *all* I knew, though I assumed that whatever they did at the meetings wasn't too outrageous or hazardous to the health. Being Catholic, I'd already had years of experience at services of infinite duration where stylized ritual and incomprehensible rote combined to elicit an outpouring of, so they claimed, grace. My personal frame of reference definitely included the conferring of unearned and unwarranted grace, bestowed, but only upon Catholics, by a benevolent though sectarian Creator.

"Does it work?" I repeated.

"Oh, goodness, yes." Marjorie leaned forward and bobbed her pink-rinsed head vigorously. She forgot Mrs. Caliguire as she launched enthusiastically into her own story, the endless saga of a drinking housewife, a narrative so boring that it put my teeth to sleep. She eventually dribbled off and asked me if I had any questions. I had thousands of questions, but none that I could formulate, and none that actually mattered as much as my original query. Not for the present, anyway. And I was disappointed in this lady. She hadn't been a little old woman with a bottle, but she hadn't been what I'd expected, either.

"I'll go to your first meeting with you," she offered. "Get permission or whatever you have to do, and call me. I'll pick you up or arrange for someone else to bring you. Then I can introduce you to people at the meeting and you'll be on your way."

Whoopee, I'm off down the yellow brick road.

She handed me a blue bound book entitled *Alcoholics Anonymous*.

"Read this in the meantime," she said. "It's the AA bible."

Wonderful. What I definitely need now is another bible. I've had so much luck with the first one.

"Do you belong to a religion?" she asked, catching me off guard.

"No," I lied promptly, having no desire to delve into my discarded Catholicism.

"Well, that's not important," she assured me. "You'll find God just the same."

Oh, Christ! I thought, as I watched her timidly twitch up the hall like an arthritic bunny. *What makes you think that I want to find God? I spend most of my time hiding under my bed hoping that God won't find me!*

I settled back on my bed and opened the book, thinking that if AA turned out to be a religiously oriented organization, I was doomed before I began.

The front of the book contained an outline of the "program" that AA people followed, a curious compendium of commonsense tactics, psychological self-evaluation, and lofty principles. In the back were testimonials written by the "redeemed," and as I read through, my spirits took a dive. They all seemed to harp along the lines of "How I stopped drinking, found God and learned to change my points and plugs." Christ!

"It's not what I expected," I complained to Alexander.

"What did you expect?" he asked sensibly.

"I don't know. But this isn't it."

"Are you going to go to a meeting?"

"I'm supposed to ask your permission."

"You have it."

"I won't be back until late. The meeting lasts until ten o'clock."

"That's all right. Tell the night nurse and come in through Emergency when you come back."

"Maybe Charlie won't like it."

"Why would he not like it? He says he wants you to quit drinking."

I'd about exhausted my supply of objections and sat quietly musing. Alexander accompanied me in silence for a time, then said casually, "As long as you'll be out Saturday, would you like an extended pass so you can stop off at home and see the kids? It's been several weeks." He gazed at his hands, detached from my answer.

I know how long it's been, goddammit Edwin, and I know how I feel about seeing them again. What do I say to them, for God's sake? That Mother is crazy and a lush and needs to be locked up? Or, more to the point, that Mommy doesn't want to come home because at home she's bogged down with despair and can't cope? That Mommy likes the hospital better because everything is pleasant and some of it is fun and here she doesn't feel like the world's prime failure? And what do I say when they ask me when I'm coming home, Edwin? Do I say "Soon" or "Never" or do I simply tell them that I'd rather stay here because here I have only to be responsible for myself, and only in a limited way? That being responsible for their happiness and welfare is making me crazy? That being the person who has to have all the answers and put everyone else first is making me bitter? That I'm dragged down by their "gimmes" and drowning in booze? Is that what I tell them, Edwin? That I'm selfish and tired and bored with the day after day of it? And if I tell them all that, can I still tell them I love them, which I do? Can I still tell them that I have never once wished them unborn; never once wished they were gone; that I've stood next to their beds while they slept, overwhelmed with pride and gratitude? That the most splendid moments in my life I've shared with them? That there have been moments when, with little arms around my neck and a soft cheek next to mine, I've felt more surely a woman than ever I've felt lying beneath a man? Do I tell them that the sight of their faces, their unwavering eyes, fills me with an unbearable guilt? Makes me want to hide, and run someplace where no one knows that I've failed them and I can pretend to forget? Don't send me home, please, even for a visit. I'm not ready. I can't bear it. "That would be nice," I said, and he nodded.

I called Charlie to tell him I was coming home for a visit on Saturday.

"Will you pick me up?" I asked.

"Do I have a choice?" he replied.

On Saturday I was ready early and sat in the parlor thumbing through a magazine. Cara bounced in, grinning cheerfully, "Want to go downstairs and get a soda?" she asked.

"No, I'm waiting for Charlie to pick me up. I'm going to be at home with the kids this afternoon and then go to an *AA meeting* tonight." I waited, expecting some sort of reaction.

"You know," she finally remarked, "you don't seem like a married person. I mean, with kids and all."

"Why not?" I asked, piqued.

"You just don't strike me that way. You're too"—she waved her arms, describing circles in the air—"I don't know."

"Thanks, Cara," I said, "have a nice soda."

She departed for the elevator and I walked down seven flights of steps, glad for the exercise, and wondering what I'd say to the kids. Charlie was sitting in the car, which was parked in the tow-away zone. He gestured frantically for me to hurry and I pulled up the hood of my car coat and made a dash through the blowing snow. I yanked open the door and slid clumsily onto the front seat next to Charlie, who immediately pulled away from the curb.

The boys were in the back seat and Jenny sat in the front between Charlie and me. "Hi, kids," I said, and leaned over the seat to give them hugs and kisses which they returned. I tried to pull Jenny over on my lap but she didn't want to come. Feeling faintly rebuffed, I settled for a kiss.

"Are you coming home now, Mommy?" Steve asked.

"Just for this afternoon," I replied. "I have to come back tonight."

"Well, when *are* you coming home?" Greg demanded. Jenny took my hand in her small one.

"As soon as the doctor says I can," I said lamely.

"As soon as he gets his new car paid for," Charlie added.

"Charlie!" I scolded. I didn't want the kids to think he was serious.

There was general silence as we went over the bridge separating the east side from the west side of Cleveland. Finally, Charlie said, "Tell Mommy about school, kids." The kids erupted into a noisy din, each wanting to "tell first." I listened as we rode slowly through the snowy streets, making appropriate comments and wondering why it was that things could seem so normal, aware that we could easily be a family out for a pleasure drive and not a family bringing Mommy home from the nuthouse for an afternoon visit. Perhaps some families are better than others at pretending. Or perhaps it was that Charlie set the tone of "nothing's really wrong," because denial is one of his defenses, and the kids because they were young and I because it was easy just went along with the game. And perhaps, too, there was not actually that much wrong in the kids' world. They had Charlie and Mother, their routines were the same, their lives basically undisrupted, and they had become accustomed to my "being sick."

I became aware that Jenny had taken my middle finger and was gradually bending it backward, glancing at me out of the corner of her eye, trying to gauge my reaction.

"Ouch, that hurts!" I said, pulling my hand away. It *did* hurt. I looked at her tiny face and the half smile, half grimace that played briefly across it.

She's angry at me. She's terribly, wretchedly angry with me. Tears filled my eyes. *I can't blame her. If I was only six and my mother went off and left me, I'd be madder than hell.*

"Don't bend Mommy's finger like that, honey," I said, patting her leg. "It hurt." *I wish I could tell you. I wish I could explain.*

I wandered around the house like a stranger, touching the furniture, picking up and putting down objects. I felt as if I'd come from another world, to one vaguely familiar, yet alien, and I wondered at my sense of displacement.

"The kitchen is cleaned up," I remarked, "even the floor."

"Daddy cleaned it up right after breakfast. He told us not to mess it up again before you got home," Greg said.

"That was nice of him," I said, and I meant it.

I felt drowsy, very drowsy, and lay down on the

floor in the living room. "Why don't you go in the bedroom and lie down?" Charlie suggested, but the bedroom was the last place I wanted to be.

"I'm fine right here," I answered. We were speaking to each other like acquaintances, very polite.

Where are we, Charlie? Where are we now? What's going to become of us, you and me? Where do we go from here? Is there anywhere we can go, or have we made too much of a mess of it? I wish I knew what I wanted.

I napped on the floor while the kids played, dragging their games and toys out of their rooms, seemingly content to be playing around me. Late in the afternoon Charlie woke me, telling me that he'd been to the store and did I want to cook dinner?

"Do I have a choice?" I said, meaning to be funny, but he took it seriously and looked disgusted. I became angry and refused to tell him that it had been intended as a joke. I went to the kitchen.

After dinner I took a shower, luxuriating in the privacy of the bathroom and the dependably hot water.

When it was time to go, I stood at the door, dreading having to say goodbye to the kids and nervous about the upcoming meeting. The kids clung to my neck as I tried to back out the door.

"I'll be back soon," I promised, trying to disengage myself from the little hands, feeling tears behind my eyes and resenting the guilt. "I'll be home before you know it. 'Bye."

I gave Charlie Marjorie's address and sank back in the seat. When we were nearly there, he said, "This'd better work, Cass. I have absolutely had it. It's hard for me to care anymore. There's just been too much."

"I hope it works too, Charlie," I said. *I've had it too. This had better work, for my sake, not for yours. Or even the kids'.*

When we arrived at Marjorie's house Charlie waited in the car while I went up to the door. A pleasant, nebbishy-looking man answered my ring.

"I'm Cassie," I said. "Is Marjorie ready?"

He shifted uneasily. "She's in the tub," he finally said.

"The *tub?*" I began to panic. "We'll be late!"

"Look," he said kindly, "why don't you go ahead without her. The meeting is just down the street—in the Women's Federal Bank. Just go in the back door and down the stairs. There will be someone there."

What could I do? I was furious.

Back in the car I told Charlie what had happened.

"Want to skip it?" he asked.

"No, you jackass. It's now or never."

We pulled into the parking lot behind the bank. It had begun to snow again. I started to open the door and hesitated.

"Want me to go with you?" Charlie asked.

"No, Daddy. I'd better do this one myself. Pick me up at ten-thirty."

I walked into the bank and down the stairs, heart pounding with apprehension. There were lights and laughing voices coming from the large meeting room. I hesitated again, feeling lost and confused.

A short, round man in a blue blazer approached me.

"Are you in the right place, kid?" he demanded, a belligerent elf.

"I don't know." *I* don't *know. And I resent the "kid."*

"I'm looking for AA," I volunteered bravely.

"Well, this is the right place, then. But you're too damn young to be an alkie," he grumped.

Fear clutched me. It hadn't occurred to me that they might not take me!

An attractive woman in a gray wig came up behind him.

"Don't pay any attention to this little bastard, honey," she said in a husky voice. "If you have a problem with booze, then this is the place for you." She extended her hand. "Hi, I'm Alice, and this nitwit here is my husband John. We're both alcoholics." She nodded at him again. "Some of us are sicker than others."

I liked her immediately and tagged along as she poured coffee from a big urn for both of us, introduced me to a blur of faces, and then planted me next to her in the front row. My knees were aching again and I wished that I had taken aspirin before I'd left home.

I looked around at the dozens of people gathered in small groups, laughing and talking. They appeared to be much like the people I'd encountered at our church bazaars or in the PTA group I usually avoided, not at all what I'd expected. What had I expected? Despite what I'd told Alexander, I hadn't actually pictured a group of red-eyed winos. But then, I hadn't expected a group of people who looked entirely normal either.

Up at the podium John called for attention and everyone took seats. The room became quiet. John introduced himself. "Hi there, I'm John and I'm a grateful alcoholic."

GRATEFUL! What the hell for?

He introduced the speaker, a tall, substantial town banker type.

Alice leaned close and whispered, "John is Ted's sponsor. Ted stays sober anyway."

I listened in amazement as Ted chuckled and chortled his way through a horrendous tale involving job losses, multiple divorces, spiraling physical and mental erosion, all due, he said, to his drinking. Everyone around me roared with laughter as Ted, with an engaging self-mockery and without self-pity, recounted disaster after disaster.

And I thought my seventh-floor cohorts were looney!

He went on, speaking softly now of loneliness, alienation, and despair. There was no laughter—only heads nodding gently in agreement, in identification, and for me, an embarrassing lump in my throat. What did I have in common with this man? He was well over sixty, yet he'd felt what I felt, had seen the same empty road stretching endlessly before him. He knew.

He recounted his call to the AA central office and

his conversation with Valdez, who, I gathered, was something of a legend. He'd yelled, "Give me someone who speaks English!" and Valdez had replied, "I don nid Inglis. I spik akahoolic."

"That was six years ago," Ted said, "and I haven't had a drink since. I'm sober and happy, and, for the first time in my life, comfortable with myself. There's one more thing I'd like to say," he continued. "In AA we each have a higher power, God as we understand Him. I choose to call my higher power God because I am comfortable with that term. But if you are new, or uncertain, or without a god you believe in, then you can call the group your higher power and be confident that the program will work for you. The important thing is that you understand you no longer have to cope with your drinking problem alone. There is somewhere to go and someone to share your burden with— and here we are." He grinned.

The meeting ended with a reading from *Alcoholics Anonymous,* a rather poetic, inspirational section entitled, "A Vision For You." It finished with the words, "Join us . . . as we trudge the road to happy destiny." I smiled. *Trudging is just not my style.*

"Well, what did you think?" Alice asked, as we stacked our folding chairs against the wall.

"It was, um, interesting," I replied.

"Not sure, huh?" she grinned. "With some people it takes a while. I was lucky. I knew right away."

"What did you know?" I asked, wondering if this straightforward, self-confident lady had ever felt as lost as I did.

"John joined AA three months before I did," Alice explained. "He came at the gentle suggestion of a judge in traffic court. Something about thirty meetings or thirty days. At first he went mumbling and with a hangdog expression. By the time he got home from a meeting I'd be loaded and he'd join me. But after a few weeks he stopped complaining and stopped drinking. It was driving me crazy. I just knew that the old goat had found some hussy in AA and was having himself a fling. Well, I'm not one to avoid issues or suffer in silence. Never was. So I decided I'd go to the next meeting with the little bastard, find the bitch and fix her wagon. His too. He looked surprised when I got in the car with him, but he always knew better than to argue when I had my mind made up. When we got here, John introduced me to everyone, including the women. I couldn't figure out which was the hussy, though I saw several possibles. But John didn't seem to be the least bit nervous. That confused me. He always looked guilty, even when he hadn't done anything. Then the meeting started and Valdez was the speaker. I thought, 'Damn, the lectures are in Spanish. How the hell does anyone stay sober?' I could only understand every fifth word, and every tenth word seemed to be 'serenity.' I sat there listening to the Cisco Kid and thinking, 'Serenity, hell. I'd be happy just not throwing up in the morning.' But by the time the meeting ended, I was hooked. And I've been here ever since."

"How long ago was that?"

"Thirteen years. All of them sober. Me and the old goat."

"You mean you've been coming to meetings for thirteen years?" I asked, boggled.

"I'm still looking for the hussy," she laughed.

Thirteen years seemed like forever. It was nearly half of my lifetime.

"Do you have to go to meetings forever?" I asked.

"No." She shook her head solemnly. "Only for as long as you want to stay sober." She patted my shoulder. "Look, honey, if you're an alcoholic, you've got a disease that can kill you. *Will* kill you if you keep on drinking. So far, there's no cure. But the disease can be arrested if you stay sober. There are other deadly chronic diseases. Diabetes for one. Diabetics have to take insulin and stick to their diets. Heart patients have to follow their routines—diets, exercise, medicine. Well, AA is my insulin, my diet, my way of arresting my disease. It's not so bad, really. The meetings are generally interesting, and in rooms like this I find the only people in the world who really, on a gut level, understand me and my problems. However, the coffee usually stinks. Can't have everything."

"I appreciate your telling me this," I began.

"Just think about it," Alice said. "And don't worry. You're going to make it."

"How do you know?" I was curious.

"You have that look about you," she smiled. "Thoroughly beat."

"That's good?"

"Sure," she grinned. "You remind me of me when I got here. I'd spent years running around yelling, 'I gotta be me! I gotta be me!' I was convinced that 'being me' meant I had a right to drink as much as I wanted whenever I wanted and to hell with anyone who thought differently—or got in my way. Then I landed here still shouting 'I gotta be me!' and the people said, 'No, you don't.' And I said 'Thank God' and gave up. I didn't know who the hell 'me' was until I quit drinking, Cassie. I only knew who 'me' didn't want to be. Now," she said, "after only thirteen years' sobriety, I think I'm probably one of the nicest people I've ever met."

I giggled, then laughed a full free laugh that untangled the knots in my stomach and warmed the ends of my fingers. "You're terrific," I said.

"Of course," she agreed. "So are you."

Alice and John walked me to the door. She gave me a big hug and said, "Take care, dear. Keep coming back. You'll make it. See you next week." She gave me her phone number and I promised to call her from the hospital during the week.

I fled up the stairs. Behind me I heard John insist, "I still say she's too young."

The cold air and snow felt good. I breathed deeply. Charlie was waiting. I got in the car and we started off for Shaker Heights.

After a while Charlie spoke. "How did it go?"

I huddled in my coat. "Okay."

"Just okay?" He looked curious. "How are the people?"

I lit a cigarette. "They sure laugh a lot. Probably

mass hysteria. Most of them looked like they could use a drink."

"Was there a speaker?" Charlie asked.

Get out of my life, Charlie. Leave me alone while I sort out my thoughts. "Yup."

"Well, what was he like?" Charlie was beginning to sound desperate.

Can't you tell I don't want to talk to you about this, Charlie? Are you so damn thick-headed you can't see I want to keep it to myself? "He was a regular stand-up comic," I snorted.

"He was FUNNY????" Charlie hissed with disbelief. "Ask him what he drinks. Your drinking does everything *except* make me laugh. In fact, when you're drunk you—"

"Shut up, Charlie!" I bellowed, and up he shut.

We were almost there. Charlie drove me around to Emergency and opened the car door wordlessly. I jumped out and slammed the door. Neither of us said goodbye. Charlie gunned the engine and I ran toward the yellow Emergency sign. I flashed the card I'd been given and the orderly buzzed me in. I ran through the maze of basement corridors, banging into pipes and bouncing off walls, overwhelmed and driven by an anxiety attack. I stood, gasping for breath and frantically pushing the elevator button. I rode to the seventh floor, hanging on to the wall and sweating profusely, then jumped off the elevator and pounded violently on the locked ward door.

"Let me in! Let me in!" I screamed, certain that I'd die, choking, in the hall.

Tinkerbell hit the buzzer and I stumbled in, ears ringing and heart thumping madly in my chest. I hung over the counter and tried to get my breath. Tinkerbell waited quietly, just letting me calm down.

Finally she asked, "How did it go, Cassie? How was the AA meeting?"

I looked down at her sweet little face and the concern in her soft, gray eyes, and my defenses went the way of the snow melting down the inside of my boot. I reached for her tiny hand, and started to cry.

"It works, Tinkerbell! The thing really works. I don't know how or why it does. Maybe I'll find out later. I just know that tonight I met a lot of people who said they're alcoholics, who said they've had the same problem with drinking I have and they don't have to drink anymore. They don't have any reason to lie about it, Tinkerbell. If it works for them it can work for me. I'm not so different." I heard what I'd just said and smiled. "I've been thinking for so long that I'm the only one, and I'm not. And I'm glad. Jesus!"

Tinkerbell smiled. "I'm glad it worked out. You're tired. Go to bed."

"Okay." I started to go, then turned back. "Alcoholism is a disease, Tinkerbell, like diabetes."

"I know that it is, Cassie, but more important, now you know it, too."

9

Dear Bobby,

Thank you for the hideous plant. When Dalton brought it in this morning I whipped off the crinkly green paper expecting carnations or daisies. What I got was a carnivorous-looking, hyperthyroid artichoke. Is this supposed to be an example of California flora or even fauna? No wonder people out there are crazy. They probably live in mortal terror of their houseplants.

I shall assume that you intended to be thoughtful and that this is not a plot to add paranoia to my list of woes. I have named the beast "Ralph," and placed him in the far corner of my room in the dark, within snapping distance of Mrs. Caliguire's bed. Either he will shrivel up and die of his own volition or gobble up Caliguire in the dead of night. In the meantime, I will feed him salami sandwiches and sleep with one eye open. How can I thank you properly? Maybe a bomb by return mail.

For God's sake, don't tell anyone, but things may be looking up. If word got out that I was feeling even hesitantly optimistic, Mother, Charlie, and perhaps even Alexander would immediately assume that I am "well" and begin inundating my semifrail person with demands for further progress. I'm not the only one looking for "a golden key that unlocks all doors," but, being the identified patient, I'm the only one under obligation to admit it.

I need some time to ponder before I throw myself headlong under the wheels of further progress. Misery I understand, but even the remotest possibility that happiness lies tightly coiled in the dark crannies of my hidden future, ready to pounce when I least expect it, fills me with dread. If I start feeling too good too fast, my nervous system will short out and I'll end up on the floor with my eyeballs rolling and sparks shooting out of my ears. So, not a word to anyone.

Here's what's happening. I have joined Alcoholics Anonymous. I say "joined" because I went to a meeting and decided that it will work for me. I told Tinkerbell (my favorite nurse) that I know it will work for me because I saw positive, physical proof that it works for other people. There were dozens of people there, all quite sober, who I am sure would not be spending a Saturday evening in the basement of a bank without good reason. Even Cleveland has other Saturday night diversions.

I told Tinkerbell that because it sounded sane, and sensible, and reasonable, and it was true. But I will tell YOU that there was something else, my dear, and I know you will understand the way you understood when we used to send silent messages across the dinner table. Remember? We would look at one another, just a glance. The glance would linger and take hold and eventually both of us would smile or begin to laugh and Mother or Dad would say, "What's so funny?" and we would both say, "Nothing." How could we explain, even if we wanted to, that while our outside selves required words, our inside selves needed nothing. Our souls predate our history and share a secret.

So you will understand when I say this: I sat in that meeting room on a straight, hard chair, next to Alice, trembling with nervousness. I grew increasingly agitated because my hands were shaking so violently. I tried concentrating on my fingers, willing the shaking to stop. Suddenly I was filled with a sense of being in exactly the right place and time. Something deep inside, perhaps another part of me, said, "Calm yourself. All is as it should be. Everything will be all right," and for a moment I felt something that was light, peace and anticipation rolling through me like a wave. Only for a moment, and then it receded, but not entirely. Whatever it was, a piece of it, or perhaps an echo, has remained with me. I am afraid to explore it for fear that it will disappear. I am content to feel it.

I haven't told Alexander about this because I am afraid that he will dismiss it, saying that it's part of my withdrawal, or even a hallucination. I don't want my experience diminished down to a "symptom," not officially anyway. If it is, and it may be, I am grateful for it. God knows I have had horrible, unbearable, terrifying symptoms. I wouldn't reject a symptom that brought me peace of mind just because Alexander could probably come up with a textbook reason for it.

And I won't tell Charlie because he just might tell me that God is speaking to me, and believe me, I am not ready for the notion that I have somehow managed to capture the attention of the Almighty. I would crawl under my bed and stay there until I was sure that God had returned to designing a better porcupine.

I tell you because I know that you won't think I'm crazy, and more importantly, because I doubt that you will laugh. (If you are laughing may a plague descend upon your innards and rust erode your private parts— I am awesome in my wrath!)

So there it is. Not much really, but an experience of a nature I've had only once before. And it seems like it was another life—when we were fifteen.

It was the summer you grew five inches and I nearly

died. Do you remember, or were you so involved with watching your feet get farther away from your nose that you failed to notice my gradual decline?

When I was hospitalized with hepatitis everyone said that it would be all right, but I continued to get worse and I knew it. I was jaundiced and couldn't eat, and finally, couldn't even drink water. I felt myself fading away, getting weaker and weaker. The doctor was very brusque and patronizing. He never smiled and never explained anything. In fact, I got the impression that he was annoyed with me for not responding to the treatment. When the cortisone shots he was giving me made me sicker, he stopped visiting me altogether and turned me over to a resident from the Philippines who spoke very little English and insisted on examining my breasts every time he came in. I was too young, too ill, and too stupid to protest.

Mom and Dad came to visit me nearly every day. Dad sat in a chair and looked mournful while Mother hopped around the room like a nervous bird, straightening my bed and dusting everything that wasn't moving. They kept up a steady stream of small talk about inconsequential things, like how you and Mary Kay were behaving and what Mother had cooked for dinner and what was on television.

No one said anything about my skin being the color of mustard and the intravenous drip in my arm, or the thirty pounds I'd lost, or the black circles under my eyes that extended down to my chin. They just chattered on about how unusually cold it was that summer and did I think the Indians had a chance for the pennant.

I lay back inside of myself and watched and tried to listen, and wondered what it all had to do with what really was going on. I was too frightened to say, "Look at me, I'm dying. I'm dying and everyone knows it and no one will tell me." I was too frightened to say that and I knew, by the way they avoided my eyes and couldn't stop talking, that it would kill them if I said it, so I didn't. I kept my secret and they kept theirs.

I had very little will left, Bobby, and much of the time I was too weak to think or care about it very much, but there were moments when I became furious, livid with having been shut out, cast out, isolated. I thought that I would die in that room, all alone and with no one to say goodbye.

Every night Mother and Dad would kiss me and say, "Goodnight. You'll feel better tomorrow, honey," and I would agree and they would leave me to go home to you and Mary Kay. How I hated you then, sweetheart, and Mary Kay along with you, both of you all caught up with the trappings of an adolescent summer, and with all the summers of your life ahead of you, while there I was, against my will and out of place and time, trying to deal with the adult business of dying, and failing, failing. I would lie there rigid with despair, hating you all, and wondering if the truth could possibly be more painful than this godawful pretense that denied my feeling and cut me adrift in an icy-cold limbo of loneliness.

Then one day I was thirsty and drank some water and didn't vomit, so I drank some more. The day after that I ate a dish of custard and walked to the bathroom. And the day after that, the doctor sauntered in and said, "Well, Cassie, the worst is over. You're going to be all right."

He poked my liver and pronounced it less swollen, and pried down my lower eyelids and pronounced my jaundice subsiding, and chuckled and patted my head and rubbed his ferrety little paws together and told me how pleased he was. He bounced out of my room grinning, exhilarated with the knowledge that I wasn't going to litter his career with failure and screw up his batting average.

For a long time after he left, I lay there feeling nothing, absolutely nothing. I was a deserted house, emptied out.

I looked out the window at the murky gray sky and the few tired, twisted trees with their sparse, grayish-green leaves and beyond that to the smokestacks pouring black and brimstone on East 92nd Street, and I heard my voice whisper, "I'm going to live."

I hadn't cried while I thought I was dying, but I felt the tears then and let them come. They were cool and a relief and washed away the bitterness and the anger, and the clammy, insidious fear. I was going to live and nothing else was important. The worst that could happen had happened to me and I'd survived. I was still there. I felt then as now, that what is past is gone and I don't have to drag it along with me, and what's ahead somehow will be all right. It's a lovely feeling, like floating in sunshine, knowing that something or someone benevolent and loving has wrapped me in kindness and is protecting me from harm.

Of course, when I was fifteen that feeling vanished quickly. Three weeks later I was back in school agonizing over algebra and bitching about pimples. But I'm older now and, oh, Bobby, wouldn't it be wonderful if I was wiser, too? Maybe I am. Maybe I can hold on to this for a while, until I can build up some all right experience behind my all right feeling. Wish me luck.

But I'm so damn timid. I was telling Alexander about the meeting and acting as though it was as relatively unimportant as a PTA gathering.

"It was very nice," I said. "I think I will probably go to more meetings." "I thought you would like it," he said, equally casual. "You may go to as many meetings as you like." He swiveled around in his chair and sat with his back to me, looking out the tiny, grimy window. He does that sometimes, Bob, and I suspect that when he does it's because he's afraid I'll read something he wants hidden in his face. I'm always tempted to run around the desk and yell, "Gotcha!"

But I don't do that. I play by the rules. So does he. This game is more important than most and the losers often die, or wish they had.

I asked Alexander if he would call Charlie and arrange for me to have the use of my car. If Alexander calls, I won't have to hassle with Charlie and the request will carry the Good Psycho-Ward Seal of Approval. Then I can go to meetings whenever I want and won't have to depend on anyone to pick me up or bring me back.

In fact, I won't have to consult anyone at all about it. I feel like the first day of school, all starched and ready and confident I can cross the street all by myself. If I don't get hit by a truck. Or struck by lightning. Or fall down in the mud.

Wouldn't it be great, Bobby, if this all did work out?

I mean, it would be so super if I could get it all together and come out of this in one piece, with my legs under me like a real person. If I could be sure that I'm not going to screw everything up always and forever, that I have choices like everyone else and can even SOME DAY make decisions (tremble, tremble). Terrific!

I could say to Mother, "Now look here, ma'am (or for all I know, maybe sir), I am a grown-up lady just like you and I have a right to do things my way just as you have a right to do things your way. There are some things I do very well and some things not well at all, but you aren't perfect either and make mistakes, too, so you have no right to sit up there on your cloud and pass judgment on me."

And Mother would say, "My dear Cassie, I had no idea of the depth of your feelings and the level of your intelligence. You are certainly correct in what you say and I love you dearly just as you are."

And then I could say to Charlie, "Charlie, I don't know how things are going to work out with us, but I can take care of myself, and if I stay with you it's because I want to and not because I feel so guilty or so frightened of facing life alone that I can't leave."

And Charlie would say to me, "Cassie, as an adult woman you will have to make your own decisions, but I hope that we will be able to work this out together because you are such a neat, nifty, spiffy person and I would hate to lose you. We will certainly have to talk a lot."

To Alexander I would say, "Thanks so awfully, Doctor. Your assistance was invaluable and if you should acquire another patient with a similar problem and think I could be helpful as an AA person, please do not hesitate to call."

And he would say, "Goodbye."

Well, that takes care of my rich, full, fantasy life. It was terrific until I came to the part where Alexander says goodbye. What am I going to do, Bobby? If I get better I won't need a shrink anymore and if I don't need a shrink anymore I won't see Alexander anymore, and the thought of not seeing Alexander anymore makes my stomach flop over and curdle at the edges. If I don't get better, I lose. If I get better, I lose. I wish to hell I hadn't thought of that. Now that I've thought of it, I'll have to tell HIM about it and we'll discuss it and it will all be very embarrassing to me. (For all I know, it won't be too wonderful for him either.) Maybe I could impersonalize it and say that I can't stand the thought of losing ANYONE. Even a stiff-necked shrink who never laughs at my jokes. I could use it as an indication of how deep-seated my disturbance really is. He'll say, "Hmmm, we'll have to work on that." And I'll say, "Yes, indeedy, we certainly will." I'll look up appropriate phrases in my *Dictionary of Freudian Terminology* under "Loss, fear of." If I work it right and keep my wits about me, I won't resolve this problem for twenty-seven years. Problem solved. See what can happen when you're talking to a friend? I should write to you every day. I could not only unravel the Gordian knot in my psyche, but appear to be busy and involved when Brunhilde, the misplaced Viking Lady, comes tapping on my door every afternoon in an effort to intimidate me into going to Occupational Therapy. She marches around the seventh floor telling all the patients that their doctor has "ordered" Occupational Therapy and they must come IMMEDIATELY. She herds them out in the hall where they mill around until she lines them up in two columns and goosesteps them out the door.

Patients are forever trying to hide by taking a shower or even a fit, but she doesn't care. Wet or screaming, it makes no difference. She drags them along anyway.

Cara is the only person so far I've seen stand up to the Dictator of OT. Cara told her that she didn't want to go, wouldn't go, and nothing could make her go. Brunhilde said, "Your doctor WANTS you to go." And Cara said, "Who cares what he wants? I'm paying him. He's not doing me any favors."

I guess that was a line of thought that B. hadn't yet explored because she was quiet for a while. Then she said, "If you don't go to OT, it will be written down on your chart and you won't get out of here." And Cara said, "Good, I like it here."

Obviously it was too late for B. to come up with the "if you don't go they'll throw you out" line, so she just scowled and made an awkward retreat, pushing her more passive charges into the elevator.

I go sometimes and hate myself for it. I sit and dab grout on a metal shell and try to decide what color ashtray I'm going to mess up that day. I listen to the conversations around me, and the tape recorder in my head jots down snatches and fragments and I smile and pretend that I am not listening in. Very often patients shuffle off to OT soon after they awaken from shock therapy and they haven't quite returned from wherever it was the electricity took them. One day I asked an older lady being treated for depression to pass me an ashtray, which she did, saying, "Icy winter elephants trumpet down the drainpipe and shatter crystal thoughts." She returned to her work with a soft, dreamy smile, her gray head bent over her embroidery hoop, while I sat wondering at the lady I knew to be a widow, grandmother, and the kind of housewife who still baked Irish soda bread with raisins on Saturday mornings. I wondered if the treatment which had temporarily disconnected her from her present reality had also temporarily connected her with a portion of another reality, remote and inaccessible except through madness, or dreaming, or the intervention of Farraday's magic machine. By evening she was fully returned and herself again, which meant that she was nattering on about her arthritic knees and her children's neglect, both of which are painful and, so far, without a cure.

I have told Alexander that I would like to have shock treatments, not because I'm convinced of their worth (the benefits, to me, seem short-lived, if in fact there are any at all), but because I'm so damned curious. I want to know what happens, where people go when they're not here. But then, they never seem to remember and my logic tells me that I wouldn't either. Yet—what if I did? What if I could remember and explain and interpret? What if I went to the place where icy winter elephants trumpet down drainpipes, and returned, and remembered, and wasn't too frightened to speak of it?

I do not say these things to Alexander because I am afraid that he would chart these thoughts and change my diagnosis and begin treating me like a person afflicted with uncontrollable flights of fancy and out of touch with his reality. In truth, I am in total touch with his reality, thoroughly at home within its walls. It's a sturdily built reality, with a foundation and keystone, and tightly caulked windows that keep out the storms. It has shape and substance and even a tradition, so that when I walk through its rooms I can hear the solid echo of my footsteps, and know that I am where I am and there are others with me whose certainty will prevent the floor from dissolving under me. For the most part I keep my fancies to myself, enjoying them as solo flights. And sometimes, Bob, oh, devious wench that I am, I tell Alexander that the random wanderings of my mind are dreams. I sit and naïvely blink and request an interpretation.

He usually says, "What do you think that means?" throwing the whole thing back on me. I catch it neatly and shrug and say, "Beats the hell out of me. If you don't know, how am I supposed to? You're the shrink."

And he says, "Well, that doesn't make me omniscient."

And I look disgusted, but pretend to agree. Isn't that just like an omniscient person, Bob? How sensitive it is of him to pretend for my sake to be mortal.

Lest you think that I am irrevocably loony, and are feeling superior, love, allow me to remind you that for the last five years we shared the same house, you walked in your sleep at least twice a week. I would awaken, hearing you crashing through your room and would wait in my bed. Presently you would drift in like Marley's ghost, but without the chains, and hover over me, mumbling something garbled and incoherent. At times you were obviously angry and at other times you seemed to be sad. I could never wake you up by talking to you and my instincts told me that shouting or shaking could be dangerous, so I would eventually take you by the hand and lead you back to your room.

I would wonder if perhaps there was something you wanted terribly to say to me and couldn't when you were awake, something so important to you that it drove you out of your bed in the middle of the night. I also used to think that you were perhaps an instrument, transmitting a message across a mystic gulf, as a medium does, that you might be the bearer of my "golden key." I would ponder these things the morning after one of your sleepwalking sessions and often it occurred to me that if I were to question you patiently and gently while asleep, the gibberish might cease and the message come clear. And I would have too, except that beneath and overriding my metaphysical concerns was the fear that a full bladder had driven you out in the night, and if I didn't hop out of bed in one hell of a hurry you would pee all over me. Which tells you more than you need to know about my personality.

Do you still walk in your sleep? Does it frighten whatever lady you happen to be with at the moment, the current in a long list of those you have so skillfully seduced as madonnas, the better to secretly despise as whores? You didn't think I knew that, did you? Bobby, Bobby. Your twig was bent the same as mine. My desperation has just been noisier than yours.

I am rambling, rambling at you, trying to connect, looking for solutions to problems I haven't even defined. You are the only person I know with whom I feel free to be confused, the only one I feel isn't tapping his foot and impatiently watching a clock, setting time limits on my resolutions. It may be because you understand so deeply and care so much, or it may be because you are so far away and don't really give a shit. Right now either one will serve my purpose.

You see, the thing that I am afraid to say is this: I came here because I was too sick and too weary to function outside any longer. I was dead to the idea of any future for me, and in a perverse way, content. Then I got all caught up in the psychiatric game and the pretense of wanting to get well, because, God knows, the very thought of continuing the struggle took more energy than I had. But, in order to get any semblance of peace and quiet around here, you have to play the game. Somewhere along the line I began to play in earnest. One morning while waiting in the parlor for Alexander, something inside of me said, "Maybe," and with that "maybe" I was doomed, already crawling around the corner and starting up the hill, quite against my will at first. Now it seems there might be a way out, a positive, responsible way, if I want it, and I am beginning to shudder and quake inside. I opened the door just a crack for hope, and in slithered EXPECTATIONS! It's goddamn scary, Bobby.

That's what I want to say, I'm scared. I'm scared that I won't make it. I'm scared that I will. I'm scared that I will make it and no one will care. I'm scared that I'll turn out to be an insufficient person sober, no one will love me, and I'll be thrown out into some vast, empty space alone, my life entirely changed. I'm afraid that everyone will think it's wonderful and expect great things of me and rally around with love and support and I'll have to go home and nothing will change.

Yet, I can't go back. There is no way to unlearn what I've learned, to erase those particular tapes, to lapse back into an innocent ignorance of the nature of my problem and its unignorable solution. So, willy-nilly, I forge ahead—timidly. But now at least one other person in this world knows that I am terrified and a little angry. I never meant to buy a ticket on this train. It was another trip I intended altogether. I'm excited too, Bob. I've never been through this territory before. When I'm not cringing under the seat, expecting imminent derailment, I'm hanging out the window enjoying the scenery.

Send me a cheery note, love. No profundity necessary. Just whisper softly in my ear and smile. Of course if you have any courage to spare, roll it up and send in a plain brown wrapper, labeled, "To a potential paragon."

Love,
Cass

10

"Goddammit! Son of a bitch! Shit!" Cara exploded into the parlor.

"You're upset," I said, making a wild guess.

Frank peered over the frayed edge of his newspaper. "Watch your mouth, Cara, you aren't too old to spank."

"Wouldn't you just love that," Cara snorted. "You fatherly types are all alike. You act so cool and all the time you're panting over little girls in sunbonnets and pink ruffled undies."

"What's the matter, Cara?" I asked. Out of the corner of my eye I could see Alexander walking slowly from the interview room to the nurses' station. He glanced my way and I looked away quickly, caught in the act.

"It's that bastard Alexander," Cara shrieked. "He's trying to ruin my life!"

"He's right behind you, Cara, on the other side of the glass. He can hear you," I pointed out.

"So what? Let him hear me!" she shrieked louder. "If I end up dead, it will be all his fault!"

"Why? What's he done?" Joanne put down her crocheting and looked concerned.

"He called my mother and asked her to come in for a session, that's what he did! A session with him and me—all of us together. Shit!" Cara flopped down on the floor and burst into tears.

"Without your permission?" I asked.

"Well, he did ask—no! No, I didn't give him permission! I didn't!"

"What's so terrible about that?" I asked. "What can happen if your mother comes in just to talk?"

"On the other hand, why the hell should she come in?" Frank inquired. "Cara is over twenty-one. Does she really need her mommy?"

Cara shot him a look, at once forlorn and furious.

"I don't need her! I don't! Alexander has this stupid idea that since I live with her I'd better learn to communicate with her. That's exactly what he said. But I don't want to live with her. I don't want to learn to communicate with her. I want to get away from her!"

"Then do it," I said, thinking how easy it sounded. *I'll tell you twenty times a day to leave your mother, Cara, and you tell me twenty times a day to leave Charlie. By the time we're both convinced we can survive without them we'll be ready for The Home.*

"You don't know what she's like, Cassie. She'll never let me go. Never! She screams and yells and threatens awful things, horrible things—"

"Like what?" Joanne asked, frowning.

"I can't tell you. You can't imagine!" Cara sobbed.

I sat on the floor next to Cara and put my arms around her. She immediately nestled into the hollow of my shoulder and I rubbed her back slowly, feeling the tight muscles begin to relax.

"Why don't you tell Alexander that you eventually want to move out?" I suggested. "Maybe not right now, but someday soon. Ask him to help you do that, get ready for it."

Cara threw herself headlong into my lap. "He won't help me," she bellowed. "He won't do a damn thing to help me! He wants me to stay this way forever!"

"No, no," I rocked her in my arms, whispering and stroking her hair. "He wants to help. He wants to help you, honey."

She continued to sob as I held her.

I love you, Cara. I can't afford to love you and I didn't think I had any love to give, any emotion for

*anyone outside of my own skin, but I do. Today you
have a need and I love you.*

I looked up to see Alexander, poised with one
hand on the door, waiting for Dalton to buzz him
out, all done, finished with us for the day. His eyes
were on me and for once I did not look away. We
stared at one another and everything melted away
except him and me and the weeping girl curled with
her head buried in my lap.

*What will we do about this child, Edwin, you and
I? Tell me how to comfort her while you go about
the healing. How did we come to share her sorrow
and her fear?*

The buzzing startled us both. He turned abruptly
and strode through the door. I watched him through
the glass, standing with his shoulders hunched, waiting for the elevator, not looking back. Then the elevator arrived and swallowed him up.

I leaned over Cara.

"C'mon, honey. Let's go down to the coffee shop
and get some ice cream."

"I don't want any," she mumbled.

"I'd like some," I replied. "Will you go with me?
Please?"

Joanne tucked her crocheting into the large canvas
bag at her feet. She got to her feet briskly and began
to tug at Cara's arm.

"That's enough crying for one day, Cara," she said
sharply. "We're tired of listening to you. I want some
ice cream too and you're going to go with us. It's
my turn to watch *you* eat."

"Don't wanna," came the mumble.

"Tough luck," Joanne spit. "You're gonna! Besides,
if we go right now, we'll be just in time to spoil our
dinners."

Cara looked up with wet eyelashes and her Norman
Rockwell grin.

"Okay," she said, jumping to her feet. "I'll have a
banana split."

Cara skipped off to her room to get her purse while

I stood shaking my head. Some of us just can't have too many mothers.

"You're terrific, Joanne," I said, patting her shoulder.

"Thanks," she sparkled, then sighed. "I wish Ronnie thought so."

Joanne, when are you going to stop? You're worth twenty of that son of a bitch. I'd learned the hard way that any criticism of the Freak of Fairmont Avenue would only result in a spirited, and worse, boring defense of his nonexistent virtues. I would wonder, with a superior air, why some women find it necessary to crucify themselves on the altar of unrequited passion, if I hadn't found myself more than once similarly spread-eagled, with nails through my palms, bleeding to death and begging for more.

In the coffee shop Joanne and I noisily sucked up chocolate syrup through collapsing straws and listened as Cara, bright-eyed and temporarily recovered, reminisced.

"Don't know why I do it," she was saying. "I meet a guy who tells me I'm wonderful, simply great, just what he's always wanted, always looked for in a woman. I get all mushy and melty and say, 'Take me, I'm yours.' He says, 'Wonderful, don't ever change.' And the next thing I know I'm following him around, leading *his* life. The me he fell in love with begins to disappear, and the weird thing is, the guy not only seems to love it, he seems to expect it, demand it even. I end up running around doing *his* thing and dropping my own, and he thrives on it."

"It's nice to share interests with the one you love," Joanne remarked. "That's part of being in love."

Cara scooped up a dripping spoonful of ice cream and banana.

"I wasn't talking about sharing interests," she elaborated. "I was talking about completely changing lifestyles and taking off on someone else's trip. And I never seem to attract the type who goes to work at nine, comes home at five, and likes to collect stamps. I attract whackos."

"Like what?" I asked, curious.

Cara waved her spoon in the air. "Well, there was the skydiver," she said. "I'm so afraid of heights that I can't look out of the window in my room, but two months after I met Ricky, there I was, bailing out over Coshocton. My life passed before me nine times before I landed. I broke my ankle and fainted dead away, but four weeks later I was back at Cleveland Hookins Airport with Rick strapping me into a parachute. I smoked three joints before we went up and I don't remember anything. I think Ricky pushed me out. Anyway, he said I pulled the ripcord just like a pro. But that was the last time!"

"You broke up with him?" I asked.

"Oh, no," Cara shook her head. "I never break up with anyone. I have nervous collapses and get hauled off to the funny farm. They eventually get tired of waiting for me to recover and go away. End of relationship."

"Neat," I laughed, "but expensive."

"That was the only one that was really dangerous," she continued. "The others were only exhausting. I fell for an unsuccessful actor named Donald and spent a summer traipsing from one seedy motel to the other while he was on the Kenly Circuit. He played the brother in *The Prisoner of Second Avenue* and had psychosomatic laryngitis. He had to force a high squeaky voice to be heard at all, and had such stage fright that he popped a dozen downers every night just to get himself onstage. At one point the lead makes a long speech while Don leans against the wall. Don always nodded off and missed his cue. One night the lead got fed up and smashed Don over the head with a lamp. That brought down the curtain. The audience demanded its money back and the lead demanded that Don be fired. He was."

"And you had a nervous breakdown." Joanne supplied the ending.

"So did he," Cara said. "He went to some hospital near Columbus and I went to California with my mother. He sent me a note six months later that he'd gotten well and gone into the plumbing business. For some reason, I wasn't interested." She looked thoughtful. "Plumbing." She scraped glop from the bottom of her bowl and licked her lips.

"One of the best, though, was Arthur." She grinned and leaned forward confidentially. "He was a Pentecostal minister my mother introduced me to when she was going through her religious period. She thought he would be a good influence on me. Was he ever! He had blond curly hair. He looked like an angel and told me, with his hand up my skirt, how Christ had come to redeem us all, *especially me.* So of course I joined his church, and his choir, and his Bible study group, and his missionary league. And because I thought it would please him, I repented, gave witness and commenced speaking in tongues, all on the same Sunday afternoon."

"Bet he loved that," I laughed.

"No, he decided I was some kind of nut and dumped me." She shook her head. "He was something else, though. If you let him rest five minutes out of an hour, he could fuck nonstop for a week. Yum!"

"Cara!" Joanne was offended. "That's enough about your lovers!"

"Well, you wanted to know," Cara said defensively, then turned to me. "Why me?" she asked. "I keep looking for the prince and all I get is frogs. You don't have this kind of problem. All you have to contend with is Charlie."

"Think not?" I smiled, and while Joanne looked disapprovingly at both of us, I filled her in on the redoubtable Donnerly.

"But he sounds neat!" she exclaimed.

"He is neat," I agreed.

"Then," she burbled, all aglow, "why don't you leave Charlie and run off with Donnerly?"

"He hasn't asked me and even if he did, I wouldn't marry him. I couldn't live with his fatal flaw."

"What's that?"

"He cheats on his wife," I hissed, and went off to pay the bill.

We returned to our happy haven and Joanne departed to wash her hair. Following suit, Cara decided to combine hydrotherapy with personal hygiene and headed for the shower.

Our conversation had left me unaccountably grumpy, whether because Donnerly hadn't asked me to run off with him or because he cheats on his wife, and for all I know, on me also, I didn't know. Or maybe it was because I cheat on Charlie and realized that though I still loved the sin, I had begun, I know not when, to hate the sinner.

I slithered down the hall with eyes downcast and hands wedged into the sleeves of my black turtleneck, pretending to be Audrey Hepburn in *The Nun's Story*. I'd long since discovered that I could sometimes change my mood or at least temporarily escape by pretending to be someone else, somewhere else.

So now I was Audrey on her way to murder the mother superior, for no other reason than having some free-floating and unexpressed hostility to discharge. I'd wallop her with a crucifix and, chuckling gleefully, leap out the window, vault over the wall, and make for the cottage of the gamekeeper, Mellors, on loan from D. H. Lawrence.

I was creeping up on the mother, when Merriweather, the Blatantly Beautiful, grabbed my arm, sending me three feet into the air.

"Good lord, Cassie, you're nervous as a cat," she gasped, still hanging on to my arm.

"You have rare diagnostic ability, Merriweather, you must be the envy of your peers."

I only assume this nervous façade to make the other patients comfortable. Beneath this twitchy exterior lies a personality characterized by iceberg calm and nerves of steel. "Are you holding on to me for support, Merriweather, or are you acting out your latent homosexuality?"

Merriweather dropped my arm and stepped back several inches. "I wish you wouldn't be so flippant about everything. You seldom seem to take your hospitalization seriously and you hide behind that superior attitude of yours."

"If I had to take every moment of this seriously, I'd cut my throat," I replied. "And it isn't an attitude. I am superior."

"If you really felt that way, you wouldn't drink," she said sagely.

Behind those false eyelashes lies a brain that's retained a few psychiatric phrases tucked in among the clutter of hints from Cosmo's *Beauty Bazaar.*

"I only drink to preserve my health and family tradition," I countered. "Irish blood doesn't flow unless it's mixed with alcohol. It clots up the brain, causing people who should be writing poetry and preparing for sainthood to join the IRA and blow up their neighbors."

Merriweather looked startled. "You made me forget," she exclaimed. "There's a priest in your room!"

"Well, don't just stand there, lady," I said, "call an exterminator. What is a priest doing in my room?" Except for Charlie, there was no one I wanted less to see.

"He said that he's your pastor and has come all the way across town to see you. But it's your option. If you refuse to see him, he'll have to go away."

Never in my life has anyone ever gone away because I didn't want to see them. People I don't want to see are forever falling into my life, popping out of my woodwork, and leaping out at me from dark corners as if they had a perfect right to do so. I couldn't imagine telling anyone that I didn't want to see him. Someone I hate might get mad at me and go off in a snit, leaving me to feel guilty until the end of time. I stand in the doorway and let my dinner burn while I'm being polite to Jehovah's Witnesses. I couldn't possibly turn down a priest.

"No, as long as he came all this way, I'll see him, Merriweather. If you hear me bellow, come running."

I scurried down the hall, expecting to find the priest giving Mrs. Caliguire the last rites. I found him standing on tiptoe, trying vainly to look out my window.

"Good afternoon, Father Dunhill. How nice of you

to come," I said, like the Hostess with the Mostest. "Do sit down."

"I'm happy to see you," Father Dunhill said, then hemmed and cleared his throat. "Well, I didn't mean that I'm happy to see you *here*. I mean that it's always nice to see you. Of course I haven't seen you in quite some time. You've been here. Or somewhere. I mean, I haven't seen you in church for a long time."

"Oh, I've been in church," I assured him. "When I go alone I usually sit in the back, but when I go with Charlie and the kids I sit right up in front where God can see me without having to strain his neck. I haven't seen *you* in church for some time. Where have you been?"

"During the summer months I said the last two masses and left the rest to Fathers Tilton and Flowers. (*That way he could play nine holes of golf before it got too hot.*) I just never went back to the winter schedule. That's probably why you haven't seen me."

"Oh."

Terrific. While I've been lurking in the back of the church, half-concealed behind the baptismal font, hiding from Dunhill, he's been on the golf course, hiding from me and whoever else in the parish might be in need of spiritual solace.

We stared at each other for several minutes. Dunhill fiddled with his collar and finally ran his fingers through his curly gray hair.

No, I'm not going to help you. Go ahead, Father, comfort the sick.

"So," he hemmed, "how do you feel?"

"Better, thank you." I waited, bouncing slightly on my bed. He sat down in the straight chair opposite me. *This is my territory, and HE's the one who feels uncomfortable.* I was beginning to enjoy what felt like the upper hand.

"Are you coming home soon?" he asked, squirming.

"I have no idea," I replied. "My doctor says that I'm not ready yet and he hasn't given me any hint as to when I will be ready."

"Charlie and the children miss you," he said abruptly.

"How do you know?" I asked, suddenly understanding the reason for this pastoral visit.

"Charlie came up to the rectory to talk several nights ago," he replied. "He's very worried about you. And the children miss you greatly. It must be very difficult being away from them."

"Yes it is," I replied. I could feel the upper hand shriveling. I lit a cigarette and offered the pack to the priest, who eagerly accepted.

"Charlie should be less worried about me than he was a few weeks ago," I remarked tartly. "In fact, he should be pleased that I'm doing something about my problem."

Dunhill blew smoke through his nose and looked interested.

"What's that? What are you doing about your problem?"

Other than my instincts, which told me that confiding in Dunhill would be a futility akin to trying to grow roses in rock, there was no reason for me not to be straight with him.

But when I want a *priest*, I'll ask for one, preferably two minutes before I croak. Just long enough for the short form of the last rites and a plenary indulgence to wing me on my way. I've already earned my death-bed plenary indulgence. For it I hauled my rebellious body out of bed in what seemed like the middle of the night and trudged my way through bitterly cold dawns to mass for nine consecutive First Fridays, not just once, but four times. So I count on my plenary. I'm entitled. I earned it.

Mary Kay has six of them, not that she'll ever need even one. She just stacked them up as a kid, instead of collecting dolls. She said that going to church made her feel good, which is a handy way for a Catholic to feel. She was always going to Forty Hours or Lenten devotions or some damn novena or other, forever trotting off with the appropriate prayer book, looking pious and coming home looking smug.

For a while Mary Kay's devotion made Mother very happy. She increased her "Why aren't you more

like your sister?" queries to me and beamed upon
Mary Kay's comings and goings. Then she started to
wonder what Mary Kay was praying for. When Mary
Kay said that it was personal, Mother assumed that it
had to do with either leaving home or the opposite
sex, or God forbid, leaving home *with* the opposite
sex. She began to tell Mary Kay that she looked pale
and peaked and was in danger of becoming a religious
fanatic, which could eventually lead only to social
ostracism or the convent, and no daughter of hers was
going to become a nun; everyone knew they were
hysterical and ended up with uterus problems, and
besides, she wanted grandchildren, and if she waited
for Cassie to settle down and become unselfish enough
to produce children, she'd wait forever, God knows.

So, having racked up enough prayer points to redeem two Magdalens, Mary Kay tapered off. Mother
relaxed and settled back to wait for the grandchildren
who never appeared, because, having renounced religion, Mary Kay took up education and got a scholar-
ship to a college out of town, out of state in fact,
which I suspected was what she had been praying for
all along. Being of unsound mind, I became a teenage
bride and shortly proved to Mother that being selfish
has nothing whatsoever to do with getting knocked-
up.

Bobby has no plenary indulgences whatever. He's
always believed that there's no point in owning something you can't use right away.

But the priest sitting across from me peering so intently had no idea that he was dealing with a woman
who had paid-up salvation insurance, nor indeed
would he have cared if I had chosen to tell him.

I reached for the ashtray next to the bed. "I'm
going to Alcoholics Anonymous," I offered, and waited
for the look of approval. There was no look of approval, just a deepening frown.

"What for?" he blurted.

"I'm an alcoholic, Father," I said cheerfully, warmed
by the golden glow of moral rectitude. "I've been
drinking for several years, and it's gotten out of con-

trol. My psychiatrist suggested AA and I went to a meeting. I'm confident that it's going to be beneficial. I suppose you're familiar with AA, I mean, in your counseling and all."

He ground out his cigarette in my ashtray. "Familiar enough," he replied. He placed a hand on my shoulder and stooped slightly so his nose was level with mine.

"You are not an alcoholic," he said sternly. "Drinking is not your problem."

"What do you mean?" I asked him, baffled at his peculiar response. Perhaps I'd disconcerted him by stating my problem so openly, face to face, full in the light, such as it was, of a Cleveland winter afternoon. Perhaps he preferred to hear his parishioners' peccadillos hissed anonymously through a wire mesh screen in the hushed gloom of the confessional.

"I don't understand," I repeated, thoroughly perplexed.

His frown became a scowl. "You are far too young to be an alcoholic." He pursed his lips and lit another of my cigarettes.

Irritation was beginning to grow through my perplexity. "I drank for as long as I could, Father," I insisted. "If I continue to drink until I'm old enough to be an alcoholic, I'll be dead. Or permanently committed to Turney Road Hospital. I *can't* drink anymore," I bleated, hating myself for my cowardice. Was I supposed to *prove* my alcoholism to this man, produce an affidavit stating unequivocally that I was a chronic and uncontrollable drinker? Did I really care about his reluctance to believe me?

Yes, I did. His disbelief worked on the tattered and shredded but obstinate reservations still clinging like cobwebs to the back of my mind. And scared the hell out of me.

He puffed rapidly, dropping ashes on the floor.

"You have a tendency to dramatize yourself. You probably do drink to excess from time to time, but that is not your problem."

I stopped bouncing on the bed and composed myself

into the posture of respectful attention which had garnered me A's in attitude through twelve years of religion classes.

"What is my problem, if it isn't alcoholism?" I asked calmly, dead certain that I didn't want to hear the answer, but also curious as to what a man with whom I'd exchanged perhaps nine sentences in five years would see as "the trouble with Cassie."

"Charlie tells me that you've been depressed for several years," Dunhill said.

"He noticed!" I grinned.

"I'm quite serious," he snapped.

"So am I," I sighed.

"Charlie mentioned that your depression began following the birth of your youngest child," he persisted.

I was puzzled. "What makes Charlie think that? I've never suffered from postpartum depression, only the ordinary 'baby blues' that everyone gets. It's hormonal."

"I am not talking about postpartum depression." He shook his head. "I am talking about the cause of your depression. Following the birth of your youngest child you saw fit to begin the practice of birth control. You have been depressed ever since, and rightly so. It's a known fact that Catholic women who practice birth control contrary to the teachings of the Church and dictates of moral law invariably experience chronic and debilitating depression. It's a direct result of the willful perversion of womanhood."

I stared blankly at his earnest, pinched face.

What can I say to you? That birth control is not *a sin; I was raised to believe it is. That my decision was not reached lightly, but only after months of trying to reconcile the realities of my life with my religious upbringing? It's true. And why is it that you who are supposedly spiritual are so enthralled with what my body is doing while my shrink is all hung up on the state of my soul, which he calls a psyche? I cannot skip down parallel paths.*

I sighed and set about respectfully defending myself.

"I didn't have much choice in the matter of birth control, Father," I explained. "My doctor told me that it would be dangerous for me to get pregnant again. I had a difficult time with my last pregnancy and almost lost my daughter."

He scowled, "You had a choice. You could have used rhythm."

"I used rhythm for the first four years I was married. And I had three children."

"Then you weren't using it properly," he insisted.

"I not only used it properly," I said, "I used it under medical supervision. My cycle was irregular, so my doctor showed me on the chart how to figure for the longest and shortest possible cycles. That left me ten days a month for sex, and five of those days were my menstrual cycle. One month Charlie had an awful flu and we had no sex at all, and the next month was lost because he was in New York on business during my safe period. We went almost three months without sex and I still got pregnant! I used it properly, all right." My face was beginning to get flushed and I could hear the quiver in my voice. *Slow down. You're getting too close to the edge. Forget it. It isn't important. Be nice. He'll go away. Agree with him. He'll pat your head and bless you and go away, and you won't have said anything irrevocable. You won't have made a priest angry. Promise you'll be good. Promise you'll TRY.*

I began panting in shallow breaths, the way I'd been instructed in labor.

Dunhill shook his head and looked away. "If you used rhythm properly, and you'll notice I said *if*, and still became pregnant, you have only one alternative—"

"What's that?"

"Your only alternative is to abstain from marital relations entirely until such time as your doctor feels you are ready for another pregnancy." He lit another of my cigarettes, looking satisfied.

"Did you tell Charlie that?" I asked quietly.

"Yes, I did," he said. "Charlie said that while it would certainly be a hardship, he would accept the sacrifice if it would result in your getting well. He told me that you were the one who insisted on birth control. He had doubts about it. Charlie is a very good man and very concerned about you."

"Charlie didn't tell you that I don't want any more children, even if I was physically capable of having a hundred?"

"No, of course not," Dunhill scowled. "In fact, Charlie said that he wouldn't mind having more. You only think you feel that way because you are selfish and immature. You have lost, or rather, perversely discarded your ability to abandon yourself to the will of God. God knows what is best for you. He will never allow anything detrimental to happen to you."

"Even if I die in childbirth?"

He shrugged. "If that is the will of God. And what more appropriate, if not sacred, way for a woman to die than bringing another soul into the world. Of course I'm not saying that that is the will of God for you. I'm only saying that if that *is* His will, we certainly must not question it. And you do not need all this," he continued, dismissing my surroundings with an airy wave of his hand. "You need to return home and resume acting like a responsible Catholic wife and mother."

I got up from the bed and walked around Dunhill, who regarded me warily.

"Please stand up, Father," I requested.

He stood and I took the chair he'd been sitting on, moved it against the wall, and climbed from it to the recessed casing of my window, where I sat, legs dangling, looking solemnly down at Dunhill, who was looking apprehensively up at me.

"Are you supposed to be sitting up there, Cassie?" he asked, moving toward the door. "Should I call someone?"

"No," I replied. "They don't care where you sit. They only care how you feel about where you sit. You can sit in the elevator shaft if you're willing to explain why."

From my perch, Dunhill was no longer bigger than

me. He looked like an aging, tired man in a rumpled black suit.

He is only doing his job. He believes what he says to be true and he is trying to help me. There's no reason to be angry. "I appreciate your concern, Father," I said softly, "and I want to thank you for taking the time to visit me."

"Quite all right," he responded. "You are a member of my parish and I told your husband that I would speak to you. And besides, I get very upset when I see more and more people these days taking themselves off to psychiatrists and places like this. Their own willful sinning is the cause of their disturbance, not some psychological mumbo-jumbo. There isn't anything else wrong with you, you know."

"You know me that well?"

"You are not different from any other young Catholic woman I've counseled. You are not unique. Or different."

I gazed out the window, for the first time seeing the view. There was another wall, red brick and encrusted with soot. An iron cylinder, rusted and corroded, stuck out at right angles to the wall and I could glimpse a bare inch of leaden sky above it. No wonder they cut the window to my room too high to see outside. The view could easily be the last straw for any depressive.

I looked back at Dunhill. "When I was growing up, my mother always felt free to enter my room whenever she wanted. No knock, no 'May I come in?' Just bang, the door would open and she would spring through like a police raid. I always felt as though she'd caught me doing something wrong, even when I was studying for school. I started to think how nice it would be when I was grown up, how free I would feel when I was the lady of the house." I paused.

Dunhill smiled. "Most little girls dream of marriage and having their own homes. That's very natural, the way it should be."

"I know it is," I agreed. "But you see, when I thought of having a home of my own, it was with the idea that I would finally have a place where I could masturbate in privacy without worrying about Mother bursting through the door."

Dunhill blanched. "THAT is NOT normal! That is downright perverse!"

"You think so?" I said, without expression.

"I most certainly do," he sputtered, "as would any rational person. I don't know what your problem is or how you got warped this way. You came from a good Catholic home and went to parochial schools and have a good Catholic husband who cares about you. What is wrong with you?"

"Maybe I'm crazy," I volunteered.

"You are *not* crazy," he waved at me angrily. "You are irresponsible. You wish you were crazy. It would solve all your problems."

"I am in the hospital because I am an irresponsible sinner and not because I am an alcoholic at all."

"No, you're not," he said.

"Well, thanks again for coming to see me, Father." I turned to look out the window and heard him walk to the door.

"Father," I called. "Did you ever wonder who left the empty pint of vodka in your confessional? Did you ever wonder about that?" The footsteps stopped at the door, but I did not turn around. "Did you ever wonder, Father," I continued, "what happened to the lady who called you one time in the middle of the night and said she was going to kill herself if someone didn't help her NOW, RIGHT NOW? and you said to pray and call you back in the morning? Do you think she killed herself, Father? Maybe she took a birth control pill and washed it down with a quart of scotch and died of a broken commandment? What do you think, Father?"

There was a long pause and then the footsteps continued out the door and down the hall, receding in the distance like a fading heartbeat. I pulled my knees up to my chest and watched the inch of lead sky slowly darken into charcoal, then into the flat, black, depthless backdrop that passes for a nocturnal Cleveland sky, as though the city was contained each night inside an overturned bowl. Claustrophobic. I could feel the depression lowering, pressing down on my head, settling over my shoulders like a cement cloak, working its way into my chest, making breathing difficult. I hunched over, feeling my bones grow heavy and cold and wondering why I had ever thought that anything would change.

I'm tired, I thought, knowing that the sudden pervading fatigue was a sure sign that depression had crossed the moat, charged the drawbridge, demolished the tower, and won the castle. I sighed deeply, then clasped my hands over my ears, detesting the sound of my own sighing. Think, I told myself, think about what *really* happened.

What? What? A priest came in without my request or, indeed, my permission, and proceeded to explain *his* view of what is wrong with me. He didn't listen to me at all. He just forged ahead. I began to get angry and repressed the anger because I knew the priest was a narrow, petty, stupid, insensitive clod. Like a donkey, he has followed the same carrot for forty years and will follow it until they lay him in the ground with full military honors, or whatever it is they do. He was patently an ass and his opinion didn't count. But—he pushed old buttons and revived old guilts and now I was feeling crummy and depressed, even though my head told me that I was right and he was wrong.

On the other hand, he was doing his job as he had been taught it, in the best way he knows. He had a real concern for the state of my soul and honestly believed that his view of my predicament was valid and it was his duty to bring it to my attention. So . . .

The lights in the room snapped on and I blinked against the sudden glare. Gloria stood in the doorway holding a tray. She started across the room toward my table, mumbling to herself.

"Don' know why, ain' no sun up in the sky, my back is killin' me," she half moaned, half hummed.

"Don't shuffle, Gloria," I called from my perch. "You're perpetuating a stereotype."

"Aaarrrrgh!" she screamed, and leaped in the air, startled half out of her shoes. The tray flew backwards over her head and crashed against the wall. Globs and blobs of orange and white stuck to the plaster and coffee dribbled down the institutional green paint. The meat bounced.

"Aaarrrrgh!" Gloria repeated, but more softly, peeping through her fingers. She saw that it was me and began to glare as I scrambled down from the alcove.

"It's only me, Gloria," I said inanely. "I'm sorry I frightened you."

"You scare me half to death," she yelled with her hands on her hips, "and then you say you sorry. You sorry a'right. You the sorriest mess I ever did see, sittin' up there in the dark, waitin' to scare the life out of folks who has to work for a livin'. You people think you can do anything you want 'cause you crazy and nobody got any feelins but you."

I put my hand on her arm. She was trembling. "Honest to God, Gloria," I said, feeling absurdly contrite, "I didn't do it on purpose. I was just sitting up there because I was depressed and wanted to think something through, and then you came in and I spoke. I never intended to frighten you. Honest."

She looked at me for a long moment and the glare began to melt from her eyes. "My heart coulda stopped," she complained. "It runs in my family. One minute tick, tick, tick, the next minute nothin'."

"Yes, I know, Gloria," I soothed, "and I am sorry and it won't happen again."

She drew herself up, becoming official. "You ain't got no business climin' up there, neither. The hospital insurance don' cover no falls from no windows—less ya pry one open and jump out the other side. Then you family could sue for a bundle and prob'ly collect and put this whole place right out of business. Thas' why they always checkin' the windows."

"I thought it was concern for the patients," I said.

"Lordy, no," she assured me. "You can always get more patients. Half the population of this town is runnin' round with a screw loose. They just ain' had no psychiatrist around to tell 'em they're nuts, so they think they just fine. But if you sue the hospital and the place closes down and you sue the asses off the doctors and *they* close down, then there go the whole ball game and it don' make no nevermind if the patients are crazy or not. Say, who's gonna clean up this mess?"

"I will," I offered promptly. *I will prove to you, Gloria, that though I did not intend to cause your fright, I am in some way responsible, so I will demonstrate both my good faith and growing maturity by cleaning up this goddamn mess.* "Where are the mop and rags?"

Gloria directed me to the utility closet, where I collected the necessary items.

It seemed like a shame to wipe the blobs off the wall. They looked like a three-dimensional Rorschach hanging there. I could see Charlie's eyes in the squash and Mother's profile in the mashed potatoes. They were separated by tiny spots of coffee which they also encircled protectively. Me? The children? Mother and Charlie! Charlie and Mother! Mama and Papa! And in the middle, the coffee spots, I mean me and the kids, the kids and me. Mother and Charlie in the kitchen drinking coffee and "talking it over." The kids and me in the den, watching television, all of us with glasses in our hands. Scotch in mine. Coke in theirs. All of us in our jammies. My God! I shuddered and quickly scrubbed the wall clean. I sat down on the floor and pondered.

I've had Rorschachs, MMPIs, Sentence Completion, Sanford-Binets, Draw-A-Person, the Taylor Whachamacallit, four and a half years of therapy, two hospitalizations, Dilantin, an EEG, occupational therapy, and a copy Alexander loaned me of *Games People Play,* and here I was gathering monumental insights from garbage on the wall!

I got to my feet and hurried down the hall, hoping that Tinkerbell would be behind the nurses' station. I could see her tiny head bobbing up and down behind the counter.

"Yoo hoo," I said, leaning over the counter. "I want to report an escaped inmate."

"Who?" she inquired, smiling.

"A few minutes ago there was a terrific crash in my room, a minor explosion as it were, and Mrs. Caliguire didn't even twitch. Not a whit. So, she is obviously deceased against the hospital rules and without her doctor's permission, which fact constitutes an escape."

"She is not deceased," Tinkerbell said.

"What is she, then?" I asked. "Someday you will have to tell me the truth. The doctors will remove her corpse and give it a decent burial and tell her brother that they did all they could but rigor mortis set in while no one was looking. They might even call it a happy ending because old Mrs. Caliguire finally made it all the way back to that giant womb in the great beyond and, besides, they really thought that her cause of death was psychosomatic; sometimes symptoms can be very confusing. Someday you will tell me the truth."

"She is sleeping," Tinkerbell said.

"I could understand her not eating, not moving, not peeing, and not twitching if she was sleeping," I persisted, "but she is not breathing. What about that?"

"She's breathing," Tinkerbell said. "You just can't see her breathing."

"What have I ever done," I demanded, "that's so goddamn awful that I should be stuck in a room with an invisible breather?"

"You are upset about something else," Tinkerbell stated.

Aha, nearly everybody around here listens or pretends to listen. This lady HEARS. Neat. "You're right," I conceded. "Earlier today Merriweather backed away from me when I made a joke, and just now Gloria jumped three feet in the air when I said hello. The entire staff is having a collective nervous breakdown and needs to be sedated. How about that?"

"I feel just fine," Tinkerbell smiled. "No nervous breakdown."

"But you are obviously not a real staff person," I

insisted. "You are a warm, sympathetic, compassionate, patient human being who has wandered in here by mistake from another time warp. You will either disappear or your intergalactic goodness shield will wear off and you'll become like all the rest."

Tinkerbell listened patiently and looked at me solemnly. "What is troubling you, Cassie?" she asked softly.

I put my head in my hands and spoke in a mumble. "I have a basketball in my stomach. It's covered with long spikes and shouldn't be there. I'm trying to think it through and be mature and the goddamn basketball is still there. And getting bigger."

"What put it there?" she asked.

I told her about Dunhill's visit, his persistent obtuseness and his obvious sincerity. I told her how I'd tried to think it through and how lousy I still felt despite all my mental machinations.

"You're trying to work through your anger without having expressed it," she said. "That is very difficult to do."

"How can I be angry at him when he means so well?" I wanted to know.

"I'm sure he meant well, according to the way he sees it," she said. "Does that mean he's entitled to dump all over you?"

"Well," I began. "He thinks he knows what it is I need."

"And if he decided that you needed to be tied up and put in a cell somewhere for your own protection, or beaten once a day until you repent, or get well, or whatever his standard for recovery might be, would you allow him to do that?"

"No, of course not," I shook my head. "But he didn't do anything awful like that."

Tinkerbell's voice was firm. "He refused to listen to you. He ignored your feelings and the validity of your experience. He used his authority to silence you. And frighten you. And, quite consciously, make you feel guilty."

I folded my hands on the counter and looked into

her soft, lovely eyes. "He beat me up, Tinkerbell," I said.

Slowly I began to smile an idiot's grin of a smile, a wide and silly smile as I felt the chill leave my bones and the cement slip off my shoulders.

"I have a right to be angry," I said. "I mean, I have a reason, a cause. Someone did something rotten whether he meant well or not and I have a reason to be angry about it. It hurt and I'm angry. I am very angry."

"Of course you are," she said.

I straightened and looked at the clock hanging over the nurses' station. Only seven o'clock. It seemed like days since I'd walked into my room and confronted Dunhill. At the thought of him I began to get angry again. Restlessly angry. I had to go somewhere, do something.

"Where's Cara?" I asked.

Tinkerbell looked at the Patient In-Out chart lying on the counter.

"She left a few minutes ago on a date. She didn't want to interrupt your conversation with your pastor so she asked me to ask you if you'll wait up for her tonight if she's late. You don't have to wait up, Cassie. She can tell you all about it in the morning," she smiled.

"I'll bet Mama waits up," I smiled back. "I think I would like to go to an AA meeting tonight."

"Are you going to stop at home?"

"I don't know. I really don't. I'll make up my mind on the way. The meeting ends at ten o'clock and I should be back at eleven. Okay?"

"Certainly. You may go to a meeting whenever you like. You don't have to ask permission. Dr. Alexander has given written approval."

"Bless his tidy little heart." I grinned and ran to get my coat. As Tinkerbell buzzed me through the door I called over my shoulder, "Tell Cara to wait up for me if she gets home first."

I was too hyper to wait for the elevator and headed down the back stairs, taking them two at a time. I was halfway down, at the third-floor landing, when it struck me. *Home, I called this place home.*

I sat down on the landing and caught my breath. *Well, it is home. In a very real sense it is home. For now at least, this is a place where I'm safe, where I can be me without anything terrible happening, where I can even be the BAD me without getting thrown out, or hit, or rejected. And I suppose that a true-blue, dyed-in-the-transference Freudian would say that Alexander is my father. Daddy. Daddy. Daddy. I could really use a hug.*

Outside a bitter wind blew scraps of paper across the parking lot. I dashed out the door with my head lowered and ran for my car, shivering. Icy fingers tore at my coat and my last remaining button popped off and went rolling under a Volkswagen. I watched it go and clutched my coat around me. With nearly numb fingers I unlocked the car and slid into the front seat, shaking and puffing billows of white frosty breath. I started the car and backed out of the lot, turning into Shaker Heights Boulevard and heading for downtown Cleveland.

The heater warmed the car and I turned on the radio and relaxed. Dalton once told me it was too bad I lived so far from the hospital. If I lived closer, she said, I could go home more often, more easily. And, of course, like a good little person, I agreed.

But the truth was I wished the hospital was farther away. The drive gives me time to think, time to breathe, silence and solitude.

In the car I don't have to deal with anyone, live up to anything, react to anything, act on anything. I can hum, giggle, sing, snarl, rehearse conversations, remember my father, cry, sort out my feelings, and let my mind wander aimlessly down paths that usually begin in gray, misty swirls and end in small dark rooms with someone's hand on my breast.

I rumbled over the bridge and turned left at the West Side Market. There was a strangely deserted stretch of road between the end of the bridge and the beginning of the crumbling stores that fronted the deteriorating lower west side. I drove past a string of sleazy bars whose garish neon lit the street and continued past Kotecki's Monuments and The Children's Home, a spooky Victorian brick edifice. When we were children my mother had often pointed to it as we passed in the bus on the way to the dentist, promising that she would leave us there if we weren't good. The Home was so old that *her* mother had made the identical threat to her when she was a child. Some family traditions are less comforting than others.

I started up the gently sloping hill to Parma Heights. The car slowed, almost automatically, as I approached St. John's Church. It was set well back from the road, surrounded by trees, serene and lovely. I pulled into the long driveway and cut the engine. The stark, contemporary steeple with its burnished bronze bell was illuminated, as was the statue of St. John spotlighted on the lawn. The bell is only for display, however. Parishioners are trolled to mass on Sundays by a recording of a famous carillon, perhaps the one from Notre Dame. Canned bells seemed appropriate in combination with the machine-stamped Communion wafers and the Suggestions for Sunday Sermon outlines mailed to all pastors monthly by the Office of the Archbishop. Soon we would be taping our confessions and receiving absolution by return mail, addressed "To Whom It May Concern."

I sat and smoked and wondered how I could experience this transient stab of mourning for the passing of customs woven into a religion which had been the second source of terror in my life, the first being my father. At the age of six I had been solemnly introduced to a God who savaged my tremulous soul, dismaying my days and besieging my nights with petrifying nightmares.

I smiled to myself. I liked the saints, though, especially the gentle ones—St. Francis of Assisi; the Little Flower, St. Theresa; St. Cecilia, who played the organ and was murdered for her faith in a steam bath. And the Guardian Angels. I loved them as a little child, fantasizing for myself a beautiful creature with spreading, translucent wings protecting me from harm, from recklessly driven fire engines and alligators lurking in my back yard. At adolescence they lost their appeal and I tended to shudder, twitch, and look over my shoulder when they came to mind, usually while I was ineptly French-kissing some equally inept peer.

But, now. Now. Now what? The angels were gone, vanished with my childhood and Freudian explanations of religious symbolism. And the Church itself had dropped many of the saints, saints we'd believed in and prayed to, saints from whom we thought we received answers. And what was left? Only that horrid, astounding, intimidating bully of a God! That intimate friend of the doltish Dunhill!

Anger crept in and began to burn a hole in my reflections. *How dare he, that stupid priest! How dare They, he and his dreadful God, troop and trample all over me, stomp me into a puddle of inconsolable despair! Label me unrepentant and a sinner!*

I flung open the car door and ran toward the rectory, chest tight and eyes stinging with hot, furious tears. I rang the doorbell, and, wildly impatient, began to beat on the door. It was opened, nervously, by a mousy, dumpy housekeeper.

"I want to see Father Dunhill; I'm Cassie Barrett," I said, quivering and attempting to appear calm.

"I'll see if he's available," she whispered, and disappeared through a door. I tapped my foot and wrung my hands, mumbling to myself until Dunhill appeared in the doorway.

"Cassie, what's this?" he asked, alarmed.

I took a deep breath. "I came to tell you, Father. I have to tell you. You are an ass and your God is a vindictive son of a bitch!"

"Cassie!"

"You make me sick," I screamed at the cowering priest. "You both make me sick and you have made me sick, and you're not going to make me sick anymore. I will never, never, never, ever speak to either of you again!"

I turned and fled out the door with his "Cassie, come back!" pounding in my ears. I threw myself into the car, locked the doors, turned on the engine, and sped away, my wheels spinning in the gravel, fleeing as though there were a dozen vicious hounds snapping at my heels. I drove blindly for nearly a mile before I slowed down.

My heartbeat slowed along with the car and I found myself thinking over and over, *I had to. I had to. I had to.*

A stern and familiar voice inside of me answered, *No, you didn't have to,* but before I could wince and accept the judgment, the smiling face of Tinkerbell floated through my mind.

"Well, Tink," I said aloud, "I expressed it. I sure as hell expressed it."

I turned the car toward Ridge Road and the meeting. I began to hum *Panis Angelicus,* and as I pulled into the parking lot a sheer irrelevancy came flashing from somewhere behind my left ear. *Dad would not be angry. My father would approve.*

Inside the meeting room people stood in groups, holding cups of coffee. I searched for Alice and found her, as usual, with John at her side. She looked at me sharply. "You okay?"

"Sure. Fine." I answered. I was beginning to feel it. "I had a minor trauma on the way over, but it's okay now. Or it's going to be."

"Just don't drink," John interrupted. "When you going to get out of the nuthouse, kid?"

Alice poked him in the ribs. There seemed to be permanent dents in his midsection. "That's her business, nitwit," she scowled. "Leave her alone."

"Actually, that's up to my doctor," I said, using my handy-dandy all-purpose excuse.

John gazed at me shrewdly. "And there's nothing you can do to hurry it along?"

"Well . . . maybe," I half admitted.

"Don't wait too long, kid. You'll get used to the easy way and won't have any muscles left for trudging the road of happy destiny."

I laughed. "That's what I'm here for, John. I'm trying to develop some muscles."

The meeting began and I settled down next to Alice feeling curiously contented and at home. The speaker was a woman who was a wife and a legal secretary.

"When I came to AA," she was saying, "I couldn't imagine living the rest of my life without even one lousy drink. Not one. I said as much to the lady who brought me and later became my sponsor. She squashed that whole idea by telling me that I didn't have to worry about the rest of my life. I only had to worry about *today*. Yesterday is gone and tomorrow isn't here, maybe never will be. I could give up drinking one day at a time. Well, it made a sort of sense and I tried it and as of now, it adds up to nearly four years of one day at a time." She grinned, looking pleased with herself. Who could blame her? And it made a sort of sense to me, too.

Later, while we were drinking coffee, I asked Alice about something that had been on my mind for days.

"What should I tell my kids, Alice? I mean, they know I'm in the hospital but, as far as I know, they don't know why."

"They haven't asked?"

"Not really. They want to know when I'm going to get over being sick and come home, but they don't seem to know what kind of hospital I'm in or why. I just say 'sick.' I don't think Mother or Charlie have said 'crazy' to them. Or maybe they have." I took a sip of the hot bitter liquid. "No, I don't think so," I decided. "Even if they were angry, they wouldn't want the kids telling anyone in school and spreading it all over the neighborhood. But I feel I have to tell them *something*. But what?"

"Tell them the truth," Alice said levelly. "Tell them that you're an alcoholic."

"My God, Alice!" I'd thought of a lot of things to tell them, but the truth hadn't occurred to me. I considered for a moment. "I'll think about it."

"You do that, honey," Alice replied, "and let me know what you decide. Call me when you can."

"Sure. Thanks. I'll do that." I waved goodbye and ran up the stairs. I thought about what she'd said all the way back to the hospital. I knew from experience that telling the plain truth could get me into deeper and more irreversible trouble than the most elaborate lie, yet, why shouldn't they know? But would they *understand*?

I returned to the seventh floor in time to join the patients watching *Whatever Happened to Baby Jane?* on television.

"Now, *that's* what I call a crazy lady," Ludwig remarked, as Bette Davis served a dead pet bird to a shrieking Joan Crawford.

Norma snorted, "If any of *us* acted like that, they'd stick us in the padded room forever and zap us every day of the week."

There was a general mumble of agreement.

Behind the glass partition separating the nurses' station from the parlor, the staff was looking decidedly anxious. Allowing psychiatric patients to watch movies about loonies is a chancy business. They might begin *acting out*, for Christ's sake. Pomeroy passed the evening medication early.

"Get out of here with your sleeping crap," Ludwig grumped, and dumped his pill cup in the wastepaper basket as soon as Pomeroy's back was turned. Good old bitchy Norma jumped up and snitched on Ludwig, who was spoken to sternly while Norma smirked and the other patients smouldered.

The fade-out found Joan dead on the beach and a group of straight citizens warily circling around Bette, more frightened of her insanity than they would have been by an invasion from Mars.

However, a great cheer went up from the patients. Joanne beat gleefully on the coffee table with her shoe and Frank did a few quick cartwheels down the hall. Everyone shipped off to bed in rare good humor.

Obviously none of us were as sick as Bette, not even close . . . so we all went to bed feeling a little saner, a little healthier, a little more in control. It came as a surprise only to the staff, to whom logic often comes as a surprise.

In the morning Cara burst through my door before I was out of bed.

"You didn't wait up," she accused.

"No, I didn't," I agreed with her. "How was your date?"

She shrugged. "He turned out to be an absolute creep," she said. "Before we even got out of the parking lot he came on with this big line about how he wasn't going to try to lay me because I'm in the hospital and probably couldn't handle it."

"And?"

"And he didn't," she sighed.

11

Alexander regarded me quizzically across the desk. He reached for his cigarette lighter with one eyebrow raised, sure sign of a question I didn't want to hear.

"What are you going to do about Charlie?" he asked.

Well, Edwin, my love, since you asked I'll tell you. I'm going to go home and whack Charlie across the upper lip, thereby driving his nose bone straight through his brain. He'll go down like a felled ox and expire at my feet, murmuring, "You shouldn't have done it, Cassie. I loved you dearly." I'll plead temporary insanity, F. Lee Bailey will defend me, and I'll bring the jury to tears with my testimony. They will then rule justifiable homicide. I'll be acquitted in my red dress and walk out of the Cleveland Court House hand in hand with F. Lee (as played by Dustin Hoffman). "I don't know," I said.

He frowned, rumpling his forehead. "You have choices, Cassie. You can go home, reconcile, see a marriage counselor—"

"You?" I interrupted.

"No," he said, without explanation; then continued, "you can do any of those things, or you can decide on a separation, divorce, whatever. You have choices."

Outside of cholera, I can think of anything I want less than choices, Edwin. Tell me what to do. Please. I'll do whatever you say, but it better turn out well or I'll blame you forever. "Do I have to decide now?" I asked, beginning to panic.

"No, you don't. You have time. Just think about it."

Wonderful. I can add that to my list of contemplations, along with what to tell the kids. Maybe I'll tell Charlie the truth and divorce the kids. Maybe I'll tell everyone the truth and run like hell! No one I know is ready for the truth, including you, Edwin. Just look at you sitting there like a doctor in a pharmaceutical ad, all professional poise and polish. What's going on there, in back of your eyes? Come out. Come out, whoever you are.

"What are you going to do about Donnerly?" he interrupted my thoughts.

"Now wait a minute. What's with all this asking me what I'm going to do about everybody?" I said angrily. "I don't know what I'm going to do about ME yet, and you want me to tell you what I'm going to do about Charlie and Donnerly. I don't know. Maybe they'll all get hit by buses! Shit!"

I folded my arms and legs and retreated, glowering.

"You'd best do something about him while you're here," Alexander said, blandly. "It'll be easier in the long run. You have to give him up eventually, you know."

"Why?" I demanded.

He stared at the ceiling. "Oh, he's not good for you, for one thing. And you don't love him, for another."

"How the hell do you know?"

"I know," he gazed at me smugly.

"You know," I repeated, wondering how. "Look," I brightened, "if I divorce Charlie then there is no reason for me to give up the affair, is there?"

"Yes, there is," he said vehemently. "It will eventually turn into a disaster."

"No, it won't."

"Yes, it will," he continued blithely. "Just like the last one."

I retreated even farther into the chair, silently furious. *You bastard. There is no connection whatever between that one and this one. Not the remotest similarity. Still. . . .*

I hadn't thought about Ray in months, maybe almost a year. But then why should I? I had gone on to bigger and better lunacies. I frowned, remembering.

Ray had been a shining knight, cleverly disguised as an advertising man. He was an old friend of Charlie's and had moved to New York following a drunken farewell party thrown by his fellow workers. Thoroughly smashed, I'd flung my arms around his tall, bony body and planted a passionate kiss on his startled mouth.

"I wish I'd gotten to know you better," I panted lustfully, knowing that he was leaving at dawn (into the valley of Madison Avenue rode the ad man) and feeling perfectly safe.

"So do I," he said regretfully, then smiled. "I know. You can write to me." He gave me a card with his business address, then crushed me to his navel. (He was *very* tall.)

The kissing was terrific (I adore kissing *up*), but I wondered as he pressed his hips against me to impress me with his bulge, why he thought I would want to write to him.

In the next seven months I wrote him one hundred and forty-seven letters, quickly progressing from the first "Hi, how are you? How's the family?" newsy type of thing to twenty-page epistles written in all-night sessions between sips of scotch. Hour after hour I labored in utter silence, seeking to create myself on paper, to dazzle this semisexy near-stranger with the brilliance of my intellect and the depth of my sensitive soul. I wrote and rewrote, crossed out and began again, plagiarized from the poets and back issues of *Esquire,* devised clever quips and puns, poured out my hopes, my dreams, my ambitions—or rather, what I felt he wanted them to be. I dramatized trivia and invented events. Toward the end of the night—and bottle of scotch—I rambled, expressing wanton, wordy yearning for his body and misspelling dirty words.

Every letter, mailed as per his instruction to a local post office box, brought one in return. Has he done this before? I wondered briefly, immediately ashamed of the thought. True love comes but once.

His letters were written in the club car as he commuted to his happy home in Connecticut. Between three martinis and the swaying train, his letters were covered with dear little blobs, sweet little squiggles, and wonderfully undecipherable phrases, all of which I took to be expressions of love. And were.

Like a true ad man, he wrote, "I love you. I want you. I need you," over and over, beating down my assumed resistance with repetition. What he lacked in panache, he made up for in monotony.

There were soon too many letters to hide in dresser drawers, so I bought a small filing cabinet with a lock where I kept them neatly bundled in groups of ten. Once Charlie asked me what was in the cabinet.

"Things," I said, and he went off to play golf, his curiosity completely satisfied.

Then, one April day Ray suggested, via air mail special, symbol of total commitment, that I tell Charlie I needed to get away for a few days and meet him in New York in June while his wife was visiting her parents in Vermont.

"Impossible," I wrote back, and "Impossible" I said to Alexander, who frowned disapprovingly every time I spoke of Ray and my paper passion, a subject which now took up ninety per cent of my office visit.

"It's not only impossible," Alexander replied, "it's potentially dangerous."

"Dangerous?" I quivered and knew that somehow I had to get to New York. Using the repetition strategy I'd learned from Ray, I assaulted Charlie with whines, wheedles, challenges, and demands.

ME: "I want to get away. I need to get away."

CHARLIE: "We'll go somewhere on vacation later this summer."

ME: "I need to go somewhere alone. I've never been anywhere without my mommy or daddy or you. I feel like a child. I want to go somewhere alone. Just a weekend. Please, Charlie?"

CHARLIE: "That's silly. No."

ME: "Why, Charlie, don't you trust me?"

Night after night I besieged him, and finally, wearily, he capitulated.

"Of course, I trust you," he said at the airport, and I flew off to be "alone" with Alexander's optimistic words ringing in my ears, "Don't come wailing to me when this thing blows up in your face."

On arrival I was crushed in a spastic embrace, smashed to a bosom even bonier than I'd remembered. I stood with my head buried in the spareribs waiting breathlessly for warm, wet, knee-dissolving kisses.

"Let's get out of here before someone sees us," he whispered romantically, and we were off, propelled by paranoia. The temperature in the car was 109, and Ray kissed me fervently as my hair grew stringy, my dress wilted, and my deodorant died. The drive was punctuated with caresses as Ray steered with his left hand and explored with his right.

Suddenly shy, despite two drinks on the plane, I patted only the safe parts, acutely aware that I was about to bed with a stranger.

Though comfortingly dark and blessedly cool, the motel room smelled of sweated-in bathing suits and mold in the air conditioner. As Ray lugged in the bags I watched, apprehensive and wishing he would hurry. I'll be all right as soon as I get in bed, I thought, as I shivered with shyness and shook with ambivalence. What if he doesn't like my breasts? What if he wants to do something freaky? What the hell am I doing here?

My agitation went unnoticed as Ray slowly and methodically unpacked his bag, neatly hanging his shirt and trousers on wooden hangers, mathematically arranging toilet articles on the dresser, precisely piling underwear in one small corner of one drawer, and carefully draping a bathrobe (bathrobe!) over the proper hook. Mother would be proud, I thought, as passion collapsed and lust expired.

Finally he turned to me, alerting my sensors— ALARM! ALARM! YOU ARE ABOUT TO COMMIT SEX!

Instead, he said, "How about a nice walk down the beach?"

"Now?" I asked.

"Sure," he said. "And then we'll come back and really *relax*." And he winked suggestively, his dark blond hair falling over his eyes.

"All right," I replied, wanting to get into bed and *get it over with!*

A nice walk down the beach ended five miles from the motel with Ray skimming brisky along and me panting and staggering after him, carrying the blanket. We lay down on the sand behind a dune, turned our bodies to the sun and held hands.

"Talk to me, Cassie," he said, but without my pen and paper, scotch and solitude, I had nothing to say. For months I'd snowed him with an avalanche of words and now that he was here beside me I'd gone completely dry, in all respects.

"So, how's business?" I asked, and he launched into a diatribe against the advertising business with which I gathered he had a love-hate relationship. He rambled endlessly on as the sun grew hotter and stronger. Suddenly he rolled on top of me, covering my face with kisses and fumbling under my bathing suit.

"I love you, Cassie," he said, rubbing me enthusiastically.

"I love you, too," I said, spitless with thirst and dying to pee.

He jumped to his feet. "Last one back is a rotten egg," he quipped wittily, and jogged off toward the motel, leaving me to gather the blanket and stumble along.

He was lying on the bed with his eyes closed when I got back. I went to the bathroom and drank three glasses of water, knowing that the MOMENT had arrived, realizing that even if I could climb through the window, I'd never be able to find the airport alone.

But he was dressed and waiting at the door.

"Let's go to dinner. I know a terrific Italian place," he said, fondling the doorknob. I dressed quickly, and chastely, in the bathroom.

Ray ordered antipasto, salad, manicotti, lasagna, veal scallopine, and two bottles of red wine, which I gulped greedily, grateful that its rapidly spreading glow was melting my inhibitions along with my fillings.

Ray ate for hours, cutting his mountain of food into tiny, uniform bites. *Tapeworms,* I thought.

Back at the motel Ray changed into pajamas and bathrobe in the bathroom while I scrambled to get into my nightgown and dove into bed. I was lying seductively lumped under the covers, blanket pulled up to my chin, when Ray emerged. Gazing lovingly at me, he got into bed.

"Let's watch TV," he said, and switched on the set.

I was suddenly relieved. I'd go home to Charlie guilt-free, as pure and chaste as when I'd arrived—chaster even, for temptation ignored is a purifying flame, even if it wasn't exactly *my* idea.

I was relaxed and giggling at Johnny Carson when Ray abruptly turned off the light and the TV and pulled me under the blanket. He petted me in long, smooth strokes, starting from left to right ranging from neck to knees. Over hills and valleys he went, methodically covering the territory. Thinking to reciprocate, I reached for him. As my hand brushed his hip, he jerked, flopped over on me and began with no particular rhythm to bounce up and down. His sharp, pointy hipbones dug into me and I lay there hoping my wincing would pass as response.

And knowing that something was wrong. I couldn't feel *anything!* We were not coupled, enjoined, attached, as it were. Either he didn't know it, or didn't know I knew it, or was determined to brazen it through in any case, because he continued on and on and on—methodically. I was thoroughly battered, bruised, and exhausted before I thought to fake an orgasm, which I promptly did or I'd be there to this day grinding away.

"I hope that was as good for you as it was for me," he said, kissing me sweetly.

"Better even," I replied, falling into a dead sleep. Travel is so tiring.

The next day was the same: a round of activities planned by my social director–host, culminating in almost-sex when the delaying maneuvers ran out. I resisted the urge to ask him how long he'd been impotent, preferring to protect his pride and not really wanting to know.

On Sunday he put me on the plane with visible relief. "Just wait until you get my next letter," he whispered.

At home, Charlie asked me if I'd had a good time. I said, "Yes, terrific," and made up some unconvincing stories about sightseeing trips I'd taken. Charlie looked dubious, but said nothing.

Later, having rebuilt my fantasy with alcohol, I wrote a looped and ardent letter to Ray. (Thanks so much for the lovely affair. I'll keep it on the mantel and polish it often.) Thoroughly drunk, I left the letter on the coffee table before I staggered off to bed. Charlie read it in the morning and blew his cork.

"You fucking whore," he bellowed, shoving me against the wall. "You fucking, cheating whore!" He slapped me sharply, threw the letter in my lap and went off to the bedroom to call Ray, while I sat weeping and panic-stricken in the corner of my living room. Ray, like the tower of strength that he was, apologized to Charlie, telling him that he was sorry for having capitulated to my "feminine wiles." His exact words.

That afternoon I was in Alexander's office, wailing that the whole thing had blown up in my face.

"Told you so," he said.

"Charlie could divorce me," I wailed.

"He could," Alexander agreed, "with justification."

"My God, what would happen to me? What would I do? Where would I go?" I wailed harder.

"You should have thought of that last week," he said sternly, no comfort at all.

"But I didn't think I'd get caught!"

"Didn't you?"

"I was depressed so I got loaded. Leaving that letter out was an accident!" I insisted.

Alexander sighed. "Wouldn't it be simpler to tell Charlie how furious you are? Do you have to kick the shit out of him?"

"I'm not," I objected. "I didn't mean to . . . I mean, well . . . what about Ray? He said he loved me and wished we could be together forever. How could he do this to me? I loved him."

"Oh? Then go to New York and get him. He'll probably accept you if you just show up. You can be together forever."

"I was with him just for a weekend," I sobbed, "and it seemed like forever."

I reached for another Kleenex, making a grand total of six gooey tissues squashed in my sweaty palm.

"I'll love him always," I whimpered. "I just don't like him. And I never want to see him again."

Charlie didn't divorce me. He remained raw and wounded, aghast at my betrayal. And righteously indignant. I remained defiantly unrepentant, insisting that my affair had been the result of his inadequacies. He yelled. I drank—and drank—and yelled in return. Together we worked out a snappy routine that featured sleepless nights, full-volume cursing that split the silence at 3 A.M., and, on those occasions when I sloshed over that fine line that divides verbal and physical drunken aggression, an encore that left us both with embarrassing bruises.

Though it had happened nearly two years ago, the game continued, with variations and time out for good behavior, right up until the week I once again landed in Alexander's platitude-lined nest. Charlie, still raw and wounded and knowing nothing about Donnerly, went right on yammering about Ray. I took my lumps for the past and my revenge in the present.

I shook myself out of my reverie and ground out my cigarette in the ashtray.

"This is nothing, absolutely nothing like that stupid business two years ago," I reiterated positively. "Donnerly is not Ray. And I am not even the lady who went winging off to New York. She was a dumb kid."

"And you are . . ." Alexander prodded.

"Right now, I'm pooped and my head aches and my bones hurt and no one could make me an offer I couldn't refuse."

"No one?" Alexander smiled.

"Well . . . nope. No one," I lied. I lit another cigarette. "I'm smoking four packs a day," I confided suddenly, wanting to change the subject. "And eating mountains of ice cream."

"Don't worry," he soothed. "You'll taper off on both. Substitution."

Untangling my arms and legs, I relaxed in the chair and stared up at the ceiling hoping to find the answers that Alexander seemed to read on its rippled plaster surface.

"Do you know what I would really like to do?" I said, in a quick, brave gush.

"No. What?" He leaned forward.

"I would like to leave here . . . oh, not immediately . . . when I'm ready, and—"

He nodded encouragingly. "And?"

"And go live in the West Side Residence for Women," I finished, breathless.

He looked puzzled.

"Why? What for?"

"I've never lived alone. I'd like to see if I could

take care of myself, I mean, really take care of myself. I went from my father's house to Charlie's house. I'm twenty-eight years old and have three children and I don't even know if I could function for a week in a room of my own, without a routine structured by someone else. I don't know if I would love it and perform like a trooper or go out of my mind and fall apart without someone around to tell me what to do. Maybe I'd hide in bed and listen for rapists at the door. Maybe I would go out in the world and do great and wondrous things. Who knows? I don't know. I would like to know." At that moment I wanted it more than anything in the world. Anything.

Alexander grimaced skeptically, riveting me with the same kind of look that I usually reserve for my children when they want to go off on some reckless adventure, like tobogganing alone. "And what would you do in the West Side Residence for Women?" he asked in words of one syllable.

"I would get a job, anything I could. There are always the drugstores and the dime stores and the May Company. And I'd learn to function. I'd have to learn. And now would be a good time. I've been away from home for a while. The kids are accustomed to a mommy who visits. It wouldn't be very much of a trauma for them. My mother is always there, loves being there, and I would be close enough so I could see them every day if I wanted. If they wanted."

"And Charlie?"

"Charlie wouldn't like it," I admitted, "but he'd get used to it."

"Charlie might divorce you," he said.

"He might," I agreed. "But he might divorce me anyway. If I go home, I mean. This way we wouldn't have to go through any more hassle, any more fighting. It might be better for everybody this way."

"Especially you."

"Maybe. But I still might fall apart."

"What if you do fall apart and Charlie doesn't want you back? What will you do then?"

I sat looking at my hands, stymied. *Edwin, Edwin,*

*you're worse than the Chinese water torture. Drip,
drip, drip.* I began to laugh.

"If I fall apart, I'll fall apart alone, without all the
expert assistance I've been getting up until now. I'll
still have you, and AA. I'll be all right."

I grinned at him, feeling light and free and very
grown-up. He did not grin at me.

"You've thought about it," he said flatly.

"Yes, I have," I replied, though at that instant I
realized I hadn't thought about it consciously.

"Well, think about it some more," he said, and
abruptly rose from his seat, dismissing me. He paused
at the door. "And get rid of Donnerly," he said, over
his shoulder.

12

There had been only one topic on the seventh floor
for days. Endlessly discussed by patients and staff
was the way in which Eleanor, the old midnight ram-
bler, finally came out of IT. Despite the stringent
precautions of the staff (they gave her a Seconal and
said, "Stay in bed, Eleanor") she was still doing her
musical bed number.

Late one night she snuggled blissfully in next to
the snoring Abdul, who, unbeknownst to us all, was
snapping out of his stupor. He immediately perceived
Eleanor as a gift from heaven, or thereabouts, and
jumped on her bones. The resulting shrieks woke everyone on the floor.

Tinkerbell and I arrived together to find Eleanor
wildly kicking and flailing about under the calmly

humping and thumping half-asleep Abdul. Quickly
we grabbed Abdul's legs and yanked. Eleanor rolled
from under and landed on the floor, where she sat,
screaming, wailing, hiccuping, and whistling through
her nose, an act that could bring back vaudeville.

Somewhat belatedly Kenny arrived, all bleary-eyed
from napping in the linen closet and madder than
hell. He screamed righteously at Abdul, who was half
hanging off the bed, blinking and looking disgusted.
As Tinkerbell led the quaking and semiviolated Eleanor off to be super-sedated with phenobarb and Oval-
tine, Abdul lay back on his bed and shut his eyes.

Kenny's record finally ran down and he finished his
tirade in a spitty sputter.

"Don't you know any better?" Kenny demanded.

"Shit, man, I didn't mean any harm," Abdul
shrugged. "I'm sound asleep and that fool woman
gets in bed with me and I roll over and think I'm
dreaming or something and start to do what comes
natural, and the next thing I know all hell breaks
loose. It ain't my fault."

Kenny jumped at the word "fault."

"How's it going to look tomorrow," he bellowed,
"when she tells her shrink *and* her husband that she
was almost raped by a patient of the opposite sex,
not to mention color. Her husband will come after *your*
ass and her shrink will come after *mine*."

"That's your problem, man," Abdul shrugged, and
turned his back on Kenny. "I didn't invite that woman
in my bed." He shook his head. "Damn shame though,"
he mumbled to himself. "That's the first time I've gotten it up in two years. It don' pay. It just don' pay."

Kenny turned and nearly tripped over me. He tried
to regain control of the situation by ordering me back
to bed. Instead I jogged down to the nurses' station,
where Tinkerbell and I discussed psychodrama as a
theraputic tool while Eleanor babbled incoherently in
the corner.

The next day, Abdul, realizing that his foray into
reality hadn't been met with a standing ovation,
lapsed back into the safety of his stupor. But Eleanor,

that formerly rambling wreck, bounced around neatly dressed, calling everyone by their proper name and carrying on conversations. She hadn't blown the whistle to either shrink or spouse and the word went out that if she continued to exhibit normal behavior, she'd be out in less than a week.

Of course Dr. Fisher took all the credit and immediately began treating or mistreating his patients the way he had Eleanor, hoping to pull it off again. No one will ever see this case written up in the APA *Journal,* but it ranks as one of the truly great cures of our time. Of course, there are those of us who know that the credit, and the fee, should go to the ubiquitous Abdul, who is at the moment in the parlor mumbling "Shazam!" at Mrs. Walker, who thinks he's her granddaughter.

13

I was on my way to meet Charlie in the coffee shop. He'd called me, a rare enough event, and left a message to call him at the office, rarer still.

Thinking that something must be wrong with one of the kids, I'd called promptly.

"They're all fine," Charlie said. "I bought Jenny new boots last night. Her old ones were developing splits. She wanted red, but all they had was white. Steve broke the frame on his glasses wrestling with Greg. I'll stop off on the way home and get them fixed."

"Ask for Herman at the optician's," I suggested. "He'll fix them in a few minutes for nothing. Unless they're beyond repair."

"Oh, no," Charlie said, "they just have a screw missing." He paused. "Hey, I just had an idea," he went on, and I could hear him smiling. "I'll bring you along to Herman and he can fix you, too."

"In just a few minutes and for nothing?" I asked, playing.

"I don't have that kind of luck," Charlie sighed.

"What do you want, Charlie?" I asked, irritated with myself and wishing I wasn't so adept at games where I was the butt of the joke.

"Well," Charlie said slowly, "if it's all right with you, I thought I would come over there at noon and we could have lunch. I think we should talk about Christmas."

"Christmas? Why should we talk about Christmas?"

"It's coming," Charlie answered. "I'll be there at noon. 'Bye." And he hung up.

For several minutes I stood in the arched green alcove that housed the patient phone, staring at the receiver in my hand. One thing about Charlie, when he's right, he's right. Christmas is certainly coming.

In fact, Christmas was bearing down on us like a foreseen but unforestallable disaster, and I was experiencing my annual urge to convert to Judaism. Already some twit, probably Pomeroy, had strung gold foil letters reading "Merry Christmas, Happy New Year" across the nurses' station. Later there would be tinsel draped over the letters, Christmas cards posted on the bulletin board, and for those who needed an added nudge into terminal depression, a Christmas tree in the parlor, all a-twinkle and a-blinkle. The staff blathered happily on about plans for the jolly holidays, apparently impervious to the ill-concealed apprehension of the patients, who slunk about trying to avoid both the letters and the blather. The patients KNEW. Christmas can make you sick. People have died from Christmas.

But why did Charlie want to talk about Christmas? It wasn't as if there was anything we could do about it. It would come, like it or not, and there we would all be, yo-ho-hoing at full throttle for the kids' sake, who would be clapping their hands with glee, for our sake.

Charlie was already seated at a booth. His eyes, teeth, and the gray in his hair gleamed orange, reflected in the glow from the walls. It was becoming. I slid in opposite him.

"So what's this about Christmas?" I asked. "Have you thought of a way to have it canceled?"

"I wish," Charlie sighed.

He ordered sandwiches and coffee for both of us.

He looked at his hands and cleared his throat. "Ahem, hum, well now," he said, cranking up. Any minute his motor would catch and he'd go chugging down the conversational highway, obstinately missing the forest and crashing into the trees. I waited.

"Are you going to be with us for Christmas?" he finally got out.

"As opposed to against you?"

"I'm serious," he frowned.

"Me, too."

The sandwiches arrived. Charlie began to munch absentmindedly.

"What I meant was, is Alexander going to release you before Christmas?"

"I don't know." He looked dubious and I shook my head vehemently. "Honestly, I don't know."

"Don't you ever ask him when he's going to discharge you, Cassie?"

"No, not so far."

"Maybe you're afraid that he'll send you home," he said wisely.

"Maybe."

Charlie looked sad. "Is it that horrible at home, Cassie?"

"Sometimes. Don't *you* think it's horrible?"

Charlie sighed. "Sometimes."

We both sipped our coffee in silence.

"Well," Charlie began again, "if you aren't going

to be home before Christmas, do you think you could help me out with it while you're here, do me a few favors?"

"Like what?" *I don't want to do you any favors, Charlie. Right now there's little I would do for you out of kindness or affection. Right now I think most fondly of you from a distance and, oddly, in the past tense.*

"If you could get a pass and pick up a few things for the kids in the afternoon, it would help me a lot. You know, toys and games and stuff like that. You could bring the presents when you come home to visit and I'll hide them. I don't know when I'm going to find the time to do everything. I just don't. I'm taking far too much time from work as it is. I get the kids off to school, dash for the office, try to cram all my work into a few hours and then dash home again."

He gazed off toward the windows and I could see the bluish circles under his eyes and lines in his face where there had never been lines before.

It isn't always easy for you, is it, Charlie? Why do you pretend that keeping it all going, keeping us all together is a matter of unchangeable, predetermined fate, and not a result of your conscious choice? You get tired, like everyone else. You could walk away.

"I'll ask Alexander," I replied. "If he says it's all right, I'll do some shopping for the kids. *Only* for the kids though. You'll have to either take care of the other relatives or ignore them. I don't feel kindly disposed toward many people right now."

"So I've noticed," Charlie said, "and so I've heard." He looked thoughtful.

"From whom?"

"Father Dunhill called me," he explained, looking somewhat embarrassed.

"And?"

"And," he said with the corners of his mouth beginning to twitch, "he said that you are suffering from moral erosion."

"What?"

"Erosion. Like urban blight."

I dropped my coffee cup. "Maybe he'd like to fill me in with sand, and plant petunias. Jesus Christ! Did you really let him say that to you, Charlie? I mean, really?"

"Well, he does have a peculiar way of expressing himself, but I think I understand what he was trying to tell me."

Charlie slumped. He had heard the message behind Dunhill's words and I felt sorry for him.

"Poor Charlie. No one has any good news for you. First Alexander tells you I'm arrested and now Dunhill tells you I'm eroded and no one gives you any hope. It all sounds so final and incurable and sad."

"Is it, Cass?" he asked softly.

"I wish I knew, Charlie. Sometimes lately I have hope that it will all get better. That I'll get better. AA will help."

"Do you really think so?" He straightened, unaccountably cheered.

"Yes," I said, trembling. *For God's sake, Charlie, don't take my word for it. What do I know?*

He walked me to the elevator.

"Listen," he said suddenly, with his hand on my arm, "last Sunday in church Father Dunhill said that he was refusing permission to the Little Theatre Group to put on *The Killing of Sister George* in the church hall because it portrays homosexuality sympathetically and is therefore a dangerous play."

"It could cause moral erosion," I nodded solemnly.

Charlie leaned over to kiss me. "It's a terrific play," he said. "Dunhill's collar doesn't make him a critic"— he kissed me again—"or a student of human nature."

We were holding up the elevator. " 'Bye, darling." As the doors began to close I watched Charlie turn up his coat collar and pull his gloves out of his pocket, preparing to do battle with the blowing snow.

I'm sure Charlie never lost his mittens when he was a kid, or tore his pants or scribbled in his history book. He goes to bed every night at eleven-thirty, always eats a healthy breakfast and returns his library books on time. Someday I am going to run him down in the driveway.

"Yoo hoo, Cassie!" I turned as best I could in the crowded elevator and saw Cara mashed in behind two fat ladies.

"Who was that adorable little gray-haired person you were kissing?" she cooed, with a gleam in her eye.

"That's Charlie," I said, grinning. The other passengers stared fixedly at the floor indicator.

"But he doesn't *look* like a pervert, Cassie. I mean, all those things you told me about whips and chains and frozen bananas . . . my!"

The fat ladies gasped.

"Charlie's a fooler," I laughed.

"I don't blame you a bit for setting him on fire while he was asleep. He should be locked up."

The elevator stopped and several people got off. Cara pushed forward and put her arm around me.

"Tell me," she said, "is the treatment working? Do you still take fits and attack strangers?"

The elevaor stopped again and *everyone* got out. Quickly.

"The citizens are restless," Cara giggled, and we arrived on the seventh floor breathless with laughter.

That afternoon on impulse I asked for a pass.

"I want to go home and make a pot roast," I said.

I was smiled upon, yuckily, by Pomeroy.

I drove home slowly, knowing what it was I wanted to do and wondering how I would go about doing it. *Out of the depths I cry to thee, Lord, Lord, hear my prayer.* Where had that come from?

How could I tell the kids? What words? If they were older, I thought, I'd give them that godawful book opened to the place where it explains "Alcoholism, the disease," but they'd probably end up thinking I had trench mouth. How specific could I get about a disease for which they don't know the cause and haven't a cure?

I hunched over the wheel and began another prayer. *God grant me the serenity to accept the things I can-*

not change, the courage to change the things I can, and wisdom to know the difference . . . and the prayer carried me into my driveway. *For an agnostic, I am becoming a whiz-bang at prayer.*

Charlie met me at the door. "What are you doing here?" he asked, surprised.

"I live here."

"You could have fooled me," he said. "How about staying with the kids while I go to the supermarket?"

"Sure," I replied. Providence was handing me a golden opportunity. Why me? Why always me?

Charlie departed in a flap of mufflers, mittens, and galoshes.

I called the kids, who seemed unimpressed with my unexpected arrival, and lined them up while I sat on the sofa.

"Well," I began hesitantly. They gazed at me warily. "You're probably wondering why I've been in the hospital for so long."

Jenny fidgeted. "Grandma says it's your gallbladder."

Steve grinned. "Daddy says you're cracked."

Greg stared fixedly, my brown-eyed boy. "Why are you?"

"Well," I plunged ahead. "Grandma and Daddy mean well, but the truth is . . . hmmmmm . . . I'm in the hospital because I'm an alcoholic. Alcoholism is a disease. It's caused by drinking too much booze. I've joined Alcoholics Anonymous. That's a place where people who have the alcoholic disease go to stop drinking. I won't have to drink anymore and I won't have to go to the hospital anymore."

I let out a long breath.

The kids remained silent.

"Well, what do you say?" I asked.

The kids stared.

Finally Steve said, "I knew you drank an awful lot of that stuff."

Greg chimed in, "I thought it made you sick. It sure did make you mad. And mean."

And then Jenny, "Is that why you're always lying on the couch sleeping when I come home from school?"

I nodded, hot with shame, close to tears.

And Jenny again, "Do you have to stay at Aka . . . Aka. . . ."

"Call it AA," I prompted.

"Do you have to STAY there?" They all looked anxious.

I shook my head. "No, no. I can go to meetings after dinner and be home again by eleven."

"Every night?" Greg wanted to know.

"Every night at first, honey. I drank every night. Then, when I'm more comfortable, I'll go three or four times a week, whatever works best."

Steve asked, "Are you home from the hospital now?"

I answered, "Not yet. Soon."

Greg said, "Then you'll be here?"

And Jenny, "Always? Forever?"

I swallowed hard and nodded. "Always and forever."

The children looked at me and then at one another.

"Can we go outside and build a snowman?" Steve asked.

I turned my head quickly. "Yup, go. I have to make dinner. Scoot." They tumbled into their coats and boots, pushing and shoving to be the first out the door. They left in an explosion of energetic whoops and I closed the door quickly against the icy blasts.

I sank back into the sofa, hugging a pillow to my tummy and rocking myself gently back and forth.

Dumb kids, I thought. No one believes me. *I* don't believe me. But those little twerps, in one minute flat, *they* have to go and believe me. I say that I don't have to drink anymore and they *believe* me. Simple as that. "Alcoholism is a disease." "Okay, can we go out and play?"

I really went and did it. I said, "Forever" and "Always" to the midgets. Big, brave me. And now I'm stuck with a promise I'm not sure I can keep.

I hugged the pillow tighter, biting the corner. "I'll keep it," I sniffed. "I'll keep the goddamn promise."

When Charlie came home with the groceries, he

found the four of us in the back yard, building a lumpy snow-person of indeterminate sex.

14

"They just accepted it, Tinkerbell," I was saying enthusiastically later that night. "They sat there and listened and accepted what I said."

"Without comment?" she asked.

"Very little," I replied, "and they didn't refer to it later at dinner either. When I was getting ready to leave I told them that I was going to an AA meeting and Steve wanted to know where it was. So I told them it was in the bank building across the street from where Grandma goes to church."

"Any comment to that?"

"Jenny wanted to know why they had Alcohol meetings in the bank."

"And you told her that they're held in different places?"

"Yes."

Tinkerbell shifted in her seat and regarded me thoughtfully. We were sitting in one corner of the parlor away from the group watching television.

She finally spoke. "The next time you're home perhaps you can offer to take the children to a meeting with you."

I looked startled.

"Oh, they probably won't want to go, Cassie, but offer to take them anyway."

"Why? I don't understand."

"It will reassure them." She shifted in her seat again

and seemed reluctant to go on. "Perhaps," she said, slowly, "they weren't quite as accepting as you think."

"What do you mean?"

She leaned forward, eyes wide and dark, radiating concern. "I'm not saying this to upset or offend you, Cassie, but I do feel that it is essential for you to be as realistic as possible right now."

"I agree. Shoot."

"Okay, think a minute. Have you ever told the kids that you were going to quit drinking?"

"No," I began, and stopped. "Oh, Christ, Tinkerbell, I have. Many times. Jesus." My buoyantly hopeful mood was beginning to fray at the edges. *Please don't unravel me completely, Tink. One solid tug is all it would take.*

"And," she continued with a little frown, "have you ever told the children that you hadn't had a drink, when in fact you had?"

"Yes," I whispered. "I've told them I was sober when I was practically falling down."

"Did they ever seem to go along with it even when you knew better?"

"Yes."

"What happened when they challenged you—if they ever did?"

I picked up my cigarettes, but my hands were shaking too hard to light one. Tinkerbell lit it for me. *All right, Cassie, go on. She isn't trying to hurt you.*

"At first one or the other of them would occasionally challenge me," I said, trying to keep my voice steady. "Steve would say he smelled booze on my breath or Jenny would say I was walking funny. Greg would begin to tell me something about school, then stop abruptly in the middle of the sentence, give me a strange look and walk away—I'd always go after him, demanding that he come back and finish."

"What else did you do?"

I leaned over, hugging my knees and avoiding her eyes. "I screamed at them. I screamed that I wasn't drinking, and anyway what I did was my business. I was their mother, who did they think they were anyway. . . . I screamed at them."

"Did you ever hit them, Cass?"

"Yes, twice—that I remember." Tears fell on my blue-denim knees and I could no longer keep my voice steady. "Look, Tink, I know what you're asking me and what you're telling me, but I can't talk about this anymore. I can't."

"I'm not trying to hurt you, Cassie."

"I know. I know," I wept. "You aren't hurting me: I'm hurting me." I cried softly for several minutes while Tinkerbell waited patiently.

"They did challenge me at first," I said, lifting my head, "and I reacted violently."

"So?"

"So, they stopped challenging." I ground out my cigarette, suddenly indignant. "But goddammit, Tinkerbell, this is altogether different! I've never been involved with AA before. I've never even admitted that alcoholism was my problem. Not really. I just made stupid promises that I wouldn't drink. This time I know I've found an answer. This time I mean it!"

Tinkerbell smiled sympathetically. "I know that you feel that way, Cassie. But children get tired of broken promises, of being disappointed time and time again. They turn off to the promise so they won't have to feel the pain. Do you expect them now to suddenly believe and accept? Can they?"

"I suppose not," I sighed. "No, I can't expect them to understand fully. But how can I convince them, Tink? How can I tell that this time it's going to be all right, that they can trust me?"

The door buzzer rasped and Tinkerbell rose to answer it. She paused and patted my shoulder.

"You can't tell them, Cassie. You'll have to show them. Stay sober and eventually they'll believe you." She smiled and walked into the hall, leaving me slumped over my soggy knees.

Stay sober, and eventually they'll believe me. I don't want "eventually"! I want right now!

Slowly I walked to my room, carefully treading on only the green tiles. "Step on a crack—hmmmm," I mumbled.

I sat wearily on the side of my bed, picked up the *Alcoholics Anonymous* book and idly flipped through the pages. On page 135 I was attracted to large letters printed in italics. "We have three little mottos which are apropos. Here they are: *FIRST THINGS FIRST* *****LIVE AND LET LIVE*****EASY DOES IT!"

I stared at the page, too tired to read further. It was advice obviously meant for the simple-minded. Or perhaps it was for the complicated mind too worn out with the confusion of it all to understand anything except simple advice.

"My dear Mrs. Caliguire," I addressed the seventh floor's incumbent recumbent, "I have three little mottos which are apropos. First, I shall continue to go to meetings and remain sober. Then, I shall allow my children to learn to trust me in their own way and their own time. And, I shall take it very, very easy because I have damned near killed myself with taking it hard. How's that, Mrs. Caliguire? Aren't I terrific? Don't I learn quickly? What's that you say, Mrs. Caliguire? It's only taken me twenty-eight years to learn that I don't know much of anything? *Tres* unkind, you old bat. Wake up and we will fight a duel. *En garde!*" I leaped to my feet and waved my arms at the unmoving form.

"What an incredible idea, Cassie!" Cara exclaimed from the doorway. "Who but you would think to try witchcraft."

"C'mon in, Cara. I wasn't trying witchcraft, but it's an idea."

"How do you stand it?" she asked. "I wouldn't be able to sleep at night with her just lying there like that. It's unnatural."

"I seem to be getting used to it. There are some advantages, too. She keeps her side of the room neat, I get all the dresser drawers, and most of the time I pretend that she's not even here. It's like having a private room."

Cara leaned over Caliguire. "Yoo hoo, lady, your bed's on fire! The sky is falling! Jesus Christ, by popular demand, is appearing in the parlor! Yoo hoo, lady." She straightened. "Not a flicker. Maybe she's enchanted. We should call a prince to kiss her and wake her up. How about Alexander?" She leered. "If he kissed me, I'd not only wake up, I'd roll over and do tricks."

"What kind of tricks?" Tinkerbell stood in the doorway holding a tray and smiling at Cara.

"Tricks that would curdle his spine," Cara giggled.

"Sounds enthralling," Tinkerbell decided. "You'll have to tell him all about it in the morning."

"Okay," Cara agreed. "I'll think of some really neat stuff before I go to bed."

"Do you actually *tell* him things like that, Cara?" I asked, amazed at her lack of inhibition.

"Oh, sure," she replied enthusiastically. "I tell him whatever pops into my head. Sometimes it's even true." She laughed. "Last week I told him that you and I wanted him to adopt us and—"

"Me?! Why did you bring me into it?"

"Why not? Anyway, I told him that we were going to go over to his house and sit on his doorstep until he adopted us."

"What did he say?" Tinkerbell asked.

"Oh, one of his usual remarks when I say something like that. He said he couldn't adopt us, but he'd pay us two dollars an hour to shovel snow off his driveway."

"What?" I yelled, astonished. "He made a joke!"

"If you can call it that."

"He makes jokes with you?"

"Sure. All the time. What about it?" Cara cocked her head to one side. "Doesn't he make jokes with you?"

I folded my arms and sat on my bed, thoroughly disgruntled and hoping it didn't show. "Sure he does. All the time," I replied, lighting a cigarette. "From now on though, please keep me out of your therapy. He's going to think that I *told* you I wanted to be adopted, that it was my idea and not yours."

"That's why I haul you in with me," Cara admitted cheerfully. "When he smiles and makes a joke I tell him that it was my idea. When he frowns I blame it on you."

"Christ, Cara!" I was really irritated. "Do you think you're so goddamn lovable that no one is ever going to get mad at you? You're like a three-year-old smearing jam all over his clothes. You think that everyone is going to forget to spank you because you look so adorable."

Cara was deflated. "Are you mad at me, Cassie?"

I sighed. "No, I'm not mad at you. Just keep me out of your jam. Okay?"

Tinkerbell smiled, her warm look patting me on the head. "You girls had better not stay up too late," she said, starting out of the room. "We're getting a batch of student nurses first thing in the morning."

"What for?" I asked.

"It's part of their training. They go from one part of the hospital to the other. This is their week to learn about mental illness. You're going to love the*m*," Tinkerbell said.

"Phooey," Cara pouted. "I hate having strangers up here. I don't even like when the library lady comes around. Why don't they all stay downstairs where they belong. This is *our* floor."

"Maybe it won't be so bad, Cara," I soothed and it sounded like a lie even to me.

"Maybe," she said, unconvincingly. "Well, I'd better go to bed."

She paused at the door, gazing at Mrs. Caliguire. "One thing you have to say for her, though. She sure found a way to drop out of the rat race."

I stretched out on my bed and sighed. "Maybe she didn't drop out. Maybe the rats won."

The following morning found me in the middle of the room, underwear-clad, bent over double brushing my hair. Suddenly the door crashed open and I heard a lilting voice behind me.

"Hi! I'm Karen and I'm a student nurse."

"How thrilling for you. For Christ's sake, close the

goddamn door!" Upside down and through my legs I could see Abdul in the hallway, gazing in his out-of-focus way at my upturned rump. I wheeled around.

"Quick, you ninny," I shouted, "before he comes out of his stupor again!"

"Wha . . . what?" she stammered as I vaulted past her and slammed the door in Abdul's face.

From the hall there came a roar, "SHAAAA—ZAAMMMM!"

I leaned against the door, panting and angry. "Now look what you've done." I shook my brush at her. "I've hurt Abdul's feelings and scared the hell out of myself."

Karen shook her head slowly and the ends of her taffy-colored hair bounced.

"I don't feel very good, either," she said and sank down on my bed. "You startled me."

"Sorry," I said, purposely curt. "Don't they teach you to knock?"

She watched me with eyes like pale blue golf balls. "It's different on other floors," she said. "Everybody is in bed and you just walk in. When something private is going on the curtains are pulled, so there isn't much of a problem."

I reached for my jeans and sweater. "Well, here you knock," I said.

"Okay," she concurred, smoothing the starched lap of her pink jumper. "When did your problems begin?" she asked brightly.

"When you opened the door," I mumbled, my head halfway through my sweater.

"I mean your mental problems," she insisted.

"That was it," I said. "I'm only a visitor here. You gave me a nervous breakdown."

"Visitors don't stand around in their underwear," she remarked.

"You haven't met Rotten Ronnie," I answered. "He came bopping in here one night bombed out of his skull in a Hawaiian shirt and jockey shorts."

"Rotten Who?" she asked, looking puzzled.

"Never mind." I began to pull on my jeans, wondering if the whole floor was full of inquisitive teeny-boppers or if I had been specially chosen.

"So when did your mental problems begin?" she persevered. "Recently?"

"No."

"Before you got married?"

"No," I answered. "Before that."

"During your childhood?"

"Before that."

"Infancy?"

"Before that."

"What?"

I grabbed my cigarettes off the table and jammed them into my pocket.

"Look, it's been wonderful talking to you but I have to run. I have to cathexe my catharsis and traumatize my neurosis before breakfast." And I sprinted through the door with Karen hot on my heels.

"Where are we going, Mrs. Barrett?" she called.

I stopped dead and she ran up the back of my tennis shoes.

"We are not going anywhere, Karen. And where I am going is my own damned business. Go away," I said sternly.

"I can't go away," she said earnestly. "I'm assigned to you. You're my patient."

"For how long?" I wanted to know.

She glanced downward, scuffing her white toe self-consciously on the tile floor, an orphan at the picnic. "Oh, about two weeks," she said.

I threw my arms in the air. "Christ Almighty!" I exploded, and turned on my heel, heading for Cara's room. I found her babbling into the freckled ear of a tall, red-headed teenager, attired like mine in a pink jumper and white blouse.

"Hi, Cassie! Let's go to the parlor," she suggested. "It's almost time for Alexander to come in. I have a lot to talk to him about this morning."

"Who's Alexander?" the redhead asked.

Cara fluttered her eyelashes. "He's my lover. Every

morning between eight and nine we make passionate love in the laundry room. It's therapeutic."

"You're kidding," the redhead decided.

I took Cara's arm. "Astute as hell, aren't they?" I said, and we marched down the hall with our pink starched shadows following right behind.

Clustered around the nurses' station and scattered through the parlor were bunches, batches, coveys, and gaggles of rosy adolescents.

"It's an invasion from the Peppermint Planet," I said to Cara as we approached Dalton, who was scanning a patient chart with a student peering over each shoulder.

"Is this the complaint department?" Cara asked, as we draped ourselves casually over the counter.

Dalton glared squintily at us and pushed an escaping wisp of hair behind the ear.

"Please," she murmured. "I don't have time this morning. Just wait in the parlor for your doctor. Go on, girls—go!" She waved the chart, shooing us like vexatious chicks. We exchanged glances.

"Frazzled," Cara said with an emphatic nod.

"Unglued," I agreed. "She's even sweating. I thought her pores were hermetically sealed."

Rounding the corner to the parlor, we were crashed into by a red-faced and furiously puffing Frank.

"That kid," he sputtered, too angry to say "excuse me." "That kid . . . she–she asked . . . that kid—!" He pointed at a sweet young thing who looked like a brunette Alice in Wonderland.

"She what, Frank?" Cara encouraged, regaining her balance.

"She asked me if my wife and I have a satisfactory sexual relationship!" he bellowed. "It's none of her goddamn business. She's young enough to be my daughter. What the hell are they teaching these kids anyway?"

"They are here to learn about mental illness, Frank," I said. "We are a learning experience."

He shook his head angrily. "What the hell has my sex life got to do with mental illness?"

"Oh, c'mon now, Frank," I winked. "We've all heard the rumors about the bizarre sexual behavior of civil servants, the decadence, the perversity, the—"

"This isn't funny, Cassie," Frank fretted. "This place is turning into a madhouse."

"He finally caught on," Cara interrupted. "All this time he thought he was at the Seaside Hotel in Atlantic City having shock treatments on the American Plan."

"You're both nuts," Frank grumped and we nodded agreeably. "I am," he said decisively, "about to take myself and my newspaper into the men's room. I will stay there until dinner time. This junior Nightingale told me that they go off duty at three o'clock. See you later."

"Cop out!" Cara called after him.

"I'm happy to hear they leave at three," I remarked as we walked into the parlor. "I was afraid they were planning to sleep with us."

"Wrong profession," Cara grinned.

"Not from what I've heard," I said sourly, then frowned at my cattiness. *I'm not the only one suffering a case of the creeps,* I thought, surveying the parlor. Joanne sat on the green, woolly sofa crocheting spastically and casting occasional nervous peeps at the student planted rigidly beside her. At the game table, two sullen-faced involutional melancholias played a mute game of Monopoly with two smiling students who kept up a running chatter hoping to lure the mutes into conversation. In another corner Ludwig slouched in an easy chair with a copy of *Slaughter, The Gun Collectors' Digest* wrapped around his face, while a little pink person perched on a footstool regarded him hopefully.

"Give the kid a break, Ludwig," I called. "Tell her about the conspiracy." Ludwig glared.

Only Margaret seemed to be enjoying the attention. She sprawled on a beige couch, her arm in an affectionate half-nelson around a student who squirmed and ineffectively attempted to wiggle away from the bombastic outpourings of the professional patient.

Gloria limped in and tapped Cara on the shoulder. "Yer shrink wants to see ya."

"Goodie." Cara clapped and bounded to her feet. "Why are you limping, Gloria?" Cara asked, winking at me.

"Well," Gloria began, "I was coming up in the elevator this mornin' on my way to work and on the fifth floor this orderly gets on pushin' a gurney. Well, this guy on the gurney, he's all doped up, see, an' anyhow he starts moanin' he's got a pain in his gut. So the orderly, he says, 'You gonna feel a lot better when they get that kidney out.'

"And the patient, he says, 'Kidney? What kidney? I got a hernia.' And the orderly, he says, 'No, you ain't, you got a bad kidney. It's ri' here on your chart.' So the guy gets all excited and starts to sit up and the orderly, he gets all excited and pushes the guy down and commences yellin' at ME to strap him in, which ain't easy to do with the guy's arms all over the place and him screamin' about havin' the wrong chart. So the door opens up and the orderly says, 'They gonna yank your kidney and that sure as hell gonna shut you up!' and he pushes the guy, who sounds like he's stranglin', out fast as he can. What a commotion!"

Cara looked puzzled. "I still don't understand why you're limping, Gloria."

"Oh," Gloria said, "that dumb bastard, he run the gurney right over my foot."

"Working here is just one long adventure in pain for you, Gloria," I commented. "Why don't you work at something that isn't quite so hazardous to your health?"

"What?" Gloria bristled. "I ain't about to give up the medical profession."

She whirled and limped off huffily with Cara in tow. The redhead followed, settling herself to wait, like a devoted Irish setter, outside the door.

Karen inched closer. "Are your children upset about your hospitalization?"

"No," I said crossly, "they love it. They run the streets like a pack of wolves, rolling drunks and shooting up heroin behind the school."

I grabbed a copy of *Better Homes and Gardens* from the top of the coffee table.

"Here," I said, thrusting it into her lap, "read a magazine." It was like trying to keep one of the kids amused at the dentist's office.

"I can't," she said, returning the magazine to the table. "I'm on duty." She turned her attention to me. "Why are you here, on the seventh floor, I mean?" she persisted.

"I went into a severe depression following the breaking of an affair with a veterinarian who gave me the mange," I sighed.

"I mean seriously," she began, but stopped cold as Norma came hurtling across the room, on her way out of the parlor at a dead run. Suddenly Norma halted and turned on the girl running a few steps behind her.

"I am going to my room!" she screamed. "I am going to take a nap. I take naps ALONE! Stay OUT!"

The student gazed after her in confusion. "Why would she want to take a nap? She just got up."

"Depressed people sleep a lot," I answered, feeling as though at least three days had elapsed since Karen bounced thorugh my door. I sank back on the sofa with my eyes closed, hoping to avoid further conversation. If this trend continued, the seventh floor would soon be reenacting *The Last Man on Earth* with patients sleeping away the days in dark sequestered rooms and roaming the halls at night in search of Vincent Price.

"Cassie, Cassie!" I looked up startled to see Cara, with streaming eyes and contorted face, standing in the doorway twisting a Kleenex.

"Cassie, he won't talk to me!" she sobbed. "He won't talk to me!" She turned and bolted down the hall.

"Cara!" I started after her, but was halted by Dalton, who blocked my way.

"Dr. Alexander wants to see you now," she said briskly.

"But Cara . . ." I protested.

"She'll be all right. You can see her later," Dalton said, pushing me gently toward the interview room. "Your doctor wants to see you."

15

I hesitated at the door, feeling like an intruder. Alexander stood with his back to me, one arm resting on the dingy window, shoulders slumped slightly forward. I coughed in a dry, self-conscious attempt to announce myself, fearful that I'd caught him unawares and unprepared.

So sometimes we do get to you, don't we, Edwin? C'mon, friend, don't stand there looking vulnerable. Sit down, tap your pencil, clear your throat, say "hmmm," look omniscient—anything. Where would we be if I should begin wanting to comfort YOU? Where would we be if I should succeed?

"What's wrong with Cara?" I asked peremptorily. "She's very upset."

He turned and sat heavily in the large swivel chair.

"You needn't concern yourself with Cara's problems," he said, patting his pockets. "You have enough problems of your own to occupy your mind." He frowned and continued to frisk himself. "Say," he said, "I seem to be out of cigarettes. Could you—?"

"Oh, sure," I said, pushing the pack across the desk at him. "But Cara is my friend. I care about her."

"Fine," he said, lighting a cigarette. "Continue to be her friend. It's good for both of you. But I'm her doctor and I don't discuss my patients with other patients."

Stuffy bastard.

"Wouldn't you be even angrier than you are now if I discussed you with anyone else, even Cara?" he asked.

"Well, yes, I suppose I would," I admitted reluctantly. *No matter how I arrange my face and craft my monologues, you read my emotions. Perhaps it goes with the profession, like a mechanic's wrench. Maybe in the final year of Shrink School you're all implanted with Emotion Detectors. At graduation you totter past the podium with nerve endings aquiver, clutching your diplomas and emitting a high-pitched whine. Maybe that's what causes me to short-circuit when you look at me. Maybe that's what causes the wavy lines on my television set. Maybe—*

"What are you thinking?"

"Nothing."

He frowned. "You are not thinking nothing. I know you. You are always thinking something."

I squirmed. "You know me." *What a truly noxious and appalling thought, Edwin. What an unnerving hypothesis.*

"As well as anyone knows you," he amended, leaning back in his chair. "Why are you smiling?"

Go ahead, Cassie. He doesn't bite. Come to think of it, he doesn't even nibble. Wouldn't you like a taste, Edwin, just a light and tickly lick?

"It's possible that you know the wonderful creature you see sitting before you," I said, wondering where I was going. "But you've never met the killer lady I keep locked in the closet, the one who snarls and growls and batters at the door."

"She's that bad?" he asked.

I nodded. "Monstrous."

"What would happen if you let her out?"

"She'd run amuck. She would butcher everyone who made her feel guilty or angry or afraid. She'd make an invasion by the Huns look like a sophomore cotillion. Havoc, havoc everywhere."

Alexander picked up a pencil and began to tap on the phone, a reassuring return to normalcy.

"I'll wager," he said, "that your lady is not as dangerous as you think. Why don't you give her a weekend pass and see what she does?"

YOU'LL wager, Edwin? Damned sporting of you. You have nothing to lose. "And what happens when we pick up the Cleveland *Plain Dealer* on Monday and find that the Terminal Tower has been reduced to smouldering rubble and the citizens are all lying in the street maimed and mutilated and crying for their mothers? Wouldn't I feel guilty for having let her loose? But enough about her. How's business?"

For once Alexander's scowl, usually the ultimate weapon, failed to modify my behavior.

"What would you people do," I said, running blithely down the path and trampling the tulips, "if they discovered that all these mental problems are chemical imbalances, or hormonal screw-ups, or chipped chromosomes? What would you shrinks do if everyone's problem could be solved with little red and green pills, if all the whackos stopped hallucinating and became used-car salesmen? Hmmmm? Would you be miffed?"

The frown, a masterpiece of its kind, deepened.

"Would you pack all your Oedipus Complexes and Sibling Rivalries off to the Mythological Beast Museum and become a gynecologist? You could announce pregnancies by shouting, "Anatomy is destiny!" at quailing ladies who were hoping for menstrual dysfunction. You could congratulate the mother of four with a collapsing uterus and varicose veins on her mature acceptance of the womanly role. You could teach battle-scarred veterans of the hormonal wars how to turn premenstrual tension into a peak experience. You could—"

"What the hell are you trying to tell me?" he demanded, his forehead a veritable mass of criss-crossing crevices.

"Nothing," I replied, exhausted. I thought his patience would never run out.

"Have you given any thought to your plans?" he asked.

"Do you mean Plan A, where I stay sober and become a brain surgeon? Or Plan B, where I jump off the High Level Bridge?" I hedged.

"I mean," he said, ignoring me, "the idea you had about leaving here and checking into the West Side Residence." He waited.

"What about it?" I asked, fencing.

"Well, ahem, hmmm, immm," he said, attempting to dazzle me with psychiatric jargon, "your instincts are basically correct. You would like to go back and live through a transition you never experienced, find your missing link, as it were. You intuitively understand that you never went through the maturation process."

What's intuitive about it, Edwin? Give me credit for knowing what I know.

"Unfortunately, at this time your instincts and intuitive feelings do not coincide with the realities of your life," he continued.

"I don't understand." A headache was beginning to poke my left eyeball.

"You are not an adolescent. You have a husband and three children."

"You're kidding. I was wondering who those people using my bathroom were!"

"You have to deal in present realities," he forged ahead. "You can't go back."

"But I'm not trying to go back," I protested, wishing I could present my points with the same facile eloquence that never failed me in my daydreams. "I'm trying to go forward. Are you telling me that there's only one path out of this swamp?"

"The reality of it is that you have a family."

"The reality of it is that I am separated from my

family," I said, my voice rising. "My hospitalization doesn't make it any less a separation. I'm just saying that I would like to continue the separation, at least for a while. Until . . . until . . . until I decide what I want to be. . . ." I trailed off lamely.

"Be? What's wrong with what you are?"

"I'll bite. What am I?"

"A wife and mother for one thing—"

"A drunk and a psychiatric patient for another . . ."

Alexander smiled smugly. "And you think that if you cease being a wife and mother you will also cease being a drunk and psychiatric patient?"

"Nothing's ever that simple," I sighed.

"Exactly," he grinned.

Exactly what, Edwin? Wait a damn minute. What have I just agreed to? Whatever it is, I've just changed my mind.

"I'm going to go to the Residence," I declared loudly, wondering if he would call my bluff, tell me to pack and go.

"That would be unwise at this time," he said, sitting back and looking disappointed.

You were expecting maybe a breakthrough, Edwin?

"Why would it be unwise at this time?"

"You're not ready for that."

"Well, what do *you* think I should do?"

Alexander touched his fingertips together. *Here's the church, here's the steeple. . . .* "I think you should go home when you leave here."

"Why?"

"You need Charlie's stability."

"What! Charlie's stability?"

Alexander's steeple collapsed, killing the people. "That's my opinion," he said, staring fixedly at my contorted face. "Just think about it. You don't have to make any decisions right away."

In that case, you're forgiven. I'll agree to anything as long as I don't have to do anything about it.

"I'll think about it," I said like a good little girl, and, satisfied, he rose from his seat.

"See you tomorrow," he said, walking out.

Thanks for warning me, love. I'll be up all night soldering my armor and oiling my crossbow for tomorrow's joust.

I walked to my room slowly while my mind hop-scotched over tumbling ideas. I don't need Charlie. I can do it on my own. It would be easier with Charlie, safer with Charlie. Charlie loves me. He wants me back. What a shitty thing to do, to return out of need and not out of love. To hell with it. I'm doing the best I can. I'm not doing anything at all. What am I doing?

"Goddammit," I said to Mrs. Caliguire, "what the hell am I going to do? What do I WANT to do? What's that you say, dear? I appreciate it, but going into a coma is not the solution to everyone's problem. But I do think it's marvelous that it's worked out so well for you."

I pulled pale blue writing paper out of my dresser drawer and fished in my purse for a pen.

Where are you when I need you, Bobby, I thought. *Better yet, where am I when I need me? Inside this crazy lady there's a normal woman trying to get out —and pack up—and move away. What normal woman needs to be trapped inside a crazy lady?*

I began my letter, mentally picturing the gold stars Dalton would soon be gluing to my chart. If I told her it was a poison-pen letter would she still give me one and a half?

Dear Bobby:

This is the blast from your past, your golden oldie, the girl of your incestuous dreams—and don't tell me that you never have them because I broke into your diary when you were sixteen. Just because I was cleverly disguised as Sophia Loren and spoke only Italian while doing weird things to your body with linguine, do not for a second think I am deceived. I have read the cartoon version of *The Interpretation of Dreams* and I am a-twitch and a-twitter with awareness, a-gush with labyrinthine explanations of surrealistic symbolism comprehensible only to qualified psychiatrists and an obscure group of gypsy wig-worshippers located in the lower Ukraine.

However, all my knowledge seems to be of little use in interpreting my own nocturnal transmissions. My latest technicolor episode of the *Charlie and Cassie Story,* featured, once again, Charlie as the captain of the good ship *Titanic.* He ran back and forth shouting that everything was fine, fine, FINE, while I sat in a deck chair admiring the sunset as the water rose to my chin.

Not once, Robert, did it ever occur to me to tap Charlie on the shoulder and say, "Excuse me, sir, I do not mean to cast aspersions on your navigational abilities, but we are up to our ass in icebergs!"

If passive resignation was an art form, I'd be Picasso. And it seems to me, or at least the part of me that scouts my psychic landscape at night and returns with messages of imminent Indian attacks or the sighting of the Promised Land lying just yonder over the hill, that my marriage holds for me all the allure and security of a kamikaze mission. I communicated this undeniably REAL feeling to Alexander, who brushed it off his lapel along with the lint and instructed me, wagging his head like a balding St. Bernard, to go home to Charlie because "you need his stability."

And what did I do? Did I vault from my designated patient chair in an explosion of wrath and assault his clavicle with the fire extinguisher? Of course not. He might decide I'm crazy and lock me up in the psychiatric ward, or even worse, say, "Get out of here, you nut!"

Did I coldly assume that he has gone deaf in one eye and blind in both ears and is therefore unable to understand what I am saying? Don't be silly. I have seen him receive messages in every medium including Morse Code, Braille, whistles, groans, and grunts, all loud and clear, Roger over and out.

Did I ever for a moment, consider the possibility that he might be WRONG, for God's sake, WRONG? Not by the hair on your chinny chin chin. After four years and untold nickels, dimes and quarters plunked into the couch meter, my vested interests in his RIGHT-

NESS is so great that I would rather be locked up in the back room at Turney Road State, salivating at the sound of the dinner bell and charted as Incurably Obtuse than admit for a fraction of a millisecond that the wild bull of the pompous could be anything even approaching mildly incorrect.

So what did I do, oh brother of misbegotten youth? I sat, clutching my herniated credulity, limp and passive-pussed externally with the shadow of an acquiescent smile playing demurely on my lips while inside I frothed and seethed, conjuring up fantasies wherein I prowl the streets beating up Honda Civics. And I continued to froth and seethe as I bowed my way backward out of the room, mumbling, "Thank you, sir. Very good, sir. Begging your humble pardon, sir, do kick me again."

But, as they say, Bob, seethe and ye shall find. What I found, after excessive rumination (which always gives me gas), is that Alexander's point of view, and it is a point of view no matter how I might wish it to be Absolute Truth and therefore the golden key, and my point of view (I have one! I have one! I found it under the bed covered with dust!) parallel but do not intersect. (Rule #4 at Shrink School: At no time shall the patient and therapist intersect, an action which could result in either a devastating emotional trauma for the patient, who may never return from banana-land, hohum, win a few, lose a few, *or* a monumental lawsuit for the therapist, who is a skilled professional and a credit to his race.)

Alexander said that I should go home because I need Charlie's stability and while we were both concentrating on Charlie as the fountain from whom this blessing flows, we let the blessing trickle through the floorboards. Alexander is right (thank God, or Freud, or his undoubtedly sainted mother). I do need stability. More than love or sex or validation from my fellow man or the escape of a meaningful relationship. More even than approval, I need stability. But Charlie's?

That, my unrivaled sibling, is where Alexander and I part company. Not that Charlie isn't stable; Charlie is a rock. He is one of those people who were born secure, steady, and dependable. He is never constipated, not even on vacation. And he is generous. For eleven years he has attempted to wrap me up in his nice, warm stability, to protect me from the guys in the black hats and the things that go bump in the night, the midnight terrors and the sunlight traumas. I've leaned on it, borrowed it, abused it, sucked it dry, rejected it, and fought it. Charlie did his desperate best to shore me up, and for good reason. Alcoholism isn't a spectator sport. Eventually the whole family gets to play. But, because it was Charlie's stability and never my own, I collapsed anyway.

So, I've tried that approach, Bob. Even if I go back and try it again sober, how far and for how long can I rely on it?

Suppose that Charlie is out on the golf course someday and a duffer bounces a bad slice off his left temple? Suppose Charlie croaks and I bury him on the eighteenth green? Then what? Whose stability do I use then? May I have yours, Bobby? Will you send it to me by parcel post, ready to assemble in the privacy of my basement or garage?

Do I go door to door in my neighborhood ringing bells and saying, "Excuse me, I'm collecting stability for a worthy, albeit erratic, person. Any little bit you can contribute will be appreciated."

Do I set up Stability Collection Receptacles in strategic locations so people can drive by and drop off their second-hand, but freshly cleaned and pressed stability? Maybe I could get Jerry Lewis to do a telethon—a forty-eight-hour Stability-for-Cassie Marathon, with him doing his frenetic "exhortations to the adoring public" bit, while I'm waiting, profusely grateful and looking attractively spastic, and donations pour in from Sioux City, Iowa. How about a Mother's March on Stability? Do you think, my dear, that our mother would march for the sake of my stability? I have a feeling that, for me, she wouldn't even stroll.

Although these are all obviously viable alternatives, and practical besides, I, in my own demented way, seem to favor another idea. Is it too freaky do you think, to feel that somehow, someday, I would like to develop my own stability? And is it freakier still to sense that stability is not something you go somewhere to get, but something you have to develop slowly over a period of time? It's not wisdom that provokes these thoughts, but experience. I've tried it the other way and it doesn't work. Even Alexander's stability, stored in a Byzantine jar on the corner of his desk and freely offered to all comers, cannot sustain me indefinitely. I WANT MY OWN STABILITY!!!

So why didn't I say as much to Alexander? Why do I nod and smile and say, "I'll think about it." when everything inside of me is yelling, NO, NO, NO? Why do I invariably react with that part of me who thinks that he knows me better than I know myself? Perhaps it's because that too is part of my experience. There have been times, many many times, when he's cut through the façade to expose parts I've hidden myself. Of course, occasionally his scalpel slips and I find myself minus a vital organ or grafted to an extra arm. He's not perfect. (Do not, under pain of death, ever repeat that to anyone. It's not true. He is too perfect.)

But somewhere in my future, Bob, there has to be a day when I'll lie in a field of buttercups watching bosomy clouds scud across a perfect sky and say, "This is what I feel. This is what I know to be true. This is me."

In the meantime, buttercups and perfect skies being rare in Cleveland, I'll have to stumble along as best I can, falling off the mountains and tripping over the molehills.

I had hoped that by writing to you I would find a resolution hidden away among the ambivalences, but I haven't. I suppose that authentic answers don't come that easily, but I keep hoping. In that respect I'm no different from my sweet friend Cara, who worships the water Alexander walks on and looks for the meaning of life in the lyrics of Simon and Garfunkle. Anything, anything, so we don't have to do it ourselves.

So I shall continue to ride my mental yo-yo, vacillating between the road to solitary self-determination at the West Side Residence for Women and a return to Charlie until such time as I am stricken with an insight so blinding and unmistakable that even I can grasp it.

Unless, dear brother, you would like to volunteer for hazardous duty and tell me what to do. Just make sure it's the right thing. Make damn sure, or my heart will turn to flint and I'll cut you out of my will. And you thought that coming into possession of my roller skates was a sure thing, didn't you?

Bobby, Bobby, why does it have to be so hard, so complicated? It isn't taking action that is so difficult, not really. The right thing has a life of its own. It demands to be done. It's trying to decide what that right thing is that's killing me. Take care,

Love,
Cassie

16

"I am responsible only for my behavior, not for what people choose to think about it," I was saying to Cara.

"That's terrific. Did Alexander tell you that?" she inquired, unwrapping a giant Hershey bar.

"No, dammit," I said, "I thought it up myself. Alexander doesn't come up with *all* the goodies."

"No need to get huffy," she said, munching around the edges. "It just sounded like something he would say. Like I'll be telling him that my life is a mess and I'll never amount to anything and I may as well be dead, and he'll say, 'Self-acceptance is the keystone of emotional well-being.' and I'll ask him what the hell that has to do with my crappy life. I think he writes articles for the *Journal* and tries out lines on his patients."

"I know what you mean," I laughed. "Once I was wailing away about the terrible fights Charlie and I were having and screaming that Charlie was a cold-hearted son of a bitch and he said, 'True self-esteem is based on a realistic appraisal of one's actions.' Stopped me cold, I'll tell you. So I said, 'And a bird in the hand is worth two in the bush. What game are we playing?' "

"What did he say?" Cara asked, licking her fingers.

"Nothing. He just started talking about penis envy."

Cara stopped licking. "You've got that, too?"

"That's what he said," I sighed. "I'm beginning to think it's universal, like dandruff."

"It made sense when he told me that I suffer from penis envy," Cara confided. "I want everything else I haven't got. Did you want some candy?"

"No, thanks," I said, thinking that only with Cara would I be saying thank you for something she'd already gobbled up.

"Still," I mused, "there's something about the idea of penis envy that just doesn't ring true. Not for me anyway. When I think of actually having one, it doesn't appeal to me at all. I'm afraid it would fall off or get bumped into or caught in the lawn mower or something. It's either all hanging out there in front jiggling around or flopping in the breeze or getting mashed in jockey shorts or caught in flies—yuk. I wouldn't be able to sleep at night for fear someone would sneak in and snip it off with hedge clippers or whack it with a baseball bat. If I ever had a social disease, I'd be waiting for it to shrivel up and turn black, and if I was ever impotent, even once, I'd never try again. As it is, if I'm impotent, who's to know?"

"Women don't become impotent," Cara laughed.

"Sure we do. Or at least I do. There have been times when I've been temporarily frigid for one reason or another. But I'm so much an accomplished actress, Charlie or whoever never had to know about it. If I were a man, the lady would know in five seconds."

"Why don't you want to tell Charlie?" Cara asked. "I can guess why with the whoever."

"Well," I giggled nervously, taking an unexpected plunge into cold truth, "besides wanting to maintain the image of the fascinating, sexy creature, the fact is that it has nothing to do with Charlie. He always presses the right buttons. Sometimes I just can't get it together, and sometimes it's booze. I can get wildly uninhibited and abandoned, which is terrific and really impresses Charlie; but everything below my neck goes numb. When I'm drinking, my sex life is all between my ears."

"Dope does the same thing," Cara remarked. "It turns on your head and that's about all. Except for grass. Grass is great for screwing. I've met women with penis envy, Cassie, but you're the first one I've ever met with a castration complex."

"I don't have penis envy," I decided. "I like the way I am. I know where everything is when I want it, but in the meantime it's all safely tucked away out of reach of the forces of evil."

"Who?"

"Amateur gynecologists," I said, casting about for another subject. I was beginning to sound like selective paranoia.

"Have you ever had a man tell you he would like to crawl up inside you and stay there?" Cara asked thoughtfully.

"Sure," I answered. "Stay there where it's safe is the way I've heard it put."

"Have you ever told a man that you would like to crawl up inside HIM?"

"And snuggle in his intestines. Hell, no. I've never for a second thought it would be safe inside a man. Or warm. Or cozy. Or anything else comforting. Maybe they haven't a gift for nurturing."

"No womb," Cara decided. "Most of the guys I know want to return to the womb. And I'm supposed to feel flattered because it's my womb they want to return to."

"Maybe Mommy won't have them," I laughed.

"Are you sleepy yet?" Cara asked.

"No," I answered. "Are you?"

As usual we were the sole post-midnight inhabitants of the parlor. By rule, the television set was switched off every night at eleven; I'd yet to meet any-

one on the seventh floor who complained or felt a
moral obligation to watch the late news, the general
attitude being "It's their world, let THEM cope with
it, good riddance, who cares."

Life in the psychiatric ward bears a certain resemblance to an ocean cruise. After three days connections
with the real world become ambiguous. Within a week
we become totally detached from the problems, pres-
sures, people, places, and things that supposedly caused
us to crack up or shut down or go bananas or do
whatever it is we did that caused society, our near and
dear ones, and the medical profession to rise up as one
and shout, "Hey, you with the crying jags and the
confusional delusional despair. You are a fruitcake!"

If, after a month spent confined within the walls of
Cleveland's answer to Shangri-la, we should acciden-
tally hear that New York had fallen into the East River,
we'd likely look up from our lunch trays and say, "New
York? I remember New York," and go on slurping
up the vanilla pudding with roughly the same emotional reaction we experienced when first hearing about
the lost continent of Atlantis. How very interesting
—and how very long ago and far away!

We landed here because we cared so much and reacted so profoundly that trivialities threw us into a
tizzy. So we learn to detach and not to care at all
and just when we have that little act down pat with
all the lines and gestures memorized, some shrinky
person slaps us with a summons ordering an immediate appearance back in the REAL world, do not pass
GO, do not collect your wits.

And as parting advice from the doctor: Don't care
so much that it makes you crazy, or so little that it cuts
you off from the joy of interpersonal relationships.
(JOY? What joy? I'm taking Gelusil nine times a day
because *joy* is eating holes in my stomach); ignore
the irrelevant (Does that mean my marriage, job, and
family, or is it flat tires, pimples, and the threat of imminent nuclear war?); concentrate on positive important goals (Glad to. Quick, tell me what they are. The
bus is waiting); discover your priorities (I had one of

those once. I lost it on my way to school along with my Wonder Woman lunch box and haven't seen it since); and be sure to call if you begin feeling badly (For Christ's sake, what made you think I'm feeling *goodly?*). You may go (Thank you, Doctor. I'll just leave through this open window. I can't tell you how much you've helped me, but perhaps my next of kin will find a way).

Cara began pacing up and down, humming "Tea for Two" and bumping into the furniture. Every night she downed two Seconal and an hour later was livelier and more hyper than before, except when she was depressed and maudlin. She reminded me of me with a pint of scotch sloshing through my interior. Unlike most members of the medical profession, Alexander seemed to feel that there was something inconsistent in prescribing sedatives for an addict, so I had been introduced to the wonderful world of insomnia. Together we haunted the parlor until the wee, small hours.

Cara wadded up the candy wrapper and made a neat toss into the wastepaper basket. She stretched like a cat, arms overhead. "I'm hungry," she complained, fingers wriggling in the air.

"So am I," I agreed. "But there's nothing to eat except saltines and lukewarm milk."

"Let's go downstairs to the employees' lounge," Cara suggested. "They have all kinds of junk in the vending machines."

"Tinkerbell isn't going to let us off the floor at two A.M.," I pointed out. "We're lucky she hasn't given us more hassle about staying up half the night. Anyone else would be in here every five minutes telling us to go to bed."

"I wasn't thinking about asking permission," Cara said, sparkly-eyed. "When Tinkerbell makes her next bedcheck, I'll run behind the desk and hit the buzzer. You hold the door open and we'll be out of here in two seconds. How about it?"

"Jesus, Cara, they'll have a fit if we get caught."

"Who are they, what can they do, and how are we going to get caught?" she asked sensibly. "We'll just get some sandwiches and pie and come right back. C'mon, it won't hurt anything."

"Okay," I decided.

We smoked and waited for Tinkerbell to make her hourly rounds. As usual, she checked the rooms on one side of the hall and sent Abel shuffling down the other side to shine his flashlight in sleeping eyes.

Cara hissed "Now," and slipped behind the desk of the nurses' station. As she hit the buzzer, I yanked open the door and held it for Cara. Without looking back, we bolted down the back stairs, taking them two at a time, like fleeing thieves. We slowed at the fourth floor, panting and laughing.

"Where's the employees' lounge?" I asked, thinking that we were like kids who run away from home without crossing the street. Some great escape!

"On this floor," Cara answered. "Right around the corner from where the surgeons hang out between mutilations."

We crept stealthily down the corridor, peering into rooms as we went, forgetting how much we resented visitors peering into our rooms. Patients moaned and groaned softly in their sleep.

"Look, they have railings on their beds," Cara whispered. "Why don't we have railings on our beds?"

"Loonies don't fall out of beds," I answered. *"We* jump out of windows. If you'll notice, their windows are open."

"They'll die of pneumonia and pollution," Cara said. "We are air conditioned. In fact, we are the only air-conditioned floor in this whole damn hospital."

"Obviously, we are a superior group of people and must be carefully preserved. Like butterflies. Or kumquats." We continued to tiptoe down the hall, watching for on-duty nurses and orderlies. There didn't seem to be any. Except for the patients, the floor was deserted.

"Where is everyone?" Cara asked. "What if someone died?"

"Without medical assistance? Never happens. Where's the lounge?"

"Right here," she said, taking me by the arm and guiding me into a gleaming yellow and chrome space. It was a plastic lemon, patterned, like the other eating areas, after artificial fruit. As was the food.

"Whatever happened to cool greens, soothing blues, soft carpets, and easy chairs?" I asked Cara. "That chair over there looks like a tennis ball."

"Beanbag," she explained. "Look, vending machines! Yummy. Let's see what they've got."

She pranced to a row of robots with windows and began reading off the goodies.

"Ham salad, chicken salad, turkey, beef, bologna, and tongue. What do you want?"

"I don't know," I said, hanging over her shoulder. "Why are the turkey and beef the same color? Why is the ham salad orange? Would you eat tongue in a hospital? Maybe I'll just have an ice cream bar."

I plunked a quarter in the ice cream machine and picked up a chocolate-covered, nut-encrusted rectangle, already melting down the stick. Cara fed the sandwich machine a pocket full of change, and closing her eyes, punched buttons at random. "I love surprises," she giggled.

"Anything that comes out of that machine is going to be a surprise, Cara. You've probably got a botulism burger." She collected her sandwiches and we kicked the milk machine until it gave us two pints, lukewarm with wax floating on the top. We spread our food on a yellow plastic table, brushing off crumbs left over from someone else's snack.

I lapped at the ice cream quickly but it dripped over my thumb, around my wrist, and inside the sleeve of my sweater. I was beginning to wish either we'd stayed on the seventh floor, or I'd remembered to bring my cigarettes.

Cara stopped rustling her waxed paper and looked up with her mouth full.

"Are you going to get well?" she asked.

I stared into her somber brown eyes.

"What kind of question is that to ask me, Cara? Did you think maybe I was planning to get sicker?"

She shrugged. "How should I know? You were here before and from what you've told me, you didn't go home the first time planning to get well."

"You're right," I admitted. *Admitting things to Cara is getting easier and easier to do.*

"I hadn't thought of it that way, Cara, and you are right. I don't know about 'well' because I don't know what 'well' means. Who's well? What's well? Well as compared to whom? We're all models of mental health compared to Caliguire, but if I have to compare myself to Alexander or even Tinkerbell, I'll just hide in the closet and give up. I plan to get *better*. In fact, compared to the way I was when I arrived, I am better. When I went home the last time, all I really wanted was to control my drinking so I wouldn't get into so much trouble. And I wanted to take charge of my life and have my own interests, which somehow translated itself into having an affair with Donnerly."

"It didn't work out too well, did it?" Cara grinned along with me.

"What can I say? Here I am," I laughed. "I must say, though, I was the captain of my ship right up until the time it sunk. Despite my dreams. Though, actually, I've never said that Charlie sunk the ship, only that he refused to believe that it was going down. Yup, I'm going to get better." I stretched, feeling happy.

"Why now? Why not last time?" Cara asked.

"Outside of not being ready, who knows? Maybe Alexander is the world's greatest shrink and only hit his stride this year. Maybe old age is bringing wisdom as advertised. Maybe the moon is in Aquarius. I get tired of forever discussing the 'whys' and never getting to the 'hows.' That's why I like AA. They're very big on 'hows.' Are *you* planning on getting well, or better?" I teased, and immediately wished I hadn't asked. Her eyes filled with tears, real ones, not the crocodile variety that were the specialty of Cara's house.

"No, I'm not," she sniffed. "I mean, I can't. I would like to get better, but I can't. I really can't do it."

She covered her face with her hands, sobbing in a quite different way from her usual shrieks and howls.

Dry, hollow, and echoing sounds twisted up from some cavern of sorrow deep inside her, and tears leaked through her fingers. I patted her shoulder gingerly, knowing that a warm supportive hug would only produce further torrents and I'd never discover what was bothering her.

"Why? Why can't you get better?" I asked and waited. The sobbing continued. "Why?" I persisted gently. "You're young and bright. You have so many options open to you. You haven't made any irreversible mistakes and you needn't take anyone but yourself into consideration. If you weren't tough and strong under all that noisy depression and helpless little-girl exterior, you'd be dead by now. It takes guts to survive your kind of craziness. OUR kind of craziness. Why can't you get better?"

Slowly two fingers of her right hand moved and a wet, red-rimmed eye peered through. A pear-shaped tear quivered on her lower lashes.

"Because, if I get well, I won't see Alexander anymore. He'll discharge me." She blinked her eye and the tear fell, immediately replaced by another.

"And I lo-o-o-ve him," she wailed, sounding like herself again.

Tell me something I didn't know about you, Cara. And don't know about myself. I folded my arms and watched her cry, wondering if I could share my own feelings and empathize with her and still be helpful. And feeling terribly embarrassed and silly and childish at finding myself, if not in the same boat with Cara, then certainly in the same troubled waters.

I was patting my pockets, hunting for a nonexistent cigarette in perfect imitation of Alexander when an unsolicited insight, perhaps my small share of the collective unconscious, flashed through my mind. Suppose I'd walked into my first AA meeting, encountered Alice and said, "I'm an alcoholic, and I just can't live without booze." And she'd said, "I know how you feel. Have a drink." Empathy would have bought me a one-way ticket down the tube, with no stopover in Buffalo. Adding my own lamentations of unrequited whatever-it-was to Cara's would only result in two dejected ladies reinforcing one another's despair and splashing tears on a litter-strewn, plastic, pseudo-imitation Parsons table.

"It's only transference," I said firmly. "And you know it."

"Is not," she said indignantly, emerging from behind her hands. "I really love him."

"Why?" I prodded, wondering how the staff could possibly enjoy this. It was like pulling wings off a fly.

"He's gorgeous," she said. "You can't deny he's gorgeous."

"Granted," I agreed. "He's young and relatively gorgeous if you are attracted to that type—which you aren't. You've told me enough about the kind of guy who turns you on and Alexander isn't it."

"I adore him and he does too turn me on," she insisted vehemently.

"You'd feel the same way if he was ninety-seven and looked like a warthog," I said blandly. "That's transference."

"I would not!" Cara shouted. "I know how I feel!"

"It's not *how* you feel; it's *what* you feel. And what you feel is transference," I said, hoping Cara wouldn't bring up counter-transference, which could only give her false hopes and me heartburn. There was no way in the world that I could convince the astute little Cara that transference/countertransference was less valid a basis for a meaningful relationship than, say, a shared passion for science fiction and Chicken Delight.

"What do you know about him? I mean, REALLY know about him, outside of his profession and a penchant for gray tweed? Huh, Cara?"

"He's a football freak."

"How do you know that?" I sighed, wondering why I didn't know that.

"He told me he went to a game once. On a Saturday."

"Terrific. And that makes him an enthusiast. For all you know, that was his day to do the macho bit. Maybe he's a secret cake-baker. Maybe he likes needlepoint. Or trout fishing. Or taking naps under the dining room table. You still don't know anything about him."

"He has two children," she stated.

"Three," I disagreed.

"Two," she insisted. "A boy and a girl. I've seen their pictures on his desk."

"Three. Two boys and a girl. I've seen the pictures, too."

"Two, dammit. There are TWO. Where the hell do you get the third one?" Her eyes darted with hot points of anger and I was ready to agree with her when I thought of something.

"Where do you sit when you go to the office?" I asked. "In the inside chair or the outside chair?"

"I sit in the inside chair next to the wall. Why?" she asked, calming down.

"Most of the time I sit in the outside chair next to the window," I explained. "When I'm trying to hide I sit in the inside chair. From the outside chair you can see that there are three kids in the picture. The little one is sort of falling off the photographer's table. Cute little brat. Looks like his father. Has on a gray tweed suit."

Cara stared blankly. "Are you kidding me?"

"Nope. The next time you go in the office, sit in the outside chair and you'll see."

"OHHHHHH!" She wailed, burying her head in the debris on the table. "I don't even know how many kids he has!"

"As long as he knows, that's all that matters." I went back to patting her shoulder. "Cheer up, kiddo. Everybody falls in love with their shrink and nobody ever knows how many kids he has. Or anything else. It isn't fatal. You'll get over it."

"No, I won't," she mumbled, "because it isn't trans-ference. It's true love and true love comes but once."

"Romeo and Juliet came but once and look what happened to them," I said tartly, realizing that I hadn't helped at all. I tried another approach.

"Look at it this way," I offered. "Even if you get better, Alexander will continue to see you for as long as you need him. He isn't going to suddenly cut you adrift the moment you show some tiny improvement or even a whole lot. By the time you're well enough for Alexander to discharge you, seeing him won't be nearly as important to you as it is now. In fact, terminating will probably be your idea."

"Ha! You're full of crap!"

"Dear sir or madam, you may be right," I gave up, reassessing my opinion of the staff. Why would anyone want a job where the people are more obstinate and impossible to deal with than first-graders on a field trip? No wonder Pomeroy weighed nine thousand pounds. Why shouldn't Dalton look frazzled? What a hell of a way to make a living. What perverse needs they must have.

"C'mon, Cara, let's go back upstairs. You can cry in the elevator."

I was depressed and peevish at having given it my best shot and failed so miserably. I was still dying for a cigarette and apprehensive about facing Tinkerbell. We had definitely taken advantage of the only person who probably wouldn't report us.

"You go," she demanded. "I want to stay here."

"You can't sit here all night crying with your head in the rubbish, Cara. I'll be damned if I'm going to go up there without you. Besides having to take all the heat, I'll have to tell Tinkerbell that you're suicidal in the cafeteria, which for once is appropriate behavior. Then she'll have to come down or send someone to rescue you and that will cause a big commotion. You don't want to cause a big commotion, do you?"

Her still-buried head jerked up and down violently. Yes, she did. That was what I was afraid of.

"Well, you pick some other time, some other way, and someone else to cause it with," I said. "We are going to go upstairs. Now."

I stood beside her and pulled at her arm. She snapped her arm and hunched over the table, determined to stay put. I could hear her teeth gritting. I walked behind her and wrapped my arms around her chest in the Red Cross "How to Save a Hostile Drowning Person" maneuver. I had her half raised from the chair when three men in white coats with stethoscopes hanging out of their pockets walked into the room. I let go and Cara fell, bouncing off the end of the chair and sliding under the table.

"For God's sake, Cara, get up!" I hissed as they walked toward us. "They're doctors!"

"Is something wrong? Can we help? I'm Dr. Marshall," one of them said. Cara crawled from under the table and I broke out in a cold sweat. Never again. God, just get me out of this one and I promise, never again.

"You startled me," I said, thinking fast. "My friend here," I went on, pointing at Cara who was brushing off her skirt, "is overwhelmed with grief. I was trying to persuade her to go home and rest. She just lost her mother."

"I couldn't lose my mother if I had a sex-change operation and moved to Cairo," Cara asserted, obviously deciding not to help. "Believe me, if that woman was paralyzed, she'd hunt me down in her wheelchair. People like my mother don't get lost. Your only hope is that, eventually, they'll get dead."

"See," I said, trying to save it. "Overwhelmed."

Somehow, Marshall didn't look convinced. "Where did this young lady's mother pass away?" he asked.

"Down the hall and around the corner in room, um, I forget," I said weakly.

"I doubt that," Marshall shook his head. "I'm in charge of this entire floor and we haven't lost any patients tonight."

"You're not trying," Cara smiled sweetly. "But the night is young. You'll think of something."

Marshall frowned sternly. "Who are you and what are you doing here at this hour?" he demanded.

"Actually, we work here," Cara said. "We're file clerks."

"The business offices are closed." Marshall fingered his stethoscope.

"We're overachievers. Work, work, work," Cara chirped.

I sat in Cara's chair and waited for it all to come crashing to a close. On the other hand, maybe it could still work out.

I rose from the chair and took Cara firmly by the arm. "We are leaving," I said. "Right now."

"You can't go." Marshall started after us. "You haven't told me who you are yet."

Cara pulled away from me and faced Marshall. "Think of us as a brief encounter, a fleeting moment of loveliness in your life, an urk—"

I gave Cara a sharp poke in the ribs and dragged her out of the cafeteria. "Goddammit, you nitwit! Move your ass before I kick it!"

I pushed her around the corner and up the stairs. Cara giggled as we leaped them two at a time and I was right behind her, swearing all the way. "Goddamn irresponsible nitwit kid . . . who needs it . . . and her goddamn mother. . . ."

I lurched against the buzzer, panting and clutching my pounding heart. Cara jiggled up and down on one foot, teary with laughter and equally breathless. Through the window I could see Tinkerbell hang up the phone as she buzzed us in. I approached the desk wishing I could apologize without feeling like a naughty two-year-old.

"Dr. Marshall just called from the fourth floor to ask if we had any patients missing," Tinkerbell said. "If you hadn't shown up at the door exactly when you did, I would have had to tell him that I had patients off the floor."

"And we would have been in a lot of trouble, huh?" Cara giggled.

"Oh," she said, casually riffling through some papers, "Alexander might have revoked some privileges temporarily and lectured you a bit, but I'm the one who would have been in trouble. At night this floor is my responsibility. You are my responsibility."

"Even when we deliberately do something stupid?" I asked, feeling more than ever like a naughty two-year-old. "That's not fair."

"Sure it's fair," Tinkerbell said. "It's more than fair. It's my job."

I watched her puttering around the desk, avoiding our eyes, waiting for something, waiting for what? Beside me Cara twitched and hopped.

"But that's dumb," she protested. "It's not like we're totally out of contact and wandered off. We didn't even leave the hospital. It's not like the time Jean What's Her Name, you know, the lady who used to see devils with watchdogs, slipped out of here during visiting hours and went jumping over snowdrifts in her quilted bathrobe and pink mules and took the seventy-three bus home to Brecksville. You people just sent someone to fetch her and that was that. What's with the big fuss about us?"

I slouched against the counter.

"I think we're supposed to know better, Cara," I said. "I think we're supposed to do better than a lady who sees devils with watchdogs."

"We didn't do anything so awful, Cassie."

"We didn't do anything so terrific, either, Cara. We can't go on just floating through life, getting into trouble and pleading insanity."

"Speak for yourself, Mrs. Barrett," Cara spit at me, eyes ablaze. "YOU'RE the one who has all the answers to everything. You're the one who has all your problems solved. What the fuck are you still here for, anyway? Why doesn't Alexander send you home to your husband, where you goddamn well belong? With Charlie and the kiddies and the house and the station wagon and the quiet little life in the quiet little suburb. Why the hell doesn't Alexander let you go?"

"Cara!" I reached for her arm. She pulled away. Tinkerbell moved closer, watching us.

"Every goddamn time you leave here to go to one of your freaky meetings someone in the parlor says, 'Isn't that wonderful? She's doing something about her problem.' Every goddamn time you walk out of here wrapped up in that scroungy old coat without any buttons, some turkey says how terrific it is that

you're going to a meeting even though you have a
headache or your legs are hurting, because you make
goddamn sure that everyone knows you feel lousy
and you're going anyway, and when you come in later
than anyone is allowed to be out, Tinkerbell always
says, 'How was it? How do you feel?' I heard about
the night you got lost driving back to the hospital
and Tinkerbell called Alexander and he was here waiting for you when you came in. Joanne told me and she
said, 'Wasn't that sweet of him? She's trying so hard.'

"Well, it wasn't sweet and it isn't terrific and it isn't
wonderful. It's lousy and it stinks and you make me
sick!" She turned and fled down the hall to her room,
arms flapping.

I stood quietly and watched her go, thinking with
some detached outer corner of my mind that she was
very upset. What I said to her had probably sounded
like a lecture, and coupled with Tinkerbell's reproof,
provoked this sudden rainstorm. Perfectly understand-
able. It would pass. Like all of Cara's thunderstorms,
it would pass. It was only when I tasted salt in the
corner of my mouth that I realized I was crying. Whatever made me think that trying to do the right thing
would end conflicts forever and make everyone love
me? Whatever made me think?

Tinkerbell touched me gently. "That's too bad," she
said.

"It's not that I don't understand how she feels,"
I said evenly, while the tears continued to pour. "I
felt the same way when my sister turned her back on a
guy she was crazy about but not ready for and went
to college. I detested her for being so mature and pragmatic. And farsighted. Funny thing, though, I always
thought that she did it because that was her nature
and she couldn't do otherwise. It never occurred to
me that it might have been painful, and she might
have been hurting, but she did it anyway. Never. Until right now. Damn!"

Tinkerbell smiled. "Do you mean 'damn' you didn't
know before, or 'damn' you know now?"

"Both," I said. "If I'd known, maybe I wouldn't

have been so hostile to her and perhaps we could have been better friends. And now that I do know, I'll have to change my attitude about her. I had her pigeon-holed as an uptight pain in the ass and now I'll have to change my mind. I hate changing my mind. A lot gets lost rounding the bend. It's like plunging off a familiar road into uncharted territory. No recognizable landmarks."

"Many people feel that way," Tinkerbell agreed.

"Well, to hell with them," I said, realizing that I had been involved in a "therapeutic" conversation and unwilling to go further. For now.

Tinkerbell thoughtfully refrained from any more probing. "Cara probably won't be angry in the morning," she said.

"Probably not. But it still won't be the same. With Cara, everybody is either THEM or US. I've taken one crummy step out of US, so with her I'm automatically THEM and that's where I'll stay unless I return to drinking, insanity, and suicide as a way of life. Then she'd feel that we were even again and all would be well. Jolly."

"Are you thinking of returning to drinking, etcetera?" she asked.

"Sure, I think about it. I'm in uncharted territory. Scary. And sometimes I wonder who the hell I think I am that I can just whoop-de-doo myself off to AA meetings and stay sober forever and ever. I know people who *aren't* flaky and have real guts who don't seem able to do that."

Tinkerbell frowned. "So you don't think you can stay sober forever and ever?" There was genuine concern in her voice and her expression.

Stop playing games, Cassie. Goddammit, stop. I smiled and patted her tiny hand. "Fortunately, I don't have to worry about Forever, Tink. I only have to worry about Today. That's all. And I think I can stay sober today. Okay?"

"That's AA?" she asked.

"That's AA," I answered. "Specifically designed for those with no guts."

"And for people who have guts but don't know it yet," she smiled. "Get on to bed. In a couple of hours there will be thirty student nurses in here asking about your childhood."

"Jesus, Tink! They've been here every day for a week! This place is turning into the seventh circle of hell. The Egyptians didn't have such plagues. Well, good night." I started down the hall and turned back.

"By the way," I said, stammering slightly. "About tonight . . ."

"Yes?"

"I'm, well I'm very, um . . . it won't happen again." She nodded and I fled down the hall, not unlike Cara.

I undressed in the dark, more out of habit than a desire not to wake the unwakable Caliguire. I had always undressed in the dark when late to bed, first in the room I shared with my sister, then in the room I shared with Charlie. What began as an uncommon courtesy quickly became a way to avoid looking at my body, which, in whatever light and whatever state, fat, thin, pregnant, nonpregnant, exercised, or sedentary, always appeared peculiar to me. From childhood on, I'd felt that everything below my neck was accidental, temporary, about to be nonfunctional or diseased and, most likely, belonged to someone else. I imagined that the real owner of the property would arrive someday to claim it and I wished he or she would hurry before the whole wretched mess collapsed altogether. I had an endless list of complaints for the landlord. Either remodel this structure or I will vacate, I would say.

Once I'd seen a marvelous story on "Twilight Zone" about creatures who existed solely as intellects—giant squishy brains enclosed in glass domes. They didn't seem to suffer in the least from their inability to enjoy pay toilets or Cracker Jacks, and for years thereafter I fantasized that I was one of those creatures unencumbered by a treacherous, uncomfortable body that required hauling around and tending to, a body that forever seemed to be moving in the opposite direction from where the real me, the part that began and ended above my neck, wanted to go. While the real me made plans for a life of prayer and work in a cloistered convent, the part south of the border went into heat and skipped off to a Spanish bordello.

My mind and body wouldn't recognize each other if they got on the same bus. Never the twain had met.

So I buttoned my pajama shirt over someone else's breasts and wondered about Cara. I hadn't been thrilled with the way I felt when I was lecturing her. I felt like THEM. I can't do that, I thought, not consistently. It would take more than I've got.

Maybe I could work out a way to be THEM part of the time, and US part of the time, to avoid most of the trouble and still have some of the fun.

What do THEY do for fun? Let's see. Charlie golfs and Mother cleans house. Yuk. Mary Kay studies. Nope, won't do. What does Bobby do? Beats me. He won't say. That sounds promising. I'll have to ask him.

"And what have YOU been doing for fun?" I asked myself out loud in my mother's voice.

"Well, I have been drinking myself into an early grave and earlier insanity," I answered.

"And has it been fun?" Mother-Me inquired slyly.

"No," I answered. "It has been a goddamn disaster."

"Then you have nothing to lose by trying another way, have you?" Mother-Me asked sweetly.

"Guess not."

I pulled up the covers, planning to ask Alexander if getting well meant that I would gradually become a composite of Mother, Charlie, him, Alice, and the last person I talk to on any given day. Would I disappear altogether? Was that Plan A, the purpose of it all, to extinguish me under everyone's blanket? Or was there perhaps another me, composed of past, present, and future, still an embryo, but waiting to bloom and grow in the sunshine. Cheering thought. Unrealistic, but cheering.

I fell asleep wondering what I would plead in days to come if I could no longer plead insanity. Probably guilty.

17

"Of all the crap!" Frank bellowed, walking into the parlor.

Joanne looked up from her crocheting. "What's the matter? What's happened?"

"That dumb broad Dalton told me I couldn't spend all day in the men's room, that's what!" Frank complained. "She said I have to sit out here as usual and com-mun-i-cate. With that." He pointed backward over his shoulder at the student nurse, who hovered, looking as though she was one insult away from bursting into tears.

"Go sit in the men's room anyway," Cara suggested.

Frank shook his head. "The bitch says that if I do, she'll have to put it on my chart, and Alexander will take it into consideration if I ever decide I want to get out of here."

"Who knows what they take into consideration?" I said, feeling fairly placid because Cara's storm had blown over. If anything, she was in an exceptionally good mood. "I think the discharge list is made up by throwing darts at the filing cabinet. If one hits your chart, out you go."

"I don't think that's the way it's done," said Joanne, who suffers from excessive reality contact.

"I don't give a damn how it's done!" Frank yelled. "I won't put up with another day of this kid following me around!"

The "kid" hung her head and sniffled.

"You're making her cry, Frank," Joanne pointed out in case he hadn't noticed.

"I don't want to make her cry," Frank mumbled, half ashamed. "I want to make her disappear." He slunk out of the parlor, followed by his very own little almost-nurse.

Joanne sighed. "Well, I know how he feels. My student arrived this morning right after Dalton gave me my insulin and I got so self-conscious with her there watching me eat that I almost choked to death on my toast."

"When I saw Alexander this morning, he asked me about something that I'd said to my nurse yesterday," Cara said. "I'd asked her not to repeat it to anyone. But she told someone who told Alexander and he got all hot and asked me about it." She reached for one of my cigarettes. "I was only kidding anyway."

"About what?" I asked, curious as to what it might be that Cara, the uninhibited, had decided was overly raw or perhaps too revealing for Alexander's ears.

"Never mind," she said with a smile to indicate that I wasn't to take it personally.

"It's going to be another long week," Joanne sighed again. "And it will take longer than that for everything to return to normal. I wonder if any of us will still be here."

"I can't imagine anyone improving enough to go home while they're here," I said, somehow appalled at the idea that I might be discharged before the students departed. I found them so distracting that I'd been unable to think, much less brood or ruminate or formulate an opinion or make a decision. Supposing I was on some arbitrary schedule known only to Alexander and his astrologer. Conceivably, I could be given the old heave-ho while the ninnies still had the run of the place.

"We'll all be here when the Strawberry Finks have returned to never-never land," I said.

"The who?" Joanne asked, dropping a stitch.

"Strawberry Finks. They look like ice cream sundaes and listen to every word we say. And, according to Cara, pass it on."

Cara giggled. "I like that name. It suits them. Look over there in the corner. Poor Norma keeps moving from chair to chair, trying to get away from hers. She hasn't got it together well enough to ask hers to run an errand, like we did with ours."

"And speaking of the darlings, here they come," I warned, watching our fluffy pink triplets approach.

Karen dropped a Mounds bar in my lap. "Here's your candy, but it's the last time," she said, as she flopped down next to me. "Dalton told us that we're not to leave the floor again to run errands. She said that you all have off-floor privileges and can get your own candy bars."

"Sweet of her to tell you that," I remarked.

"Would you like to go for a walk after lunch?" Karen asked.

"With you?"

"Sure."

"Nope."

"It would be good for you."

"I was afraid of that. Nope."

"We'll walk down to the square and go to the drugstore."

"I said I don't want to go. Why the drugstore?"

"I need some toothpaste. We could kill two birds with one stone."

"Kill your bird on your own time. I don't want to go."

"It's not good for you to be cooped up here all the time. You'll get sick."

"I wasn't cooped. I was committed. And, goddammit, I *am* sick. Cara," I shouted, "let's go to the ladies' room!"

Cara scrambled to her feet. "Okay," she said, and to the Finks, "don't move. We'll be right back."

She was right on my heels as I barged into the rest room and slammed the door. "We have to do something about this," I whispered for no particular reason. "They are driving me crazy. What made me say I was committed? I'm beginning to feel the way I did when I first got here, helpless and like a volcano about to erupt. This is not progress."

"We could all break out after lunch," Cara suggested. "A mass escape. What could they do if we all headed for the door at once?" Her eyes gleamed.

"No, that would leave them in here and all of us milling around in the parking lot freezing to death and missing our dinners. What we want is just the opposite. What could we do that would be effective? If we do something crazy, no one will pay any attention to us."

"When do they now?" Cara inquired.

"Hmm. I've noticed that even Dalton will pay attention if I'm serious and sensible and act like I'm thinking whatever it is through."

"Hey, we could go on a sit-down strike!" Cara burbled, hopping on one foot.

"What kind of sit-down strike could we pull off?" I asked. "Half of us never get up to begin with. What is it we could refuse to do? Get well? It would take three months before anyone noticed. Go to OT? Most of us have taken to telling Brunhilde where to go when she comes after us, anyway. Have shock treatments? They'd just borrow a few orderlies from elsewhere and turn this place into a real snake pit. Maybe we could refuse to eat?"

"No!" Cara shouted.

"Well, that's it," I said. "Anyway, if any of us were capable of a real sit-down strike, we wouldn't be here. It takes sustained effort. What is there that isn't a sustained effort, something, if possible that would require only twenty seconds and no effort at all?"

"How about a petition?" Cara asked. "You and I could write it up and it would just be a matter of getting everyone to sign it."

"That's the best idea yet," I decided. "I'll go back to my room and write it up. You pass the word to everyone who's functional or plans to be to meet in my room after lunch."

The door swung open and Karen's pale blue eyes and taffy hair appeared. She looked like she'd been decapitated on the doorjamb.

"Well, here you are," she gurgled. "I was worried about you."

"Hurry," I said to Cara, giving her a nudge out the door. "I can't hold out much longer."

"Okay," she said, and vanished in the direction of the parlor. I walked slowly toward my room with Karen, constant Karen, faithful Karen, at my side.

"What are we going to do?" Karen asked as we passed Ludwig and his shadow in the hall. He looked ready to give himself up to the conspiracy.

"I'm very tired, dear," I said. "I am going to take a nap. Why don't you play cards in the parlor and wake me up in about an hour? If I sleep too long, I won't sleep tonight. Okay?"

"You people take more naps," she complained. "I suppose it's a form of escape from your problems."

"That's right."

"And indicates depression."

"That's right."

"*Deep* depression?"

"Could be."

"Psychotic depression?"

"Possibly."

"Suicidal depression?"

"Hope not."

"When did you begin thinking of suicide, Mrs. Barrett?"

"Arrgh!"

"Are you thinking of suicide now?"

"I'm thinking of homicide, you nitwit. Get out!"

I threw myself on my bed and pulled the blanket over my head. I could feel Karen watching me. After a few moments of silence I heard the door close. I peeked cautiously over the edge of the blanket in case she was still there waiting for me to emerge. She was gone.

I removed the writing paper from my drawer and sat down.

Across the top page I scribbled: "Get rid of the kids or we'll burn the goddamn hospital down."

I crossed it out, and wrote underneath: "Remove the Strawberry Finks by noon or a bomb will go off in the shock treatment room."

Having discharged my hostility, I tore up the paper

and began again. I was writing when Cara slipped in the door, looking backwards over her shoulder like James Bond trapped in Goldfinger's den.

"I'm supposed to be taking a nap," she said. "How's it going?"

"Here, read this. Tell me if you have anything to add." I handed the paper to her.

She read aloud. "We, the undersigned, view the presence of student nurses as an invasion of our privacy and, further, as detrimental to the therapeutic process. We respectfully request their removal from the seventh floor. Immediately."

"Even sooner," Cara said. "I like it. What therapeutic process?"

"I could say 'the alleged therapeutic process,'" I smiled, "but why quibble? Did you tell everyone to come here after lunch?"

"Sure," Cara said. "I'm not positive how many will turn up, though. I got a lot of blank stares. Joanne, Frank, and Ludwig for sure. Norma and Abdul possibly. Margaret is suffering from ambivalence. She LIKES them."

"I know. They're an untapped resource, a new audience. I'll bet some of them even ask her where the bodies are buried."

"I asked the new lady with the red curls and orange rouge, but she just stared. I heard her talk to Dalton, though, and she seems to be in contact."

"In contact with Dalton anyway. That's not saying too much. Well, we'll just have to wait to see who shows. We can't really expect the people who are really out of it to do anything, or even to care."

"You know that older man who has the wife who looks like a fireplug and the kid who looks like a narc?" Cara asked.

"You mean the copper-plumbing salesman?" I said, wondering what a narc looks like. "I know who you're talking about."

"I heard that Dr. Fisher gave him three days to come out of his depression or he's going to start shock treatments."

"Three days? Why not two—or one—or an hour and a half? As long as Fisher is playing Beat the Clock, why not stand there with a stopwatch and give him ten seconds flat. Why three days?"

"Who knows? Maybe it's his lucky number. Anyway, he might be here. I told him about it and his eyebrows quivered."

"Terrific. What made me think we were going to accomplish anything with a petition signed by people whose only sign of comprehension is a quivering eyebrow?"

Cara and I ate our lunches together in her room, accompanied by probing questions composed by Karen and the redhead.

"Have you ever considered going into law?" I asked Karen.

"It's almost time for occupational therapy," Karen remarked, glancing at her student nurse special.

Cara wigwagged at me behind Karen's back, looking as though she was trying to bring me in for a three-point landing on an aircraft carrier.

"Wrong," I yawned. "It's time for another nap. Chewing has exhausted me."

"But you just woke up," the redhead said. "You can't take another nap."

"Sure I can," Cara and I said simultaneously.

"See you later," I waved to Cara and walked across the hall to my room, closing the door behind me. Several minutes later Cara slithered into the room. Right behind her came Joanne on tiptoe.

"What are we doing?" Joanne whispered, then jumped at the sharp knock on the door. Cara answered the door to find Ludwig and Frank arguing in the hallway.

"What do you mean, this is dangerous?" Frank was asking Ludwig. "This should be right up your alley, sneaking around hatching plots, having secret meetings, outwitting the staff. Not that outwitting the staff is such a big deal. I had a bigger challenge when a water main broke on Prospect and I had to improvise a reroute.

THAT was a big deal, outwitting the city of Cleveland."

"This *is* dangerous," Ludwig's voice rose. "THEY know who we are. There could be reprisals."

"THEY are psychiatric personnel, Lud," Frank snorted, "not the Gestapo."

"When the reprisals begin, remember who warned you," Ludwig insisted.

"Hush, Ludwig," I said. "THEY'll hear you."

"You sound just like Ludwig," Cara commented, and indeed the dividing line between Ludwig's fantasy THEM and our real THEM had dissolved. I watched Ludwig and wondered how paranoids ever learn to distinguish between their fantasies and the people who really are out to get them. What happens to a paranoid who gets sued for divorce or fired from a job? Does he show up in his doctor's office saying, "See, I told you so!" Does the doctor try to explain that while wives and employers are indeed out to get him and that is known as reality, Martians, Communists, and the Mafia are not and that is major mental illness. Why should the patient believe him? The reality of it is that wives, employers, Communists, and the Mafia all exist and are capable of malevolence. And just because Martians have yet to appear on "Meet the Press" doesn't mean that they're not out there waiting to conquer the third planet from the sun, God knows why. Unless they need the water and are hard up for amusement.

Another rap on the door and Cara opened it a crack to admit Norma, who skulked through soundlessly and stood in the middle of the room glaring and clutching her purse to her bosom.

"We're glad you came, Norma," I said, trying to put her at ease. Actually she was perfectly at ease doing what she did best, radiating hostility and weirdness. I was the one who was shaking with discomfort, and wondering why I ever started this. "I think we should just sign this and that will be all there is to it. Then Cara and I will present it to Dalton and—"

Another tap at the door. I was beginning to feel like the leader of the local cell.

Abdul wafted in and seated himself on the floor. "Shazam," he observed.

"He's in better shape than I thought," Frank remarked. "I didn't think he understood anything that's going on. I wonder if his doctor knows."

"Shazam, Shazam!" Abdul yelled.

"Don't worry. We won't tell anyone," Frank assured him. "But I'll stop feeling guilty when I beat you at poker."

I handed my pen to Cara who leaned over my desk to sign the petition. Another knock. We all looked at the door, startled. I opened it to find the copper-plumbing salesman surrounded by student nurses. I slammed the door quickly and the knocks became more insistent.

"Go away," Frank bellowed.

"Let us in," Karen called. "You're not taking a nap."

"Yes, we are," I countered. "It's a form of group therapy."

"Let us in," she insisted. Abdul moved in front of the door, effectively blocking it.

"What are you doing?" Karen cried, evidently frantic at the idea that something secret and unobserved by the official observers might be going on behind my closed door. Abdul began to waver as the students pushed against the door in a concentrated effort. To discover what? A group debauch? Human sacrifice in progress?

Frank motioned to Joanne. "Here, give me a hand with this," he said, pushing the dresser I shared with Caliguire in the direction of the door. They propped the dresser against the doorjamb, and Ludwig, inspired by Frank's take-charge attitude, lifted the only chair in the room to the top of the dresser.

"There! Try to get through that!" he yelled at the door. Surprisingly, it looked as though they might. The door wobbled on its hinges and cracked open a fraction of an inch.

Frank looked around for another piece of furniture. There was none. With a yodel of glee Cara began dragging Mrs. Caliguire's bed toward the door. "Here," she said, huffing and puffing away. "Help me."

Ludwig and Frank helped her swing the bed against the door while Caliguire, oblivious, snored on.

"There," Frank said. "That should hold it." And it did, long enough for us to sign the petition. Abdul declined to accept the pen, but stood guard over Caliguire. When he thought no one was looking, he solicitously pulled the blanket over her shoulder and patted smooth the sheet.

Having signed the petition, we gazed at one another in the spirit of Now What?

"I'll just take this down to the desk," I said bravely. "You can all go back to doing whatever it is you were doing."

Frank and Ludwig pushed Caliguire back to her gloomy niche, Joanne removed the chair, and Cara and I shoved the dresser to one side. Cautiously we opened the door and peered out into the empty hall.

"They gave up," Cara said, crestfallen with disappointment. She had been looking forward to a noisy and dramatic scene, a sort of irate villagers against Dr. Frankenstein confrontation, complete with torches.

I walked down the hall with Cara tagging along behind me. Everyone else melted away to their respective rooms.

"Well," Dalton remarked as we approached the desk. "If it isn't the revolutionaries." She turned her back on us and busied herself with the afternoon medication tray. She rattled the pills as she dropped them into paper cups. Through the partition I could see the students sitting in the parlor, heads together, whispering.

"We just want to give you this petition, Miss Dalton. All you have to do is pass it on to whoever is responsible for having the students here. We are not trying to cause anyone any trouble. We just felt we weren't being listened to and we have a right to be heard. That's all."

Dalton reached for the paper with one hand while

continuing to pour pills with the other. "What do you think you've already caused, if it isn't trouble?" she asked. "The students are upset, the floor is disrupted, medication is late. What do you call this?"

"The voice of the people," Cara answered. "Democracy at work."

"Games," Dalton snapped. "Silly, adolescent games. You people don't make the rules here. When the patients start making the rules it isn't democracy, it's anarchy."

"I agree," I said, "but we aren't requesting anything unreasonable. We sincerely believe that the presence of the students is not beneficial to the patients and we chose this way of saying so. Please, just pass on the petition. Okay?"

"I'll pass it on," Dalton agreed, "and of course, it will be in your charts anyway, but I assure you it will do no good. You cannot dictate policy in this hospital."

"Well, at least our feelings will be on record." I turned away and hesitated. "Look, Miss Dalton, I know this is an aggravation to you, but all other things aside, isn't it better for us to do something positive and actually harmless, than to continue to grumble and hide out in the bathrooms? This effort required a certain amount of discussion, agreement, and teamwork. I think everyone whose name is on that petition should get a gold star for occupational therapy today."

"You would," she grumbled, turning her back on us again.

"I am becoming a positive thinker," I whispered to Cara as we walked off.

Although the petition was never again discussed, the Finks disappeared from the floor. When asked, Dalton sternly replied that the students had been rotated to another service, according to hospital schedule. Our petition had nothing to do with it.

We wisely refrained from gloating.

18

Tinkerbell hit the buzzer and I shivered my way through the door, stamping snow off my boots.

"I'm frozen to the bone," I chattered. "I wish we had a roaring fire in the parlor."

"We almost did," she said. "Mr. Michaels left a cigarette smouldering in the sofa. Abel put it out with a vaseful of mums. Why don't you stand on the register to thaw out?"

"I remember doing that when I was a kid. My feet fried before my kneecaps unfroze."

"Well, a cup of coffee wouldn't hurt," she smiled. "The kitchen is officially closed but you may go in if you like." She tossed me a key chain studded with keys of all sizes.

"Why, thanks," I said, delighted, feeling like a friend. "I'd love a cup of coffee. Would you like one?"

"Sure. Sugar, no cream."

Minutes later I returned to the nurses' station with two steaming cups.

"How was your meeting?" Tinkerbell asked, sipping.

"Fine," I replied. "The speaker was a man about my age. Evidently his drinking career was characterized by countless vain attempts to be Errol Flynn. He drank, gambled, loved and left women, quit jobs when he was bored, drifted around the country, even punched out a cop who tried to arrest him on a drunk-driving charge. He made it all sound very jolly and exciting. He certainly enjoyed talking about it."

"If it was all so jolly, why did he quit?" Tink asked, squinting through the steam.

"An excellent question," I grinned. "One doesn't give up the good life for no reason. It seems that his macho dream came to a crashing conclusion one night when he came out of a blackout and found himself draped around a police officer crying because his mother had run off and left him when he was five. The policeman told Gary to knock off the sob story. He said that *his* old lady had run off too, so what, and threw him in the drunk tank. It continued to happen. Every time he had a beer, a shot, anything, he ended up with his arm around some stranger's neck crying for momma."

"He must have been frantic," Tink remarked.

"He was destroyed. Anyway, Gary worked with a man who wasn't shy about saying he was in AA. Gary told him that his drinking was getting out of hand, though he couldn't then tell him in what way. The friend brought him to AA and he's been sober for eighteen months. And now he can talk about what happened to him. That impressed me. I doubt I'll ever have the ability to be that open."

"Give it time," Tink said. "When you're more comfortable, you'll loosen up. There's no hurry."

"I'm not actually worried about it. Still, I doubt I'll ever stand up in a group and talk casually about my drinking behavior. I know I'll never reach the point where I can laugh in that one-step-short-of-bragging way. But then, it's usually the men who do that. The women are more apt to discuss feelings."

Tink nodded in agreement. "Women are more comfortable in dealing with feelings than men are."

"That's true. But it's more than that. Women never get together to slap each other on the back and swap drinking stories. You never hear anyone say, 'Wow, she can really put away the booze.' Not with any admiration anyway. A man who boozes, brawls, and chases can swagger around like a Hemingway hero no matter what he feels inside, and often people will react

to him that way. A woman who does the same thing
. . . well, there's a name for it. A man with a drinking
problem can still feel like a man. A woman with the
same problem feels less than a woman. I know I did."

"I can understand why you would feel that way,"
Tink said. "Do you still?"

"No," I said firmly. "Not since the first time I talked
to Alice. She gave me one of those looks of hers, very
direct and semifierce, and said, 'Don't ever forget that
alcoholism is a disease, Cass, and a disease is a disease.
It has no more to do with weakness of character or
moral turpitude than cancer does.' I bought it. I
bought it because it's true. I can feel sorry about a
disease, but I can't feel shame."

"So you aren't ashamed of it?" Tink said.

"Not anymore. It wouldn't do me much good anyway. Alice told me that if I want to whimper and
whine and slink around feeling guilty, I can, but she
doesn't intend to watch me wring my hands or listen
to my delusions of rottenness. She called the game before I had a chance to play. How about that?"

"I think I like Alice." Tink smiled.

"So do I. She's blunt and direct with an iron core
of honesty that I trust absolutely. She cares enough
to tell me what I need for survival, not just what I
would like to hear. You and Alice are dissimilar,
Tink, yet you both impress me as strong people who
really care."

Tinkerbell waved her hand in a dismissing gesture.
"I've always been surrounded by strong people," she
said. "Some of it must have rubbed off. Someday, I'll
tell you about it."

"When you're more comfortable, you'll loosen up,"
I grinned.

She laughed. "That's what's wrong with words of
wisdom. They're easier to deliver than to act on. Okay
Cassie, I'll play fair. I also have a brother who lives
in California. His name is John and he's two years
younger than I am. I learned about disease in nurse's
training, about faulty defenses and destructive be-

havior. And, of course, I needed to learn concepts. But nearly everything I learned about the beauty and potential of human beings, I learned from John."

"You two are close?" I asked, wanting them to be. *Bobby. Bobby.*

"Emotionally very close," she replied. "Though we write less than we once did and seldom phone, our communications seem to have a sustaining quality. I've heard from him only three or four times since the last big earthquake in California. I called to see if he was all right and he said he'd weathered the quake with less fright then he'd felt in Ohio during tornado alerts. He said, 'I finally found out how fast I can strap on my legs.' And he laughed."

"His legs!" I said, astonished.

Tinkerbell leaned both elbows on the counter. Slender fingers framed her tiny heart-shaped face.

"Johnny was born without legs," she said, "and with only one arm. His left arm ended in a flipperlike appendage just above the elbow. It had to be amputated."

"How awful," I said quickly, "and how awful for your poor mother," I added, thinking of my own three with their healthy, sturdy-limbed bodies.

"That's exactly what everyone said to my mother. 'You poor thing,' they would say, and Mother would smile and say, 'I don't know what you're talking about.' Not that she denied that anything was wrong. She took Johnny to the best doctors we could afford and followed their advice. She never seemed to suffer from the guilt that's so common in parents of handicapped children or, if she did, she kept that particular burden to herself. She never allowed it to spill over onto Johnny and me and she never allowed me to feel guilty for being whole. 'John is John and you are you,' she would say to me, 'and you both have strengths and limitations. Take care of your own life. John can take care of his.' Mother never felt sorry for herself. She never felt sorry for John."

"I couldn't do that," I interrupted. "I would hover."

"Most of us would," Tink agreed, "but Mother told

me once that her primary obligation was to prepare
John for the time when she wouldn't be there to help
him. My father wasn't able to handle the situation.
He left when Johnny was six weeks old." Tinkerbell
suddenly laughed, warming to a memory. "When
Johnny was fitted with his first legs, Mother acted as
though the wheel had just been invented. They were
enormously expensive contraptions and required a
long training period. Mother was there every minute,
filling Johnny's head with visions of what he could
accomplish with his new legs. The visions all added
up to freedom and independence. Well, as you are
acutely aware, Cassie, freedom and independence can
be frightening. Exploring brave new worlds can be
thrilling, but usually the brave new world is a strange
rocky place and must be explored one step at a time.
So it was with John."

"What happened?" I asked, leaning on the counter.

"At first, when Johnny wanted something, he
would ask me to get it for him as he always had.
Mother would stop me, saying, 'Your legs are as good
as your sister's. Get it yourself.' And Johnny would
pout and go without. Mother would say, 'I'm going to
the drugstore for a soda. If you'd like to come along,
put on your legs.' If Johnny refused, Mother and I
went alone and didn't bring home a soda for Johnny.
Mother hid the wheelchair. Eventually, with grum-
bling, Johnny began doing things for himself. Mother
forced him to learn to strap on his legs with one hand.
He would call to her to come help him and she would
call back, 'I'm cooking your breakfast. You'll have to
dress yourself.' Once Mother and I had the flu. She
tucked me in bed next to her, and said to Johnny,
'Thank God we have you to take care of us!' He
fetched and carried for nearly a week, even changed
the bed when I was sick in the middle of the night.
By the time we were well, Johnny was the man of the
house. Mother used to tell him to forget what he
didn't have and concentrate on what he did. He'd say,
'What do I have?' And she'd say, 'A good mind, a
kind heart and an Irish gleam in your eye, more than

enough to get you through the world.' So he grew and coped. And laughed. One day we were at the art museum and one of those awful, officious ladies walked up to Johnny and said accusingly, 'You're crippled!' as if his being handicapped was a personal affront. Johnny grabbed her hand and kissed it, nearly sending the lady into fits. 'How can I thank you, dear lady!' he exclaimed. 'But for you I never would have known!' "

I laughed. "He sounds very special."

"Oh, he is," Tink agreed. "Once, when he was in the ninth grade he came home from school complaining that his history teacher was such a mean, bitter bitch that her class was an agony for everyone in it. No one liked her, he said, and most of the kids got even by pulling every rotten trick they could think of. If only she'd loosen up, just once, he speculated, the kids wouldn't be so hard on her. Then he thought about it for a while. 'You know,' he finally said, 'I think that everyone is handicapped in one way or another. Mine just shows.' "

She reached for her coffee cup and sipped slowly.

"I learned from him, Cassie, and from Mother I learned that everyone needs help and support until they get their legs under them and then a loving, but firm shove and lots of encouragement once they do. I learned that facing reality makes most of us stronger and that everyone has the ability to do *something* for himself, no matter how small and inconsequential that something may appear to others. And I firmly believe that everyone, all of us, have the ability to look beyond ourselves and care for another human being. There are exceptions, of course. There are the incurably insane, those whose lack of contact is complete, but most of us, even the sickest, have resources."

"Shredded and shattered and buried though they might be," I sighed. "Now I understand why you're so compassionate and seem to read people so well. But you'll never know how it feels to be, um, defective."

"Are you sure about that, Cassie?"

"Of course I'm sure. You're one of the most caring, involved, and giving people I've ever met."

She leaned closer. "If I'm so caring, so involved, why do I choose to work at night when there are relatively few patients around? Why don't I work days? That's when the action, the heavy involvement, takes place. That's nitty-gritty nursing. Why don't I do that?"

"Why—why—" I stammered. "I don't know. Why don't you?"

"Because I have limitations like everyone else," she said, eyes warm and steady on mine. "I prefer involvement on a limited basis, caring on my terms, the way I handle it best, the way I'm most effective."

Disappointment must have played on my face. She placed her little hand over mine.

"Don't idealize me, Cassie. Don't make the mistake of comparing my outsides with your insides. You know only that I appear to be all strength and self-actualization, all commitment and serenity. I have weaknesses also. I know what they are and accept them and work to change the few I can. But don't place me, or anyone else, on a pedestal. People aren't meant to live on pedestals and, in comparison, you'll always fall short. And, inevitably, you'll be disappointed when the pedestal dweller turns out to be human after all." She smiled. "I'm standing on this side of the counter, Cassie, and from where I'm standing, I have a clear view of *your* strengths."

I smiled. "You are like Alice, Tink. She shared a part of herself with me, too. You care."

"I care," she nodded. "Would you like some more coffee?"

"No, thanks," I said. "I'd better go to bed. Dalton will be in bright and early to throw me out so she can prepare Caliguire for her shock treatment. Caliguire doesn't talk, but she's beginning to snap, crackle, and pop."

"Oh, Cassie," Tink called after me. "I nearly forgot, we've been so busy talking. Cara asked me to tell you to stop in before you go to bed. She had a call from her mother this evening and got upset. You don't have to do it. She's probably asleep by now, anyway."

Damn, I thought. I wanted to pull my blanket up to my nose and think about how the brightest full moon has a dark side, so why should I walk around feeling like the universe's sole permanent eclipse.

"Okay," I decided. "I'll stop in her room for a minute. And hope she isn't crying. Sometimes Cara's crying dries up my tears, and I need them."

Quietly, I pushed open the door. "Cara," I whispered, "are you awake?"

"I'm awake." The voice, thin and whiny, floated from a far corner of the room.

"What are you doing? Why aren't you in bed?"

I groped for the wall switch and turned on the light. Cara sat on the floor, face to the wall, head bent over her lap.

"What are you doing?" I asked again, becoming annoyed at her inexhaustible need for dramatic variations on the depression theme. "Get off the floor," I demanded.

"No," she answered, like any normal two-year-old.

"C'mon," I said, softening at the pathetic slope of her thin shoulders. *I've felt this way, lost and abandoned and wanting to hide in the dark, hoping someone will care enough to come looking for me.*

"We'll go ask Tinkerbell if we can make hot chocolate," I suggested.

"Don't want to," she said.

Damn, now what? I've tried the soft approach because I care and the hard approach because you make me angry. I'm too tired to be objective. What now, Cara?

I leaned over to pat her shoulder, then recoiled with shock and a cold horror that writhed up my spine. Her hands rested limply in her lap and her wrists were covered with blood.

"What have you done?! My God! Cara, what are you doing?!"

She stared at me with large tearless eyes.

"Killing myself. I'm killing myself," she said listlessly. Her face was yellow and sunken and years older.

"Jesus Christ!" I snapped out of my shock. "Stay right here," I ordered her, fearful for some reason that she would run, flee, disappear. I ran out of the room.

"Tink," I yelled, halfway down the hall. "Come quick! Cara's in trouble!" As upset as I was, I couldn't bring myself to scream "Suicide" down the seventh-floor hall, for fear of rousing all the sleeping innocents. Then, too, Cara's folly might catch on, like hula hoops. "Come quick," I yelled again, and she was already on her way.

"What?" she asked.

"Cara . . . slashed her wrists . . . in her room . . . on the floor," I explained breathlessly. Tink patted me in passing and sped into Cara's room. I followed one step behind.

Tinkerbell kneeled on the floor next to Cara examining the wrists she meekly extended.

"Superficial," Tink said quietly. "Lots of blood, but the cuts aren't very deep." I had a feeling that her words were more for me than for Cara, who didn't seem to be listening.

"What did you use, Cara?" Tinkerbell asked. There was no answer. "You have to tell me," she said sternly. "Now, what did you use?"

"My car keys," Cara whispered.

"Your car keys?" I said. "You mean you've been sitting here in the dark hacking away at your wrists with your car keys?"

Cara nodded yes. A sudden picture exploded through my mind—nine-year-old Bobby lighting a firecracker, throwing it into a milk bottle, and running like hell. It was just that dumb.

"Well," Tink said briskly, "you'll have to come up to the desk so I can take care of that. Right now."

Cara struggled to her feet. "Will Dr. Alexander be angry?" she asked in her baby voice.

"Who knows," Tink shrugged and led her out of the room. She glanced at me as she passed, almost imperceptibly shaking her head. I knew the look was meant to be significant—but of what?

Tinkerbell washed the myriad surface scratches with

an antiseptic, holding Cara firmly as she flinched. As Tink wrapped gauze around her wrists Cara began to look something close to cheery. I had to admit that the bandaged wrists were rather impressive, if you happened to be the type impressed by suicide attempts. Unfortunately, I am. You can have your Mount Everest climbers and first men on the moon. Their risks pale in comparison to the suicide attempter, frantically acting out his death wish, desperate to outmaneuver the rescuers who, hopefully, will beat down the door just in time to save him, not that he wants to be saved, you understand. But if people won't let you alone to die in peace, what can you do? Raw nerve and timing. And cowards need not apply.

"We'll take the bandages off first thing in the morning," Tink said, sounding as though she was giving a lecture on a boring subject. A shadow of disappointment crossed Cara's face.

"All you'll need after this is some antibiotic ointment," Tink went on. She tied the gauze and patted the neat bandage, then turned her back on Cara and reached for a chart. Cara watched her, looking like one of the Send-money-or-this-child-will-starve waifs featured on foreign missions' guilt posters. Tink wrote a quick note, then turned back to Cara.

"There," she said briskly. "Now, Cara, if you ever decide to do this again, don't use your car keys. You can't possibly kill yourself that way and you just might damage the tendons in your wrist permanently."

I gasped at Tinkerbell's cold approach. Cara's eyes blinked with astonishment. "Furthermore," Tink said, "it's almost impossible to commit suicide with a horizontal slash regardless of what instrument you use." She held Cara's wrist, palm up, lightly in her hand. "If you are serious, take a sharp, straight-edge razor and cut here, vertically, along the vein." She traced the pale blue vein with a pink-polished fingernail. Cara snatched her arm away.

"You're making fun of me!" she accused.

"Quite the opposite," Tink assured her. "I am taking you very seriously. You say that you have decided to kill yourself. I'm showing you an efficient way of doing just that. If, in fact, that is what you want to do. If it isn't, I see no reason for you to mutilate yourself inadvertently."

"I hate you!" Cara yelled, and fled down the hall, sobbing. She paused at the door of her room. "I hate both of you," she screamed.

"For Chrissakes, shaddup!" Frank's sleep-blurred voice floated out into the hall.

"Shaddup yourself!" Cara hiccuped. Norma emerged from her room, weaving perilously and hanging on to the wall.

"How are we supposed to sleep in this madhouse?" she demanded furiously, "with lunatics screaming in the middle of the night—"

"I'm not a lunatic," Cara responded. "I'm depressed."

"Like hell!" Norma shouted into the dark cavern of Cara's room. "You don't need a shrink. You need someone to turn you over his knee and give you a good old-fashioned—"

Cara appeared at the door of her room, hands on hips and chin thrust forward. "You and who else. . . ." she began.

Tinkerbell deftly bridged the closing gap between them.

"Ladies," she said softly, "it's time for everyone to go to bed. Right now."

Norma and Cara glared at each other for fifteen seconds before Cara vanished back into her cave and Norma wobbled into her room.

"Good night, ladies," Tink called, and walked to the nurses' station, where I stood shaking my head in amazement.

"How do you do that, Tink?" I asked. "You never raise your voice."

"Easy," she grinned. "I just told them that they wouldn't be allowed to do something they didn't want to do anyway."

"You are the O. J. Simpson of the seventh floor," I laughed. "Graceful and good at what you do."

"Your praise is acknowledged and appreciated," she smiled.

"I'll miss you when I go home," I said abruptly, flushed with embarrassment at having laid my pygmy emotion all naked and quivering on the counter.

"I'll miss you, too," she said quickly. "But you'll have Alice."

"True. But having Alice won't prevent me from wishing I could see you. It's more than support and encouragement. I like you." I paused awkwardly, then rushed on. "How old are you, Tink?"

"Twenty-seven. Why?"

"Maturity," I sighed, "seems to have very little to do with age. Alice is fifty-one and she told me she grew up five years ago. I'd like to call her and ask her to be my sponsor. Would you mind?"

"If she wouldn't mind, I certainly wouldn't," Tink replied. "Use the patient phone."

I fished through the trash dump of my purse for Alice's phone number.

A sleepy voice answered the phone. "Yes?"

"It's Cassie. Were you asleep?" I asked, suddenly aware of the late hour.

"I get up for work every morning at five A.M. What do you think?" Her voice lost its brittle edge. "What's the problem, Cassie? Are you drinking?"

"No," I said, chagrined. "I'm at the hospital. How could I drink?"

"Well, you could have gotten into the rubbing alcohol. What's the matter, then?"

"I'm calling to ask you to be my sponsor," I said, wishing I had waited until morning.

"So the spirit moved you in the middle of the night, and you couldn't wait until the sun came up." There was a low, throaty, chuckling noise. "I think you're an alcoholic, kiddo. Impulsive."

"I apologize," I said, smiling. "Will you be my sponsor?"

"And tenacious," she said, with more throat gurgles. "Before the excitement of your inspiration carries you off in the clouds, let me tell you that not everyone likes the way I sponsor. I'm tough. No sympathy. If you want a hand-holding bleeding heart, you'll have to look elsewhere."

"Of course I'd like a hand-holder. I thrive on it. But I like the way you stay sober and your attitude about it. That's what I want. What do I do?"

There was a long silence. "Okay, the first thing you do is never call me in the middle of the night unless you're on the verge of taking a drink. Then, call me anytime. If you have a medical problem, call your doctor. If you have a legal problem, call a lawyer. If you have an emotional problem, see your shrink. If your marriage is coming apart at the seams, see a counselor. If your kids are sending you shrieking into the closet, see . . . whoever it is people with kids see. I am an alcoholic, not the Oracle of Delphi. I know about booze. I can't solve your problems. If you want to talk to me, come to meetings. You'll find me at three a week, and I'll be happy to listen or provide a shoulder for a ten-minute cry, or give you a pat on the head. On nights when I'm not at meetings, don't call me after nine o'clock. That's when I go to bed."

"You would have made a marvelous marine drill instructor, Alice," I said.

"Change your mind?"

"Nope," I said with bravery I didn't feel. *Good thing you're not a surgeon, Alice. Someday I'd find myself biting a bullet while you methodically saw off my leg.*

"Another thing," she continued. "If you do drink, tear up my number and forget my name. I won't talk to you drunk."

"Okay, okay," I said, startled. Her toughness was far less appealing directed at me.

"And until you come home from the hospital, read part of the book every day," she ordered.

I sighed. "I don't like the book, Alice."

"I didn't say like it," she said, patiently. "I said read it. And don't forget about nine o'clock. That way you get self-discipline and I get my sleep."

"A mutually advantageous arrangement," I said,

thinking that I'd already had self-discipline preached at me unceasingly during four years at St. Theresa's Academy, always by nuns who regularly lost their tempers, their manners, and their minds. "Good night, Alice," I said.

"Good night, Cassie," she yawned. "See you Saturday."

I waved my good night to Tinkerbell, who sat at the desk making notations on charts, and walked slowly to my room.

What have I gotten into? I thought. "Whatever it is, I'm in."

In my room I picked up the book and randomly read a section. It had something to do with taking a moral inventory, a terrifying and insurmountable project, I decided, especially for one who had been busily stockpiling sins.

19

I stopped at the nurses' station on my way to the parlor. Dalton looked up from her chart and smiled. "That color looks nice on you," she smiled, showing the gold caps on her back teeth.

"Thanks," I said, wondering how to take the compliment. I was dressed like a depressed Fascist, entirely in black. I decided that she merely wanted to say something nice to me and gave her an A for effort.

"I'm going to go home this afternoon for a visit," I said casually. "I'll see the kids, make dinner, stuff like that. I won't be back until after my meeting."

"Okay. Be sure to sign out." She went back to her

chart and I breathed a sigh of relief. No searching questions, no "meaningful" statements about my children, no allusions to a permanent return home. Just "I'm going" and "Okay." Like a real person.

In the parlor Frank silently handed me a section of the newspaper in the manner of a man who is accustomed to sharing the morning paper over the breakfast table. I settled back to read the review of a play recently opened at the Hanna Theater, one of those English imports fraught with symbolism that reviewers regard with awe and audiences with confusion. This one involved two emaciated men, one of them hungry, a deathbed wish, and a bronze crocodile.

"Listen to this," Frank remarked. "A man in Elyria is divorcing his wife because she allows her pet goat the run of the house. And she says that the goat is more companionable than her husband. And smells better." He laughed.

Gloria waved to Frank from the doorway, summoning him to the interview room.

He was back before I finished the article, holding a pink slip in his hand, and grinning from ear to ear.

"Well, I guess I'd better call Barbara and tell her to come and get me. I'm already packed."

"Frank, you're going home!"

"Yup," he grinned.

"How do you feel about it? Did Alexander say you're ready?"

Frank shook his head. "No, Alexander didn't say I was ready. *I* said I was ready. I told him I wanted to go home."

"What about your job?" I asked.

"That's what he wanted to know. I said, 'If I can't drive a bus, I can't drive a bus.' That's all there is to it. I'll have to learn to live with it. It could be worse. Some guys my age aren't working at all. I am. It's as simple as that." He grinned, suddenly self-conscious. "Better call Barbara," he mumbled and started for the phone.

I looked after him, smiling. *So it's as simple as that, Frank? Eight weeks in the funny farm, fifteen shock treatments, hours of agonizing introspection, and it's as simple as that. It isn't, it wasn't, and you are something else.*

I stared over my newspaper, picturing Frank on the phone in the hall softly telling Barbara to pick him up, and hurry. I smiled as I saw Barbara's excitement. I could almost hear her say, "Now? You're really coming home? Right now? I'll be there in a half hour."

I saw Frank smiling as he hung up, and frowning as apprehension settled in to smother his excitement. Then shaking his head vigorously, shaking it gone. And straightening his shoulders, lifting his head, his decision made and not to be retracted regardless of the apprehension, regardless of the price. And the excitement returning, not as great as it was at first, tempered by the reality of 'What will happen? How will I do?' but there nonetheless. I could just imagine. More than imagine. Somehow I knew. I tuned in on Frank in his state of developing health, and felt warm, and quietly strong, solid and steady somewhere deep inside myself. So this is what it feels like, I mused, and cuddled myself, mightily pleased.

I looked up to see Alexander standing at the nurses' station, smiling faintly and writing rapidly on a chart. Probably Frank's.

Aren't we all pleased with ourselves? And don't we all have reason to be?

Alexander handed the file to Dalton and strode briskly across the hall to the interview room. I wanted to be called next. It would be nice to enter the interview room with good feelings to report and examine and explore. Alexander would smile and the air would be full of positive charges. I would go home for the afternoon, full of energy and affection for the kids, ready to cope with anything. Well, almost anything. As long as it didn't involve stray animals, arithmetic, or mysterious red spots.

"Where's Cara?" Gloria leaned against the wall squinting and looking put upon. "Where is that girl? The doctor wants her right now, this minute, in a hurry."

"I haven't seen her, Gloria. She's probably in her room or in the ladies' room," I answered, thinking that I hadn't seen Cara all morning.

"I'll go look in her room," Gloria sighed. "But she should be in here. You people are all supposed to be in here in the mornin' so a body don't have to tramp all over the floor huntin' you up. When the doctor has to wait he gets mad and yells at Dalton and she gets mad and yells at me."

"I never hear anyone yell at you, Gloria," I interrupted.

"Well," she drawled, "there's the honest kind of yellin' with hootin' and hallarin' and then there's the kind they do here where they act calm and hiss through their teeth. Sneaky. Well, this ain't gettin' Cara."

Gloria heaved herself down the hall sighing, and leaving me nodding at her back in agreement. My eighth-grade teacher, Sister Wilbur, had a way of hissing through her teeth. Though she never raised her voice she existed in a state of perpetual fury, and deceived no one, least of all the thirteen-year-olds sentenced to her care.

Gloria was back within two minutes, wide-eyed and confidential.

"Don't that beat all," she whispered. "She said she ain't coming. She don't want to see him. I told Dalton." She took a deep breath. "Don't that beat all?"

I watched Dalton knock on the door of the interview room, then vanish inside. Seconds later Alexander emerged, jaw squared and mouth compressed into a tight, firm line. He walked slowly down the hall. My chest tightened. *Don't do this, Cara,* I silently implored. *Whatever it is, change your mind before it's too late.*

Alexander politely knocked on Cara's door.

"Come out, Cara," he called. "I want to see you."

"No," came the muffled answer. "I don't want to."

"You're upset," Alexander responded firmly in an even voice. "Come to the interview room and we'll talk about it."

"No."

"We can't work it out unless we talk, Cara."

"We can't work it out, anyway. You don't really care how I feel. You're just playing shrink. I don't want to play."

Alexander frowned and rubbed the back of his neck with his right hand. He looked tired.

"That's enough, Cara. I'm waiting."

He waited, as he usually did at the elevator, body apparently relaxed but head slightly forward, expectant, anxious to get on to the next thing.

Slowly the door opened and Cara's puffy and tear-streaked face appeared. She blinked at Alexander, whose frown deepened.

"Now we'll talk, Cara," he said and turned on his heel. Cara followed quietly, her eyes on his back.

"Wait," she called. "I forgot my cigarettes." He stood at the door. I could hear Cara slamming open dresser drawers and muttering under her breath.

"You'll have to get along without your cigarettes, Cara," Alexander said firmly. "Come now."

"Goddammit," Cara yelled. "I want my cigarettes! You'll have to wait. I'm looking."

"I can't wait any longer," Alexander said, and strode purposefully down the hall and into the interview room. Seconds later Cara flew out of her room and tore breathlessly down the hall clutching her cigarettes, a big grin on her face. She disappeared into the room and slammed the door behind her.

I returned to my chair in the parlor with the peculiar sensation that I'd witnessed a domestic argument. It was like one of those hassles Charlie and I so often had, arguments with no principles at stake, no issues to be resolved, just a clear contest of clashing wills, an argument ad infinitum that left no one the winner and both of us isolated. How strange to see Cara and Alexander play identical roles.

The buzzer sounded and I looked up to see Barbara at the door, wearing a big smile. Dalton buzzed her in. She waved in passing and scurried down to Frank's room. A moment later they were at the nurses' station arm in arm. Frank was carrying a suitcase. He handed a paper to Dalton, who said, "Well, now you're all set."

"Yes, yes, I certainly am," Frank replied, grinning.

I moved into the hall, not wanting to say goodbye in the parlor and making a mental note to effect a midnight departure when my time came to go home. Some goodbyes are harder than others and I could picture myself leaving the hospital in an emotional storm, totally unglued. What a thrill it would be to have a nervous breakdown in the parking lot ten minutes after having been discharged.

"Good luck, Frank," I said, offering my hand.

"Thanks, thanks," he said. "Barbara and I are going on vacation for a couple of weeks and then it's back to work. I've goofed off long enough."

"I guess." I laughed. "Have a terrific time. Both of you."

I gave him a quick hug and a thump on the back. He looked shyly pleased and gripped my arm.

"You take care now. You're going to be all right, you know," he said.

"I know. I know." I squeezed his hand, smiled at Barbara, and took off for the ladies' room, wishing I could either stop feeling teary because I would miss Frank or stop feeling embarrassed because I was teary. I ran water in the sink, feeling good for Frank and sorry for myself. But why? I wouldn't want to be going home today. I caught sight of myself in the mirror and knew. I wanted to feel what Frank was feeling, hopeful, and alive, anticipating tomorrow, and though apprehensive, unafraid of today, with someone's warm hand in mine, someone who wanted to go on a vacation with me.

I dried my hands and walked back to the parlor, glancing at the clock.

The door to the interview room crashed open and Cara ran out crying. Alexander followed close on her heels, face grim. At the door to her room Cara whirled and screamed, "You can't do this to me!" She stared at him white-faced, but he ignored her and walked to the desk, where he spoke to Dalton in a low whisper.

She nodded and he returned to the interview room. Three seconds later he emerged dressed in his overcoat and hat, and without a glance in the direction of the parlor, was buzzed through the door. He turned up his coat collar as if expecting a blizzard in the hall; then, irritated with the slowness of the elevator, he went down the steps. I watched him go, knowing that I would be in Cara's room in a few minutes listening to her side of what had happened and wishing I could, like Alexander, just grab my coat and run. Therapists can vault the wall when emotions heat. Friends remain on twenty-four-hour call.

"What happened?" I asked, bracing myself as I walked into her room. She was pulling sweaters, stockings, underwear out of the dresser and heaping everything in the middle of her bed. She'd stopped crying but her face was grim, tight, angry, and very, very pale. She began tossing small jars and tubes containing makeup on top of the clothes. There was a dusty explosion of powder as a box landed upside down, filling the room with the scent of Tabu.

"Cara, what happened?" I demanded.

She was in the closet, snatching garments off hangers and throwing them backwards over her shoulder into the middle of the room. She scooped a wrinkled black skirt off the floor and added it to the pile on the bed, then threw herself face down on the bed in the middle of the mess.

"He discharged me," she moaned.

"He what? Why?"

"I don't know. He doesn't care if I die," she began to wail. "He just doesn't care."

I sat down on the side of the bed and absentmindedly began to stroke Cara's hair. What could I say? That he did care? That he cared so much that he was throwing her out? Would she feel any better if I said that Alexander was wrong, terribly wrong, perhaps even dangerously wrong? And how did I know, how could I possibly know what was in his mind? I could only hope there was more than anger I'd seen so clearly written in his face.

"What did he say to you?" I asked. "He must have said something."

Cara rolled over and rubbed her eyes. She grimaced and sat up. "He said that my therapy is not a game. It's serious work. And if I am not ready to take it seriously, I'd better leave and make room for someone who really wants help."

"And what did you say?"

She shrugged her shoulders. "I said that I didn't want to leave."

"And?"

She hauled a suitcase out of her closet. "And he said that it was no longer my choice."

I picked up a sweater and began folding it. "But didn't you tell him that you do take your therapy seriously?" I asked. She didn't answer. "Well, didn't you?"

"How can I convince him of that when he's obviously made up his mind?" she answered, shoving clothes into the suitcase.

"You could have tried," I said, exasperated. "I think all he wanted from you was some indication that you were ready to settle down and do something constructive . . ." I knew while I was saying the words that I should keep my mouth shut. She didn't want to hear that. It wouldn't help. Maybe it wasn't even true.

"You sound just like him sometimes. You know that, Cassie? You really do. The two of you just bore the living shit out of me. Where's my curlers?"

I picked the curlers off the floor and handed them to her.

"Here," I said, trying to make up. "Let me fold those things. You'll never get them all stuffed in the suitcase that way."

"Okay." She settled herself on the bed and watched me pack her suitcase. Dalton walked in carrying two official-looking forms.

"Will you sign these, please?" she said coolly.

"Sure." Cara signed the papers with a flourish, equally cool.

"Would you like me to call a cab for you?" Dalton asked.

"No, my car is out in the parking lot. *If* I can get it started."

"You will," Dalton said blithely, and bustled out of the room all efficiency and starch.

I snapped the suitcase shut. "There. All set."

I looked at Cara sitting on the bed staring into space. It had all happened so fast that I didn't know what to say. I didn't know how I felt. Though Cara appeared calm, I knew she must be feeling terrible, awful, devastated. And suddenly, I began to feel guilty, like a favored child watching her disowned sister get pushed out into the cold.

"What are you going to do?" I asked.

"I don't know." She was struggling into her coat.

"Did Alexander have any suggestions?"

"Yep, the son of a bitch said I should get a job or go back to school. He knows I'm too goddamn depressed to do either one, the bastard. Maybe I'll go visit my aunt in Columbus for a while. She has a huge house and a ton of money."

"How long will you be gone?"

"I don't know. I have an appointment with Alexander a week from Tuesday."

"And you're going to keep it?"

"Sure, why not?"

"I thought you were furious at him."

She gave me a contemptuous look and picked up her suitcase. "What's that got to do with it?" she asked.

I followed her down the hall to the nurses' station. My legs seemed to be made out of lead.

Dalton handed Cara the money they'd held for her and she received it with less emotion than she would show if we were going downstairs to the coffee shop for a chocolate soda.

"Well, 'bye now," she said to Dalton and turned abruptly away before Dalton could say anything to her.

I walked her to the door. There were so many things I wanted to say to her. Half-formed sentences scrambled and tumbled in my mind while I stood si-

lent, as mute as I always was in one of my recurring
dreams where I stand in the middle of a rushing,
flashing crowd, unable to move or speak.

"Take care of yourself," I finally stammered. "Take
care." I hugged her fiercely, teetering on tears. *Please
don't go.*

"You, too," she said, shaking herself. She glanced
over her shoulder, nodding at Dalton to buzz her out.
She opened the door, then turned back to me with a
solemn smile and eyes brimming with mischief.

"I'll be back, you know," she grinned. "Here, I
mean. I'll be back."

The elevator door opened, she tossed her suitcases
in, punched the button, and waving cheerfully, disappeared. I watched for what seemed like hours, somehow expecting her to return, then sighed and walked
back to the nurses' station.

"She said she'll be back," I remarked to Dalton.

"Oh."

"Yes." I twisted the wedding ring on my finger and
pulled it off, balancing the slender gold circle in a
crease in my palm. "You know, that's the first time
I ever heard Cara say anything that even vaguely resembled a plan for the future. She's coming back.
What kind of goal is that? Shit."

I walked into the parlor and slumped in an easy
chair. *Small wonder I have the feeling that nothing
ever works out. Nothing does. That isn't depression,
it's reality. What's the point of getting better if it just
erects an unbreachable wall between me and a friend,
a person I care about? What good is it when all that
bright and sunny laughter turns to hostility for her
and guilt for me, when we gaze at each other at the
moment of goodbye and have nothing to say.* Cara
hadn't hugged me back.

And what is the point when the doctor I trust to
care and to help and to know what is best could so
calmly and coldly cast me out, because if he had done
it to Cara he could do it to me. As far as I could see,
significances aside, all Cara had actually done was to
lose her temper, in a childish way certainly, but still,

that's all it was, a loss of temper. Express your anger, Alexander was always saying. Let it out, don't bottle it up. You'll be healthier.

Terrific! Except when the anger was directed at him. Then, watch out patient, the doctor will get you and he's in a much better position than you are to express *his* anger. To express it and hide behind his profession and rationalizations, to climb up on his pedestal and look down his nose, and call his anger therapy and say in well-modulated tones, "I'm doing this for your own good." And who the hell can argue with that? Not the patient. Least of all the patient.

Getting well. Highly touted, overrated, and lonely, lonelier, loneliest.

Going home for the afternoon had lost its allure. Challenges are for masochists, I decided. Through the glass partition I saw Dalton watching me. My eyes met hers and she walked into the parlor.

"Still going home, Cassie?" she said in what she thought was an offhand manner.

I had to get out. "I'm leaving now," I said, and a few minutes later was walking out the door. I got off the elevator at the lobby and headed for a bank of phones against the wall, phones I'd always imagined as gripped by weeping relatives calling the next of kin with death-watch bulletins. I had to look up the number in the directory, it had been that long. I spoke briefly to a receptionist whose voice I failed to recognize, then waited, heart thumping.

Finally, the deep, familiar voice on the other end said, "Well, hello."

"Hello, Tom," I said, breathless.

20

Twenty minutes later, furious with myself, I was half hanging off a scuffed and smelly seat, jammed in beside an obese lady in a red wool trimmed with imitation rat coat, swaying around curves on the Shaker Rapid Transit. Glowing with excitement, I'd run from the lobby to the parking lot and been dismayed to find the headlights of my car on and the battery dead. How could I have been so stupid, so frantic for the warmth and security of the seventh floor! To leave my lights burning and my door unlocked while I bolted across the parking lot in my usual style with private demons nipping at my heels. When would I feel safe anywhere except at meetings and in the hospital?

But now it wasn't safety I was seeking. It was excitement and involvement, and, yes, Donnerly. I smiled at my reflection in the sooty window. At least my luck wasn't all bad. Donnerly had said that he had to be downtown, just a quick business stop, and would I meet him there. And I'd said yes, and we'd cast about for some meeting spot, some place I could get to without having to walk far in the bitter cold, he'd said. We'd have lunch at P. J.'s or the Tavern and then— and then. The "then" was understood and I'd always liked the way he never seemed to have the need to make snively little jokes.

He just asked me, as usual, what time I had to be home. I'd quickly said that I needn't be home until eight or nine, which startled him, as I usually had to be home in time to fix dinner. He hadn't asked about it directly, though he did say, "How long have you been home from the hospital, Cass?" I'd taken the easy way out and told him that I'd been home for two weeks and felt better, much better, thank you, I really needed the rest.

"And how about meeting me at the Soldiers and Sailors Monument, Tom."

"Is that convenient for you?"

"Sure. I can park underground at the terminal, and just run across the street. Besides, it's romantic."

"Romantic?" he laughed. "It's dark and gloomy and full of winos hiding out from the weather and the cops. What makes you think it's romantic?"

"Because it's dark and gloomy and full of people hiding out. It reminds me of Casablanca."

"You've been to Casablanca?"

"No, and I don't have to. I can go to the Soldiers and Sailors Monument. It's foreign and exotic and a half hour away from home. The best of both worlds."

"Hmmmm," he rumbled in his own special soft, sexy, purr-hum, "the best of both worlds. For you it's the monument and for me—well, it's you. I've missed you, Cass. More than I thought I would. More than I should." He laughed, lightening it up, giving himself space. "But this isn't getting us together, is it?"

"No, it isn't." I smiled into the phone. It was our usual three-minute pre-meeting conversation, about nothing, going nowhere—his way of making contact, checking me out for a hint of reluctance or rejection. He was invariably polite and friendly, like a man I might have met at a cocktail party calling for the first date. And me, I was the eternal high school girl trying to appear sophisticated, laughing lightly, whispering rendezvous plans and thinking my mother would kill me if she found out. I'd never, not once on forty-seven separate occasions, felt like an adult woman having an adult relationship, committing an adult sin with an adult friend, stranger, lover.

Evidently the conductor was dedicated to the prevention of napping on the Rapid Transit. He brought the car to a screeching, jarring halt. As I lurched forward into the aisle, an enormous meaty paw grasped my coat collar and yanked me back into my seat, nearly choking me in the process.

"Gotcha," my seatmate rasped, settling her bulges more comfortably.

"Thanks," I croaked. "I think the conductor is a retired getaway man."

"It's not all his fault, honey." She shook her chins at me mournfully. "I take up so much room I got you hanging out there in the aisle. Most of the time people won't sit next to me. They just pass me by, glaring for all they're worth, madder than hell. Sometimes someone will say something nasty, like I should pay two fares or why don't I rent a U-haul, or two of them will sit behind me and talk about me as if I was deaf. You'd think I like being this size. Believe me, honey, I've tried everything. I was on the water diet and couldn't get two minutes away from the bathroom. I tried the high-protein diet and nearly went broke buying meat. The shots damn near killed me, and when I was taking the pills I was up at three o'clock in the morning scrubbing floors. I even had my thyroid checked out. Nothing. If I do lose a couple of pounds, I gain it right back the second I go off the diet."

I could sympathize with her frustration. "Have you ever tried Weight Watchers or Overeaters Anonymous?" I asked.

"I went to an Overeaters meeting once because I was curious and it was free," she said. "But, honey, all that running to meetings and losing weight on the buddy system. I mean it's silly. If you want to eat cake, you call somebody up and they talk you out of it. It's nothing but a crutch, honey, a crutch for weak people." She sighed and all her layers and bulges jiggled.

She humphed in her throat. "How do you stay so skinny, honey?"

I laughed. "It doesn't seem to be a problem for me."

"Some people don't know how lucky they are," she moaned and turned away to look out the window.

All you do, lumpy red lady, is drink between a pint and a fifth of booze a day. If you're like me you won't be hungry, even when you can remember you haven't eaten. The fat will melt away in no time, and you'll be blissfully happy. If you don't mind loose, yellowish skin, red blotches, circles under your eyes, puffiness, gastro-intestinal disorders, chronic nausea, and, eventually, that gray-and-washed-up-on-the-beach look so popular with medical school cadavers. It's really no trick at all.

I caught sight of my reflection in the window and was momentarily jolted to see how healthy, how filled out, and, well, almost glowing I looked. I'd gained five pounds and lost that pinched and wasted look, that tight-mouthed and haunted-around-the-eyes appearance that had increasingly dismayed me the last six months of my drinking. Tom would be pleased. I sat straighter on my corner of the seat. *I* was pleased.

Big Red made another bid for sparkling conversation. "You going Christmas shopping?"

"Well, yes," I replied, wondering how she would react if I told her I was on my way downtown to screw someone else's husband. She'd probably tell me she didn't want to hear any more about the buddy system.

"Me, too," she said. "I hate it. The stores are too hot and crowded and everyone's rushing around looking tired and miserable. I've got too many kids and too little money. Christmas is nothing but work anymore. No fun at all. Except for the kids. Wish I had more money this year. I hate to skimp on Christmas. It seems to me that there should be one day in the whole year when everyone gets what they want."

"Everything they want." I echoed and stared at my reflection. The lady in the window stopped smiling and stared back, looking less pleased than she had. *What would I ask for,* I thought? *What will be my request on that magical day when everyone gets what they want?*

I frowned and thrust my hands deeply into my pockets. There was a broken cigarette in one pocket and a few pennies in the other. I clinked the pennies and shredded the cigarette, becoming increasingly confused. I couldn't think of anything I wanted. Nothing. There had never been a time in my life when I couldn't think of anything I wanted. Usually there were dozens of things I felt deprived at not having. Though my list of necessities might change frequently, there was always something. And now, well, I just couldn't think of anything.

I slithered down in my seat and contemplated the tops of my black fur-lined boots. I tried to picture the gorgeous suede coat about which I'd nagged Charlie before I decamped for the funny farm. I just had it fixed firmly in my mind, gracefully draping in rich, elegant folds, when a thought flashed behind it: *I don't need it. I'm sober*.

I froze in my seat and the fine hairs on the back of my neck *prickled. Goddamn*, I thought, *that's what I call an insight!* I couldn't wait to tell Alexander. Immediately. I knew I could reach him at the office. "Hey," I would yell, "I had an insight on the Rapid Transit!" And he would say, "All right, why not. What is it?"

And I would say that what I have has become less important to me than what I am. That what I am right now, sober, is something I had despaired of, thought impossible. That I'd truly felt hopeless and alone, at the mercy of a terrifying and overwhelming problem over which I had no control; now I was no longer alone and without hope and I certainly had a way out if I wanted to take it.

I shuddered and glanced at my reflection. The lady looked frightened and suddenly smaller. *Hey, lady,* I asked my shrinking image, *are you ready for this?*

It occurred to me that this was the first time I'd ever been on my way to meet Tom without at least one large, quickly gulped drink. To relax, I always told myself, as I chewed a package of Lifesavers in the car. As the warm glow spread from my stomach outward, I'd been able to slip smoothly and easily into the warm, laughing, responsive lady Donnerly obviously wanted, the graceful, witty, uninhibited lady I wanted to be. And had been, on forty-seven separate occasions.

And now? Now there was a knot in my stomach instead of ninety-proof scotch, and a growing fear that the lady of Donnerly's affection had slipped away unnoticed, leaving only me behind.

I licked my lips, tasting lipstick. My mouth was dry. Perhaps when I actually saw him, when his arms went around me pulling me into the circle that had always, however briefly, shut everything out, when we kissed, perhaps then, summoned by Tom's exuberant affection and open-hearted warmth, the graceful lady would return.

And perhaps she wouldn't.

Why does the idea of pretending seem so difficult now, I wondered. It never did before. I've always enjoyed the temporary escape from my life, the temporary escape from me.

Maybe that's the problem. I've spent the past weeks, delving into myself, exploring, trying to discover— what? I've admitted to others things that I'd never dared admit to myself. I've said, "I'm wrong," and "I'm sorry," and "I want to try."

Hell, I mumbled to myself, *I wanted to stop drinking, not give up my acting career.*

And what if I can't have one without giving up the other, I thought, wishing I could return my sharply barbed and cumbersome insight. What if being sober means you have to live your life inside your own skin with no outside excursions allowed? What if?

I thought of Frank.

Well, I shrugged at my reflection, *if I can't drive a bus, I can't drive a bus.*

The car lurched and screeched, but this time I was firmly braced against the seat ahead of me. Big Red heaved to her feet and ploughed into the aisle. People parted before her like bowled-over tenpins and I followed closely, riding her wake out the door. I walked slowly up the steps and into the arcade, the maze of shops and stores beneath the Terminal Tower. I wandered aimlessly past Harvey's Coffee Shop. There was a checker set displayed in the window. I moved closer, thinking it would make a nice gift for Steve, who, unlike his mother, has a liking for games with specific rules.

I sat at the counter and ordered a cup of coffee. Somewhere inside me there was an empty space beginning to grow and I longed to fill it up or seal it off, to deny it existed before I could begin to feel the gnawing pain that comes with empty spaces. I wanted to believe that I hadn't reached a decision, hadn't closed a door. But I had and I knew it. It was done and it was right and it was too late to change my mind.

I wouldn't run through the slush and traffic to the monument. I wouldn't meet Tom. He would be angry and he would have a right to be angry. It would be kinder, and, yes, far more mature to see him and explain.

But I'm too vulnerable to be kind, I thought, and, God knows, not mature enough to explain and then leave. If I saw him, I might—I might—no might about it. I would. Pain began to gnaw the edges of the empty space.

I paid for my coffee and was halfway to the Rapid Transit entrance when I remembered the checker game, and turned back.

While the saleslady wrapped the set, I noticed a tiny locket in the shape of a kitten with a curled tail, and next to it a funny crossed-eyed frog bank, all warty and covered with green fuzz. I bought them for Greg and Jenny, wondering if Charlie would approve of my presents. Charlie. Would Charlie approve? Suddenly I wanted to tell Charlie about today, about Donnerly. I wanted to say, "See, Charlie, I gave him up because I can't pretend anymore. I can't run back and forth between two lives trying to escape from myself. I'm one woman with you and another with him but the moment I'm alone I disappear. I can't pretend that there aren't any consequences and I don't have any choice. And I can't pretend that it's all your fault. Not anymore." I wanted to say that; I wanted Charlie to approve. Look at me, Daddy, see how big I am. But I wouldn't. I hoped to God I wouldn't.

I wrestled my awkward bundle onto the Rapid Transit and balanced it on my lap. My reflection was there in the window where I'd left it. *Hello there, lady, haven't I seen you somewhere?* This conductor seemed more benevolent and we swayed gently along. I thought of Donnerly, waiting in the monument, and winced. The gnawing grew sharper and a dull, pounding throb started behind my eyes. *How could I? How could I? I'm sorry. I'm not.*

I had to stop thinking about him. I pictured myself with Alexander making the explanations I couldn't trust myself to make to Donnerly. He would nod, look impassive, make noises of objective approval, and ask me how I felt. I would tell him.

But what the hell was I going to say when he asked me why I called Tom in the first place? He won't like that at all. How would he react, I wondered, if I told him the truth, the truth that crept in between a cup of coffee and a fuzzy cross-eyed frog—that I called Donnerly because I was lonely for Cara and upset, angry, furious with Alexander for discharging her—that I have a terror of loneliness and no tolerance for pain. What would he say?

Snow was falling as I got off the car and the cold air, which should have banished my headache, didn't. I walked the distance to the hospital briskly, trying to remember a time when I hadn't felt tired. I wanted the warmth of the floor, the silence of my room, the softness of my bed. I wanted the oblivion of sleep, of not having to think. I leaned against the wind, willing one foot in front of the other.

The elevator was crowded and I clasped my bundle, standing first on one foot and then the other, exhausted and impatient. I was surprised to see Tinkerbell behind the desk, already on duty. It was later than I thought. She buzzed me through.

"Hi," she greeted me. "Been shopping?"

"Yes," I replied, yawning. "I'll show you what I got later. Right now I'm going to take a nap."

"Okay. I'll see you after dinner."

Dropping my bundle and coat on the floor I stretched out and fell into an instant sleep, dreaming that I was walking on a desolate, craggy, mist-shrouded landscape. Suddenly Charlie appeared in a swirl of fog and informed me that he was leaving immediately for Tibet and had no idea when he would return. He had been assigned to edit the memoirs of the Dalai Lama, he said, and since Cleveland was short on branch lamaseries, it was necessary for the mountain to go to Mohammed, so to speak. He said he hoped he had enough clean handkerchiefs to last, then turned and disappeared back into the fog, leaving me open-mouthed and silently screaming, "Wait, Charlie! Wait for me!"

I awoke curled in a ball with my fists clenched. I was cold to the bone and felt hollow, emptied out, a cavern of bereavement. Somewhere inside me a little girl whimpered, wanting to go home.

"Shit," I mumbled, rolling off my bed. I kicked my coat under the bed and pulled a heavy black sweater out of a dresser drawer. I pulled it over my head and stretched out again on my bed.

"Oh, shit and double shit." I rolled off my bed, retrieved my coat, hung it in the closet and slammed the door.

"Did you hear me, Caliguire? I said 'SHIT!' Did you hear me?"

"What's bugging you?"

I jumped three feet. It was Kenny, who'd entered my room quietly, carrying my dinner tray.

I waved my arms angrily. "For God's sake, can't you knock?"

He placed the tray on my table and shrugged. "How can I knock when I have my hands full? What's wrong, anyway?"

"Nothing. Nothing's wrong." I turned my back on him and he left.

I started to eat the cold and tasteless dinner, then pushed the tray away. I sat, staring at my bitten fingernails, unable to focus on any particular thought and still cold, despite the sweater. As I reached for a cigarette, there was a light tapping at my door.

"Come in," I called, too tired to get up.

Tinkerbell came in quietly. "Dr. Alexander is here, in the interview room, and he wants to see you."

I felt a clutch of alarm. "Anything special, Tink?" I asked, wondering why I felt so panicky.

She touched my shoulder lightly. "No, I don't think so. I think he just wants to see some of the patients he missed this morning."

I lit my cigarette. "Okay."

We walked down the hall together. "You haven't had a very good day, have you?" she asked me.

I smiled, more at her perception than her question. "I don't know. It isn't over yet."

Alexander was waiting for me. The harsh overhead light made him look stern, tired, and somehow unhealthy.

I probably don't look any better, I thought, seating myself.

"You went home today?" he asked, lighting a cigarette.

"No, I didn't go home."

"But you went out."

"Yes." I folded my hands in my lap and waited.

He swiveled his chair around and sat with his back to me, looking out the window at nothing, at blackness.

"You're upset," he said.

I watched the smoke curling up from the cigarette in his left hand. It drifted across the desk mingling with mine.

"I'm angry," I said, "angry about Cara."

"Why?"

"I, hmmm—I think you were wrong to discharge her."

"I have my reasons for discharging her."

"I'm sure you do," I was astonished to hear myself say, "and I have my reasons for being angry." I held my breath, thinking, *Now I'll find out what happens when I say what I think.*

The wall clock ticked, magnified to a metronome in the silence.

"Where did you go today?" he asked softly.

I ground out my cigarette. "I went downtown to see Tom Donnerly."

The chair whirled around and both his hands came crashing down on the desk. "You what?" he thundered.

"But I didn't see him," I blurted, surprised into defensiveness and frightened down to my shoes. *Don't do this to me, Edwin. Don't come at me with emotion and scare me this way.*

Alexander glared at me across the desk and I shrank in my seat, feeling constricted, suffocated. My eyes were wide open and I put one hand on my chest, feeling my heart slip and flutter in the beginnings of an anxiety attack. *Don't do this. Please.*

He took a deep breath and looked away. He stared upward at the ceiling for several seconds. When his gaze returned to me his face registered mild annoyance.

"What made you decide to see Donnerly?" he asked. "And why didn't you?"

I waited until I was breathing normally. "I just thought," I began, "I mean, I felt . . . I don't know. I guess it was an impulse . . . or something . . ." I trailed off, twisting my fingers and refusing to look up.

I wanted nothing more than to leave this room, run down the hall and slam my door behind me. A few hours earlier I'd been frantic to talk to him. Now all I wanted was to get away from him—from the man who'd frightened me and denied Cara, the man we'd expected to supply us with the missing parts of ourselves.

I waited, knowing his silence would eventually force me to speak. *Who are you, Edwin? Who are you to me? Who do you think you are? Who the HELL do you think you are to frighten me this way? And who am I to let you?*

I untwisted my fingers. "Do you have a cigarette?" I asked him.

"Oh, sure. Here." He pushed the pack across the desk at me. I lit one, blowing smoke through my nose.

"I was feeling, well, twitchy, so I called and asked him if he was free this afternoon and he said he was. He's always twitchy." I smiled at Alexander and tossed the cigarette pack back at him. He caught it neatly.

"I see. Well, if it was just a simple matter of, um, twitchiness, then why didn't you see him?"

I busied myself, brushing invisible lint off my lap.

"My period started on the Rapid Transit," I said, not trusting myself to look at him. "There wouldn't have been much point in seeing Donnerly, would there?"

I could feel Alexander's stare.

"I guess not," he said finally.

You do that, Edwin. You go ahead and guess— or guess not. It doesn't matter. If I tell you about it someday, and I probably will, it will be because I want to and not because I feel frightened and intimidated. But not until then.

"As long as we're on this general subject," he remarked casually, "don't you think it's about time you wrote that letter? To Donnerly, I mean?"

"Now?"

"Why not? Of course it would reduce your options the next time you get, um, twitchy, but I'm sure you'll be able to think of other alternatives. Less potentially disastrous alternatives. Unless you are emotionally involved to a far greater extent than you have told me. Are you in love with him?"

"No," I said quickly. "And he isn't in love with me. It's not one of those things." *Why do I continue to debate this? My decision was made hours ago. Why am I refusing to write the letter?* I felt a sudden twinge and knew. Writing the letter would make my decision final, irrevocable. If I wrote telling Tom not to call me again, he wouldn't. He'd be angry at my coldness and insensitivity, but he wouldn't call. He'd respect my decision. Did I want that? Did I seriously, wholeheartedly want that?

"If I can't drive a bus, I can't drive a bus," I said.

"What?" Alexander frowned, puzzled.

"I think this would be a good time to write a letter."

"You're sure?" He seemed pleased but puzzled at my sudden decision.

"Yes, I'm sure."

"All right." He opened a desk drawer and produced paper and pen.

Just like the Hilton, I thought, wondering what to write.

He read my mind. "Just say that he is not to call or contact you again and sign your name," he directed.

I scribbled, feeling absurd to be writing so stiff and formal a note to a man with whom I'd—I'd—oh God, I'm going to miss you, Tom Donnerly. You were my passion put to use.

"Sign your name," Alexander nudged. "Here." He thrust an envelope into my hand. "Address it and I'll take it along with me when I leave."

"Wait a minute," I objected. "What's the rush?"

"Why not?" he asked. "Then it will be done and you won't have to worry about it anymore."

I was beginning to be amused. If I hadn't made my decision previously, I might have reason to feel somewhat pressured, if not railroaded. I scribbled Donnerly's business address on the front of the envelope and handed it to Alexander.

"Well, that's that. I'll see you in the morning," he said, and was gone before I could say good night.

I sat staring at the space where he'd been. *That's that is right,* I thought. *Now it's really done.*

I leaped from the chair. *No! Come back, I've changed my mind. Give me back my letter.*

I ran to the nurses' station. Tinkerbell looked up from her chart.

"Is he gone?" I asked.

"Yes," she said, "he just went out the door. Is there something wrong?"

I leaned against the wall. "No, no, it's all right."

"Sure?"

"Sure. I'll see you later."

I walked to my room, stepping only on the green tiles. It's all right, I told myself. It will be all right. It has to be all right. It can't be anything else but all right. Somehow, eventually, it will be all right.

In my room I picked up my brush and pulled it through my hair, slowly at first, then hard and fast enough to make my scalp tingle. I caught sight of myself in the mirror. I leaned closer.

"Hey, lady, how do you feel now?" I asked the creature in the mirror who stared, looking vaguely angry, obscurely sad. "Since you got up this morning you've lost a friend, lost a lover—no, let me rephrase that—*given up* a lover, been crushed under an avalanche of insight, refused to share that insight with your grand and glorious physician, written a letter making a decision final, and—let's see—skipped your dinner. So how's by you?"

She regarded me steadily, then began slowly brushing.

"Pooped, huh?" I continued, beginning to enjoy the conversation. "Yeah, me too. You know, besides being angry at Alexander, I think there might be another reason for not confiding in him. I already know that what I did was right. For once I didn't need anyone else to tell me so. Not even him. Isn't that nice, lady? Isn't that spiffy?"

She nodded at me and we both smiled.

"I just thought of what I want on that magical day when everyone gets what they want," I said.

She nodded encouragingly.

"Besides being sober," I said, "I want me. I want me solid and steady and clearly defined, living inside my own skin. Whatever I am. Whatever I turn out to be. How about you?"

She nodded.

"It ain't easy," I sighed, then remembered something Alice had once told me at a meeting.

"All AA promises you," I repeated her words to my image, "is sobriety and a fighting chance at everything else. Are you ready to fight for your chance, lady?"

She nodded, beginning to look sparkly around the eyes.

"All right then. So am I. Let's go." I snatched my coat out of the closet, threw it over my arm, and went off to a meeting.

21

"What in the world are you doing?" Joanne piped from the open door of my room.

"Wait, let me get down."

I was perched, clutching the wall like a mountain climber with acrophobia, one foot on the bedside table and the other on the headboard of Mrs. Caliguire's bed. I leaped backward into space and landed with a thud that rattled my teeth.

"There," I said, rubbing my hands together with satisfaction.

"There, what?" Joanne demanded. "You looked like you were planning to jump on poor old Caliguire's head."

"No, I'll leave that to her doctor. Look up there, over her head. Isn't that gorgeous?"

Joanne's eyes traveled upward to the clump of greenery and white, waxy berries dangling from a red ribbon hanging about twelve inches from Caliguire's upturned and oblivious nose.

"Cassie, why would you hang mistletoe over Mrs. Caliguire's head?"

"Why not? It's Christmas, even if she doesn't know it. I hate to see her left out."

Joanne looked skeptical. "I think you just like the idea of hanging mistletoe over an unconscious old lady. You're incorrigible."

"Thank you. I certainly hope so. Want some mistletoe for your hair?"

"No, thanks. I'd feel silly. Aren't you coming down to the parlor? I looked in just a minute ago, and Kenny has all the equipment out, ready to trim the tree."

"I saw the tree when the maintenance man brought it in this morning. It looks like Woody Allen."

"Looks like what?"

"You know," I explained patiently, "it's all scrawny and scraggly, its branches are spindly, its needles go every which way, and it looks like one solid cough would kill it. Woody Allen."

"I won't tell anyone you said that," Joanne laughed and ran her fingers through her red hair. Her earrings, shaped like round Christmas ornaments, bobbed and glittered in the dim light, adding a festive dash to her plain white blouse and black skirt.

"Tell anyone you like," I said. "I've always had a thing about Christmas trees. They have as many personalities as cats. The first year Charlie and I were married I insisted on buying a Christmas tree because I felt sorry for it. It was a dwarf of a tree, bent, twisted and misshapen. I named it Quasimodo. Charlie tried for four hours to hammer Quasimodo into the tree stand. He finally gave up and hung it from the ceiling with picture wire. I thought that was very inventive of him." I laughed. "But he said he'd never again take me with him to buy a Christmas tree."

"Did he?"

"Oh, sure, but after that Charlie always had the last word. One year he picked out a short, squat, bristling, and unfriendly Douglas fir, just because it had a straight trunk. I named it Brando and it sat in a corner of the living room with its branches crossed and glowering. Most of its needles fell off before Christmas morning. I took him down early. The next year I was smarter."

"You went without a tree?"

"Never! Before we went out I mellowed Charlie down with a four-star dinner and about eight cups of eggnog. We came home with the best tree we ever had. It was massive and regal, a patriarch of a tree. I named it Orson Welles and wanted to keep it forever." I sighed, remembering.

"What kind of tree are you having this year?" Joanne asked.

"I don't know. When I talked to Charlie he said that they had the tree and were going to trim it, but he didn't describe it. I'll find out in the morning."

"Are you going home early?" Joanne asked.

"Of course. I asked Dalton and she said that I can go as soon as I get up. I'll be home in time to go to eight-thirty mass with Charlie and the kids."

Joanne smiled. "I thought you've given up practicing your religion."

"What has going to Christmas mass got to do with practicing my religion? I also leave cookies out for Santa Claus."

"Sure."

Joanne was exercising the annoying habit she had of looking wise about something she thought only she understood.

"What are you going to do tomorrow?" I asked.

She brightened. "Oh, I'll be gone even before you are. Ronnie is picking me up first thing, at seven, and we're going to spend the day with my sister and her family. I'm really looking forward to it. I haven't spent a whole day with Ronnie since I was admitted."

Which is why you look like a human being, Joanne, instead of a collection of bones that's being evicted from its crypt.

"That sounds terrific," I said.

"Let's get into the parlor," she urged, "before they finish the tree."

"Okay," I said, thinking that Christmas Eve was a good time to practice being agreeable.

Boxes, some bursting with gold and silver baubles, others with red and green tinsel ropes, were scattered over the floor of the parlor. Woody shrank against one corner, his trunk and stand coyly concealed beneath a sheet marked "Property of Shaker Heights Hospital." From ancient dusty speakers hung precariously near the ceiling, Andy Williams offered a reminder that "there is no place like home for the holidays," just in case some of us might be suffering from the delusion that plastic holly strung across the door to the shock-treatment room and top-hatted Styrofoam snowmen taped to the glass panels of the locked ward door constitute the ultimate in holiday cheer.

In the chairs that rimmed the room, patients sat stiffly, like children coerced into dance school, assiduously avoiding each other and Kenny, who was unwrapping ornaments and scowling.

"C'mon, gang," Kenny said. "Put some of these ornaments on the tree. We're supposed to be having fun."

"Who says?" I asked Kenny.

He glanced up at me from the pile of glitter and tissue paper that surrounded him.

"The general idea is for everyone to gather in the parlor, trim the tree, socialize, communicate in a meaningful way by expressing their true feelings about Christmas, and have fun," Kenny said, annoyed.

"Then you can consider it a success," I pointed out. "Everyone seems to be expressing their true feelings about Christmas, all right. It looks like Yuletide at the Wax Museum."

Kenny scrambled to his feet. "Look," he said, "I had to put up one stupid tree for my mother before I came to work today and I'll be damned if I'm going to do another one without help."

"And now *you* are expressing your true feelings about Christmas, Kenny," I said. "Isn't this a wonderful party?" From somewhere behind me came a soft snicker.

"Here, I'll help." Joanne picked up a red tinsel rope and began to drape it on the tree.

"I should hope so," Kenny groaned, not knowing when to leave well enough alone. "After all, this is for you."

"So who asked us if we wanted a tree—or a party?" Norma demanded, eyes flashing. "Nobody came out and asked me, that's for sure. I would have told them straight off—screw it. I would have said, 'You can take it and shove it, that's what you can do with Christmas,' but nobody asked. Did anybody ask you?" Norma looked around, expectantly, but no one answered.

"Nobody asked me," I volunteered quickly. I hadn't heard that many words out of Norma since the day she was admitted.

"See?" Norma said. "Nobody asked. So you can make us gather in the parlor, but you can't make us have fun."

"Shazam," Abdul remarked from the corner where he was nodding off.

"Aha," Ludwig exclaimed, leaping to his feet, "now I understand. They herd us all into the parlor and while we're sitting in here like sheep, they're searching our rooms!" Ludwig took off at a dead run.

"What's he got in his room and why would anyone want to search it?" the copper-plumbing salesman inquired politely.

"Well, um, he just gets nervous about people going into his room," I answered, not wanting to explain Ludwig to a relative newcomer. "I'm Cassie," I said. "What's your name?"

"Ted. Ted Kreeger," he said. "And I can understand how the guy feels. I don't like anyone poking through my things either. I never let my wife clean off my desk"

"You work at home?" Joanne asked.

"No—well, yes. I guess you could say that," he smiled affably. "I do my studying at home and that's my real work, of course. The other, the copper-plumbing sales, that's only temporary, till I get my degree and start my practice."

"What practice?" Joanne asked, looking at me conspiratorially. Another Ludwig, her eyes remarked.

"Veterinary," he said, smiling. "I'm studying to be a vet, specializing in farm animals. That's all I've ever wanted to be. Used to follow Doc Taylor, he was the local vet, all over the country. My folks had a small place near Xenia, mostly vegetables and some winter wheat, smack-dab between two of the finest dairy farms in the entire area. We had a pond on our place, small but pretty, and I used to lie on the bank in the heat of an afternoon with my legs cooling in the water and watch the grazing cows on the other side of the fence. And I'd be thinking how I'd be taking care of them when I grew up, how I'd go around the country like Doc Taylor and get to know everybody and how glad everybody would be to see me coming. Folks down near Xenia will call a vet for their animals before they'll ever call a doctor for themselves. *Anyway*," he continued, "I started school and took a part-time job with Midwestern Plumbing to put myself through; my folks didn't have much. And then I met my Betty, finest thing that's ever happened to me, and we got married. I had to go to full time at the job and slow down with school a bit, and then the twins came. You should see those two. Can't tell them apart to look at them and yet they're as different as they come, real individuals. All Hank wanted was to be on whatever team was going, baseball, football, track, basketball, it made no difference long as it was sports; while Harve, he didn't know a baseball bat from a shellie bean. All he wanted to do was listen to music, and I don't mean junk, I mean Beethoven and Bach and like that. That's his mother's doing." Ted smiled. "She loves that kind of music and she had Harve listening to nothing but the best right from his high chair."

"Are your boys still at home?" Joanne asked.

"They're in their last year at Ohio State." Ted grinned. "Both in Business Administration. That's *my* doing. 'Be practical,' I said. 'Study business and you can make a place most anywhere.' And they listened. Hank wants to work for the John Deere Corporation after graduation. He's already had an offer. And Harve says he thinks he'll go to California and do something in television, maybe records. Still got music on his mind. They're both good students, too. Good boys."

"But what about you?" Joanne nudged. "Did you quit school?"

"Oh, no.'" He shook his head adamantly. "I just postponed it some. Dad died and Mom sold off the place and came to live with us. Now, that's a woman for you. Never complained, never once interfered with me and Betty and the kids, always cheerful and humming in the kitchen. Betty calls my mom her best friend. How often does that happen, I ask you? She's still with us. Slowed down a bit, of course, but she cans peaches every summer and all our neighbors get jars of green tomato relish. No, ma'am, I never quit. I just kept going to school when I could and working overtime when I couldn't and some years were easier than others. I had to postpone school for a long time after Emily was born. She had this condition and the doctors said . . . well, never mind . . . anyway, it was a long time ago. But she's okay now," he smiled, "and that's the important thing. She started nurses' training but dropped out a while back. She's finding herself, Betty says, and soon as she does, why you're going to see the prettiest little nurse that ever graduated from St. John's, you just wait."

"How much longer do you have to go to school before you can practice?" Joanne asked.

Ted reached in the pocket of his gray cardigan sweater and pulled out a pipe. He began to ream it out with a fuzzy blue pipe cleaner.

"Not long," he said softly, "not long at all now. Then we're going to sell the house in Lakewood and move back down to Xenia. Not long at all now."

"How the hell old are you?" Norma demanded.

"Why, I'm fifty-three," he said, startled.

"You're never going to finish school," Norma snapped, "or practice veterinary, or move to Xenia. It's all talk." She hugged her purse to her bosom and leered gleefully at Ted, who'd turned pale and sat motionless, staring at the carpet.

Sweet Jesus, Norma, shut your goddamn vicious mouth! I wished desperately that Cara were here to say something caustic to this unfeeling woman. I wished Cara were here to say something nice to me.

"I don't know why Ted shouldn't finish school," I said quickly. "Last year I took some classes at Baldwin Wallace and there were three—no, four—people in my history class who were as old or older than Ted. They all planned to finish school. Three had already decided on career changes. Ted will do the same."

Ted pulled a tobacco pouch out of his pocket.

"Older than me?" he asked.

"At least two of them," I said, refusing to feel guilty about lying to a man whose dream had run out of time. And what did I know anyhow? I'd arrived in class on Tuesday and Thursday evenings late, breathless, half crocked and knowing I wouldn't be able to concentrate well enough to retain anything. My mind functioned like a steel sieve, and I'd paid no attention to anything or anyone. Somewhere in the vastness of Baldwin Wallace night school I was sure there had to be students Ted's age and older.

"Why not?" said Ted, nonchalantly tapping tobacco into his pipe, and I relaxed, feeling good.

"There isn't anyone searching my room," Ludwig announced as he came back.

"Of course not," Kenny said.

"They probably heard me coming and snuck out," he insisted. "Or finished searching while I was still in here watching Kenny break ornaments."

"I wouldn't be breaking them if you people were helping me," Kenny flashed. "How would you like it if you were trying to do something nice and everybody sat around with their thumbs up their nose making nasty cracks?"

"You're paid to trim the tree, kid," Ludwig said.

Kenny threw a tinsel rope into the box. "Well, I'm not being paid to listen to nasty cracks. You guys can abuse someone else." And he stalked out of the parlor.

There was a long silence.

"He's got a point there," Ted remarked. "We were pretty rough on him."

"What do you mean—we?" Joanne asked. "You didn't say one nasty word, Ted, and I was helping."

"It's his job," Ludwig repeated obstinately, "and he can damn well put up with it."

"Amen," Norma agreed. "The only good thing about this rotten place is being able to say what you think, nasty or not. If I said 'Screw Christmas' anywhere out there, people would treat me as if I'd tried to assassinate God."

"Well," Joanne said, looking like a ruffled hen, "I think it's one thing to say you hate Christmas if that's what you really feel, and another thing to give someone who's trying to be nice a hard time, even if it is his job. After all, it's bad enough that the poor guy has to work on Christmas Eve. I'm sure he'd rather be home with his mother."

"I wouldn't go that far," Ludwig said.

"But it is too bad he has to work tonight," I said. "Joanne is right about that." I was beginning to feel guilty about teasing Kenny, and I could see that I wasn't alone.

There were patients there whose names I didn't know, most of them older and not very verbal. I didn't want to know them better. To my mind, in its never-ending search for fresh sources of acute anxiety, they resembled a certain large and clannish branch of my father's family, a group who began to die off in dizzying succession, one after the other, in the middle years of my childhood, leaving me with the impression that I'd spent my fourth-, fifth-, and sixth-grade after-school hours tiptoeing across the plush wall-to-wall at Corrigan's Funeral Home.

"If you ask me, someone ought to go apologize to that boy," said a disapproving voice from the brown corduroy sofa, "AND," she added vehemently, "help with the tree." It was either Mrs. Carlisle, Mrs. Dreyfuss, or the one referred to as Bunny, three undistinguished, and to me indistinguishable, involutional melancholias who seemed to be permanently planted on the sofa, where they wove ragged potholders on lap looms and gossiped in whispers.

"Not me," Ludwig sputtered.

"Or me," Norma agreed.

"Oh, for heaven's sake," Joanne sighed, "I'll go. What's the big fuss?"

"And I'll hang some of these ornaments on the tree," I said, wishing I'd stayed in my room.

"Me, too." Ted laid his pipe in an ashtray and picked up a plastic-candy cane.

"You're putting them all on one side," Norma complained. "It's going to be lopsided."

"Here," I said, handing her an ornament, "stop complaining and start hanging."

"All right, all right." She hung the ornament on a bottom branch and stepped back. "There," she said, "and now we need a few more above this one." She scooped a handful of ornaments out of a box and began threading them with hangers. I watched her quietly for a moment, then turned to Mrs. Carlisle or whoever.

"Here," I said, laying an ornament on top of her lap loom, "would you please put this on the tree while I put hangers on the rest?"

"Okay." She heaved herself to her feet, then turned back to the sofa. "C'mon, Bunny, give us a hand." Both of the ladies rose and were soon rooting around in the ornament box. Ted's eyes met mine and we both smiled. Ted handed an ornament to an elderly gentleman in a striped bathrobe who looked at it, then at Ted, said, "Thanks, son," and placed it in his pocket.

"No, no, Mr. Hodges," Mrs. Carlisle clucked. "Put it on the tree, the tree." She took him gently by the elbow, led him to the tree and helped him hang the ornament.

"There, isn't that pretty?" she said, smiling. He nodded and she handed him another ornament, which he placed in his pocket.

"What's this?" It was Kenny, with Joanne at his heels.

"Welcome to the seventh-floor Christmas party, Kenny," I said.

"Yeah, kid," Ludwig said. "Welcome back. What did you steal out of my room?"

"I haven't been in your room," Kenny said automatically. "Now this is nice, really nice."

"Kenny," I whispered confidentially, "just hand an ornament to each person who isn't taking part and ask him directly to put it on the tree. It works!"

"Yeah?" Kenny said, surprised. "Good idea."

Within a few minutes nearly everyone had an ornament or clump of tinsel in his or her hand and was placing them on the tree, except for Mr. Hodges, whose pockets bulged.

"It's shaping up, isn't it?" I remarked to Ted. "I think I'll go ask Tinkerbell if we can bring the tray with the punch and cookies in here, just for tonight."

"Good thought," he said. "I'll help."

Tinkerbell agreed, promising to visit the parlor when the tree was finished. Ted removed cans of punch from the refrigerator while I arranged vanilla wafers on a large plastic tray.

"Wouldn't it be nice if we could have something special tonight?" I said.

"Like what?" Ted asked.

"Oh, I don't know, um, like pizza! Wouldn't that be terrific! I haven't had a pizza in—well, since I got here."

"That would be nice," he agreed, "and it would seem more like a Christmas party anywhere instead of group therapy here."

"You know," I said, excited, "we could call the Pizza Man down at the Square and get a delivery. I'll bet it wouldn't take very long. I've got some extra money and we could get just enough for everyone to have a slice or two. What do you think?"

"I'll kick in, too," Ted smiled.

"I'll get the cups and things together and you run down to the parlor and ask who wants pizza. Okay, Ted?"

"Sure," he said, and was gone.

I took plastic cups out of the utility drawers and arranged them on the tray with the cookies. I was hunting for pitchers when Ted returned.

"Everybody thinks it's a terrific idea," he said. "Well, almost everybody. A few people just stared, Mrs. Carlisle said it will add nine inches to her hips, Norma said pizza gives her gallbladder attacks but she wants some anyway, and Ludwig said that this is the chance they've been waiting for to poison him and he wouldn't touch it with a ten-foot pole. But he gave me a dollar to help pay for it."

"You may not know it," I laughed, "but what you just got was an overwhelmingly enthusiastic response. Would you call while I take this to the parlor?"

"Sure, I'll ask Miss Andover if I can use the desk phone."

I walked back to the parlor carrying the heavy tray and whistling "Jingle Bells." It was nine o'clock and I suddenly wondered if the kids were in bed yet. And if they were, what Charlie was doing. Had Mother dropped in or was he all alone with only the cat to keep him company on Christmas Eve? I shook my head, trying not to feel miserable and guilty about something beyond my control.

"Here we are," I announced, placing the tray on the coffee table.

I was pouring punch when Ted walked in, looking flushed and angry.

"What's the matter?" Joanne asked.

"What's the matter? I'll tell you what's the matter," Ted stormed. "Pizza Man won't deliver to the psychiatric ward. That's what's the matter."

Everyone stared at him.

"Why?" I demanded. "What did they say?"

"I gave them the order," Ted explained, "three large plain, and four ditto pepperoni, and when I told him where to deliver it the guy thought it was a joke. So I put Miss Andover on the phone and he told her no way, we're not making no deliveries to no nuthouse, and hung up."

"Who the hell does Pizza Man think he is?" Norma

yelled. "Our money is every damn bit as good as anyone else's."

"Does he think," Joanne snapped, angry for the first time, "that we're a bunch of raging lunatics in some sort of Bedlam, plotting to trap innocent deliverymen?"

"Call the police," Ludwig shouted. "My civil rights have been violated!"

"I thought you weren't going to touch it with a ten-foot pole, Ludwig," Norma said.

"What's that got to do with it?" he answered. "Delivering pizza is their business. What I do with it is my business. They have no right to refuse delivery. Call the cops."

"Somehow, Ludwig," I said, "I don't think the Shaker Heights police department wants to hear about your inalienable right to order pizza. Especially on Christmas Eve."

"You're right," he agreed. "Pizza Man operates interstate. Call the FBI."

Joanne sat on the floor, surrounded by tissue paper and remnants of broken ornaments. "What's the use?" she sighed. "We can't even order pizza on Christmas Eve. What's the use?"

There was a long silence. People avoided looking at one another, while Andy Williams, who obviously was in no imminent danger of being rejected by society, crooned on, "Chestnuts roasting on an open fire . . ."

"Are those lights on the tree the kind that blink off and on?" Mrs. Carlisle broke the silence. "Because if they are the kind that blink, when we turn them on someone could have a fit."

"What?" Joanne asked, looking stupefied.

"My Arnold couldn't look at blinking or flashing lights. Used to give him fits. Once a police car stopped us for speeding and Arnold sat staring at the flashing red light on top of the police car and by the time the officer got to our car Arnold was having a full-blown fit and we had to rush him to the hospital. So I thought if those were the kind of lights that blink, we'd better not turn them on. I noticed that some patients here take Dilantin like Arnold did, so I thought . . ." She turned to me and smiled.

"The lights don't blink," Kenny said.

"Thank you for thinking of it, though," I said, genuinely touched by her concern.

"You're welcome," she said matter-of-factly. "Now, why don't we clear away this rubbish and turn on the lights and have our punch and cookies," she said, like a woman who's spent a lifetime being a mother and a den mother and a room mother and a field trip mother and a PTA chairmother and a grandmother.

"I'm too depressed," Joanne sighed, and several people agreed. "You're forgetting about Pizza Man."

"So who's forgetting?" Mrs. Carlisle said, briskly stuffing papers into an empty box. "Fuck 'em."

Norma gasped, Joanne blanched, and I began to laugh, joined a second later by Ted, Kenny, and, surprisingly, Ludwig. And, in another moment, by everyone else.

"A noble sentiment, Mrs. Carlisle." Ted scooped up a handful of tissue. "Here, allow me." He dumped them in the box.

With the refuse cleared away, we called Tinkerbell, who joined us promptly. Kenny plugged in the tree to the accompaniment of "oohs" and "aaahhs," and Joanne and I passed around punch and cookies. We nibbled and chatted, watched the softly glowing lights and finally fell silent in the darkness, listening to the old familiar carols drifting through the parlor.

"Shazam," Abdul said softly.

"Merry Christmas to you too, buddy," Ludwig replied. I sighed contentedly and stretched, wiggling my toes.

"Who needs Pizza Man?" I said.

Apparently no one did.

22

"My God, I've overslept!" My feet hit the floor and I grabbed my bathrobe from the end of the bed, pulling it on as I ran down the hall. I was relieved to see Tinkerbell still at the nurses' station. I wasn't yet 7 A.M.

"Merry Christmas," I waved to her on my way to the shower. Minutes later, clean but still wet, I was back in my room yanking clothes out of drawers and slapping on makeup. Then I was on my way down the hall, my coat over one arm and a large rectangular box, my gift to Charlie, securely tucked under the other. I reached the desk, breathless.

"All set," I said to Dalton, who had just replaced Tinkerbell.

"Merry Christmas," she said, trying to look cheerful.

"Same to you," I smiled. "Cheer up. You should be off duty in time for your Christmas dinner." She didn't look thrilled.

I scribbled my name on the In/Out register and headed for the door. Just inside the parlor door Joanne sat perched on the edge of an easy chair, looking small and forlorn, as though she had a thorn in her paw.

"What are you doing here?" I asked. "I thought Ronnie was picking you up at seven."

"That's what he said," she nodded. "Something must have come up. But I do wish he had called." She blinked at me, making a whimpering sound, a pathetic little noise that filled me with compassion and a fleeting impulse to set her hair on fire.

"Maybe something did come up, Joanne." *It's more likely that something's gone down; about a fifth I would imagine.* "Look," I said, dismayed with my inability to walk out the door and leave Joanne to wait in vain, like Miss Haversham, for a vanished lover. "Didn't you say that you were going to spend the day at your sister's?"

"Yes, why?"

"Well, I'm going home right now. I'm late, in fact, and if your sister lives anywhere near where I'm going, I can drop you off."

"But what about Ronnie?"

I'm sure that Christmas in the drunk tank will provide him with glowing memories for years to come. "Miss Dalton can tell Ronnie where you are when he arrives, Joanne. How about it?"

"Well," she said, looking less like crying, "I was just going to call Marge and tell her that I don't know when I'll get there but . . . that certainly would be nice."

"Okay, but hurry," I said, glancing at the clock. "Charlie and the kids are waiting for me." *All in their places with bright shiny faces, and silent ambivalence spelled out in their eyes.*

I hopped up and down on one foot, a-jiggle with impatience, while Joanne took several maddening minutes to sign out and convince herself that Dalton understood her apologetic and meandering message to Ronnie.

"C'mon, c'mon," I said, hustling her out the door.

"Oh, my God, stop running, Cassie," she gasped as I dragged her across the parking lot through blinding snow. "I've got a pain in my side."

"Almost there, Joanne," I said, and dragged her faster.

"Cassie, you can't see!" she shouted as we roared out of the parking lot.

"I can see fine," I said, wondering what was ahead of me. "Now, where did you say your sister lives?"

"On Riverside Drive, north of Kammas Corners."

"Rocky River! That's Rocky River!"

Joanne nodded. Rocky River was nowhere near where I was heading. I would be going home in a tremendous zigzagging arch, terrific if you want to take in the scenic delights of the west side of Cleveland, but not too wonderful if you were picturing an irate husband peering at his watch and muttering about inconsideration and irresponsibility.

"Okay, Joanne," I sighed. "Rocky River, here we come."

I pushed the accelerator halfway to the floor, hoping the defroster would take care of the ice so I could see something.

We were barreling across the High Level Bridge when I hit a patch of ice and skidded into a spin. Mammoth iron guardrails blurred all around us.

"God in heaven, we're gonna be killed!" Joanne shrieked.

"Hang on," I shrieked in return, swerving the wheel first to one side then to the other, unable to remember whether you're supposed to turn into or away from a spin. We wobbled, slowed and spun out. I pulled the car over to the side of the bridge. Joanne and I looked at each other, wide-eyed and breathing hard.

"If this had been a regular morning with rush-hour traffic, we would have been killed," Joanne gasped.

"If this had been a regular morning we wouldn't be playing whirling dervish on the High Level Bridge. We'd be back at shrink city watching Pomeroy shove Thorazine down Abdul's throat."

I turned left and took off again, as fast as I had before, hoping that the adage about lightning striking twice applied equally to patches of ice. I noticed Joanne was riding with her hand on the door handle and her eyes tightly shut. I turned on the radio.

"Relax, Joanne," I said, hunched over the wheel. "Listen to Christmas carols."

"Adeste fidelis," I sang along with the Mormon Tabernacle Choir as we sped through deserted holiday streets.

The Mormons came to their usual fortissimo conclusion and I listened, fascinated, as the announcer informed us that an FDA report just released listed three substances I'd eaten regularly since childhood, my disposable fold-up raincoat, and the air even now hanging over my hometown as probable causes of cancer. We then rejoined the Mormons, who, apparently untroubled by such mundane matters, swung into "Joy to the World."

"Did you hear that?" Joanne, who was not a Mormon and therefore troubled, asked with her eyes still closed. "What next? Last year the doctor prescribed a new wonder drug for my grandmother's strep throat. He said it was twice as effective as penicillin."

"Was it?"

"I don't know. Three days later she died from an allergic reaction."

"Jeez, what did the doctor say?"

"He said we could probably get a refund on the rest of the prescription. Every time you turn around these days you hear about something else that will probably kill you. It makes life seem so—dangerous."

"No," I disagreed. "Actually it makes life very simple. All you have to do is avoid eating, breathing, and coming in contact with anything invented after 1945."

A light turned red in front of me and I pumped the brakes frantically, hoping for dry pavement. The car jerked like the Bubble Bounce at Cedar Point and Joanne's eyes flew open.

"It's okay," I soothed. "We're almost at your sister's house. There's St. Theresa's Academy."

"My niece goes to school there," Joanne said. "The grounds are lovely but the school looks like some Middle Ages fortress. I've never been inside."

"I have," I said, smiling. "I went to high school there."

"I wouldn't have thought it," Joanne said. I frowned. Cara once said that I didn't seem to be the type who had a husband and three children, and now Joanne is surprised at my having been what was referred to in these parts as an STA girl. What kind of impression did I give people anyway? Was it my personality in general or the fact that I said openly that I was an alcoholic that made people assume I hadn't a husband, children, religious affiliation, or any of the accouterments of normal life? Maybe they assumed that I grew up in an orphanage, went to reform school, and spent my life in dimly lit bars fulfilling romantic fantasies for the local Willie Lomans in exchange for a scotch on the rocks.

"What was it like—St. Theresa's, I mean? How did you like it?" Joanne asked.

"They have fixtures for gas lights still in the walls. And no showers in the gym. Showers had never been installed and the nuns didn't want us to see each other naked anyway. Girls periodically threatened to call the Board of Education and report the school for violation but, as far as I know, no one ever did. The nuns were like nuns everywhere, some cranky, some pleasant, and all damned clever at dragging religion into algebraic equations or chemical formulas or Shakespeare. They were all similar except for one wild-eyed, red-haired lay teacher, who insisted that the rampant moral decay in this country was deliberately created and fostered by Jewish movie producers. She could never explain exactly what Jewish movie producers would gain by destroying the country, but she used part of every class to warn us that young people who went to the movies every week became Communists before they were old enough to vote. Our typing teacher, Sister Roberta, also taught chemistry. She lived in mortal terror of Bunsen burners and prayed for the stigmata."

"What's that?" Joanne asked.

"It's a Catholic thing," I said, not wanting to explain. "When I was at St. Theresa's, the biography of Theresa Neuman, the German mystic, was going around and everyone was praying for the stigmata. The next year we were all praying for new basketball hoops for the gym. We didn't get either one. Sister Camilla used to say, 'Storm heaven, girls. Storm heaven,' and we'd all pray our knees to the bone in chapel, but we never got anything we prayed for except the time we said a novena that Sister Margaret Mary would recover from the measles even though no one seriously expected her to do anything else. And then we had to attend a mass of thanksgiving. I spent more time with Sister's measles than I did with my own."

"Did you get in trouble in school?" Joanne asked, sounding as though she thought I must have.

"Oh, no. I was quiet and a good student and no behavior problem at all. I did as I was told and kept my opinions to myself. I never got in trouble for anything I did or said, just once in a while for something I wrote."

"Like what? Turn here, Cassie. This is Marge's street."

"Well, once in English we had to write an essay. We were given a choice between 'My Favorite Character in the *Merchant of Venice*' or 'What Would Happen If Christ Came Back Today?' Everyone was doing *Merchant*, so I chose the other, and somehow missed the point, which was that Christ would be very disappointed if he came back and saw how worldly and materialistic we all are. I saw it literally and from another point of view and turned in a paper that had Christ preaching a sermon in Brecksville Park surrounded by picnicking families and college students and moony lovers and an industrial league softball team, plus a couple of cops and winos on benches and a few of those people who come to feed ducks and frown at everybody who isn't old. I had Christ saying, 'Be nice to each other, you're all you've got.' And 'Blessed are those who listen, for they shall be listened to,' and things like that. I made Saint Peter a tool-and-dye maker at Republic Steel, and I was Mary, sitting at the foot of Christ and not having to do the dishes because I had chosen the better way. I finished it with Christ multiplying hamburgers and fries for the hungry multitudes and everyone sitting on the grass feeling good and singing 'Holy God We Praise Thy Name,' which was my favorite hymn. Well, the shit hit the fan, I'll tell you. Sister Agnes said it was blasphemy and the principal threatened to call my father, not my mother, mind you, my father, AT THE OFFICE. It was ghastly, let me—oh, here we are."

"My goodness, so soon," Joanne said.

"Time flies, etcetera," I said, nearly pushing Joanne

out the door. "Have a wonderful Christmas, Joanne."

"Thank you, I will." She reached back and grabbed my hand. "And thank you so much for going out of your way like this. It was so nice of you."

"It was nothing. What are friends for?" I said through gritted teeth.

"I just know Ronnie will be furious because I didn't wait," she sighed.

"He isn't the only one, Joanne," I hissed, shooing her into a snowdrift. I slammed the door, narrowly missing her coat. " 'Bye now."

I raced up her sister's street, zooming around the corner and up Riverside to West 220th Street.

I jostled over potholes and careened around road barriers on Brookpark Road, now in its fourteenth year of reconstruction. Snow blowing across the road in front of the airport made visibility difficult and I had a flashing picture of myself ending up draped tastefully around a telephone pole.

Charlie and the kids were getting into his car as I squealed into the driveway.

"Park in the street, hurry up," Charlie called. "You've made us late."

"Damn," I muttered, stopping the car at right angles to the curb. "That's good enough."

Charlie had the motor running as I threw myself into the front seat.

"We'll have to stand in the back of church," Charlie said angrily. "Where the hell were you?"

"I'm late because I was doing a good deed for another patient," I snapped.

"Wonderful. Why don't you try doing your good deeds at home for a change?"

"Why don't you go to hell, Charlie?"

"Merry Christmas, Mommy," Jenny said from the back seat.

My crackling anger at Charlie crumbled and dissolved, replaced by anger at both of us. How could we fight on Christmas Day? I peeked sideways at Charlie, who looked none too happy either.

"Merry Christmas, sweetheart," I said, twisting sideways in the seat so I could see all three of them. "I'll bet you can't wait to open your presents." No one answered.

Because it was only eight-fifteen we managed to find a pew together and filed in seconds before Father Dunhill shuffled, yawning, out of the sacristy and onto the altar. As he made the sign of the cross I suddenly wondered if the old fool had a family, someone to share the day with, or if his Christmas began and ended with the solitary celebration of mass.

"Unbutton your coat," I whispered to Jenny. "It's warm in here. Tell the boys, too."

I reached for the missals arranged on the rack on the back of the pew and handed one to Jenny. Charlie had already given missals to the boys but none of the children were following them. They gazed around the church as I always had, taking in the Christmas transformation. Masses of poinsettias covered the altar, and on either side towered not one but two stately Christmas trees, alive with tiny, twinkling Christmas lights.

The altar boys wore red cassocks which I knew were cotton but had the look of velvet in the flickering candlelight, and Dunhill's vestments were a wonderment of gold thread and intricate embroidery.

The elementary school choir, led by a round, perspiring nun, sang "O Little Town of Bethlehem" in soft sleepy voices, and I knew, having sung in the choir for five years, that they had been practicing since October, were singing the hymn for the four thousandth time and didn't care if they never sang it again. I also knew that the nun hadn't slept all night worrying about her choir, and once the mass was over and the congregation streamed down the aisle, the children would peer over the railing at their audience, sing, "We Wish You a Merry Christmas" lustily and at the tops of their voices and then go home with their families asking, "Could you hear me? Was I okay?" and glowing with pride.

I looked over the children's heads at Charlie, who was reading his missal and seemed to be humming along with the hymn.

Charlie looks as though he belongs, I thought, and

felt a sharp twinge of envy for his complacency, or perhaps it was acceptance. When we were told from the pulpit that there were inexplicable mysteries that must be accepted on faith alone, Charlie, untroubled by a rebellious nature and, for all I know, afflicted with faith, accepted this, seeming to feel it was right and proper to do so. My usual reaction was, "Who says? I'll believe it when I see it." Which provided me with a certain intellectual independence but left me without Charlie's built-in insulation, the ability to accept the unfathomable and unchangeable, so useful for weathering emotional storms and random vicissitudes.

The choir went into "Hark the Herald Angels Sing," with the second sopranos slightly off-key. The offertory bell rang and everybody reached in their pockets for fatter than usual donation envelopes.

If I had the choice where else would I be, I wondered, watching Charlie hunt through his pockets for his envelope.

What nonsense, I decided, riffling through my purse for loose change. I had a choice and I'm here. The idea of not seeing my children on Christmas had never even entered my mind. Nor had the thought of skipping Christmas mass. And it had absolutely nothing to do with the practice of religion.

Ever since I could remember, and most likely before that, I'd attended mass pressed between my brother and sister, with Mother and Dad on either end, listening to Mother's whispered admonitions to unbutton our coats before we caught cold and Dad humming along with the hymns. Year after year, without prior consultation we'd entered the pew in the same order, first Mother and Mary Kay, then me, Bobby, and Dad. We'd sung and prayed, lost our rosaries and mittens, scratched and giggled, been slushed and glared at, gone to communion and listened to sermons, right up until the unexpected year when Mary Kay and I were taller than Mother and Bobby's chin came up level with Dad's.

Now I was the mother. My children stood in the pew between their father and me and I could see through clouds of incense to some future Christmas when their children would stand next to them. I smiled at the thought, knowing that deep inside I was, like all natural rebels and would-be revolutionaries, a secret sucker for tradition.

As we walked out of church, children hung over the balcony railing bursting with "We Wish You a Merry Christmas," joined by the red-faced sister with wimple askew, beaming from ear to ear.

When we got home the kids tumbled out of the car and raced to the porch, excited at last, eager for Christmas. The wind had come up and snow clouds hung heavy in the northwestern sky. We'd have snow, courtesy of Canada.

"C'mon, Daddy, open the door," Steve called impatiently.

"I'm coming. I'm coming," Charlie grinned. "What's the hurry? You'd think it was a special occasion or something," he teased.

"Charlie, I'm turning blue," I said, not really complaining.

"And a very becoming shade it is, my dear," he said, opening the door with a flourish. "Hang up your coats first, kids."

I hung up my coat while Charlie plugged in the tree.

"I can't imagine what that is," I laughed, pointing at a tall, thin cardboard box with handlebars sticking out the top.

"Oh, boy, oh, boy," Steve shrieked, running to his new bike. "I hope it's a ten-speed."

I looked at Charlie. He nodded.

"I want one, too," Greg said, not looking up from the package he was unwrapping.

"Next year, when you're big enough to handle it," Charlie said, and Greg, blessed with his father's pragmatism, nodded agreeably.

"Look, Mommy," Jenny called and I turned to see her holding up a dress. "Isn't it beeeautifoool?" she cried.

It was beautiful, red velvet and white lace with a full skirt and ribbon sash.

"Oh, it's gorgeous, Charlie," I sighed. "She'll look

like the altar boys in church this morning. Where did you find it?"

"I saw it in the window of that little dress shop on the mall," Charlie replied. "There are white leotards that go with it. I showed it to your mother and she said that a dress like that needed a pinafore, and I said, 'You're right. What's a pinafore?' So she told me and I got one. It's in that smaller box over there."

"Can I wear it today to Grandma's?" Jenny asked.

"*May* I wear it," Charlie corrected. "Sure, honey. There's some coffee in the kitchen, Cassie. I made it before church."

"I'll get both of us a cup, Charlie."

My kitchen was immaculate, spotless in the way it was only when my mother had blitzed through, armed with a bottle of Lysol, a bucket of scalding water, three acres of cleaning rags, and more energy than the Minnesota Vikings. I poured the coffee.

"Was Mother here?" I asked Charlie. "Did she come over to clean?"

He looked up from tying a silver ribbon on a small square box. "She dropped over last night so I could run out and get a few last-minute things, and when I came back she was washing down the walls."

"On Christmas Eve?"

"She said that she just wiped some jelly off the wall next to the refrigerator and when she saw the difference, well, it just got out of hand."

"That's dumb, Charlie, washing walls on Christmas Eve."

Charlie frowned. "I should think you'd be grateful, Cassie."

"Well, I'm not," I said bitterly. "I know I'm supposed to be grateful for all the help she gives me, but somehow I'm not. Every time Mother comes over and begins cleaning I feel, well, criticized. I want to put up a sign on the front door that says, 'This is my house and my dirt and I like it this way, so leave everything the hell alone.' "

"That's childish," Charlie remarked, concentrating on his ribbon.

"But that's the way I *feel*," I insisted.

"Childish," Charlie said.

"Oh, Charlie, for God's sake—" I stopped, remembering Christmas.

Charlie handed me the square package. "Merry Christmas, Cassie."

"Why, thank you," I said, and began untying the ribbon Charlie had just finished bowing. While I unwrapped the package Charlie hauled a holly-decked carton from under the tree and dumped it at my feet.

"This is for you, too," he puffed.

"My goodness." The small package was a bottle of Chanel No. 5, my favorite perfume.

"Thank you, Charlie, I'm all out," I said, dabbing behind each ear.

"Open the other one," Charlie prompted.

I pulled off the paper and tore open the carton. Inside were about twenty-two small blue bound volumes.

"What's this?" I asked, removing one of the books. On the side in silver letters was printed *Othello*.

"It's the complete works of Shakespeare—plays *and* sonnets," Charlie said, grinning. "I thought you'd like it. You like Shakespeare. Don't you like Shakespeare?"

"Why . . . um . . . sure I like Shakespeare. I mean, I've always liked . . . but it's such a strange . . . whatever gave you the idea, Charlie?"

"I just thought it was something you wouldn't buy for yourself," he said.

"That's for sure. But what an unusual combination, perfume and Shakespeare." He smiled, taking it as a compliment, and indeed, though I was puzzled at the wondrous workings of his quixotic mind, the gifts did appeal to me. A lot.

"This combination isn't as unusual as some I've come up with," Charlie said.

"Like what?"

He sipped his coffee. "Two years before we were married I was going out with five girls, all casual, but I felt I had to get them Christmas presents. For some reason, each one thought I wasn't going out with anyone else."

"Why would they think that?"

"Who knows? I'm not the type who talks about other people I'm dating and I guess they just assumed . . . you know how women are . . ."

"Yes, I do."

"Anyway, I gave each of them a bottle of perfume and a black umbrella."

"How weird."

"That's what they said." Charlie laughed.

"How did you ever decide on that?" I asked, curious.

"Easy. It was Christmas Eve and the perfume and umbrellas were on adjoining counters on the first floor of the May Company. I grabbed five of each and ran all over town ringing doorbells and telling each one I'd love to stay but I had to fly home to New York because my grandfather had died. Then I went home, drank some eggnog and went to bed, exhausted. I spent the next three weeks describing my grandfather's funeral on dates. By the time I got to the fifth one I'd worked Grandpa up to an honor guard by the Knights of Columbus. I think that's when I decided to get married."

"That was a year before you met me. I was still in high school."

Charlie nodded. "I know, but I'd already decided to get married as soon as I met someone suitable. Then you came along and I thought, what the hell, she isn't much, but she's young and strong, she can carry bundles—"

"Charlie!" I threw a sofa cushion at him and he ducked, laughing.

I jumped to my feet and ran to the door.

"Hey, I was teasing," Charlie called.

"I know. Just wait. I'll be right back." I ran through the swirling snow and snatched the package from the front seat of the car. I was shivering when I handed the package to Charlie.

"I almost forgot. Merry Christmas."

While he opened the package I sipped my coffee and looked around the living room. The tree was hung with every ornament we owned and a few that I didn't recognize. Lights marched up the branches with more precision than I'd ever managed. "Hello, Mary

Poppins," I said to the tree. "You are practically perfect in every way." There were pine boughs on the mantel along with the fat red candles that I'd arranged there every year we'd lived in the house. On the coffee table where I always placed it was the manger on a sheet draped to look like snow, and behind it, the pine cones I'd sprayed green to resemble Christmas trees. Bulging stockings hung on red ribbon from the mantel and greeting cards were taped to the archway over the door. The windows were covered with plump Glass Wax snowmen and fantastic snowflakes the size of napkins. Charlie had done it all. Of course the tree and the manger were for the kids, but they'd never have noticed the pine cones and candles and cards taped over the arch. I noticed.

"The house looks lovely," I said.

"The kids did the windows," Charlie said, pulling a red plaid bathrobe out of the box.

"Do you like it?" I asked, feeling guilty because I'd given Charlie's gift less than five minutes' thought. I'd just whooshed into a store and grabbed the first thing I saw in the men's department. Well, the second thing. The first thing was cotton spandex bikini briefs in fluorescent colors embossed with words like "Dynamite."

"Try it on, Charlie," I urged.

He slipped the bathrobe on over his clothes and turned slowly.

"It fits," I said, feeling silly. *How could a wraparound robe not fit?* "How does it feel?"

"Warm," he said. "And soft. Thank you." He leaned over to give me a kiss. I quickly pecked him on the cheek and pulled back, but he stayed where he was, nuzzling my ear. "You smell nice," he said.

"It's your perfume," I said, beginning to get nervous.

"The perfume smells nice, too," he nuzzled. "You, um, must be tired, getting up so early and all. Wouldn't you like to have a little, um, rest?"

"I'm not tired, Charlie."

"Wouldn't you like to rest anyway?"

"The kids . . ."

"The kids are busy with their presents."

I struggled past the still-nuzzling Charlie and slipped out of the chair, panic-stricken. I couldn't just come home and slip off to "rest" with Charlie as if nothing had happened, nothing was wrong. If I did that, I might as well tell Charlie that I'd be coming home, that I'd be a good little girl and everything would work out fine. Charlie would think, "Well, that's that, now back to business," and go cheerfully on, oblivious to the fact that I wasn't at all sure if it would work, or could, or if I wanted it to.

"I'd better fix breakfast before we all starve, Charlie. Did you get bacon and eggs?" I was impressively efficient.

Charlie seemed not so much annoyed as tired and, something I'd never before known him to be, wistful.

He nodded. "There's bacon and eggs and that braided coffee cake you like from the bakery. I think I'll go take a shower."

I was setting the table with one eye on the cooking bacon when I heard Charlie call from the other end of the house.

"Cassie, come here. Quick."

"What is it, Charlie?" I called. "I'm cooking."

"Hurry, Cass. It's an emergency."

I turned off the gas under the bacon and ran down the hall to the bedroom. Charlie was standing behind the door.

"What's wrong?" I asked, frightened.

"This situation has just come up and we must do something about it," he said, reaching for the buttons on my blouse. "Immediately!" I saw that the bathrobe was definitely too large with nothing on under it.

I pushed him away. "Charlie, the breakfast—"

"Later," he said, unzipping my skirt.

"But the kids—"

"They're busy with their presents," he said, pushing me into bed. He jumped in beside me.

"Now, isn't this better?" he whispered, pulling me close.

"Urk," I replied, tangled up in the folds of his bathrobe, then, "Charlie, did you remember to lock the door?"

We settled down into a variation of our own particular pattern, a seldom-deviated-from routine, a practice which *Cosmopolitan* warned was boring, stagnating, and ruinous to a marriage. I didn't know about that, but I did know that no amount of therapy would ever bring me to the point where I could walk into a room with a stranger, as Cara did, or said she was able to do, and say, "Look, Buster, this is what I want you to do." It had taken months, maybe years of persistent trial and error with shyly veiled hints and endless, polite "That was fine, really it was" from both of us before we each discovered what the other enjoyed, responded to, and wanted. Charlie, only slightly less shy than me, knew where I wanted to go and how to get me there, and in turn, over a period of time, I'd been able to reach through his natural reserve to the passionate man underneath. Now we had an intimate knowledge of one another and our own pace, our own rhythm, our own consistent satisfaction, and to hell with the marriage manuals. In bed, at least, we trusted one another. And shared.

With a sigh I nestled into Charlie's shoulder thinking that though my marriage certainly didn't provide the electric ego-boost of a weekly rendezvous with the demonstratively appreciative Donnerly, neither did it require that I be the Bernhardt of the bedroom or anything but what I was, a basically shy lady who craved affection, the comfort of familiarity, and the security of someone who wouldn't vanish at three A.M.

How embarrassing, I thought, wiggling my toes, I'm a closet monogamous heterosexual. A failed swinger. Ick.

I nudged Charlie, who was half asleep. "If I come home, I want to smoke in bed," I said.

He opened one eye. "You can smoke in bed as long as you don't drink. I'm always afraid you'll set the bed on fire." He sat up abruptly. "What do you mean *if* you come home? Of course you'll come home. What else would you do?"

"I do have other options, you know," I replied, wishing I hadn't said anything. Christmas Day. Christmas Day.

"No you don't. You'll come home where you belong. That's the end of it."

It's not the end, I thought, but I won't argue today. I took an old housecoat off its hook in the closet and wrapped it around me as I headed for the door. Charlie stood next to the bed, shrugging into his robe.

"Charlie," I said, with one hand on the doorknob, "the last year or so has been devastating for both of us. You'll have to admit that."

He nodded. "Let's not get started on who did what to whom," he said.

"I'm not. I'm not," I said quickly. "What I'm saying is that so much has happened, there's been so much damage, that, well, wouldn't it be easier if I just sort of walked off into the sunset? Wouldn't it be simpler, Charlie?"

He picked up a hairbrush from the dresser top and studied it for a moment, then looked at me.

"You're my wife," he said. "We have a family, a home. People can't be discarded, and families smashed, just because it's easier. If it was that simple, I would have divorced you this year."

"But if we're not happy, Charlie . . ." I pleaded.

"Happy?" Charlie said angrily. "What's happy? You expect life to be a fairy tale with happily ever after and violins. You take kids' colds and going to the supermarket and the nights I have to work late as a personal insult."

He came toward me waving the hairbrush. I backed into the doorjamb wishing I'd kept my thoughts to myself.

"That's the difference between us," he stormed. "You're a romantic and I'm a realist. Well, this isn't fairyland, you're not Cinderella. You're a woman named Cassie who has a husband and three children who desperately need to depend on her. I'm not Prince Charming. I'm Charlie. And every morning I go off to edit mundane books in an ordinary office downtown. I spend as many hours doing things I dis-

like because they have to be done and it's part of my
job as I do the things that give me pleasure and satisfaction. I battle traffic twice a day and look forward
to pulling into the driveway at night because it's *my*
home and *my* family, and, goddammit, I love you.
And it sure as hell isn't easy."

Charlie, the nonromantic idealist, glared at me as I
cringed, overwhelmed by his uncharacteristic vehe-
mence. I searched my scattered thoughts, trying to
think of something to say.

Finally. "Would you like your eggs scrambled or
fried?"

The glare vanished and his forehead wrinkled with
puzzlement, then amusement glimmered in his eyes.

"Fried would be fine," he said. "Over easy."

Later that day, bundled and booted like an Eskimo
family, we were on our way to Mother's house for dinner. The children, reluctant to leave their new and
enthralling possessions, were each allowed to bring one
item with them. Greg rattled a box containing a baseball game with at least three dozen separate pieces.
Steve held a book whose cover depicted a minute
spaceman being menaced by a gigantic three-headed
green person, and Jenny had all but disappeared under an enormous floppy-eared stuffed dog she had
positioned on her lap so "he can look out the window."
The kitten locket nestled in the hollow of her neck.

I'd enjoyed breakfast, listening to the children bab-
ble about their gifts, and observing Charlie's quiet
pleasure in presiding over the head of the table. After
breakfast, I cleared the dishes away, then read the
paper sitting next to Charlie on the sofa. While he
showered, I puttered around the house, beginning to
feel less like someone visiting a stranger's house full
of unfamiliar objects. The bedroom clothes hamper
was full, so I swept up a load of laundry, carried it
downstairs and stuffed it in the machine. It took me
several long seconds to remember what buttons to
push, and as I heard the water pour into the machine, it occurred to me that the last time I'd carried
laundry down those stairs the trees outside the window
were scarlet and gold, the air was full of October

crispness and I was full of scotch. I'd been smashed to
the gills and forgotten to add soap. It also occurred to
me that upstairs in the cupboard over the sink was a
bottle of brandy, a bottle of scotch, and quite probably several others.

"If you don't drink, you don't get drunk," I said to
the washing machine, who gurgled. I went upstairs to
take a long, hot bath.

Wonderful aromas filled Mother's house as we
tracked snow in the back door.

"Come in. Come in," she called from the kitchen.
"Take off your boots and hang up your coats."

The kids scattered coats and boots all over the entry
hall and ran off to tell their grandmother about their
presents. I put things in order and followed more slowly. Mother held a large spoon in one hand and was
tucking stray wisps of hair behind her ear with the
other hand as she tried to listen to three children yammering simultaneously. Charlie was eating a piece of
cheese hacked from a brick of cheddar arranged on a
wooden tray with crackers.

"If you'll look under the tree in the living room,"
Mother was saying, "you'll each find a package with
your name on it."

Whooping, they disappeared around the corner, leaving the kitchen heavy with silence.

"Merry Christmas, Mom," I said, leaning over to
kiss her on the cheek. There were beads of perspira-
tion on her upper lip.

"When are you coming home?" she asked. "God
knows you look healthy enough. Merry Christmas."

"Soon, Mother," I replied, thinking that God might
know how I looked but He didn't know how I felt
and I didn't really feel "healthy enough," whatever
"enough" was.

"You've been saying 'soon' for six weeks," Mother
persisted. "I'm getting tired of 'soon,' your kids are
tired of 'soon,' and Charlie is wearing himself into the
ground. I don't want to hear 'soon.' I want to hear
tomorrow, or next Wednesday, or a week from Monday afternoon at two o'clock."

"I have to do what Dr. Alexander tells me and he

hasn't said anything yet about when I can go home," I said, beginning to get exasperated. "Can I help you with anything, Mother?" I asked to change the subject.

She shook her head. "I would have appreciated some help two hours ago, but now everything is just about ready. You can set the table if you want, if you think you're up to it," she said with what could have been a sneer.

"Fine," I said, relieved at having something to do.

She handed me her best tablecloth, dripping with ecru lace and carefully ironed.

"Use this," she said, "and tell the kids not to spill. I'll get the napkins."

She placed the napkins on top of the tablecloth.

"I don't think much of that Alexander," she said. "Any doctor who thinks it's perfectly all right for a mother to be away from her children for three months is just stupid. It's not as though you're actually sick or anything. Not sick sick. If everyone ran off and hid in a hospital when they got a little down in the dumps, if *I* had done that every time things got tough while you were growing up, well. . . . You've got to keep going whether you feel good or not. Like I do."

The exasperation was deepening into anger and I held the linen before me like a shield.

"I think it's more complicated than that, Mother," I said and stopped. *Christmas Day. Christmas Day.*

"Well, don't be surprised if twenty years from now YOUR children are on some psychiatrist's couch telling him about YOU." She turned with a flourish and began beating the bejesus out of the mashed potatoes.

I set the table, wondering if Mother thought that I crammed all my therapeutic hours with complaints about her. Yet, I couldn't tell her that I never talked about her. I did. And I couldn't reassure her that I never expressed hostility or bitterness, or never, with my gift for not-too-subtle sarcasm, caricatured her in any way. I did. And somehow I didn't think she'd believe that my rambling APA-approved stream-of-consciousness verbalizations sometimes contained references to her that were tinged with affection, humor, and a grudging, very grudging, admiration. But they were. Once while waiting to see Alexander I'd drawn a quick sketch of Mother nailed to a cross with a crown of thorns on her head and a balloon coming out of her mouth that read: "After all I've done, this is the thanks I get."

"Alexander doesn't have a couch, Mother," I said, walking into the kitchen. "I sit in a chair."

She continued beating. "For what Charlie is paying, you should lie down on a couch. By the way, you just missed a call from Bobby."

"When?" I said, wretched with disappointment. "When did he call?"

"While I was taking the pies out of the oven, about ten minutes before you got here. I nearly dropped the mince."

"Well, how is he? What did he say?"

"He said I should tell you Merry Christmas and he'll write to you soon, don't hold your breath. I've never gotten a letter from him yet."

"How *is* he?"

"He's having Christmas dinner with some girl's family, he said. Someone he met at work. I said, 'Are you serious about this girl, Bob?' and he said, 'Now Ma,' as if I shouldn't even be interested. I asked him when he's coming home for a visit and he said, 'Now, Ma.' Every time I ask him anything except how's the weather out there, he says, 'Now, Ma,' like his life was a CIA plot or something. I spend my whole life asking my children when they're coming home. Everybody says 'Soon' but nobody ever shows up. Ha!"

"Did Mary Kay call?" I asked, desperately wishing I'd been there to talk to Bobby. Even if it was just for a minute and all small talk, we could have made contact.

"No, she hasn't called yet. She usually calls sometime after dinner. She sent me a Christmas card with a note on it that said she'll be spending the holidays studying for finals. In January she should have her master's degree."

"Then what?" I asked.

"Who knows? She doesn't. She said she needs a

doctor's degree to teach college and she wants to teach college. She'll be in graduate school forever."

"She'll be the first advanced-degreed professional in the entire family," I said, chartreuse with nausea-producing envy.

"That won't keep her company in her old age," Mother snorted. "Not that having kids will, either. Look at me."

"It's a terrific accomplishment, Mother," I said, making myself feel worse. "You've got to admit that."

"Yes, it is," she agreed. "Your sister always was a hard worker. I just wish she was—"

"Sometimes you miss her," I finished for her.

She dumped the potatoes into a bowl. "You keep me so busy with all your foolishness that I don't have time to miss anybody," she muttered. "Cleaning two houses . . . get the serving spoons, Cassie."

I poked through the silver for the large slotted spoons.

"Ask Charlie to come carve the turkey," Mother directed, "and fix us a drink before dinner. Oh, Bobby was promoted."

"To what?" I asked. "Charlie," I hollered in the direction of the living room.

"He's the director of something," she said, lifting the huge turkey out of the oven. "Whatever it is, he's the director of the whole thing in California."

"That's terrific," I said, hunting for the gravy ladle. Charlie strolled in munching a cracker. "Charlie, Bobby's been promoted to director of something."

"What?"

"Mother doesn't know. What can you be the director of in the insurance business?"

"With his background, probably sales," Charlie said, smiling. "Now, isn't that great. He's a sharp guy."

"Now he'll probably never get home," Mother sighed. "Charlie, fix us a drink."

"Okay," Charlie said, reaching for the bottle on the top shelf. "You should be proud, Helen," he said to Mother, "everyone is doing very well."

Oh, sure, I thought, watching Charlie pour scotch

into glasses. Mary Kay is grabbing off every degree offered by the University of Detroit and a few they'll create just for her; Bobby is rising like a rocket in the insurance business and getting away with being mysterious about his life; and here I am, good old creepy Cassie, on temporary leave from the nuthouse and one drink away from a two-month binge. If someone were to ask me what I do, I would say that I'm a professional percher. I have developed the fine art of remaining precariously perched on the edge of disaster. Of course, I take a spill every now and again, but then I haven't yet received my degree in disaster or been promoted to disaster director. Shit.

Charlie paused in mid-pour. "What will you drink, Cassie? What will you have?"

I looked at the bottle. *I'll have a quart of scotch, a gallon of gin, a shot of heroin, and a suicide pill.*

"Have you any Coke, Mom?" I asked.

"Hmmm? Oh, sure, I got some soda for the kids. It's in the pantry."

I got a Coke from the pantry and returned to the kitchen. Charlie handed me a glass full of ice cubes. "Is this going to bother you, our drinking, I mean?"

"No," I said, not knowing if it would bother me, but thinking this would be a good time to find out. *The world isn't going to lock up the booze just because I can't handle it. I have to find out sometime what bothers me and what doesn't.*

"You're sure?"

"I'm sure."

"Tell the kids to get ready for dinner," Mother said.

The kids were sprawled in the living room. Wrappings littered the floor and they were each absorbed in a game or puzzle. Jenny was reading to her dog.

"Look, Mommy," she said, "I can read most of the words myself. Grandma gave me a book that has the same words we have in first grade."

"That's neat," I laughed. "You all go and wash up for dinner. It's almost ready. And pick up the papers and ribbon. It looks like a blizzard struck in here."

Though reluctant to tear themselves away, they got up. I sat on a hassock watching and sipping my Coke while they scooped up the glittering debris. Jenny and Greg ambled in the direction of the bathroom, but Steve slowly walked back to me. He stood silently in front of me wide-eyed and solemnly owlish behind his glasses.

"What is it?" I asked. "Is something wrong?" He looked like a deflated balloon.

"Nope," he said, with his hands behind him. I could feel the clenching.

"Mom," he said, then faltered.

"Yes?"

"I'm thirsty. Could I have a sip of your drink?"

"Why, sure, honey. Here." I held the glass for him and he took a gingerly sip, glanced up at me over the rim, and took another, longer drink.

"It's Coke," he announced with a grin, his face all smoothed out and eyes crinkling. "It's Coke."

He turned and walked away, while I sat, unable to move. My son. My little boy was checking me out. Tinkerbell was right. Acceptance wouldn't come overnight. Cold shivers slithered in waves up my back and a noise, halfway between a laugh and a cry, burst out of my throat.

"Steve," I called after him.

"What, Mom?"

"You can have a sip of my drink anytime you want," I said, tears beginning to roll down my cheeks. "I mean, anytime you feel like it you just ask me and you can have a sip of whatever I'm drinking. You understand?"

"Sure," he said, ignoring the tears. "I was just thirsty." And he ran off to join his brother and sister, leaving me curled on the hassock.

I won't disappoint any of you.

Dinner was noisy and boisterous and everyone ate too much and then ate some more. Mother had cooked enough for an army of starving Hessians and kept reminding us that she had two pies and vanilla ice cream in the kitchen, plus a fruitcake that Bobby sent from California, home of the Date Growers' Association.

Halfway through the meal, she jumped up from the table, returning with a box.

"Look at this," she said, pulling a vividly mottled scarf in horridly clashing colors from the tissue paper. "Your Aunt Irma sent this mess to me. I wouldn't hit a dog with it."

"Mother!" I said, laughing. "She probably shopped for half a day and thought it was beautiful."

"Either she didn't give a damn what she sent me or she's a fool and wasted her money," Mother said. "I'll never wear this." She stuffed it back in the box and then paused, struck by a sudden thought. "You don't suppose she's going blind, do you? I'll call her tonight."

I grinned at Charlie, who grinned back at me.

"Do you have to go to an AA meeting tonight, Mommy?" Greg asked with his mouth full.

"Not tonight," I answered. "They have a meeting tonight, but I'm going to wait until tomorrow."

"How come they have a meeting on Christmas?" Steve asked.

"Oh," I answered, "they have them every night, so people who have a problem can go whenever they want, whenever they need to. There's always someone to talk to when you feel bad or you're scared."

"I never get scared," Greg said, attacking his pile of potatoes.

"You do too," Steve said, poking him.

"Knock it off," Charlie commanded.

"I don't know why you want to go to those meetings anyway, Cassie," Mother said, frowning. "And hang around with all those awful people."

I knew that a few months ago, or maybe just weeks or even days, I would have replied angrily, feeling a need to defend myself and explain, explain, explain how I felt. Perhaps it was the half ton of delicious food I'd consumed, or the tree blinking in the corner, or the children across the table, but the bile didn't rise and I felt no need.

"The meetings are very nice, Mother," I said, "and besides, I'm one of those awful people."

"You're not," she glowered. "No one in my family—"

"Helen," Charlie interrupted. "She's doing the right thing. And she's doing a good job."

Mother looked surprised. "You approve?"

Charlie nodded. "I approve."

"Do you want mince or pumpkin or both?" Mother asked.

We did the dishes with a great clang of pots and half a box of detergent.

"Six hours' cooking, two hours' cleaning, and all for an hour of eating," Mother sighed.

Mary Kay called and told us how nervous she was about her upcoming exams and how she was sure she hadn't studied enough. Of course she would get A's and we would all say, "What were you worried about, kid? We knew it all along."

It was late, almost time to go. I tried to relax in the living room, dreading the thought of having to return to the hospital. The room, with the tree and the children, by now quiet and beginning to be sleepy, seemed so cozy and warm. Charlie was at the table in the kitchen playing checkers with Steve, who was concentrating with a fierce scowl. Jenny looked up from her puzzle, then rose from the floor and sat on the couch next to me.

"I wish you didn't have to go, Mommy," she said.

"I was just thinking the same thing," I sighed, pulling her onto my lap. "But I do."

She sighed and her little face looked pinched and clouded.

"Remember when you were little," I said softly, "and I used to wrap us both up in the brown afghan and rock in the rocking chair?"

"When I had colds and stuff," she nodded.

"Yes."

"That was a long time ago," she said.

"Too long," I replied, beginning to rock her awkwardly on the straight-backed sofa. She made a soft purring noise and nestled against my shoulder.

"What are you doing?" Mother asked, walking into the living room. She was carrying knitting needles and a ball of blue yarn.

"Just rocking Jenny," I whispered. "She's a sleepy little lady."

Mother settled herself on the couch. "She's too old to be rocked," she said. "You make a baby out of her."

"No I won't, Mom. Besides, everybody needs to be rocked sometime."

"Ha. That's what you think. I don't."

I glanced over at her. She was staring straight at me with her tiny jaw squared and thrust forward, a small, fair, fine-boned, pugnacious lady. I smiled at her ferocity.

"But you rocked me when I was small. I remember the chair—it seemed so huge—with a yellow chintz seat. And your mother must have rocked you."

"No, my mother never rocked me." The small chin quivered just a little.

"Never?" I asked, truly surprised.

"Never. Not once. She wasn't the type." The quiver became a tremble and the mist that rose to wash the pale blue eyes didn't quite extinguish the indignation burning through. "And the only reason I rocked you so much is that you had a hard time teething. You and your brother both. You weren't easy babies, Cassie."

"I know," I said automatically, staring at her.

"And your sister a year later. You wore me out, believe me." The mist was gone, the chin once again solidly square. "All three of you in diapers and I had to . . ."

She went on. I heard her voice rise and fall in a kind of cadence but I was no longer listening to the words. I cradled my daughter and stared at my mother, at a fifty-nine-year-old lady who had tears in her eyes, who suppressed emotions unacceptable to her, who capped her hurt with anger in order not to cry, who needed to cry, longed to cry because her mother had never rocked her, never wanted to, and now, never, ever would.

I stroked Jenny's cheek, thinking that perhaps Tinkerbell was teaching me to hear instead of just to listen, and knowing that it would be a while, hopefully a good long while, before I heard only the whining and ignored all the whys.

I smiled at Mother, who was making her points with jabbing knitting needles. *I hear what you're saying, Mother. If I were a widow and had to say Merry Christmas long distance to my children, if I had to shovel the snow off my walk in the mornings, and the only child I ever saw resented my cleaning her house, if I worried about my grandchildren and was told it was none of my business, if I lived alone and was often lonely and my mother had never, not even once, rocked me when I was a child, then Mother, I would cry, too.* I felt tears in my own eyes and bent over Jenny, brushing back the hair that had tumbled into her eyes.

"What's wrong?" Mother asked.

"Nothing," I said. "I think I'm feeling a little down because I have to go back to the hospital in a few minutes."

I could feel her stiffen, then sigh. I felt her hand on my arm. "Don't feel too bad, Cassie," she said. "You'll be home soon."

"All right," I said. "But I have to go now."

Mother got up and started shooing the children into their coats and hats. She dashed around with the kind of energy she always has when she feels angry or sad and doesn't know what to say.

Charlie went out the door with a load of presents under his arm. "I'll put these in the car," he called, "and be right back."

I shoved my feet into my boots wishing I could think of something to say, something to show that I understood just a fraction more, something to show that I cared. I always think of those things in retrospect and too late. The best conversation I ever had with my father was one week after he died.

I was ready. The children kissed and hugged their grandmother, and Charlie caught her in a rib-cracking embrace. "Terrific dinner, Helen. Thank you."

"I'll be over tomorrow, Charlie," she said.

I wrapped my arms around her and leaned down for a kiss. "That was a wonderful dinner, Mother. It was perfect. You worked so hard."

"It was nice, wasn't it?" she said.

"Better than that. Do you really like the bathrobe we gave you?" This was our year for bathrobes, it seemed.

"Oh, sure," she said, "I'm going to put it on as soon as you leave."

"Fine." I started out the door. "Mother," I said, with the door partway open, "do you think you could teach me to knit someday? I mean, I know I have ten thumbs, but you make such nice things, and, well, I thought you could start me out on something easy. . . . How about it?"

"Of course. I'll be happy to show you. Anytime. As soon as you come home."

Or even if I don't, I thought, thinking that I could also learn to knit at the West Side Residence for Women. I smiled. She seemed pleased.

"Take care," I called. "I'll phone you in a few days."

"I won't hold my breath," she said, waving.

As I settled myself in the car next to Charlie I looked back at the house. Mother was standing, silhouetted in the window with the Christmas tree twinkling behind her, still waving.

The drive home was silent. The children were tired and I wondered briefly what Charlie was thinking.

As we pulled in the driveway I whispered, "I have to get out of here fast, Charlie. This is very hard tonight and I feel terrible."

"Go ahead," he said, either understanding or not wanting to argue.

I kissed the kids quickly, before they had a chance to come fully awake and jumped in my car.

The snow stopped before I turned off West 25th Street and I flipped on the car radio. Usually I was so expert, so proficient at examining my feelings, at deciding exactly how I felt. Once I delved just below the surface there were no mysteries. But now I was itchily aware of new feelings, some fledgling, not-ready-to-fly feelings, and I didn't know how to sort them or know where they would belong once I had them tidily labeled. And I was tired.

The elevator still reeked of old overcoats. I punched the button for the seventh floor, then, changing my mind, punched the lobby button.

In the lobby I reached for a phone and dialed my number. Charlie answered.

"I just wanted to tell you, Charlie," I said breathlessly, "I had a very nice Christmas. I left without telling you that. Everything was . . . well, pleasant and lovely and nice."

"Everything?"

I heard what he was saying. "Everything," I said firmly.

"I had a good day too, Cass," he said. "One of our better Christmases I would say. Not perfect, but very, very good."

"Yes. Well, I just wanted to say good night . . . and Charlie . . . I put some laundry in the washing machine. You'd better put it in the dryer."

"I already did," he laughed, "and I had to wash it over again."

"Why?"

"You forgot the soap."

"Oh, Charlie, I'm sorry. Good night."

"Good night."

I went to the seventh floor wondering if I was going to do the same dumb things sober that I had done drunk. Woe.

Kenny buzzed me through the door.

"Where's Tink?" I asked.

"She's down the hall somewhere," he answered. "The troops are coming back all shot down."

I walked down the hall wondering what he meant. I poked my head in a room and saw Norma standing next to her bed, dressed in her coat. She had her back to me.

"Hi. Just come in?" I asked cheerily. "How was your Christmas?"

With a snarl of rage she turned and swatted me full in the face with her purse.

23

Norma had not had a good Christmas and she was certainly not alone. On December 26 the seventh-floor parlor was full of frayed and battered psyches. Evidently Christmas was an unmitigated joy only for the people who inhabited department-store brochures and seasonal television specials. For everyone else the day seemed to be a trip across a mine field seeded with resurrected family feuds, exacerbated loneliness, emotional excess, and the inevitable disappointments that arise when expectations fall far short of reality. We sat waiting for our shrinks in total silence. I pretended to read the newspaper, thinking that it had only been luck, an uncharacteristic willingness on my part to keep my mouth shut, and the obviously conscious cooperation of Charlie and Mother that had prevented disaster at my Christmas.

"So you had a good day," Alexander said when I saw him.

"Yes," I replied, "I did. In fact, considering all that's happened and is still happening, and all the intense emotions and undercurrents of anger and confusion, and all the questions that weren't asked and things that everyone refrained from mentioning, I would say that Christmas dinner at my mother's house was one of the peak accomplishments of civilization."

Alexander laughed. "I wouldn't go that far," he said.

"You weren't there. It reminded me of when I was little and my brother and sister and I would fight over a game we were playing. My mother would come in and yell at us and say, 'Stop all this arguing or you'll have to go to your rooms.' So we would settle down and play quietly and after a while she'd come back and say, 'See how nice you can play when you want to?' Well, yesterday we all played nice."

"It sounds charming," Alexander smiled.

"It was. But anyone can play nice for one day. It didn't solve anything. Charlie and I have the same problems we've always had, and as for my mother, well, I think I understand her a little better, but it's definitely a one-way street at this point. She can be so abrasive at times. Then I react and we fight and the whole thing starts all over again. I can't see that changing one bit. It was a nice Christmas. That's all."

"Okay," he said. "Maybe for now, that's enough."

"Maybe," I replied, dubious and waiting for him to say something about going home. But he rose from the swivel chair, stretched and yawned.

"Haven't worked off my Christmas dinner yet," he commented, patting his tummy.

Christmas dinner, Edwin? You ate Christmas dinner? Then you aren't Jewish. It's not that I thought that you were Jewish. It just never occurred to me that you weren't. I just assumed that I'm involved in a system where all doctors are Jewish and all patients are Catholic.

"Is there something you want to say?" he asked. "You look as if you have something on your mind."

"Oh, no," I quickly replied, "my mind is a total blank. Scout's honor."

"Sure, it is," he smirked, and ducked out the door.

I walked back to my room wondering when Alexander planned to raise the question of my departure. There had to be some reason for my continuing residence on the seventh floor. I grinned to myself. Maybe Alexander was enjoying my company and couldn't bear to think of seeing me only once a week. I laughed out loud. It might be a fantasy, but it was certainly more fun to think about than the idea of an ongoing and perhaps intractable disease.

"May I talk to you for a moment?" a voice hissed from behind me. I turned to see Norma.

"That depends," I said, backing off. "How do you feel? Where's your purse?"

She winced and a faint red flush crept from her collarbone to her forehead.

"I'm sorry about that," she whispered. "When you came in last night sounding like you were on top of the world and asked me how my Christmas was, well, I don't know. I just lost control of myself, that's all. I didn't know what I was . . . well, I shouldn't have, but you're so . . . so goddamn aggravating." She was beginning to look angry again and I took three steps backward.

"Why am I aggravating?" I asked, puzzled. I'd never done anything to her.

She shrugged. "Oh, it's you and your damned AA and the way you seem to have it all figured out. You know what your problem is and what to do. . . . It's just so damn simple for you."

Simple! I gaped at her. *This crazy woman thinks it's simple! Simple! Calculus is simple. Space travel is simple. A cure for cancer is simple. My life, you idiot nut, is anything but simple. If it's so simple, why am I still here?*

"Why are you still here?" Norma asked.

I jumped, thinking perhaps I'd spoken out loud. Had I, she would be whacking me again, not asking questions.

"Beats me," I replied.

She glanced around furtively and lowered her voice even more.

"I shouldn't be asking you this," she said, "and I expect you'll say no, but you're the only one I can ask, the only one here who has a car and I wondered if maybe you would, well, ummm—" She stopped, blinking rapidly.

"What? What?" I prodded, hoping she wouldn't ask me to help her escape.

She put her hand on my arm. "Would you . . . could you," she hissed, "drive me to Mount Olive Cemetery?"

"Whatever for?" I asked, snatching my arm away.

I could only imagine what she had in mind, what perverse and bizarre—

"My husband is buried there. I would like to visit his grave."

"Oh."

"I haven't been there for months," she continued, white-faced and trembling. "I really feel I need to . . . would you?"

I couldn't think of anywhere I wanted less to go. And I couldn't think of any reason to refuse.

"If it's all right with Dalton and your doctor—you have Fisher, don't you?—then I'll take you," I said, wishing I could think of a way to squirm out of it. "My father is buried there."

Minutes later she was in my room saying it was peachy with Fisher and Dalton. Within a half hour I was once again negotiating the ruts on Brookpark Road, with Norma, who resembled a pale, coiled spring, twisted in knots on the seat beside me. I watched her nervously out of the corner of my eye and made occasional stabs at conversation.

"I'm surprised you were able to get permission so quickly," I said. "Romping midst the tombstones doesn't seem like an activity they would encourage."

"I didn't ask if I could go," she snapped. "I lied."

"But you said you had permission."

"Just keep your mouth shut. I won't tell."

I've been had, I thought, curiosity overcoming my anger. I wondered why this is so important to her.

"Do you have any children?" I asked, trying again.

"They're in a foster home." Her eyes glinted dangerously.

"Oh."

We drove through massive iron gates flanked by marble angels on great gray stone pedestals.

"Turn to the left," Norma directed. "He's buried near the statue of Saint Paul."

"My father is somewhere over in the Saint Peter section."

"You can visit his grave."

"No, thanks. Tell me where to stop."

I drove slowly over gently sloping hills while Norma craned her neck out the window as if uncertain where to stop.

She grabbed my arm. "Here! Here it is. Stop."

I pulled over to the side and watched as Norma got out of the car and walked slowly up the slight incline. Small, uniformly sized headstones were laid out, like extracted teeth, in neat rows. I decided I'd better get out of the car and go with her, remaining close in case some demonic spirit caused her to run away, although I hadn't the vaguest idea what I would do if Norma decided to take flight. The favors I did for people certainly seemed to turn out less than well. Ronnie had never arrived at Joanne's sister's, and somehow she had come to the conclusion that it was my fault for persuading her not to wait. Would a convent still take me, I wondered, trudging the incline in Norma's footsteps.

Norma stared down at the grave, white-faced and as rigidly frozen as the stone angels. Her arms were tightly folded across her body in a viselike self-embrace. I shuddered, imagining cracked ribs. I looked down at the headstone.

"Why, he was young," I said. "Only forty-one."

She nodded curtly, then said, "A year before he died the doctor told Ralph he had cirrhosis. Told him he'd die if he didn't quit drinking. He quit for three weeks, then went right back to it. Said there were more old drunks than old doctors."

I sat down on a tombstone. "How hard for you."

Her face remained impassive, her voice a monotone. "I nursed him the best I could. Tried to hide the liquor. Used to pour it down the sink. He'd just go get more. He used to get drunk and scream that I was against him. Me and the doctor. In league, he said. He actually died of pneumonia. It was a blessing."

She fell silent, but her mouth began to move as though her jaw was about to come unhinged. Still no sound.

"Maybe we'd better go," I said apprehensively.

Her blank, glassy eyes widened and bulged and

suddenly she wore a gargoyle's mask, a face so distorted that it sent blood and terror pounding in my
ears.

"Norma!" I said sharply, but she wasn't hearing.

Her back arched with an audible snap and, flinging
her arms in the air, she threw herself on the grave.

"I hope you're happy, you son of a bitch," she
screamed, flailing the stone with her fists. "I hope
you're proud of yourself, dying like that and leaving
me with two little kids to raise." Sobs blended with
her screams and I was afraid she'd choke to death. "I
tried to tell you. Would you listen? No. Not to me, not
to anybody. Well, I hope you're happy. I'm in the
goddamn nuthouse and your kids are with a rotten old
whore who doesn't feed them enough! Have another
drink, you son of a bitch! God help me. Oh."

Her screaming subsided and she sobbed deeply, lying flat on the ground with her arms over her head.
I reached in my pocket for a cigarette, lit it and
smoked, waiting.

The sobs became a low moan, until finally she sat
up and wiped her wet, dirt-smeared face with her
sleeve.

"I'm freezing," she said.

She stood and began brushing the dirt from her
coat. Without another word we walked to the car.

Two blocks from the hospital she said, "Let's stop
for coffee. The hospital makes theirs with dishwater. I
haven't had good coffee in weeks."

"Sure thing," I said, and headed for a nearby How-
ard Johnson's.

We had coffee and apple pie and talked about our
children.

Back at the hospital, Norma went up ahead of
me, while I bought candy bars in the coffee shop.

"There's a message for you," Dalton greeted me.

"Oh, no," I replied, expecting, as always, the worst.
It was a phone number I didn't recognize.

"Who is it?" I asked Dalton.

"I don't know," she shrugged. "The ward clerk took
the call. You don't have to return it if you don't
want to."

"Yeah, I've heard that tune before," I said, heading for the patient phone. "And collected the demerits."

A familiar voice answered, "Hello."

"Why, Cara. How the hell are you? What a surprise!"

"Can you meet me for lunch?" she asked, panting. "At Stouffer's on the Square?"

"I guess so. Sure. What's wrong?"

"I'll see you in an hour. 'Bye." And she hung up.

Christ, I thought, clenching the receiver. What the hell is going on with her? I'm not sure I'm ready for this.

Stouffer's was full of old ladies with cameo pins, eating chicken pot pie.

I divided my time between putting out cigarettes and fiddling with the silverware. I should have known she'd be late. Then she was beside me in a cherry-red coat trimmed with dark fur, all glowing and radiant.

"You look terrific," I said, as she sat down.

"You don't," she remarked, settling in. "It's that black dress and institutional pallor. When are you getting out?"

"As soon as Alexander—I don't know."

"You're waiting for Alexander to stamp 'CURED' on your forehead and send you off into the big, bad world all by your onesies?"

"Alexander must have a reason—"

"Bullshit. He does what he wants to do just like everybody else and you think he has reasons because he's a psychiatrist. You're stupid, Cassie."

"He's done fairly well with me so far," I protested, wishing I would stop allowing Cara to push me into defending what I wasn't quite sure of myself. "He seems to know what he's doing."

"Crap. He flies by the seat of his pants."

"Are you still seeing him?"

"No."

"Oh, I see." And I did.

"I have something better."

A waiter appeared at my elbow. "Would you ladies like a drink?"

"I'll have a daiquiri," Cara said.

"And I'll have a Coke," I added, picking up the menu.

"Have a real drink," Cara said suddenly. The waiter was still there, crouching at attention.

I stared at her, amazed. "You know I can't," I said quietly.

"Just because Alexander says you can't?" she sneered. "Big Daddy says the naughty little girl can't have any?"

"I don't remember Dr. Alexander ever saying that. He just—never mind."

"If the naughty little girl has a little drink, then Big Daddy won't love her anymore," she went on in a high-pitched singsong.

"Cara, stop." The waiter looked bored.

Her eyes flashed. "You're a grown woman. Why don't you do what you want to do and to hell with him!"

"I'm doing what I want to do, Cara," I said softly. "I'm an alcoholic."

"If that's what you want to believe. If that's what you let him call you—"

"He never said it. I did. That's the way it is."

The waiter coughed. "Then it will be one daiquiri and one Coke. Would you care to order now?"

"Chicken pot pie," I said, unable to think of anything else, yet not in the slightest upset. I think I just won one, I thought, feeling peaceful.

"And I'll have a hamburger with everything on it," Cara added, evidently in the best of humor.

Our drinks came and I told her about Norma.

Cara listened, dunking a celery stick into her drink.

"She's such a hostile bitch," she commented. "Old Ralphie was probably glad to croak."

"She's been through a lot, Cara."

"Haven't we all?"

Our lunches arrived. "Tell me about this something better," I said, poking at my pie.

"You just won't believe how fantastic it is, Cassie," she bubbled. "My new boyfriend, he's a dentist I met at one of my mother's cocktail parties—"

"How's your mother?"

"She should get leprosy. Anyway, Axel just went through it and he said it's changed his life. Completely. And I'm going next weekend."

"Where? For what?"

"New York. There's this man named Montgomery Talbot who gave up the magazine business—he was a research assistant—to develop this program. He says that one day he woke up and looked around him and saw all these people leading miserable, unfulfilled lives and he decided to do something about it. So he developed this program called Life-Crash."

"A true humanitarian. What's the program?"

"Well, Axel says that they lock you in a room with fifty or sixty people and two therapists, personally trained by Montgomery Talbot. You're not allowed to go to the bathroom and there's only one break for a peanut butter sandwich and when they unlock the doors seventy-two hours later, you're a different person."

"I would imagine, what with kidney failure and malnutrition and all—"

"Goddammit, Cassie, I'm serious," she shouted. The hum of conversation ceased as people turned to stare.

"Okay, okay. But what really happens," I asked, "and do you honestly think you can permanently change your life in a meaningful way with seventy-two hours of therapy?"

"Talbot is supposed to be very dynamic, and it's better than seeing Alexander for the rest of my life."

"I don't care how dynamic he is. It sounds like a TV dinner, 'Therapy flash-frozen and ready to serve. Heat and eat.' Another golden key. You still haven't told me what happens."

"Well, I'm not sure exactly. Axel says I'll have to experience it for myself. You can't get it secondhand. But he says that Monty says—everybody calls him Monty—"

"Cute."

"Monty says that people cause their own diseases with their own minds and that they also have the power to cure them, and even better, to prevent them from ever starting."

"Physical things as well?"

"Especially physical things. Monty has the power, Axel says."

I lit a cigarette and blew smoke through my nose. "Then Monty claims to be immortal."

Cara blinked. "What do you mean?"

"Well," I said, flicking an ash into the ashtray, "if he claims he can prevent disease with his mind, then he will never get sick, and if he never gets sick, then he will never die. Unless he gets run over by a tugboat."

"I don't know." Cara shook her head. "I don't know that he claims to be immortal. I'll have to ask Axel."

"And if he's right and all disease is caused by the mind, but he can't prevent getting sick himself, why the hell should you go all the way to New York to be locked in a room with peanut butter sandwiches?"

"There's more to it than that, Cassie. Axel says that Monty has given him a new lease on life, has completely turned him around, shown him a new way of thinking, of living—"

"How's he done that?"

Cara's eyes sparkled. She grasped my hand, wringing it in her enthusiasm.

"By telling him that he must take the responsibility for his own actions, his own life," she gurgled. "By pointing out that reality is to be accepted, life to be lived, joy to be experienced, pain to be worked through—"

"But, Cara," I interrupted, "that's the same thing Alexander has been telling you for two years." She dropped my hand.

"Well, Monty must say it differently," she pouted, "or there must be more to it than that. Axel says that he's a changed man and he's tried as many things as I have. Before this he couldn't even find a therapist who would help him stop smoking and lose weight."

"So now he's stopped smoking and lost weight."

"Not exactly. But now he knows why. He says he found out it's his own fault, his own responsibility."

"Good for Axel," I laughed.

"It's nothing to laugh about," Cara said angrily. "Axel says he tingles with awareness, and when he wants to quit, he'll quit. He just doesn't want to—yet. He's given up chocolate, though."

"Bully."

"You should talk," she huffed, "with your AA. You have to keep going forever."

"I have a poor memory, Cara. If I went to Life-Crash, I'd come home and a week later forget I'd been changed."

"I don't laugh at AA," she said indignantly. "You shouldn't laugh at Life-Crash."

"That's true." I softened. She had a point.

"And it's helped so many people." She was gurgling again. "One of the men in Axel's group said that he found the courage to tell his wife that the reason he hadn't been home in eight months is because they're separated."

"You mean she hadn't figured it out? He should hold on to her. Women like that aren't easy to find."

"You're laughing again," she accused.

"Sorry," I said, straightening my face. I reached for her hand. "Cara, I really do hope this works for you. I hope it's everything you want it to be and you come back feeling wonderful and all together . . . and—"

"I expect to," she said positively.

"Can I drop you anywhere?" I asked, suddenly feeling sad and wanting to go.

"No. I'm going to do some shopping here at the Square and then Axel is picking me up for dinner. He's shortened his office hours so he can have more time for life."

"Huh?"

"Real living, he says, instead of just existing. Although, since Monty, he likes his work better. He told me that he's overcome his aversion to saliva and now views his patients with unconditional positive regard."

"You can't ask for more than that," I grinned.

We paid the check and strolled out the door, arm in arm. Cara walked me to my car. Large snowflakes fell and were caught in her dark hair. She looked like a watercolor of the enchanted Snow Princess in one of

my childhood fairy tales. The Snow Princess in search
of Prince Charming or, failing that, a mystical guru
with a magic potion.

I threw my arms around her. This time she hugged
me back.

"Take care, honey. Take very good care of yourself."

"You, too," she whispered.

"And call me sometime when you get back."

"I will," she promised. "And you call me when you
get out."

I nodded and got into the car. I drove back to the
hospital wondering why Cara always left me with an
urge to go after her, wrap her up in a blanket, and
take her home where it was safe. And then spank her.
I felt extraordinarily lonely. We hadn't exchanged
phone numbers.

"Returning Christmas presents?" Tinkerbell asked,
as she buzzed me through the door.

"No. I had lunch with Cara."

"How is she?" Tink asked.

"She's buying another brand of snake oil."

24

I had just seen Alexander and was back in my room,
pondering. We seemed to have entered some sort of
limbo. He watched me and I watched him and
though he talked, there seemed to be no sense of ac-
complishing anything. Just trivia, and rehashing, covering old, familiar territory, smoking one cigarette after
another.

It's almost as though we're companions, I thought, *marking time and waiting for something. It's all pleasant enough, but God, it's making me edgy. What are we doing? What's going on?*

I stretched out on my bed, thinking I'd take a short nap, and maybe come up with a significant dream. I was running out of material for the trivia mill.

My door opened and Dalton entered with a very old man who looked as if he had a light socket sticking out of each ear.

She stood at the foot of Caliguire's bed.

"Guess what, Mrs. Caliguire," she gushed. "Your brother's here and you're going home!"

"What?" I shouted, leaping off my bed. "She's going where?"

"Home!" Dalton repeated, looking enraptured. "Isn't that wonderful?"

"It's ridiculous!" I exploded. "She hasn't moved! She hasn't twitched! She hasn't opened her goddamn eyes in—ever! Not once! How the hell can she go home?"

Dalton glared at me. "Dr. Fisher says that Mrs. Caliguire is ready to go home and he certainly knows more about her case than you do. He is a doctor. You are a patient. He knows, you don't. Now I'll thank you to be quiet while Mrs. Caliguire gets ready to go home."

"Who's she?" the old man asked in a quavery voice.

"I'm Cassie Barrett," I said. "We share this room."

"Loom? What loom? I don't see any loom," he said, looking around.

"Oh, God," I sighed.

Dalton took Caliguire's clothes out of her half of the closet.

"Here we go," she said cheerfully, approaching the bed. "Upsy daisy."

I fled down the hall and pounded on the counter at the nurses' station. Pomeroy refused to be distracted from her crossword puzzle.

"May I help you?" she mumbled.

"You're goddamn right you can help me," I screamed. "You can tell me why Caliguire is going home in the same shape she arrived in while I am still here collecting dust in the goddamn mausoleum for misfits! Why? Just tell me why?"

Pomeroy glanced up and smiled sweetly. "Her doctor has released her and yours has not. What's an eight-letter word for a kind of circus?"

"Shaker Heights Hospital. But, goddammit, Pomeroy, she's no better. If anything, she's worse!"

Pomeroy smiled. "She's going home, Cassie, so obviously she must be better. Now, mustn't she?"

"No, goddammit," I exploded, then gave up. "The word is 'carnival.' " Pomeroy was like the proverbial brick wall. I'd save it for Tinkerbell. She'd have a sensible answer.

A few minutes later Dalton pushed Caliguire past me in a wheelchair. She was all mashed to one side, slumped and sound asleep, or unconscious, or dead. I'd never know. Her brother shuffled along behind, looking confused.

"Goodbye and good luck," I said, under my breath. I started back to my room thinking that it would really be no emptier than it had been before.

"Pssssst." It was Gloria, lurking in an alcove.

"What is it, Gloria?"

"You don't know why Caliguire is going home?" she said, shaking a finger at me. "You're sure dumb."

"Because she has been restored to health, as any fool can plainly see," I said, very annoyed. "Another fabulous recovery, another minor miracle from medical science."

"She was on Medicare," Gloria whispered. "Her time was up."

"Oh, Gloria," I said, dismayed. "That's terrible."

"That's Fisher," she shrugged. "The second your time is up, out you go."

"Christ, that's not right."

"That's policy."

"That's awful."

"That's life."

"Then who needs it?" I shouted, ran to my room and slammed the door. I threw myself on the bed, sobbing and perplexed. Why was I carrying on so about Caliguire? She didn't mean anything to me. Then I recognized the cold clutch of fear in my stomach. If it could happen to her, it could happen to me. I'd heard the bell tolling. Slowly I rose from my bed, went to the closet and pulled on my coat.

"Where are you going?" Dalton asked.

"Home to fix dinner for the kids," I said, signing the register, "then to an AA meeting."

"How nice," she said, in a voice honey-coated with approval.

"On the other hand, I may go downtown, get loaded and pick up a sailor."

"That's not funny, Mrs. Barrett."

"I didn't mean it to be. Buzz me out, Dalton."

Dalton's hand hovered over the button. She looked momentarily undecided, then hit the buzzer.

"Come right back if you feel upset," she called after me.

Sure, I thought, running down the stairs. As long as my insurance is up-to-date.

By the time I neared home I was calmer. That's life, Gloria said, and she was right. It wasn't easy, it wasn't fair, some of the time it wasn't even worth living but it sure as hell was life. So who promised you nirvana, Cassie?

The lights in the living room were on as I pulled into the driveway behind Charlie's car. He's home early, I thought.

As I opened the door the odor of cooking food drifted out. Pork. And potatoes.

"Anybody home?" I called, somewhat nervously. I'd always called before I came home, to announce my arrival and get the lay of the land, so to speak. And to give Charlie a chance to prepare, I suppose.

"What are you doing here?" he asked, popping out of the kitchen. He had a head of lettuce in his hand.

"I live here."

"You could have fooled me," he grinned. "I didn't know you were coming home."

"Neither did I." I hung up my coat. "I just thought I'd go to the meeting at Women's Federal Saving tonight, and as long as I was in the neighborhood, stop in and fix dinner. But you're already started. What are you doing home so early?"

"Oh, I don't like to keep your mother too late. She gets tired. And the kids can't be left alone. So I leave work as early as I can." He frowned. "I'll probably lose my job one of these days, but—how about some help in the kitchen?"

"Sure. Where are the kids?"

"Downstairs in the basement. Steve is riding his bike in circles and the other two are being highway patrolmen. Jenny is the siren and Greg writes the tickets."

"Who thought that one up?"

"I did. Do you know how hard it is to fix dinner with everyone crowded into the kitchen?"

"You're kidding. Tell me about it." We grinned at each other.

Charlie chopped lettuce while I peeked in the oven. There was a small pork roast surrounded by whole potatoes, four of them.

"I'll have bread," I said.

"Hmm? Oh, the potatoes. No, we'll split a potato and we'll both have bread."

"Good deal."

I set the table and Charlie poured milk and made tea. *This is my week for feeling companionable,* I thought, peering through my kitchen window into the frosty blackness outside.

"Charlie, I can see clearly out of the window."

"Your mother was here."

"Hey, I can see the moon. Look, Charlie, it's full."

"Watch out for werewolves aprowl," Charlie said.

"I will," I promised, still staring at the bright silver surface with all its craters sharply etched. Maybe there was something to be said for clean windows. *I can always let it get dirty again,* I thought, *if I decide I like it better that way.* I shook my head. What was I thinking?

"Call the kids," Charlie said. "They'll be surprised."

"Okay." I went to the head of the stairs and called, "Yoo, hoo. Are there any hungry people down there?"

"Mommy!" I heard Greg's voice shout and a second later they were tumbling up the stairs. "Hey, Mommy!"

"Hi," I said, kissing heads as they appeared. Steve was flushed from riding his bike.

"What's for dinner?" Greg asked, scooting past me.

"Daddy made pork. Wash up."

"Yum," Jenny enthused.

Dinner was much more relaxed than Christmas had been, closer to normal, I thought, trying to remember when we'd last had a "normal" dinner. I hadn't eaten with the family very often in those last months. Usually I'd put the food on the table and retreat to the bedroom with a drink. When I'd fixed dinner at all.

"You aren't eating," I said to Steve, who sat with his fork in his hand, listlessly picking at his food. "Don't you feel well, honey?"

"Come here, Steve," Charlie said. "Let Mommy feel your head."

"I don't want to," he scowled. "She's always feeling my head. She can feel Greg's head."

"Come here this minute," I ordered. He walked to me reluctantly. More than any of them he didn't like being sick, seeming to feel that the extra fuss wasn't worth all the hassle that went with it. Unlike his mother, I thought, reaching for his forehead. Mommy loves fuss.

"He's burning up, Charlie," I said, startled. Steve's forehead was dry and very hot.

"Here, let me feel." Charlie reached for him. "You always exaggerate."

"Well, you can't tell the difference between normal and a hundred and twelve," I snapped. It was true. He couldn't.

"He is warm," Charlie agreed. "And he was coughing after school. Your mother said he looked peaked."

"Nobody's looked peaked since 1938," I said. "Let's stop all this feeling and take his temperature."

"I'll get the thermometer," Charlie said and went to the bathroom.

"Let me see your throat," I commanded, holding a large tablespoon in my right hand.

"Aw, Mom," he said, but his protest was feeble.

"Open up."

"How is it?" Charlie asked, returning with the thermometer.

"Bright red with white streaks," I said, popping the thermometer in Steve's mouth. "I think I'd better call Dr. Halston."

"Get the temperature first," Charlie advised. "If you kids are finished eating, you can go watch television."

"Does Steve get to stay home tomorrow?" Greg wanted to know.

"Probably," I said, reading the thermometer. It was just over one hundred and three.

"Rats," Greg said, and disappeared.

"Look, Charlie," I said, not wanting Steve to hear how high his fever was.

"You know I can't read those things," Charlie whispered. "What is it?"

I told him. He whistled. "Call the doctor."

A few minutes later I walked into the bedroom, where Charlie was helping Steve get into his pajamas.

"What did he say?" Charlie asked.

I frowned. "He said it sounds like an upper respiratory infection similar to the one Steve had last year. He said it's going around again and we should keep him warm, give him aspirin and lots of fluids and bring him in to the office tomorrow."

"Maybe your mother could—no, I'd better do it," Charlie sighed. "She doesn't know where the doctor is. If I miss any more work . . ." He leaned down to button the pajama top. "How you feeling, fella?" he asked.

Steve didn't answer. His eyes were glassy.

"I'd better get the aspirin," I said.

"I tucked him in bed," Charlie said, walking into the kitchen, where I was hunting for aspirin. "It's on the bottom shelf."

"Here it is," I said, wrestling with the childproof cap. Charlie took the bottle from me.

"Here," he said, plopping two in my hand.

"That's one of the things I can't stand about you, Charlie," I said and marched off to give Steve his aspirin.

Two hours later I was sitting in the living room smoking and glancing nervously at the clock. We'd put Greg and Jenny in bed and Charlie was reading the paper.

"Isn't it time for you to go to your meeting?" he asked, peeking over the headlines. "Bay Village Woman Spots UFO," it read.

"It's past time," I replied. "The meeting has already started. I hate to leave when Steve's sick. I feel guilty."

"No need," he said, folding the paper. "I can take care of him. He'll be fine. Go to your meeting."

"It's just that sometimes his fever doesn't go down when he's sick. You know that. It just gets higher and higher."

"Dr. Halston says he'll grow out of it," Charlie said. "And I'll check him every half hour or so. Go ahead."

"Are you sure?"

"Yes, it's okay."

Even with permission, official, certified, sanctified permission, I was unable to move. I remained in the chair.

"I can't go," I said.

Charlie said nothing.

"I have to go," I said. I squirmed, stymied.

Charlie just sat quietly and watched me.

"What are you going to do, Cassie?"

"I don't know," I groaned, miserable. "What do you think I should do?"

"I don't know," he said. "I can't say."

There was no sound except the whistling of the wind outside and a branch of the tree in the front yard that rapped rhythmically against the porch overhang.

"I'll stay here until it's time for the meeting to be over," I said finally. "And then I'll go back to the hospital."

"Okay with me," Charlie said, and resumed reading his paper.

I turned on the radio and something by Puccini filled the air. I sat down again and hunched in the chair, tapping my foot nervously.

"Read a magazine," Charlie suggested.

"Wouldn't you like to talk to me?"

"About what?"

"Nothing," I sighed. I read a magazine.

Every half hour I crept into the room where the boys were sleeping and hesitantly touched Steve's forehead. I didn't want to wake him.

"How is he?" Charlie asked.

"Still hot, Charlie. Very hot." I frowned. "It's almost eleven o'clock. I have to go."

I sat down again and waited for another half hour.

"He's still burning up," I said, after I checked him again.

"When does he get his aspirin?"

"Not for at least an hour. Charlie, this is awful. I'm going to call the hospital."

"What for?"

"I'm going to tell Tinkerbell that Steve is sick and I want to stay until morning. I just can't go back with him running that kind of fever."

"Suit yourself," Charlie said, without any emotion whatsoever.

Cold fish, I thought, dialing the hospital. Charlie had never seen any of the kids through a medical crisis on his own. Let him see how he likes it for a change.

"Seventh floor, Miss Andover."

"Tink, it's Cassie."

"What's wrong, Cassie? Where are you?" She sounded alarmed.

"I'm at home. And I'm all right. But my son is sick," I explained hastily, wondering if Dalton had passed along my remark about getting loaded and picking up a sailor. I almost said "honest" but stopped just in time, feeling very childish.

"Which son?" she asked, remembering that I had two. "What's wrong?"

"It's probably just an upper respiratory infection. He's going to see the doctor in the morning. But the problem is that he runs these terribly high fevers when he gets sick, and, well, I just don't want to leave him. I want to stay here until morning."

"I know how you must feel," she said, sounding sympathetic, "but it's against hospital rules for you to stay out overnight, for any reason."

"Maybe if I called Alexander?"

"That would just put him on the spot," she said. "It isn't his rule. It's policy. If you stay out overnight, it's an automatic discharge and I've never known them to take anyone back under those circumstances."

"Never?"

"No. They can't set a precedent. I'm sorry."

"I am, too," I said. "It looks like I'll have to come back then. Oh, dammit, Tinkerbell," I groaned.

"I am sorry, Cassie. Look, here's what I'll do. I know you won't sleep tonight, so I'll let you camp out in the parlor and you can call home from the phone at the nurses' station every half hour if you want. And tell your husband to call the floor if there's any change and I'll get you to the phone. Okay?"

"That's really nice of you. I appreciate it." It was better, but it was far from okay. "I'll see you in less than an hour."

"I'll be waiting. Don't be too late. 'Bye, dear."

I hung up. *I'll never forget that lady,* I thought, *not as long as I live.*

"What did she say?" Charlie asked.

I explained about hospital policy.

"Then you have no choice," Charlie said sensibly. "Just tell me what to do before you leave."

"Give him two more aspirin in an hour," I said, beginning to wish I'd never come home. No, that wasn't true. I wished I didn't have to leave. "Be sure to check him every half hour. If he doesn't feel any cooler, you'll have to wake him up and take his temperature."

Charlie winced.

"I know," I said, "but you'll have to do it. If it gets to one hundred and five—"

"One hundred and five!"

"It's gotten that high, Charlie. Remember, I told you. Four times during the day when you were at work and once when you were in New York on business."

"I knew it had gotten high, but one hundred and five!" Charlie looked stunned.

"Are you sure you can handle this?" I asked anxiously.

"Sure I can. I just didn't know how high it got, that's all. What do I do?"

"If it goes to one hundred and five, pick him up out of bed and—Charlie, this is awful." I started to cry. "I feel just terrible about leaving like this and—"

He put his arm around me. "It isn't your fault. You didn't make hospital policy and you didn't make Steve sick, and you mustn't blame yourself. I understand."

I snuggled into his shoulder. *I wish I was ready,* I thought desperately. *I wish I knew what I wanted to do with my life, about Charlie, about me, about us. I wish I could just decide right now and be done with it. I'm not ready. I don't know. I can't come back and have everything just go on the same. The way it was. Oh God, it was killing me.*

"I understand," Charlie repeated. I straightened and looked at him. He did. At this moment, about this situation, Charlie understood.

"Let's go in and check Steve and then I'll tell you the rest," I said.

"And then you'd better fly," he nodded. "It's nearly midnight."

As we entered the room I heard a dry, raspy breathing. Each breath seemed to catch in the middle, stopping, then continue haltingly on.

"My God, is that Steve breathing like that?" Charlie clutched me.

"Get the thermometer. Quick, Charlie," I said, flipping on the light.

Steve's face was chalk-white except for two scarlet blotches, one on each cheek. He'd kicked off his blanket and lay sprawled, with his chest violently heaving up and down.

"Steve. Wake up." I shook him, but he remained limp, refusing to awaken.

"I'll have to take his temperature rectally," I said,

taking the thermometer from Charlie. I rolled Steve over. He didn't resist.

"Oh, Charlie."

He held my hand. "Now, now," he said, looking worried sick. "It's going to be all right."

"It's one hundred and six, Charlie," I gasped. "Turn on the shower. Hurry. Make it cold."

Charlie hurried to the bathroom while I struggled to get Steve out of bed. He was a dead weight and I could only half lift him.

"Here, I'll take him," Charlie said, slipping an arm under Steve's shoulders. Steve moaned but didn't wake up.

"What do I do now?"

"Get into the shower with him, Charlie," I said, crying and pushing him toward the bathroom. "Hurry, before he has convulsions!"

I held open the shower door while Charlie struggled to get in with his burden.

"Okay," Charlie shouted, and stood directly under the cascading, icy downpour holding his son in his arms. Steve gasped with shock and screamed, trying to twist away from the deluge of freezing water.

"He's slipping, Cassie. I can't hold him!"

"Here, Charlie, I'll help." I jumped into the shower and shivered as frigid needles hit me. The water was so cold it burned.

"I've got him on this side, Charlie. Hold on."

We stood in the shower with our arms around our boy, shaking with cold and fright, trying to restrain him and keep him from falling and hold him under the water at the same time.

"It's all right, Steve. It's all right. Mommy and Daddy are here," I said over and over, more to myself than to him. Suddenly I could feel the fever draining from his body. The wet skin through the soaked pajamas was cooler.

"It's working!" I shouted to Charlie. "It's working!"

He nodded. He'd felt it, too.

A few minutes later I backed out of the shower, with my arms still around Steve. He was wide awake and sobbing. I reached for a bath towel.

"Take off his pajamas, Charlie," I said. He was already pulling them off.

"I'm sorry, honey, but we had to do that," I said, rubbing Steve down. His teeth chattered, and he looked both exhausted and furious.

Charlie took a towel out of the linen closet and began drying Steve's hair. "That's a rotten thing to do to a guy in the middle of the night, isn't it, Steve?"

"I'll get his clean pajamas," I said. When I returned to the bathroom Charlie was holding Steve, wrapped in towels in his arms. He no longer looked furious, just very, very tired.

"Here you go," I said, and we dressed him.

"Can I go to bed now?" Steve asked as Charlie buttoned his pajama top.

"Sure, it's about time." Charlie picked him up and carried him to his bed. I brought the aspirin. Steven swallowed two, grunted, turned over, and was asleep before we could turn out the light.

"He certainly got over that fast," Charlie remarked. "Probably too worn out to cry."

"And he's been through it before," I said.

"He has?" Charlie looked surprised. "That's right. You told me something about having to give him a cold shower once before. But I had no idea it was anything like that."

"That's exactly what it was like," I said. "It was the time you were in New York. An upper respiratory infection. Of the type the doctor persists in calling simple."

"How did you ever manage it alone?" Charlie asked. "It took two of us just now."

I thought back. "I don't know," I said. "Maybe he wasn't quite as big and strong then. Anyway, you do what you have to do. There wasn't anyone else here."

Charlie's arm went around me and he pulled me close. "I'm glad you were here, Cass. I was wrong. I couldn't have handled it alone."

"Neither could I," I admitted. "Not this time. Charlie, did you just say you were wrong?"

Charlie's arm dropped away. "If we don't get out of

these wet clothes, we'll both have a simple upper respiratory and spend the next week pushing each other into cold showers."

"What a stunning idea," I laughed, walking to the bedroom. It was all right. I'd heard what I'd heard.

I began shivering all over again as I removed the clammy clothes. I reached for a sweater, then changed my mind.

"Is it all right if I wear your new bathrobe?" I asked.

"Sure, but don't you think you'd better be getting dressed?"

"Sometimes Steve's fever goes up again. The time you were in New York I had to shower him twice."

"Oh, no," Charlie moaned.

"Oh, yes. Would you like some coffee?"

"Tea?"

"Tea it is."

I put the water on to boil and waited, looking at the phone. It isn't my fault, I thought, but it is my responsibility. I picked up the receiver and dialed the hospital.

"Seventh floor. Miss Andover."

"Tink, this is Cassie. Steve is having a bad time. He's gotten through one crisis, but I'm not certain he won't have another. I can't come back tonight."

There was a long pause. "I understand, Cassie, and it's your decision," she said finally.

"Thanks, Tink. I'll be back in the morning."

"All right," she said. "Take care."

I hung up. It's done, I thought. I'm not ready, not even close, but it's done. I poured the water in the teapot—like Steve, exhausted to the bone.

"Here," I said, handing Charlie his cup, a yellow mug with Snoopy on the side, the kind of good china found in houses that also contain children.

"I heard your phone call," Charlie said.

"And?"

"And it's all right with me."

"I'll have to go back in the morning."

"I know."

"Alexander will probably have to discharge me."

"So you said."

We stared at one another, each trying to read the thoughts behind the other's eyes. Charlie's hazel eyes were as calm and steady as I knew mine weren't.

He cleared his throat. "Do you know how that lady in Bay Village knew that was a UFO she saw in her back yard?" he asked.

"No. How?"

"It had UFO written on the side in big Day-Glo letters."

"Oh, Charlie."

"Honest," he said, sipping his tea.

We sat and sipped tea, checking Steve at half-hour intervals until we woke him for more aspirin at 4 A.M. His fever had stayed down.

"Do you think it would be safe to go to bed for a while?" Charlie asked.

"I think so," I said. "I'll set the alarm for six. I want to be back at the hospital before Tinkerbell goes off duty at seven. I . . . well, I'd like to thank her. She's been very special to me."

"She sounds like a nice person." Charlie yawned.

I set the alarm clock and lay down next to Charlie, who was already sound asleep. I pulled the blanket up to my chin and closed my eyes, but, fatigued though I was, I couldn't fall asleep. I stretched, feeling all the familiar grooves and lumps in the mattress.

I haven't slept in this bed for three months. I smiled in the dark, thinking that "resting" with Charlie on Christmas morning couldn't be classified as sleeping, although it did have a restorative quality all its own. I giggled softly, remembering that the first time I'd seen this bed, four delivery men were carrying it into our first apartment. It was a week before our wedding and raining and they'd almost dumped it in the bushes. Charlie opened the door for them as they came in. "Here comes the playpen," he whispered, and I said, "Charlie!" and blushed to the roots not so much because I was a virgin but because I'd been thinking the same thing.

I lost my virginity in this bed. On our wedding night we'd eluded some mischievous friends of Charlie's and returned to our apartment to spend the night before we left on our honeymoon the next morning. I'd been nervous and Charlie more so, but when we got on the Florida-bound plane in the morning, we'd been man and wife and glad of it. And looking forward to the next night.

The children had been conceived in this bed and my labors began here, waking me out of three sound sleeps with irrefutable evidence that it was time. With Greg I'd felt my water break and rolled over the side onto the floor to avoid drenching the mattress. I landed on my tummy with a thud and Charlie was furious.

"The mattress! Screw the mattress!" he had fumed. "We can get another mattress. I only have one wife and one whatever it's going to be!" He hauled me to my feet and carried me to the car. Greg weighed nine pounds and arrived squawling, undented by my dive.

I sighed, remembering the nights I'd lain in this bed with a drink beside me, trying to sip my way into oblivion and shut out the world. And the nightmares, the grotesque, unrelenting nightmares, that began with me being pursued by nameless horrors and ended with me on the floor, or being shaken awake by an angry and troubled Charlie.

And the fights, the hours-long, screaming, yelling fights, with bitter words and angry accusations, the ugly, barbed, and thrusting recriminations, meant to wound, meant to tear. You do this and you do that. You don't do this. You don't do that. You don't care. No, it's you who don't care. I wish you were dead. I wish YOU were dead, too. I wish I were dead. Why aren't we all dead? We are all dead. Why did we ever get married? I'm sorry we did. So am I.

They usually ended with one of us leaving the bed, departing it if possible with a painful parting shot, more razor words, dragging a blanket, looking for a less hostile camp in which to sleep. Charlie went most often to the living room sofa while I preferred an old ratty chair that squatted in the basement with a pint bottle hidden in its broken springs. Eventually, cold and uncomfortable, the wanderer returned after first determining that the inhabitant of the bed, the battlefield, was fast asleep. Even after the fiercest fights we invariably awoke in the morning, drawn together in sleep spoon-fashion, with Charlie's arms around me and my hands holding his. Our bodies remembered and took comfort, while our minds tenaciously, stubbornly chose to forget.

Charlie snorted softly in his sleep, a cross between a snore and a hiccup. I pulled the blanket up over his shoulders. *You'll never be Prince Charming, Charlie, or Romeo, or Cyrano, with his gift for expressing emotion. You'll never listen to me every time I want you to, every time I need to be listened to and heard. You'll always miss points and ignore what you don't understand and remain obstinately oblivious to my fluctuating moods. You'll never comprehend the part of me that needs and greeds and longs and dreams— sighing after what? Maybe things that never were, or things that once were, but got lost along the way and are no more. Maybe childhood griefs. And there will always be a part of yourself that you'll keep locked away and hidden, will never share with me. Perhaps you keep it hidden even from yourself. Charlie. Charlie.*

I glanced at the clock in the quickening light. It was nearly six. I rose, yawning, and clicked off the alarm button. I hadn't slept at all.

In the bathroom I splashed water on my face and looked at myself in the mirror. The brash light from the overhead lamp cast purple shadows under my eyes. My cheeks were sunken, my hair stringy, my eyes dull. I looked as if I'd just stumbled out of a wreck.

"You aren't exactly Cinderella or Juliet or the fair Roxane yourself, lady," I said to the bedraggled creature in the mirror. "You are Cassie, and in this dawn's early light, I see less than perfection." I grinned. "But good morning anyway, and welcome to Wednesday. Ready or not, here it comes."

I dressed quietly, not wanting to wake anyone. I tiptoed to the side of the bed and looked down at Charlie.

"You're a kind man," I whispered and leaned down

to kiss him, "and you care. Deep down you care." He didn't wake up. I checked Steve, who was cool, and left.

I drove through empty streets, feeling surprisingly alert. I stretched at a stop light, feeling for the knots and sharp edges that usually roamed free inside of me. There were none.

Tinkerbell buzzed me in.

"Thanks for understanding about last night," I said. "I'm sorry I caused a problem with policy. Are you in trouble?"

"What about last night?" she said with a smile. "Nothing happened last night."

"What?"

She leaned over the counter. "I never reported you missing," she whispered. "The morning shift isn't here yet. It's all right. You won't be discharged."

I held on to the counter. "Why . . . why, thanks, Tink. What can I say? You really went out on a limb."

"Not really." She shook her tiny head. "If Dalton had come in, I would have had to report you. I would have been reprimanded for not calling Alexander, of course, but I could have explained it to him. He would have understood."

"Yes, he would."

"Now go catch some sleep before Alexander comes in. How's your boy?"

"Oh, he's better, much better."

"Good. Oh, by the way, Joanne went home last night."

"She did? Why so suddenly? She didn't say anything about it."

Tinkerbell shrugged. "She said she couldn't stand it anymore. She missed Ronnie. She signed herself out."

"Oh, Tink, what a mistake!"

"Who's to say," she said. "Go get some sleep."

25

I felt someone tap my shoulder and I sat bolt upright, thinking I was at home.

"How's Steve?" I said, rubbing my eyes.

"I don't know nothing about any Steve," Gloria replied, "but Alexander's down in the interview room asking if you died."

"Jesus!" I scrambled to my feet and ran down the hall, then slowed to a walk. I'm not Cara being bad, I thought. No need to run.

I walked in the door and he scowled.

"You look like you slept in your clothes," he said.

"I guess I did. Sleep overtook me."

"You look like it jumped you from behind," he growled.

"You made a joke!" I laughed, delighted.

"I make a lot of jokes," he frowned.

Not with me, you don't, Edwin. Never before with me. "Yes, you do," I said agreeably. If he cherished a witty self-image, who was I to interfere?

"Well?" he said, expectantly.

"Well," I said, crashing headlong out of limbo. "I want to go home."

His eyes widened. "You do?" They narrowed again. "Do you mean you want to go home, or you just want to get out?"

"I want to go home," I said firmly.

"To Charlie?"

"And the kids. Yes."

He folded his arms. "Since when—and why?"

"Since now, and because it's time."

"Just like that."

"Just like that."

He swiveled his chair until he was facing the window.

"Only yesterday you were telling me that you're not ready," he said.

"If I wait till I think I'm ready, I'll celebrate my ninetieth birthday on the seventh floor. And you'll be treating me for senility."

"Who'll be treating me?" he asked.

Another joke?

He swiveled around, facing me again. He lit a cigarette and offered me one. I accepted gratefully, having left mine in my room.

"Now I want to know why, Cassie. What about the West Side Residence for Women?"

"It will still be there, later, if things don't work out. But I have to try, Dr. Alexander. I owe it to the kids, and to Charlie. I owe it to me. I haven't tried for a very long time."

"And you want to try now?"

"To whatever extent I'm able. I screwed up on my own territory, I'll have to work it out on my own territory. Anything else would be running away. At least, that's what I feel."

"I see." He ground out his cigarette and immediately lit another. "You and Charlie play some pretty destructive games, you know," he said.

"I know we do. And I know that the games are reciprocal. But the worst ones are the alcoholic games, and if I don't drink, we can't play. It's got to get better."

"Do you have an idea that Charlie will somehow change?" He stared at me intently.

I laughed. "I'm done with trying to change Charlie. He'll have to change himself. I've got all I can do with changing me."

Alexander smiled. "So, you expect it will get better?"

"Charlie is as sick to the soul with the way things

were as I am. He doesn't talk about it, but in the weeks past his attitude has shown it. Charlie may have, um, potential."

"If you've miscalculated, if he hasn't, then what?"

I put out my cigarette. "I'll give it six months. If it's not better, I'll start talking about the West Side Residence for Women again. I'm not a masochist. Am I a masochist?"

"Well," he hedged, smiling, "to some extent, most of us are."

Us, Edwin?

He stood, rubbing his hands together. "Let's see," he said efficiently. "I'll write your discharge and you can leave anytime today. Then I'll see you in my office next Tuesday morning at ten. Is there anything else?"

I stood facing him. *Is there anything else, Edwin? Yes, there is. I'd like to throw my arms around you and hug you and kiss you—tell you that you snatched me back when I was drowning and no one else cared or I thought no one did, and I'll love you forever, whoever you are, and never, ever forget you, wherever I go, whatever I do. And thank you, thank you with all of my heart.*

I extended my hand like a grown-up lady. "I'd like to thank you," I said, blinking back tears. "You've really helped me. It's meant a lot—your support, I mean."

He looked surprised, but shook my hand. "Thank you," he said. "I was just doing my job."

I held on to his hand. "And I like you a lot," I blurted, flushing.

He stiffened, then relaxed. "Hmmm. Well, I like you too," he said easily, opening the door for me.

"You know," he said, as I walked through the door, "I'd say that we both did a pretty fair job. Actually, we both did damned well." He turned toward the desk and I beamed at his back.

You may drive me bonkers and be pompous as hell, but you're awfully good at what you do. And for that, Edwin, I forgive all the rest.

"See you Tuesday," he called absently, not looking up from his chart.

"Okay, 'bye now." I skipped to my room feeling lighter than air.

I was stuffing the last of my not so worldly possessions into the smaller of two suitcases when Gloria appeared in my doorway.

"What you doing?" she asked.

"Packing. Going home. Quitting this mortal coil. Shuffling off to Buffalo. Departing this vale of tears. Shaking this dust from—"

"Sure hope you do better than Joanne," Gloria sighed, gazing upward.

"What about Joanne? She left last night."

"Well, she's back this morning. Just came in."

"Where? What happened?"

"She's in her old room. The sheets ain't cold yet, and there she is, tween them again. And a fine mess she is too. This time—"

I was already running down the hall toward Joanne's room.

"Joanne, Joanne, what happened?" I yelled, rounding the corner. I stopped in the doorway. "Oh, my God!" Dalton stood next to her bed tinkering with the control on an IV bottle. Joanne was white and still, unconscious beneath the sheets.

"Is she dead? Is she dying?"

"Nope," Dalton said casually. "She came close, but she'll be all right."

"What happened? Tell me."

"It's none of your business," Dalton said, starting to push past me.

"Goddammit, Dalton, I've been discharged. I'm no longer a patient, and if you don't tell me what happened, so help me, I'll throw you out the goddamned window."

"It's hermetically sealed."

"You bitch." I grabbed her by both shoulders. She froze.

"Well, as long as you're here as a friend of the family," she said, "I'll tell you."

I relaxed my grip. "So tell me."

"She went home to surprise her marvelous husband. She found a trail of clothes that led from the front door to the bedroom. In the bedroom, in the bed, she found the owner of the clothes, glued to husband Ronnie in an act of adultery. So, of course, Joanne immediately slashed her wrists with a butcher knife. Her husband got out of bed long enough to call an ambulance. By now, I would imagine he's back in bed, reglued." She shrugged and walked out the door.

I looked down at the still form on the bed. "Joanne, Joanne," I whispered, "you did it for nothing. He still doesn't care. He doesn't even notice. He won't be sorry after you're dead. He won't cry at your funeral. He'll be somewhere else, drunk and crying for himself."

I turned and walked back to my room, where I caught sight of myself in the mirror. "You're not Joanne," I said loudly.

I put on my coat and picked up a suitcase with each hand.

Good Lord, I'll get a hernia. Where did I get all this junk? I must have thought I would stay forever.

I lugged my load to the desk. "I'm ready," I said softly, wanting to be gone before anyone came out to say goodbye. This wasn't exactly the middle of the night but it would have to do.

"Oh, are you going?" Pomeroy asked. "For good?"

"I fervently hope so," I grinned. "Not that it wasn't fun."

"Home?" she cross-examined.

"To assume my rightful place in the bosom of my family. To shoulder my responsibilities, resume my obligations, live my life—"

"Don't fall down the steps and break your neck," she interrupted. "We'd have to list you as a suicide. One a day is enough. Sign here."

I scribbled my name. "I'll take the elevator," I promised. "Buzz me out."

"Be good," she called, hitting the buzzer.

"Better than that, I'll try to be happy." I dragged my suitcases through the door. As I waited for the elevator, I looked through the glass to the nurses' station, the parlor, and the long narrow hall with rooms on each side. *A part of my life. A short part, but what a difference. Part of me grew up in there. Who says adolescence is a happy, carefree time?*

I carried my suitcases into the elevator thinking about the contrast between the sick, drunken, oblivious, death-ridden lady who'd stumbled in that door and the lady who'd just walked out. I reached for the button and dropped a suitcase on my foot.

"Hot damn," I said, rubbing my instep. "She's not altogether gone."

Snow swirled in the parking lot as I jammed my suitcases in the back seat. I drove slowly home, enjoying the sights like a tourist. Everything looked new, and very, very dear.

There are things between Charlie and me that I'll never tell Alexander, I thought, *and there are things between Alexander and me that I'll never tell Charlie. And that's as it should be,* I decided, pulling into my driveway.

I left my suitcases in the car. Charlie was home, in the living room with the kids.

"We just got back from the doctor's," he said.

"What did he say?"

Charlie's eyes twinkled. "It's a simple upper respiratory infection," we said in unison, and laughed.

I took off my coat. "I'm home."

"So I see. Alexander discharged you?"

"Yes, but not the way you think. Tinkerbell never reported me. I could have stayed."

"Then why?"

"I told him I wanted to come home," I said, watching him closely. "I told him I was ready, it was time. I'm here because this is where I want to be."

Charlie opened his arms. "Forever?" he asked.

I sighed. "Charlie, eleven years ago we said forever. This time, let's just try it one day at a time."

"That sounds good to me," he said with his arms tight around me. "I'm still a realist, you know. And always will be."

"I know, Charlie. And I'll always be a romantic. What matters more is that we're both survivors."

26

Dear Bobby,

Just a line to let you know that I am alive, yea verily, and breathing. In less than an hour Mother will be here toting enough fried chicken to feed all those starving children in Europe we grew up feeling guilty about and the Barrett clan will be off to Cedar Point for a Fourth of July picnic. The outing was my idea, inspired by a conversation I heard between Jenny and Alicia, her little friend from next door. Alicia said, "What are you gonna do on the Fourth?" Jenny replied, "Well, usually we stay home. Daddy cooks steaks and Mommy gets drunk."

That set off a class A remorse attack which I had to nip in the bud. The last time I had one I brooded all day instead of going to the supermarket and ended up serving soup and peanut butter for dinner. Given the choice, Charlie and the kids would prefer roast beef to remorse, and, incidentally, so would I. I repeated Jenny's conversation to Charlie, who said, "That definitely does not sound like a golden childhood memory."

I suggested Cedar Point and he agreed, although driving long distances on national holidays in blistering heat with three restless children and a wife who gets carsick is not his idea of bliss. or, indeed, anything a sane person would voluntarily attempt. Right now Charlie is in the basement rooting around for an old sand pail to be used for throwing-up purposes. Little things mean a lot.

Mother called Mary Kay and invited her to join us. Mary Kay experienced her annual attack of hedonism, had the book amputated from the end of her nose, and will meet us there, eyes blinking in the unaccustomed sunshine, for an afternoon of unrestrained frivolity. For the past several years our relationship has consisted of Mary Kay eyeing me apprehensively while I sniped at her from behind a barbed barricade of booze and hostility. Wouldn't it be interesting, and fun, if we turned out to be friends? Truthfully, Bob, I haven't the slightest idea what Mary Kay is really like. I know only the label I've assigned to her.

Two weeks ago Mother confided to me, in strangled whispers, that she called your apartment one night and (don't tell Charlie) a GIRL answered. She was, Mother said, breathing heavily! I told Mother that smog does that to people and everyone in California sounds like a blond starlet or obscene phone caller. Despite my reassurances, Mother is beginning to suspect that you may have lost your virginity, Robert. And she'd so hoped to see you married in white. She expects to see you show up one day with a scarlet A tattooed on your bosom. And why not? It pays to advertise.

Still, don't you dare commit marriage without bringing her home for me to meet. I need to be certain she adores you completely and will save you from bullies who crouch behind bushes holding snowballs packed around rocks. I promise not to tell your intended about the time Mother came home and thought she heard a girl upstairs in your room. She pounded on your door and you sweetly invited her in for a heart-to-heart while poor Sue Ann Krumhover sat outside on your windowsill for two hours in the pouring rain. Not a word from my lips. Just send ten dollars a month forever.

And how am I, you ask? Hark! I can hear you.

First of all, best of all, I'm sober. Still and yet and hopefully always. I was terrified when I first came home from the hospital, afraid I wouldn't make it. I skulked around the house jumping at shadows and anxiously waiting for the kids to come home. Being alone unnerved me, assailed my defenses. I forced myself to call Alice daily, or if she wasn't available, someone else I'd met at a meeting and liked. One day, suffocating with panic, I called Alice and screamed that I couldn't stand it anymore.

"Stand what?" she asked calmly.

"Fear!" I yelled. "I'm terrified. I'm drenched and shaking. I can't stand it."

"What are you afraid of?" she asked, even calmer.

"Everything! Nothing! I don't know what I'm afraid of," I said. I was crying.

"Have you been thinking about drinking?" she asked.

"Yes. No. I don't know," I admitted, ashamed.

"Well, you called me instead and you're telling me how you feel. That's good," she said.

"But I still feel terrible," I protested.

"Here's what you do," she said briskly. "Drink some orange juice with honey if you have it, or a Coke, take a hot bath, and call me back in half an hour."

"But what good will that do?"

"Don't ask. Just do it," she commanded.

A half hour later I was telling her I felt better and she was saying I thought you would. We repeated this routine frequently in those initial weeks. Sometimes just talking for a few minutes would do it, though I took so many hot baths that my skin stayed permanently puckered. Sometimes she told me to read the book and the darned thing has grown on me to the extent that at times whole passages will float into my mind unbidden and I find myself braced, soothed, and once again willing to trudge that road. It may or may not lead to happy destiny, Bob, but it most definitely leads away from the looney bin and cemetery. On one memorable morning, Alice instructed me to wash windows.

"Let's not get drastic," I said, but did as I was told. I was huffing and puffing through my ninth window and swearing because I'd sprayed backward and had an eyeful of Windex, when I was stricken with an insight, which can be dangerous when you're perched on a ladder. I hauled myself out of the shrubbery and ran into the house.

"Alice. Alice," I bellowed into the phone. "I just realized that it doesn't much matter what I do as long as I don't drink. When I get busy doing something else the urge passes and with it, the fear."

"You just realized that?" she said, laughing.

"I should have known," I said, humbled.

"Don't feel bad, honey," she said. "I knew a guy who

took nine years to realize that the reason he couldn't sober up was that he kept on drinking. Taking alternative action just never occurred to him. But you see, it works. Just be sure you call someone and let them know how you feel when you think about drinking. Okay?"

"Okay," I agreed, hung up and went to look at myself in the mirror. There were twigs in my hair and smudges of dirt all over my face. I had never looked more ravishing.

"Hi there, sober lady," I beamed. "Congratulations. You know what to do in an emergency and you can do it. You can cope."

So, Bob, the anxiety attacks grew gradually less overwhelming and the phone calls to Alice less frequent. Now when I feel upset or fear hovers on the fringe of my basic contentment, I do the things that Alice taught me. I even repeat her words to myself, and I feel better. Not always immediately, but eventually, and each time it works I feel more and more confident that it will continue to work. I go to three or four meetings a week. Charlie never says a word about the evenings he spends alone after putting the children to bed. He just helps me on with my coat and says, "Have a good time."

Two months ago, I became depressed. I don't know why. Maybe it's cyclical. I mentioned my depression to Alice at a meeting.

"Hang in there, don't drink, and it'll pass," she said, pouring herself a cup of coffee.

"When?" I demanded. "I've felt awful for over a week."

"Who knows?" she shrugged. "Hang in there, don't drink, and it'll pass."

I was steamed, Bob. I was knotted with suffering and she was making like a goddamned parrot. I hung in there and didn't drink. It passed. Grr. Trudge. Trudge. Trudge.

Last night at a meeting I sat across from a young man. He was hunched into himself and glanced around furtively as if expecting someone to challenge his right to be there, or worse yet, walk up and say something friendly. His hands shook and some of his coffee spilled. I reached for a napkin and began mopping it up.

"Sorry," he mumbled, looking very embarrassed.

"It's all right," I heard myself say. "I know how you feel. I've been there myself. Don't worry. It gets better. Much better."

"You alcoholic?" he asked.

"I'm not here for the coffee. Sure I'm alcoholic."

"How long you been in, been sober?"

"Six months."

"This thing work?" he asked and unhunched half an inch.

"This thing works," I said, answering the only question that was ever important to me.

"Six months," he sighed. "Wow, six whole months. I haven't been sober for six months since I was seventeen."

"Welcome," I said, smiling. "I'm Cassie."

And so it goes, Bobby. From Alice to me, to this newcomer Joe, and from him to the next person and on and on, ripples in a pond.

I could go on about AA forever, Bob, and I think I just have, but nothing outside of alcohol has ever had such an impact on my life. I'm learning about experiencing growth rather than perfection, and I can see it, feel it in myself. I'm still impatient with my progress and beat my fists against my limitations, but even so, I understand that if this, today, is all there is, all I get, it is better by far than what I had.

So much for wild enthusiasm. Mother taught me how to knit. My first effort was less than a major success.

"It looks like your cat threw up a fur ball," Mother said. "Throw it away."

Mother has always believed in discarding fatally flawed first efforts. I'm sure that somewhere we have a cross-eyed older brother who limps and breeds snakes.

Finally, on May 15, I presented Jenny with a gold-and-white scarf, the dropped stitches carefully concealed. It was eighty-two degrees outside but she wore it anyway.

"One thing I'll say about you," Mother remarked, "you're tenacious."

Ho, ho, ho. Trudge. Trudge.

During my first weeks at home, Charlie and I circled each other warily, like courting birds or uneasy strangers. We hadn't been so shy since our honeymooon days when Charlie would break off in the middle of heavy petting, stretch, yawn, say, "It's sleepy time," and duck into the bathroom to dress in blue and white striped pajamas. And I walked around in crampy misery for six days, too mortified to tell Charlie that I was in dire need of a laxative until one night at dinner when he remarked that I didn't seem to be eating and why were my eyes bugging out.

At first Charlie thanked me so fervently for breakfast every morning that I was convinced he'd been awake all night praying for cornflakes and toast. I washed his socks out by hand, gray ones and black ones and brown ones, hung them neatly in rows and tucked them tidily into a corner of his dresser drawer. We were polite, considerate, thoughtful, and entirely unnatural.

One night we forgot and slipped into an argument. I was screeching at Charlie and he was clamoring at me, when he suddenly stopped and went white in the face. He walked away from me without another word.

I watched him for a moment, sitting tight-lipped and tense on the end of the couch. I sat on the couch and put my arms around him.

"Whatever happens," I said. "Whatever develops between us. I don't need to drink about it."

"Are you sure?" he asked.

"Positive," I said. "I might put arsenic in your tapioca, but I won't get drunk at you."

He searched my face for some sign of doubt or vacillation. Finding none, he seemed satisfied.

"Then, will you stop screwing up the goddamn checkbook!" he bellowed, and we went at it again, this time with both of us grinning. We've never had a more comfortable fight. We've had others since, most of them concerning the day-to-day trivia that strikes marital sparks, none particularly serious or lacking resolution. I tend toward volume and personal slurs while Charlie is a master of stylish invective, hurling every derogatory word in the thesaurus—except one. In six months' time, not once has Charlie called me a drunk. I really should stop calling him Toulouse.

I must sound like a looney yet, Bobby, saying that better fights denote an improvement, but once our communications consisted solely of me babbling incoherently at Charlie while he retreated further and further into a shell of silence. Now, along with creative disagree-

ments, there are quick kitchen kisses, laughter at private
jokes, and the kids' exploits, a friendly smile and, "Hi,
how was your day?" and a growing sense of family, a
growing sense of *us*. It's not perfect, Bob. Sometimes it
isn't even great. But it's better, much better. Charlie
gives me presents. Last month he brought me a Long
Island duckling, something he said he'd seen and
thought I would like.

I think about the hospital often, about the people I
met and the lessons I learned or hope I learned there.
When I think about it there's a weird kind of nostalgia,
a sensation I can only describe as homesickness. I'd
like to go back, just to visit, Bobby, only to say hello.
But I haven't and probably won't. It was a safe place
for me, at one time the only safe place, and even now,
though I have other safe places and other people, there
are moments when I would dearly love to hear that door
lock securely behind me and see Tinkerbell's warm,
welcoming smile. Then the mood passes and I know I
am where I should be and don't belong there anymore.
But, I'll never forget, Bobby, or cease being grateful.

I still see Alexander on a regular basis and will for a
while. I was right when I told Cara that improvement
does not result in immediate abandonment, though I
really wasn't quite sure at the time. Still, I was willing
to risk. He still nods and says "Hmmm" just as he always has, and we return occasionally to some of our
old subjects. But now there are new ones, along the
lines of "That's terrific. What's next?" And we seem to
smile at each other a lot. And why not? When a doctor
does his part and a patient does hers, the results are
worth smiling about.

Recently, without warning, he said, "Cassie, do you
love Charlie?"

And I replied, "Did you ever doubt it?"

"Not for a moment," he said.

I received a postcard from my friend Cara. She is in
an Oregon commune that seems to be composed of
aging hippies who believe that Paul McCartney is dead.
They eat sunflower seeds and play Beatles records backwards. She says that she's madly in love with an ex-
Yamaha mechanic from Jersey who is now heavily into
meditation and hang-gliding and has helped her find
her center. It sounds like her belly button is missing.

But she certainly seems happy enough, and, as Tinkerbell once said, "Who's to say?"

I think about Norma and her children and wonder how they are. And about Joanne and I wonder if she's still alive. What good is anything, Bobby, if at the end you come to your deathbed with no one to hold your hand. I think about everyone, everything.

I drove past the West Side Residence for Women and noticed that in no way does it resemble a golden key. It's still there, should I want it, but the magic is gone from its walls. What I wanted, personhood, has nothing to do with a place, and the art of becoming, I find, can be practiced anywhere. Even in the supermarket. Alas. Trudge. Trudge.

I think about you. Come home for a visit. When you do, we'll put on the coffee and talk about Dad. If you're ready. I am—now. I think I began to get over his death when I was able to feel that he's out there somewhere approving of me. It's taken a very long time and I have memories to share. With you.

Got to run. My potato salad is congealing. Rather attractively, too.

Take care, darling Bobby. Beware of earthquakes and sharks and girls who say you'd be perfect if only . . .

Think of me.

Cassie

ABOUT THE AUTHOR

JOYCE REBETA-BURDITT is a screenwriter who lives in Burbank, California, with her husband, three children, three cats and one dog. *The Cracker Factory* is her first novel.